Praise for
THE CAT'S MEOW

"A charming romantic caper ... Steamy, between-the-sheets action, sensitive soul searching and a tail-twitching denouement all add to the feline fun." —*Publishers Weekly*

"In an offshoot of Carmichael's extremely funny series featuring Miss Piggy the dog, Titi the cat takes center stage and makes it her own. This is another laugh-out-loud romp!" —*Romantic Times* (Top Pick!)

"Everyone will enjoy this highly entertaining tale, but fans of Carmichael's Piggy stories will especially delight in Titi and her pithy cat wisdom." —*Booklist*

"Entertaining ... The best part of *The Cat's Meow* is the heroine, Mckenna Wright. Rarely are romance readers treated to a total, er, witch of a leading lady, but that's the only word for Mckenna." —*Contra Costa Times*

GONE TO THE DOGS

"[Emily Carmichael] will have readers wagging their tails in delight.... [Her] scenic descriptions of the northern Arizona setting, insider's peek into the world of therapy pets, and loveable characters, both human and otherwise, make this lighthearted romp worth savoring."
—*Publishers Weekly*

"Carmichael's spunky canine heroine will win even more admirers in this terrifically funny and captivating installment in her ongoing adventures."
—*Booklist* (starred review)

FINDING MR. RIGHT

Praise for
EMILY CARMICHAEL

A New Leash on Life

Emily Carmichael

BANTAM BOOKS

A NEW LEASH ON LIFE
A Bantam Book / December 2005

Published by Bantam Dell
A Division of Random House, Inc.
New York, New York

This is a work of fiction. Names, characters, places, and incidents either
are the product of the author's imagination or are used fictitiously.
Any resemblance to actual persons, living or dead, events, or locales
is entirely coincidental.

Bantam Books and the rooster colophon are registered trademarks of
Random House, Inc.

ISBN-10: 0-553-58635-1
ISBN-13: 978-0-553-58635-0

Printed in the United States of America
Published simultaneously in Canada

www.bantamdell.com

OPM   10   9   8   7   6   5   4   3   2   1

A New
Leash on Life

chapter 1

THE DOG days of summer had begun in earnest—the true dog days, that is. Dog shows. Obedience trials. Agility trials, hunting tests, herding trials, tracking tests, and so on, all summer long. Not that these activities didn't pop up during the winter months. They did. But the true frenzy blossomed with the spring flowers, new grass, and tender green leaves, as dog fanciers everywhere planned their dog-show itineraries, packed collars, leashes, brushes, and chow, and looked forward to summer competition and fun.

June in Arizona brought soaring temperatures in the desert and a thaw of the last snow in the mountains. In those same mountains, the first dog show of the season took place outside among the pines of Flagstaff, where competitors gasped for oxygen in the seven-thousand-foot elevation. One of those gasping stood at the entrance to Ring 12, but her rapid breathing came from a case of nerves, not lack of oxygen. She was accustomed to the thin air. She was also accustomed to the tension of waiting to compete, but that didn't make the wait any easier.

Fun, Jane Connor reminded herself as she stood with

her dog Shadow, waiting to go into the obedience ring. *This is fun. Fun, fun, fun.*

Of course it was fun. Dogs were the love of Jane's life. In fact, they *were* her life—her livelihood and her recreation. More than a hobby, dog training and handling were the things she did best. Competition was her life's blood, and winning was to her soul like air was to her lungs.

All in good fun, of course.

"This is fun," she repeated quietly to the alert young golden retriever sitting in perfect heel position at her left side. Shadow looked up at her with a doggy smile on his face. His dark brown eyes seemed to laugh. No matter the stress of the moment, Shadow always had fun.

The judge in Ring 12 was taking his time filling out paperwork. The ring steward had called Jane's number a good five minutes ago for this runoff—the American Kennel Club's version of a tiebreaker. Any bobble or hesitation in this performance could spell defeat, and waiting at the gate built tension to an almost sickening level. Jane could feel her focus slipping, minute by minute. Couldn't these people be a little more on the ball?

Finally, the judge finished writing, stuck the paperwork beneath a weight to guard it from the wind, and looked up at Jane with a smile. "Number two-five-one?"

Jane made the effort to return the smile. "Yes, sir. Two-five-one."

"Good. Come on in, please."

Quietly she commanded Shadow to pay attention, then they stepped into the ring and she surrendered the dog's leash to a ring steward.

"You are tied for a placement in this class," the judge told her, as if she didn't already know. Earlier that morning she and Shadow had done a bang-up job in Utility class, the most difficult level of obedience competition. She and Shadow needed a high placement in the class to earn points toward Shadow's obedience championship title.

Today he really did deserve those points, because his earlier performance had been nothing short of flawless. Hand signals, scent discrimination, retrieving, jumping—he'd done it all with style and enthusiasm. The judge hadn't specified, but Jane suspected this was a runoff to determine first place.

"This will be a heel-off-lead exercise," the judge explained. "Are you ready?"

Jane took a deep breath. Glancing down at Shadow, she checked that the dog's attention was riveted on her. "Ready!" she declared.

"Forward," the judge ordered.

They marched around the ring at the judge's direction, performing the peculiar dance of the obedience competition ring. Forward, halt, fast, slow, left turn, right turn, and more of the same choreography—no vocal commands allowed in Utility class, only hand signals. But Shadow caught every signal, his eyes never straying from Jane. They moved together like experienced dance partners, never missing a beat.

If the dog faltered a bit in one turn, lagging just a hair, it was still only a sliver away from perfection. And his final slide into a sit might have been just a tad crooked. But all in all it was a superior performance, especially considering that the wind was wreaking noisy havoc with all the tents and shade canopies on the show grounds, threatening to turn them into kites, and worse still, a kid with popcorn sat not five feet from the ring, his aromatic bag of buttery treats held exactly at golden retriever nose level.

"Awesome!" Blonde-haired, blue-eyed Jenny Sachs clapped Jane on the shoulder as she left the ring. "Good going, Jane!"

Jenny had been standing at ringside with the other Utility exhibitors awaiting the presentation of awards and scores. This morning Jenny's little Shetland sheepdog had flunked the class when he had knocked the bar from a jump, but Jenny didn't seem to mind the zero score. She always seemed to have fun—win, place, or lose. Sometimes Jane wished she had Jenny's carefree attitude.

"You think it was good?" Jane asked Jenny.

"Excellent! Really."

"I thought there was a little lag on the about turn."

"Half point, if the judge saw it at all. Uh-oh!" Jenny's voice dropped ominously. "Look who you're up against."

Jane turned to watch her competitor walk into the ring. He had a smile on his face and a tiny black and white dog at his side. This puny little dog had earned the same score as Shadow? Jane thought. Amazing.

"A papillon, of all dogs!" she scoffed. "Give me a break!"

"This pap is very good," Jenny warned. "I watched her at the Albuquerque trials last month. It's just disgusting that a dog can be so cute and so smart at the same time."

Jane made a face.

"Well, Shadow, too," Jenny revised. "Shadow's smart, and cute as a bug, too."

Now Shadow looked disgusted.

"I mean, handsome. Shadow is handsome. Gorgeous. Oh, my! Get a load of that heeling."

Jane's heart sank as she watched. The papillon pranced at her handler's left side like an animated dust bunny, not budging an inch from perfection no matter what the man did. She looked like a gremlin wind-up toy with her delicately fringed butterfly-wing ears, her toothpick legs, and her perkily curled tail.

The man in the ring was not as accomplished as his dog, however. He clearly didn't have the practiced perfection of an experienced competitor. With such a small dog he should have shortened the length of his stride and taken more care to keep his big feet out of the little pap's way. His turns were not quite square, and he stopped too fast when the judge gave the order to halt. All of that should have put the little dog at a disadvantage, but instead, she compensated for his small blunders, adjusting herself flawlessly to the difficult pace and folding herself into a precisely straight sit when her master stopped.

The best part of the performance, Jane had to admit, was that the peculiar pair seemed to have such a good time together. The man positively beamed when he looked down at his toy-sized dog, and the dog's tiny jaws gaped in a self-satisfied grin. They were truly an example of what dog sport was all about, a pleasure for any obedience trainer to watch—unless that trainer happened to be in direct competition with all that perfection.

"Wow!" Jenny exclaimed as their performance ended. "Did you see that?"

"I did," Jane growled.

"Your handling was way better."

"You don't get points for handling."

"Well . . . I still think you probably won."

"Not a chance." Jane tried to sound casual. "That little papillon deserves first place." She glanced ruefully down at Shadow, who grinned up at her, his big tongue lolling from his mouth. Unlike Jane, Shadow didn't seem to care who won.

Jane's prediction was right on the money. Five minutes later she stood in the ring with six other qualifying exhibitors. Twenty dogs had been entered in Utility class, but only these few had earned the minimum score required to pass. Jane pasted a smile on her face while she accepted second place, applauding with the others as the papillon and her handler soaked up the glory of first place, along with the obedience championship points the win afforded them.

"Losing builds character," Jane told Shadow when they'd returned to the relative privacy of her shade canopy. "It's an opportunity for us to show good sportsmanship, you know. You did your best, big guy, and so did I. That's the important thing."

Shadow pretty much ignored the lecture as he walked into his portable exercise pen, slurped a few mouthfuls of water, then curled up on his dog bed for a nap in the shade provided by the canopy.

"Fine. Be like that. You don't want to discuss it? Well, neither do I."

Jane had been on top of the heap for a long time. Ever since she had started training and competing with dogs as a teenager back in Wisconsin, she'd been a natural. She'd started out with a German shepherd, then had taken top honors with a sheltie. In her mid-twenties, she'd gathered titles and blue ribbons in both obedience and herding trials with her border collie Idaho, who now lived a life of retired ease at the Bark Park, Jane's kennel and training business in Arizona.

And then had come young Shadow, now eighteen months old and well on his way to earning his obedience trial championship.

"You'd be a lot closer to a championship today if you hadn't let that little sissy dog squeeze in front of you," she told the golden retriever.

Shadow opened one lackadaisical eye, then shut it. Jane snorted in disgust. She had gotten too accustomed to being the best. Sinking back into the pile of also-rans took some getting used to. Not that she intended to stay there. Dropping into a canvas folding chair, she took off her ball cap and scrubbed her hands through a bad case of hat hair. Hopeless. Her mop of red frizz was far less disciplined than her dogs. Not that she really cared. As far as she was concerned, an act of Congress couldn't make Jane Connor look like anything besides what she was—a horse-faced, frizz-headed woman rapidly closing on middle age. Sometimes she looked at herself in the mirror and wondered if a little more attention to femininity might be worth the trouble. But the answer always came up negative. She had more important things to worry about—like running a business, making a living, and winning competitions.

But not today, obviously. With a sigh, she scraped the thick mass of hair into a ponytail and fastened it with a rubber band.

"Hi there!"

Jane jumped up at the greeting, finding herself confronted by none other than the conqueror of Utility class and his little mouse of a dog, who had just popped around the corner of her enclosed canopy. Jane's face grew warm. She hoped he hadn't heard her crack about "that little sissy dog."

"Uh . . . hi." She tried for a smile but was only half successful.

"Absolutely gorgeous golden retriever."

"He thinks so."

"Well, he should. Handsome fellow."

Jane was surprised to find that the man topped her own five foot ten by at least four inches. When she had seen him in the obedience ring, she'd been so wrapped up in losing that she hadn't paid any attention.

Awakened by the arrival of an admirer, Shadow got off his bed and wriggled his way to the near side of the pen—wriggled because his tail worked so hard that the rest of him wagged back and forth as well. The man laughed.

He had a combustible laugh, Jane noted. It was one of those sounds that could spread like a wildfire, making everyone around him want to laugh also. She hadn't really noticed much about him during his victorious performance in the runoff. The disgustingly perfect little dog had captured all her attention—that and the man's less-than-perfect handling.

But she noticed him now. He was a man, she admitted, that most women would notice. He had an open, amiable face that probably made grannies want to pinch his cheeks. His black hair lay in a conservative trim that might have been a bit nerdy, but somehow fit him. Dark, deep-set eyes sparkled with good humor. Khaki slacks and a sweater didn't exactly show off his physique, but his shoulders stretched from here to there very nicely, and he had enough height to place Jane at an unexpected disadvantage.

Jane did not like being at any kind of a disadvantage, especially with some guy who had just left her in the dust in a competition.

"My name's Cole Forrest, by the way, and this"—he glanced at the little papillon who sat politely at his side—"is Dobby. We wanted to stop by and say what a nice job you two did in the ring today."

"Jane Connor." She nodded and stuck her hands in the pockets of her jeans. "And this is Shadow." Shadow waved his tail at the sound of his name. "Did you say the pap's name is Bobby?"

He laughed again. "Not Bobby. Dobby. My daughter named her after the house elf character in the Harry Potter series."

"Ah." A daughter.

"I saw you and Shadow in Open today and again in Utility," Cole said amiably. "Really nice performances."

The fellow was simply trying to be a gracious winner, Jane reminded herself, though the compliment sounded a bit condescending to her. As if she needed condescension from some dork whose dog had to save him from amateurish handling mistakes. But then, she might be a bit sensitive on that score.

"Thank you," Jane said, laboring to be polite. "She's a cute papillon. Did you show her in Open as well as Utility?" Open class was one level below Utility, and most truly competitive dogs showed in both classes. "I didn't see you there."

"We were in the ring early. Didn't qualify. Dobby stood up on the down-stay. She was distracted by a kid screaming at ringside."

"Oh. That's too bad. It's hard to prepare a dog for something like that." Jane managed to stifle a smug grin. "Your Dobby does very well," she added generously, "for a toy breed." It was her turn to be condescending.

If he noticed, he didn't take offense. "Not too many toys seem to be in competition. Dobby's my first try at this. Actually, she's my first dog since the collie I had when I was three."

His first dog. Criminy! Not only beaten, but beaten by a novice handler. How humiliating!

"Terrific," Jane choked out. "Congratulations on your win."

Shadow gave a soft woof, not loud enough to be rude, but a reminder that he deserved a bit of attention, too. Dobby's ears—easily the biggest appendages she owned—perked in the golden's direction. Cautiously the tiny dog eased forward and poked her nose through the wire exercise pen, just a millimeter or so, but enough to extend a friendly invitation to become acquainted. Shadow responded in kind, carefully touching his nose to hers.

Apparently satisfied that the big golden retriever posed no threat, Dobby squeaked out a little bark and commenced a delighted little dance. Shadow answered with a considerably more substantial bark. He bowed, his tail waving in anticipation of a friendly romp.

"Sorry, Shadow," Jane said, watching them. "You're too big to play with her."

"She's a flirt," Cole admitted, glancing up. "Never gets intimidated by the size of the competition. Dobby's willing to take 'em all on, both in play and in the ring."

If that wasn't a direct challenge, Jane had never heard one. "Dobby should remember that tiny little morsels like her get squashed by the competition if they're not careful."

Cole's smile acknowledged the comeback, and his eyes made a quick survey of Jane that made her want to straighten the wild red ringlets of her hair and hide her chapped lips beneath some lip balm. His gaze infused the air with a peculiar sort of tension that was more than the acknowledgment of rivalry. Not a big tension. Just a tiny current of electricity.

Cole Forrest's wife should keep him on a leash, Jane decided primly. That electricity of his should be confined to home. And evidently his little Dobby had a similar current of her own. Shadow vibrated with pure joy when the papillon sidled up to his pen and batted her eyes in an almost human fashion. Cole chuckled and leaned over the pen to give Shadow a pat.

All very entertaining, Jane acknowledged wryly, but she wished the fellow and his teacup-sized wonder dog would move on. She wanted to shop the vendors to find Shadow a reward for winning Open, and Idaho needed a toy as well—compensation for getting stuck with Jane's friend Mckenna while Shadow had fun at the shows.

"I won't keep you," Cole said finally. "I just wanted to pay our respects." His smile hinted at the devil inside. "It's always a good idea to size up the competition, don't you think?"

"Never hurts," Jane said, raising one brow slightly. "It's going to be a long summer. Hope the little mouse there has some staying power."

"I guess I'll find out."

His hundred-watt smile matched the combustible laugh, Jane noted, and it was much too confident for someone with a bad case of beginner's luck.

"I think from here we're going to hit some agility trials," he told her. "So we'll be out of the obedience people's hair for a while."

"Glad to hear it," Jane said, trying to keep the relief from her voice. "Not that it wouldn't be fun getting a bit of revenge in a rematch."

"We're always glad to provide a bit of fun," he replied, then grinned again. "Next time, we're aiming to take both Open and Utility."

She had to admire his nerve. "Good luck," she said with a laugh.

"Thank you." He called to his little mouse. "Dobby, if you lean any harder against that pen, you're going to push it over. Come back here. We need to get going."

Dobby obediently peeled herself off Shadow's pen and, giving the golden retriever a last longing look—which the dog reciprocated in full measure—trotted back to her master.

"She falls in love with anything four-legged and male. Constantly." Cole shook his head.

A dangerous problem for any female, four-legged or two-legged.

"Nice meeting you," Jane lied as they left. *Just don't come back for a while.* Bad enough to go down in defeat to a pip-squeak dog without having the pipsqueak's owner sending those little electric tingles through her veins.

Shadow woofed longingly.

"Forget it," Jane advised, leaning down. "She's not your type. Though he's—I mean *she's*—interesting, I'll confess." Picking up a leash, she dangled it temptingly in front of Shadow. "You want to go shopping? Get a new toy?"

Shadow promptly lifted a supplicating paw.

"Okay, then." She snapped the leash to his collar and opened the pen. "We'll forget all about that silly little dog." And her master with the nice laugh and the poor handling technique. Jane grinned and shook her head. "Losing turns me into such a bitch. Shame on me. Bad Jane."

THREE LONG rows of vendors crowded the backside of the grandstand, and the aisles between the rows crawled with people and dogs who had braved the chilly wind and occasional blasts of dust to peruse their wares. Holistic canine remedies crowded the shelves of one booth where an otterhound lay on a table getting a therapeutic massage. The banner above the booth read RICK TOLLESON, DVM,

ANIMAL CHIROPRACTOR AND NATUROPATH. Jane waved to Rick as she went by. He exhibited at all the shows, and everyone knew him. Next door, a Purina distributor handed out dog food samples and brochures. The next booth displayed collars, leashes, harnesses, portable exercise pens, kennels, and grooming supplies. And so on and so forth.

Jane and Shadow wove their way through the crowd with practiced ease, heading for a booth boasting two huge plastic tubs filled with stuffed dog toys. Stuffed likenesses of cats, lizards, foxes, mice, ducks, chickens, dinosaurs, and monkeys spilled out of the tubs in delightful profusion. Some squeaked, some grunted, and others whistled. Shadow, a focused shopper, went directly to the toy he wanted. He delicately plucked a fuzzy yellow duck from the pile, chomped down once, and lit up in a silly grin when the toy in his mouth went "Quack quack quack *quack* quack quack" in a fair imitation of a real duck.

A familiar feminine voice commented from nearby, "Now, if that's not an obnoxious sound, then I've never heard obnoxious."

Jane looked up to find tall, blonde Kathy Harris standing next to her. Kathy had a beagle—a breed renowned for their single-minded focus on sniffing everything within nose-reach—and had somehow found the courage to train and compete in obedience with the little hound. Jane had always admired her perseverance. With a golden retriever like Shadow, a handler worried about placing second rather than first. A beagle handler had to worry about simply passing the exercises.

"Shadow always goes straight for the most expensive toy," Jane commented. "And the noisiest. Where's Beau Dudley?"

"Home relaxing. I'm stewarding in the conformation ring today, so the dog got to stay home." Kathy's expression shifted, becoming sly. "And just who was that hot number I saw at your shade canopy a few minutes ago?"

"Hot number?"

Kathy nodded. "Definitely hot. Black hair. Good biceps. Nice tush."

Jane laughed. "How would you know if his biceps were good? He was wearing a sweater."

"Trust me. I can tell. When you've been on the hunt as long as I have, you develop a sort of X-ray vision. But you ought to know. You're—what?—thirty-five and still single?"

"Thirty," Jane supplied. "Thanks for adding five years. And for your information, the guy was not that hot. He's the upstart who took first in Utility."

Kathy's brows went up. "Oooooh! Surely not with that little piece of fluff he had with him!"

"Surely he did," Jane confirmed ruefully. "That piece of fluff is one heck of an obedience dog."

Kathy grimaced. "And you finished . . . ?"

"Second. Shadow and I got the lowly red ribbon. The papillon and Shadow both earned a score of 197, but the pap's score had a plus beside it for winning the runoff."

"Ouch. That hurts. Still," Kathy said with a smile, "he's hot."

"Married."

Kathy raised a brow. "You went so far as to ask?"

"No. Unlike some, I don't jump on a guy the minute he's within jumping range. He has a daughter. And I imagine that daughter has a mother somewhere."

"Oh. Figures. Are you going to pay for that poor duck or just let Shadow slobber it to death?"

Shadow still held the duck in his mouth, and everyone within hearing was being treated to a concert of "quack quack quack *quack* quack quack." Jane took the now thoroughly slimed toy from his mouth. "Pick another one for Idaho, big guy."

The dog didn't need a second invitation. He dove into the tub and came out with yet another duck.

"Not a duck, fur-brain. Put it back. Back!" she repeated.

The dog complied. He dove in again, this time coming up with a chartreuse dinosaur.

"Good boy. Idaho will like that one."

Kathy followed Jane to the cash register. "Did you get his name?"

Jane smiled wryly. "The married hottie?"

"Having a daughter doesn't mean anything."

"I'll bet it does to the woman who bore her."

"He could be divorced or widowed."

Shaking her head, Jane gave the toys to the clerk, along with her credit card. "He didn't look like the divorced type. He looked like the married-for-life type. But what do I know? Go get him if you want him, Kathy."

"Two for twenty or three for twenty-five," the clerk told her.

"Okay. Throw in a monkey."

"Really?" Kathy said. "You don't mind?"

"Why should I mind? A monkey for five dollars extra is a good deal."

"No!" Kathy heaved a dramatic sigh. "The guy! You don't mind if I go after the guy? After all, you saw him first."

"Be my guest. He's all yours." Jane took the bag and gave it to Shadow. "Your toys, pal. You carry the bag."

"Very cute," Kathy declared, drifting along with them to the booth next door.

"He was kind of cute," Jane admitted. "And you're right. The biceps were good."

Kathy grinned. "I meant Shadow's cute, carrying his own little bag."

Jane felt her face heat. "Well, of course Shadow's cute. But he prefers to be called handsome."

Kathy laughed. "Got to go now. I'll let you know how it goes with the hottie."

"You do that."

Jane returned Kathy's friendly wave as the woman disappeared into the crowd. How glad she was that she was happily single. Being on the prowl just had to wear on a woman.

After a little more shopping—a new pin brush for Shadow and a new cushy dog pillow for Idaho—Jane and Shadow took their purchases back to their canopy and then set off to watch the golden retrievers show in the conformation ring. Jane considered conformation competition the canine version of a beauty pageant. She wanted to spend all that time primping her dogs about as much as she wanted to spend so much time primping herself. Though it could be argued, Jane mused, that the dogs deserved primping more than she did. After all, they were prettier.

They got to the ring just as the Junior Dog class began— juniors being twelve to eighteen months old. Jane spotted a vacant metal folding chair and grabbed it. Shadow woofed quietly at the sight of all those fellow retrievers parading around the ring.

"Don't even think about it," Jane warned. "You have better things to do."

Shadow sighed.

"Not that you couldn't win, big guy. Sure you could. But who has time for that kind of fluffy stuff?"

Nevertheless, Jane cheered enthusiastically when a friend's dog took the win. As a crowd of well-wishers engulfed the winning pair, Jane started to head back to the obedience rings.

"Hello there! Wait, please. You're Jane Connor, aren't you?"

Jane turned and saw a woman pushing through the crowd toward her.

"Yes," she replied cautiously.

"And this must be Sunshine's Shadow Stalker!" the woman gushed, crouching down to retriever nose level.

At Jane's puzzled look, the woman held up a show catalog—the book that listed all the day's exhibitors, including the handler's name and full address and the registered name of the dog. "Researched both of you," the woman admitted. She stood and held out her hand in a friendly fashion. "Angela Gardner. I've been wanting to catch up to you all day so I could introduce myself, but you two don't stay in one spot for very long."

Short, blonde, and chunky, Angela wore neatly pressed blue jeans, a rather expensive-looking sweater that showed off her generous figure, and perfect makeup. Startling blue eyes twinkled from her plump face, and her smile twinkled as well, if that was possible.

Jane was sure she had never seen the woman before.

"You don't know me," Angela confirmed. "But I know you. You and Shadow and your border collie Idaho."

"Oh?" Warily, Jane took a step back.

The woman laughed reassuringly. Not one of those half-hearted feminine titters, but a genuine, straightforward belly laugh. "Don't run." She laughed again. "I get that a lot. Sometimes I come on way too strong. Comes with the territory, I guess. I'm with Animal World."

"The cable network?"

"That's the one. Actually, let me tell the strict truth. Technically, I'm not *with* Animal World. But close. Can we talk? Can I buy you a hamburger or something? I have a proposition that I think you might like." She reached down and scratched Shadow's ears. "Shadow, too."

"Well . . . sure. I guess." After all, how many people offered to take your dog out to lunch?

They bought hamburgers and iced tea at the food concession and found an empty—if rather sticky—table where they could talk.

"Lord above, but I'm hungry," Angela complained. "I could eat two of these puny hamburgers, but then I'd have to put in an extra thirty minutes exercising. Either that or buy larger jeans. I'll bet you're one of those women who burn off every calorie she eats. You look like it. Of course, you're tall, so that makes a difference. Do you work out?"

Jane blinked in surprise at the verbal barrage. "I guess lifting fifty-pound bags of dog food every day counts as working out. I own a kennel and training center in Cornville."

Angela grinned. "I know that, too. Like I said, I did my research. Amazing what you can find through Google."

Hooray for the Internet. Jane wasn't sure she liked the idea of her life being so easily available to anyone with curiosity and a computer. Privacy was a precious commodity that was fast dying, roadkill on the information superhighway.

She took a bite of hamburger, chewing slowly to buy herself time to think of a response. Shadow looked longingly at her half-eaten meal, but Jane ignored him.

"So . . ." Jane began. "You've done all this research. Why?"

"Good question. Like I said, I'm with—well, not *with*—Animal World."

"How can you be with and not with at the same time?"

"I'm a freelance television producer. I sell stuff lots of places—cable news, the History Channel, and so on and so forth. But mostly to Animal World, because I really am crazy about animals, and I'm good at making the kind of stuff that animal lovers just eat up. Did you see *Putting the Squeeze on Boa Constrictors?*"

"Uh . . . missed that one."

"Too bad. It was one of my best. How about *Zoo Nurseries?* That was a miniseries."

"I really don't have time to watch much television."

"*Dog Heroes: Where Are They Now?*"

"Nope. Sorry. I'm sure I would have liked that one."

"It was excellent. A real heartstring-puller. Not to toot my own horn, but I'm very good."

"I'm sure you are." Jane handed her last bite of hamburger to Shadow. "But what does this have to do with me and Shadow?"

"Everything!" Angela said, waving her hands in an

expansive gesture. "Absolutely everything. Animal World has changed how America regards our furry friends. Dogs have hit the big time. Animal lovers are glued to their sets watching dog shows, agility trials, stupid pet tricks, documentaries on service dogs, therapy dogs, cell dogs. They can't get enough!"

Jane gave her a noncommittal nod.

"The country has gone crazy over dog athletes. And that's where you come in. I want to do a documentary about you and Shadow. Sort of a miniseries canine reality show. You're the perfect subjects. You compete in almost everything."

"Not quite everything."

"Close enough. Anyway, you're a top-flight competitor, with a gorgeous dog that the audience will absolutely fall in love with. A Lassie for the twenty-first century."

"Lassie was a collie."

"Doesn't matter. America loves golden retrievers. They're one of the most popular breeds in the country. I tell you, Jane, you two can be stars."

Jane wondered if she could get away with simply getting up and running.

"Now, here's my plan," Angela said. "You let me and my cameraman film you doing a summer tour of agility, working toward your agility championship . . ."

"You did do your research."

Angela grinned. "I told you I'm good."

"Google again?"

"American Kennel Club website. The AKC has a great site, by the way. I got Shadow's registration number from a catalog and looked up everything he's doing."

Scary.

"Actually, Angela, Shadow and I are concentrating right now on the obedience championship. He's doing very well in agility competition also, but this summer is for obedience."

Angela grimaced. "That's great, but to the general public, obedience competition is dull, dull, dull! Everything is so rigid. Heel, sit, a few jumps and retrieves—not easy, I know, but deadly dull to the uninitiated. No noise. Not much action. But agility—now, there's a dog sport that engages the audience! Tunnels, jumps, weave poles! Dogs zipping up and down the A-frame and dog-walks. And there's always the occasional handler that trips and plows up the ground with her face. That always adds interest. Kind of like a crash at a car race."

"But..."

"We could make a whole summer tour out of it. Most of the expenses would be covered by my production company. The series would be a reality show for the canine set. It's an untapped market, and Animal World loves the idea. I've already pitched the proposal and all but have a contract in my hand."

Jane closed her eyes, imagining the nightmare of a camera following her everywhere. "It wouldn't work, Angela."

"Of course it would! If you're worried about money..."

"No," Jane denied rather sharply. "Look, I'm hardly star material. Age thirty, look thirty-five, I'm a professional fade-into-the-background sort of person."

Angela lifted one brow. "Give yourself some credit, Jane. When you're competing, you shine. I've watched you."

Flustered, Jane couldn't think of anything to say.

"You're a natural, sweetie. Shadow, too, of course. Your audience is waiting."

"No." Jane shook her head. "No. Definitely no. I have a business to run."

"The Bark Park, right?"

The woman really did do her research. "Right."

"So you'll be there most weekdays. Most of this will be weekend stuff. You must have someone who steps in for you."

Jane grimaced. "I can't, Angela. It's an interesting idea,

and I'm sure you'll do wonderfully when you find the right person, but no. I really just don't want to." And to cut off further discussion, she stood up.

Angela sighed, obviously disappointed. "You're sure?"

"I'm really sure."

"Just think about it." With an engaging smile, Angela pressed a business card into Jane's palm. "Call me when you realize what a good thing this would be."

Jane took the card—only out of courtesy. The day she let someone turn her life into a sideshow, that would be the day hell became an ice-skating rink. As she walked back toward her canopy with Shadow, she laughed out loud at the very notion.

chapter 2

BY THE time Jane folded up her canopy, loaded the van, settled Shadow into his crate, and got on the highway, the sun was sinking toward the western horizon. Driving from the high country of Flagstaff toward her home in the Verde Valley, she left the tall pines behind. Here the hills were covered with juniper and scrub grass, and as the terrain dropped in elevation, the juniper thinned out to make room for mesquite, acacia, and prickly pear cactus. Even with long shadows stealing across the landscape, the rough mesas and deep arroyos seemed to pulse with summer heat. A haze of smoke smudged the western sky, glowing orange with the dying rays of the sun. From the location of the smoke, Jane guessed the fire was somewhere on the eastern slopes of Mingus Mountain—the high country that separated the Verde Valley from Prescott Valley to the west. Even sixty miles away, Jane's nose twitched from the sharp smell of smoke. Her allergies would rage tonight.

This happened every spring. Arizona burned. Almost a decade of drought had desiccated the forests and rangelands until they were tinder waiting to explode. A cigarette thrown from a car, an unattended campfire, a lightning strike—anything could set the country ablaze. The fires would last until the monsoons of July and August brought rain, but that relief was nearly two months away.

Jane sneezed, then sneezed again. Damn, but she hated fire season!

Her part-time kennel-sitter, Suzy Crider, helped her unload when she arrived at the Bark Park, which was both her home and her business. Suzy was fortyish, short and slender, but a career grooming dogs had given her a set of muscles that would make a weight-lifter proud. She had no trouble tossing about dogs, heavy equipment, or anything else that needed tossing.

"So how did it go?" Suzy asked as they carried the heavy canopy into the storage shed.

"Won High Combined. First in Open. Second in Utility."

"Super."

Jane merely snorted.

"What? You have to win first place in everything?"

"Of course not."

"So why the long face?"

As they hefted the canopy onto its hooks on the wall, Jane grimaced. "This is not a long face." She leaned wearily against the storage shed wall. "This is a kicking-myself-in-the-butt face, a 'why wasn't I sharper?' face, and also a very tired face." With a sigh, she brushed tendrils of hair from her face and fastened her ponytail more securely. "It was a strange day," she explained. "The guy who took Utility showed this tiny little papillon, and he was a dork, but the dog did everything right."

"A dork?"

"Well, maybe not a dork." Jane smiled, thinking of Kathy setting off on the chase. Good biceps, indeed. And the fellow had possessed a very nice smile. She remembered that smile, and the memory gave her a little warm jolt.

And she had to admit that any guy with the chutzpah to

sport a sissy little papillon on the end of his leash had to have something going for him. One of those things was a disregard for image that Jane had to admire.

"He was a nice enough guy," Jane admitted.

"Good-looking?"

"Good enough. Kathy Harris went off in hot pursuit."

"Kathy Harris will pursue almost anything with external plumbing." Suzy occasionally showed her English setter, and she kept up with the show gossip.

"That's true." Jane grinned. "Poor guy."

They returned to the van to drag out the rest of the equipment. Loading it all onto a dolly, they wheeled it toward the shed.

"So what made the day so strange?" Suzy asked as she muscled the dolly over the threshold. "Losing to the papillon in Utility?"

"No." Jane chuckled. "Wait until you hear what happened right before I left. Some television producer bought me a hamburger and floated a proposition to make me and Shadow stars of some agility reality show."

Suzy nearly dropped the pen she was unloading from the dolly. "Wow! A television producer! Was *he* good-looking?"

Jane laughed. "Will you stop with the good-looking? It was a woman. She wanted to follow me around at this summer's agility trials and make it some big dramatic thing. She was aiming to get it on Animal World, is what she said."

"Cool! You're going to be famous!"

"Not! I told her to take her cameras and stuff them. Politely, of course."

Suzy responded with wide-eyed amazement. "Why?"

"Oh, please, Suzy. Can you imagine me on television? With a camera following me everywhere? I couldn't blow my nose or scratch without the whole world watching."

"Oh, Jane! Duh! They edit out that sort of stuff."

"Oh, yeah, and I would look so good on the little silver screen. Godzilla Goes to the Dog Show. I don't think so."

"Oh, garbage! So you're not a *Cosmo* model. Who cares? This is about the dogs, right?"

"Unfortunately, I would have to show up as well. Besides, I want to work Shadow in obedience this summer, not agility."

"But this is such a great opportunity!"

Jane scrunched her face. "An opportunity to be gaped at by millions. No, thank you."

"Oh, phooey! Jane, you should start letting people into your life. You don't, you know, not even your friends."

Jane grabbed the ground mats and shoved them onto a shelf with a little more force than necessary. "I let people into my life! I have a whole raft of friends—you, Nell, Mckenna, and a lot of show people."

"None of whom are as close to you as your dogs."

Jane snorted. "Bull!"

"Geez! I'd love to be on television, maybe pick up some dog food sponsors, have people know my name, have breeders want to place their very best puppies with me. I can't believe you turned it down."

"I still have the producer's card if you want to give her a call," Jane said with a chuckle. "It's right in my fanny pack. Maybe she'd consider making an English setter a star."

Suzy tilted her head, considering it, then grimaced. "Nah! They wouldn't want an also-ran, and Edsel will always be an also-ran. They want a contender, and that's you."

"A contender who has her hands full contending with the other exhibitors," Jane said firmly. "Forget dealing with a television audience."

Suzy shook her head, and they walked back toward the van.

Finally, they'd finished unloading. While Jane and Suzy had worked, Shadow had run madly about the yard in front of Jane's double-wide trailer, celebrating his homecoming with games of chase, jump, and whirl-in-place, punctuated by intense sniffing to ascertain what might have changed while he had been away. Now, having run off some of his energy, he sat panting on the patio, waiting for Jane to give him attention.

Watching him, Jane smiled fondly.

"Mckenna called a time or two," Suzy said as they walked toward the house. "She says that Idaho has been good, but he hasn't taken his eyes off the driveway since you left him at her place. He really missed you."

"Poor old guy. It's tough being retired. He adores Mckenna, and I thought he'd be happier with her for a couple of days rather than staying here. Next time I'll take him with us, just for company."

Jane paid Suzy, thanked her profusely for watching the kennel over the weekend, then saw her on her way. The evening chores had to be done—feeding the dogs in the kennel, and checking on her "guests" to make sure their pens were clean, their water fresh, and no one had decided to eat his or her dog bed. Picking up Idaho in Prescott would have to wait for the next day, Jane decided, so before beginning work, she phoned Mckenna.

"Hey there!" Mckenna answered her phone. "How did the trials go?"

"Fine. Got High Combined. How's Idaho?"

"Missing you. But he's been schmoozing with Clara. You've never seen such an odd couple—bouncy, always-on-the-run Idaho and fat old Clara, whose favorite position is sprawled flat on the carpet. But they're good friends, for some reason."

"Of course. Idaho loves everyone, and Clara is very lovable. Would you mind the boy's company for one more night? I'm really too tired to drive the fifty miles over to your place this evening. Plus I have all the kennel chores."

"Leave him. If Tom had his way, he'd file adoption papers on that dog. He thinks Idaho hangs the moon."

"Not a chance. Idaho is my main man. Besides, Shadow would drive me crazy without Idaho to entertain him."

"Say, that Hassayampa fire isn't close to you, is it? We've been hearing a lot about it on the news. It just started last night, and it's already burned three thousand acres. So far it's only twenty percent contained."

"I don't think it's that close. I don't see anyone in the area packing up their stuff to leave. The smoke is thick, though. My sinuses are objecting. Wish the wind would change."

"Well, you take care. We'll see you tomorrow."

Shadow chastised her with a look when she hung up the phone.

"Don't worry, big guy. You'll see Idaho tomorrow. If you can't do without his company tonight, then *you* drive over to Prescott."

With a disgusted whuff, the dog jumped onto the sofa and sprawled there in weary disappointment.

Two hours later, after feeding all fifteen boarding dogs, letting each of them into a play yard to exercise, hosing out a pen where one client had been particularly messy, putting kibble out for the boarding cats, cleaning litter boxes, and checking the grooming shed to make sure Suzy hadn't left the coffeepot on (which was her habit), Jane threw a hamburger patty into a skillet and rummaged in the fridge for salad makings.

She ate a solitary dinner while watching the ten o'clock news. Not much had changed in the world since she had left on Friday. The Middle East was still a mess, Washington politicians were trading accusations and excuses in the latest scandal, and the farmers in the Midwest were making doomsday predictions about the drought.

If they wanted to see drought, Jane thought, then those tractor jockeys should come out west.

On the local news, the Hassayampa fire rated a ten-second update. The blaze was indeed only twenty percent contained, but just now it threatened no structures, the newscaster said. A bigger fire burning in the Catalina Mountains near Tucson got much more attention.

Still sprawled on the sofa, Shadow was too tired to take up his usual station near the table as Jane ate. Even the prospect of a scrap or two couldn't lure him from his snooze. Competition was fun for dogs, but also exhausting, especially for a young dog. Shadow was so well behaved that Jane often had to remind herself how young he was. At eighteen months, he had scarcely climbed out of puppy-hood.

"Hey, Shadow!" she called. "Prewash time."

The big golden head lifted from the sofa cushion, ears tilted forward. Tradition in Jane's household dictated that dogs did not get fed from the table, but at the end of any meal, they got to prewash the plates before Jane put them into the dishwasher. Usually the plate Jane put on the floor had little besides crumbs, but the dogs regarded the job as their sacred privilege.

Weary as he was, Shadow was up to the task. As he licked his way through hamburger juice, a few pieces of lettuce with ranch dressing, and a bit of mustard, Jane chuckled. "See, Shadow, there are some advantages to not having Idaho here. You get the dinner plate all to yourself."

Shadow licked his chops.

"Come on, then. Let's leave the dishes and sit outside for a while."

This, also, was a nightly ritual. Jane's old mobile home boasted a roofed patio—"patio" being a fancy term for con-crete slab—that ran the length of the trailer. A large fenced-in yard planted with sturdy Bermuda grass doubled as a play area for her dogs and a training yard for her obedience classes. A long bench under the roof provided a place for spectators to watch the classes. (People dragged a surpris-ing number of relatives and friends to watch their efforts to train Fido.) The bench also afforded a perfect place for Jane to sit on a nice evening, to think about the day and plan for tomorrow. It was her perch to watch the brilliant stars in the winter sky, smell the cactus blossoms that perfumed the spring, marvel at midsummer lightning displays, revel in the welcome relief of autumn's cool air.

Tonight, however, the stars struggled to make themselves known through a veil of smoke. The only season that Jane didn't like was late spring, which was the heart of the Arizona wildfire season—dry, dusty, hot, and usually smoky. Her sinuses complained, her eyes itched, and her heart cringed at the thought of all the creatures endangered by the flames.

Lying beside the bench, Shadow sneezed.

"My thoughts exactly," Jane agreed.

Still, she settled into the seat feeling content. A hundred feet from the house, a security light illuminated the kennel building, which held her office and three wings of indoor-outdoor pens. On the other side of the kennel stood the grooming shed. No cut-rate steel prefabs these. The woman who had built the Bark Park, run it for ten years, then sold it to Jane, had been a wealthy widow who could afford a class act. People who pulled into the long driveway saw a first-rate operation, where they could safely leave their pets in comfort. Sometimes when Jane looked at the place, she still couldn't believe that it was hers, bought and paid for. Through hard work and know-how, she had transformed the Bark Park from a mere hobby operation to a decent living for herself, boarding and grooming dogs, teaching obedience classes, hosting the occasional workshops for agility, herding, and tracking.

The kennel required hard work, but Jane didn't mind. All her life she had wanted to work with animals. During the years she had spent at the university earning a business degree, she had had no intentions of doing anything other than setting up her own animal business.

And that was what she had done.

"Life is good," she told Shadow.

Shadow sighed and laid his muzzle on the toe of her sneaker.

"Yeah, yeah," Jane told him. "I know. The place seems lonely without Idaho. But we'll go get the old man tomorrow, and then things will be back to normal. But you have to appreciate the present for what it is, even if it's not quite perfect. Be grateful for the good things of each moment in time. Somebody great said that, or something like it, I think." Jane had earned a minor in philosophy at the university. Talking philosophy with her dogs, she had since found, was far superior to talking philosophy with fellow students and professors.

"Yessir, it simply doesn't get any better than this," she told the dog.

A brief image flashed through her mind—Cole Forrest and his little mouse-dog delighting in their victory. For just an instant she suffered a flash of loneliness. Suzy had accused her of not letting anyone into her life. In a way, she had been right. Jane was a loner by choice. Not because she didn't like people. She did. But when one lived alone and worked alone, solitude became a habit. Dealing with people became an effort. Privacy became the norm.

Not that she didn't have friends. Certainly she did. But she didn't share much of herself with anyone. Would life be better, Jane wondered, if she had someone like Cole Forrest, with his easy smile and broad shoulders? And his charm. And yes, she had to admit it. The man possessed charm in spades.

Shadow looked up at her, as if sensing deep thoughts. Jane dropped a hand to caress his golden head.

"Nah," she said to the dog. "I've got you and Idaho. We do just fine together." Jane couldn't picture herself, at the entrenched age of thirty, handing even partial control of her life to someone else—like her mom, who had felt compelled to consult with her husband before something as minor as changing the brand of coffee that she bought at the grocery. The purchase of a dress or a pair of shoes had called for a veritable summit conference.

It would take more than a nice smile, broad shoulders, and a ton of charm to lure her from comfortable independence. Men like Cole Forrest looked good at first sight, but once you got to know them, they grew warts. That was a little piece of wisdom Mckenna had once shared with her, and Mckenna had to have dated every hunky guy between the Pacific Ocean and the Mississippi River.

Of course, Mckenna was now happily married, and she might no longer subscribe to that particular philosophy. Jane would have to ask her someday.

She yawned, coughed a bit at the pungent odor of smoke, and stood. "Ready for bed?" she asked Shadow.

The dog rose and stretched elaborately, as if agreeing that it was about time they turned in.

But when they went through the door, the dinner dishes awaited them, piled sloppily beside the sink.

Jane uttered a colorful expletive, then brightened. "We'll leave them," she told the dog. "They can wait until morning."

One of the advantages of living alone was the ability to go to bed and leave dirty dishes in the sink. That privilege alone could substitute for a lot of the benefits of togetherness.

JANE WOKE to an insistent pounding at the front door that catapulted her into heart-racing alarm. A glance at her alarm clock told her that dawn was still four hours away. Shadow raced back and forth through the bedroom door, hurrying Jane along as she pulled on a pair of jeans and a T-shirt.

"Hold your horses!" she called out in a sleep-roughened voice. "I'm coming." *And this had better not be the neighbor's troublemaking kids playing pranks.* She grabbed a cast-iron skillet from the top of the stove, just in case something more dangerous than mischievous kids waited at the door.

The late-night intruder was neither a kid nor a serial killer. It was George Marcos, Yavapai County sheriff's deputy, with his uniform shirt only half tucked in and his hat askew. He looked as if he had been rousted from bed as well.

"George! What the hell?"

"Hey, Jane! We're evacuating everyone south of the highway. The wind's shifted, and the fire is headed here fast."

"What?" Her heart jumped in alarm.

"No time to talk! Leave now. Don't pack, just leave. The fire caught us with our pants down, and it's right over the ridge. There's no time to fool around." He was already trotting toward the front gate, where the lights atop his squad car turned the smoky night a flashing blue. As he hurried out the gate, he repeated his warning. "Leave now!"

For a few seconds Jane stood frozen in denial, sure that George's midnight intrusion was some kind of cruel joke. Wildfires generally calmed during the night's cooler temperatures and milder winds. Then she realized that large gusts were shaking the trailer, rattling a loose gutter and singing through the patio wind chimes. Smoke was everywhere, along with stinging, choking ash. A sullen orange glow outlined the ridge to the west. George was right. Hell was headed their way.

The sight of that ominous orange glow inspired a sharp stab of fear. She couldn't just up and leave, condemning fifteen client dogs and two cats to roast in their pens. Unthinkable. But she didn't have time. She could see the first flames topping the ridge, barely a mile away.

Shadow barked, infected by her panic.

"Do something, Jane, idiot! Do something!" she told herself.

Dammit! She would *make* time! No way could she leave all these animals to such a horrendous fate.

She grabbed the van's keys from their hook beside the door and ran to the garage, Shadow leading the way.

"Go, go, go!" she urged herself as she threw every dog crate she could find into the big van. There wouldn't be enough, but that was just too bad. She would have to make do.

Someone grabbed her from behind. Jane shrieked and whirled to face a firefighter in his bulky suit and helmet.

"Get out of here!" he shouted at her. "This area has been evacuated."

"I'm going! But there's a whole pack of dogs in the kennel building that have to go with me."

"Leave without them! Look!"

The fire had crested the ridge and was now eating its way downhill through the dry scrub vegetation, straight toward them. Firefighters were desperately trying to clear a firebreak that would protect the few homes and businesses tucked among the brushy hills, but even Jane could see it had little chance of succeeding. Even as she watched, the firefighters started to retreat.

She ignored the firefighter and headed for the kennel building.

"We're not holding this line, I'm warning you!"

"I'll go as soon as the animals are in my van."

He reached out to grab her again, but she swatted his hands away. "Go fight the fire!"

He spat into the dust. "You're on your own, then."

By the time Jane emerged with the first two dogs—a big poodle and a miniature schnauzer—he was gone. The firefighters were retreating, moving to a battlefront where they had more chance of holding the line. The fire was a quarter of the way down the ridge.

When she brought out the second pair of dogs—a Labrador retriever and a mastiff—the fire crackled halfway down the slope. By the next pair, a collie-shepherd mix and another Lab, the whole ridge danced with fire, and burning embers were landing in the front yard.

"Shadow!" Jane shouted. "Get in the van!"

The golden retriever leapt into the front passenger seat and barked a plea for Jane to join him.

"Stay there, buddy," she warned. "I'll be along."

On the next trip she brought three dogs—two cocker spaniels and a shih tzu. Thick, hot air seared her lungs. But she couldn't leave yet. She returned to the kennel to bring out two rat terriers, a dachshund, and a German shepherd.

The van nearly vibrated with the barks and howls of alarmed dogs. When she emerged with the last two dogs— a Lab mix and a beagle—the fire front burned a mere two hundred feet away and seemed to fill the whole landscape. Dry juniper and mesquite exploded like small bombs. Grass withered and charred. A hellish wind whipped smoke and ash through the air in fiery whirlwinds. Jane could scarcely see. Her eyes streamed. Her throat threatened to close.

The cats came out on the last trip, yowling and clawing at their carriers. Jane threw them on top of the mastiff's crate and rushed for the van's driver's seat, where she had to displace a dachshund and a rat terrier to get in. Shadow shared the front passenger seat with the collie mix and schnauzer. The shih tzu and beagle crowded their heads anxiously between the seats. In their crates, the others continued to bark, howl, cry, and otherwise sound the alarm.

By the time Jane shoved the key into the ignition and the engine roared to life, the grooming shed had begun to burn.

chapter 3

COLE FORREST propped his feet on his desk and stared moodily out the window at the sun rising over the Sandia Range. He remembered as a kid staring at the same mountains, looking out the same window, only back then this room hadn't been a home office. It had been his mother's sewing room, complete with a fancy Singer sewing machine that could do every stitch imaginable. That machine had produced clothes for the entire family—his mom, his dad, his sister, and himself. Shirts, skirts, dresses, trousers, even pajamas and nightgowns. When Cole was very small, that machine had fascinated him, and he'd sat for long periods of time watching his mom sew.

Not that he remembered back that far. His older sister Nancy had told him the story, citing it as evidence he was from another planet. Or had suffered a brain transplant at birth. Or whichever story she had conjured up at the moment. Nancy had had an active imagination. She still did, making big bucks as a nationally syndicated cartoonist. No self-respecting newspaper could get by without having *Slugnuts* on their comics page.

All the memories—his parents, his sister, this old farm-house where he now sat on the outskirts of Albuquerque, New Mexico—all these images of the past overlay a world that was in ways still the same, yet so different. He heard his daughter playing in the yard where he had once played. Her high, piping voice harangued poor Dobby with a series of nonsensical commands. The poor dog would be thoroughly confused by the time his housekeeper got here and distracted Teri with other entertainments. Thirty years ago, he had harassed his own dog, a long-suffering collie, with similar games.

But thirty years ago, he hadn't played against a background sound of traffic. And his mother hadn't worried about him dealing with drugs, guns, or terrorists in school.

"Yo, bro!" came a comment from the doorway. "You in a blue funk?"

Jerked back to the present by the arrival of his friend and business partner, Cole slid his feet from the desk and smiled. "No funk, Henry. Just looking out the window and remembering what the view used to look like before the foothills over there got eaten up by developers. No wonder Nancy doesn't ever want to visit. When you grow up in a place and collect great memories, seeing everything change just sort of eats away at all those warm recollections."

Henry laughed. "Tell it to Hallmark. Man, you're the only guy I know who has fond recollections of childhood." He dropped his long, lean body into a threadbare armchair. "Come to think of it, you're the only guy I know who still lives in the old family homeplace. How old is this farm-house?"

"I don't know exactly. I think it was old when my folks bought it."

"Well, old is picturesque, but air-conditioning is what counts on a day like today. It's no wonder you want to move. What I don't understand is why you have to go so rural on me and move to . . . where?"

"I have applications in at community colleges in Cottonwood, Arizona; Farmington, New Mexico; Glenwood Springs, Colorado—"

"Podunk, Nowheresville," Henry added. "Man, I just don't understand this urge to become a hayseed."

Henry Mason had grown up in rural Georgia in a poor black community, made the move from poverty with a full-ride basketball scholarship to the state university, earned top grades in the computer science curriculum, and after graduation declared that the Georgia backwoods had seen the last of him. He had moved his widowed mother to Albuquerque, talked his way into a good job with a computer firm, and now, eight years later, moonlighted at the local community college where Cole had taught mathematics and computer science for the past five years. Over the last eighteen months, Henry and Cole had created Southwest Computer Consulting. Henry specialized in the hardware end of the business, while Cole took care of troubleshooting software and setting up networks.

"You can have the big city," Cole told Henry. "Crowded freeways, pollution, cracker-box houses springing up everywhere there used to be open land and clean, uncluttered hills—I've had my fill of it. I want to raise Teri someplace where she can listen to birds instead of sirens and see blue sky instead of a brown cloud."

Henry made a face.

"You'll do fine with Southwest Computer on your own."

With a snort, Henry agreed. "That's a fact. I'm going to be rolling in money before too long. But you're going to starve on a community college teacher's salary."

"Don't worry about that. Small-town businesses use computers, too. I'll just do another start-up. In the meantime, Teri and I will have the whole summer to ourselves, roaming the country, having fun with Dobby at the trials, while the realtor puts this place on the market." The trials would be fun. Dobby liked agility even better than she liked obedience competition, and Cole was eager to see if such a tiny dog could hold her own in the sport. She might be as good as she was at the obedience trials—beating out the "top guns."

Thinking of one of those top guns made him grin. The touchy redhead with the golden retriever certainly did not like to come in second. What was her name? Jane. That was it. Jane. Too bad she wasn't going to be at the agility trials. He wouldn't mind coming up against her again. He liked her style—straightforward, no-nonsense, and not afraid to throw a few darts his way.

"What's that smile about, man?" Henry asked. "You look a million miles away."

Cole shook his head. "Just looking forward to the summer. I really am. Did I tell you that Nancy signed her half of the house over to me?"

"That's nice, man, but why shouldn't she? How many millions does she have?"

Cole grinned and stood. "A few."

"I can't believe that sister of yours got herself engaged without talking to me. If she wanted to turn all that money into community property—well, hell! I would've married her."

"I'm sure she'll be devastated to hear that she blew it. Come on." Cole slapped his partner on the bicep. "We've got time for a little one-on-one before meeting with Stan."

Henry followed him out the door. "Fool, I don't know why you insist on subjecting yourself to this humiliation. You know I'll wipe up the driveway with you."

Cole grabbed the basketball as they walked through the mudroom. "I need something to keep me humble after beating you ten straight games at Third Universe."

Henry grumbled. "That doesn't count. You wrote the program for that stupid game."

Cole threw the ball hard at Henry's chest. "Play ball."

· · ·

SEVERAL HUNDRED miles west, the sun rose over Arizona's Mogollon Rim, and Jane woke up with the nightmare stench of smoke still in her nostrils. Her throat was raw. Her lungs hurt with every breath. And she was hot. Suffocatingly hot. Two warm furry bodies pressed against her, one black and white, one golden. And on her chest, sphinxlike, lay Mckenna's Burmese cat, Nefertiti. Slanted amber eyes gazed down into Jane's with seeming concern. If Jane didn't know better, she would have thought that Titi knew something was wrong and wanted to comfort her. She did know better, though. Even considering Titi was a certified therapy cat, she was still a cat. And cats were, well, cats.

Dogs, on the other hand, took a person's troubles as their own, and Jane could feel anxiety rolling in waves from Idaho and Shadow. They crowded close to her both to comfort and be comforted. Jane closed her aching eyes and hugged both dogs.

"It's okay, boys. We'll be all right."

She couldn't put much certainty into her voice, though. Everything she possessed had gone up in smoke. Insurance would help, of course, but some things simply couldn't be replaced—her business files, her books, her photos of her parents and all the dogs who had kept her company from the time she was five. The dog art that she had accumulated over the years. Her trophies, Idaho's obedience championship certificate, all the title certificates from the American Kennel Club, United Kennel Club, Australian Shepherd Club of America.

All gone.

At least she had saved the boarding animals. If they had died on her watch, she wouldn't have been able to live with herself.

The animals! What had happened to her charges?

Jane threw back the bedcovers and pried herself from under Titi's weight. She wore one of Mckenna's T-shirts, she noted—the one stating "Cats Are People Too." Mckenna must have somehow gotten her out of her smoky clothing, because Jane certainly didn't remember doing it.

She swung long legs over the edge of the bed and sat up. Big mistake. A truly awesome pain speared through her head, front to back. Only sheer determination kept her from throwing up all over Mckenna's carpet. Dropping her head into her hands, she groaned. Why didn't she just die right now? Then she wouldn't have to deal with all this.

Idaho and Shadow jumped off the bed and began seeking her hands with wet, cold noses, looking for assurance that she was okay. Nefertiti brushed against Jane's bare legs, rumbling as she wound between her calves. The animal attention didn't make the pain go away, but somehow it did make her feel as if survival might be possible.

"Head about to fall off?" asked a voice. "Smoke will do it every time."

Jane looked up—squinting—to see Mckenna regarding her with sympathy. As usual, she was smartly turned out. She stood in the doorway wearing neatly pressed jeans and a silk knit shell with a matching pottery-bead necklace, her sculpted black hair perfect, her makeup flawless. All in all, Mckenna looked remarkably together, considering that the world was coming to an end. But, oh yeah, it was only Jane's world coming to an end.

Mckenna shook her head. "Your sinuses must feel like they're on fire."

"Something like that," Jane rasped, then turned her attention to the important stuff. "The animals, Mckenna. God, tell me they're not still in the van. I did manage to tell you I brought the dogs and cats from the kennel, right?"

"It was the first thing you said. And the last. You passed out."

"No way!"

"Way." Mckenna grinned. "Your Superwoman rep is tarnished for good. Don't worry about the menagerie. Tom and I got them all settled in the barn, and they're quite comfortable. Except for that freaking schnauzer. What a mouth on that dog! And I'll bet every word he utters is a German curse."

Jane managed a faint smile. "Figi's mama spoils him terribly."

"Yes, well, I hope his mama comes and picks him up very soon, before I'm tempted to take him in for surgery on his vocal cords." She moved over to the bed and helped Jane stand. "I'd wager that a nice warm shower and then some breakfast would make you feel better. You're one shade paler than paste. Come on. I'll help you to the bathroom."

The shower worked a miracle, and when Jane stepped out of it she found her own clothing, the jeans and T-shirt she had been wearing the night before, neatly folded on the bathroom counter, smelling of laundry soap. She put them on, then pulled her wet hair into a long ponytail. Her hair seldom looked good by anyone's standard, but this morning a patchwork of singeing added a bit of unique interest to the mop.

Jane grimaced at herself in the bathroom mirror, then shrugged. As a concession to vanity—every woman had *some*, after all—she wound her springy red ponytail into a fairly neat pile and fastened it with a butterfly clip she found in the bathroom drawer. Trust Mckenna to have spare beauty aids in every bathroom in her house.

By the time she walked into Mckenna's kitchen, Jane felt almost human. Not quite, but almost.

"You're beginning to look as if you might live," Mckenna told her. "Sit down. Bacon and eggs are almost ready, and there's toast and jelly on the table. And I fed the dogs, so don't believe the story they're telling you."

A pathetic story indeed. Idaho, Shadow, and Tom's geriatric Labrador, Clara, sat beside the kitchen table with starvation in their eyes. Titi regarded them from on top of the refrigerator, intent on making sure that the dogs didn't get a handout unless the cat got a share.

"Forget it, guys," Jane said. "The jig is up. Now lie down."

Plainly disappointed, the dogs oozed toward the floor in reluctant obedience while Jane played with a piece of toast. In spite of the rumbling in her stomach, she wasn't really hungry.

Would her life ever be the same?

"Tom at work?" Jane asked.

"Yes. He has a big trial coming up. *State versus Forbes.* Big drug bust. He really wants to win this one."

"You could've gone to work, too. A one-woman practice like yours can't afford for you to be lollygagging around home taking care of me."

Mckenna laughed. "Leave you alone after what happened? Right. By the way, since all your records, including phone numbers, are toast, I phoned the local radio stations, and they're going to announce that anyone who had an animal boarded at the Bark Park should pick it up here. And I talked to the newspapers, too. Not the Prescott paper, but the little rags over in the Cornville-Cottonwood-Sedona area. Though I suppose these folks are out of town, or they wouldn't have dropped off Fluffy and Fido at the kennel."

"Most of the animals were due to go home this morning."

"Good. Then Tom's horses can have their barn back." She set a plate of sunnyside-up eggs and two strips of turkey bacon in front of Jane, along with a cup of steaming tea.

"What's the news on the fire? Have you heard?"

"It bypassed most of Cornville and headed out into the brush north of Bill Grey Road. The news this morning said it's about sixty percent contained, so they're getting a handle on it."

Jane set her jaw, wondering if she would ever lose the image of her grooming shed catching fire. No doubt the rest of her home had followed. She would have to find the courage to go back and look, and to drag whatever she could from the ashes.

Mckenna pulled out a chair and sat, looking across the

table at Jane intently. "That was a brave and wonderful thing you did, Jane—saving those dogs and cats. You're a heroine. I'm just so proud of you."

Jane shook her head. "No one would have left those animals to roast."

"Almost anyone would have," Mckenna argued. "Most people would have grabbed the personal dogs and the cash box and run for it. Give yourself credit."

Jane groaned at the reminder. "Oh, man! The cash box. I had about three thousand dollars worth of checks and credit card receipts that are now ash. Damn!"

Mckenna squeezed her hand. "That's what insurance is for, sweetie."

"MY INSURANCE is what?" Jane shouted into the phone receiver.

"Expired," a bland voice on the other end of the line replied. "As of May thirtieth."

Jane sputtered. "That's impossible. My payments are up to date."

"No, ma'am. We received no payment for the period ending May thirtieth."

"But I mailed it! I'm sure I mailed it!"

"We didn't receive it," droned the voice, uninterested, uncaring that Jane's life lay in ashes and smoke.

"It must have been delayed in the mail!" She tried to keep her voice from squeaking.

"If we receive it, then your policy will be reinstated."

Like that was going to happen when the insurance company discovered the insured property had just burned to the ground. Or at least that was what the sheriff's office had told her. Jane would be allowed back into the area in a day or so to see for herself.

"Is there anything more I can do for you, ma'am?"

An invitation to drop dead sprang to Jane's lips, but she

stifled it and settled for slamming the phone into its cradle. It wasn't the woman's fault that Jane's payment had gotten waylaid in the mail.

Mckenna peeked in through the doorway. "The Carlisles are here to pick up Bucky. Uh-oh. From the look on your face, I'd guess trouble."

"The insurance company claims my policy is expired."

Mckenna let out a long breath. "Are you paid up?"

"I thought I was. But of course all my policy paperwork is toast. And my bank statements, too."

"Would you have a record in your checkbook?"

Jane saw a spark light in Mckenna's eyes. Since Mckenna had traded in her law practice defending the rich and famous for a legal crusade benefiting the put-upon, she had acquired a passion for tilting at windmills.

"You did save your checkbook, didn't you?"

"I keep the check register on the now-melted computer, but I think I have an old-fashioned version in my handbag. I usually record checks in both."

"Okay, then we can deal with this."

"But first I'd better see Bucky on his way."

Bucky's owners were tearfully grateful that their dog, a collie-shepherd mix with a huge coat of hair and a sweet expression, hadn't been cremated alive in the fire.

"If there's anything we can do for you," Mr. Carlisle told Jane as his wife hugged the dog and cried into its plush coat, "just name it. We should give you a reward. . . ."

"No, you shouldn't," Jane demurred, fighting back her own tears. "Of course I got him out. You trusted him to me, and I take that seriously."

"Are you sure? It doesn't seem right. . . ."

"I'm just glad he's fine. That's enough reward, believe me."

"If we can help—"

"I'll let you know." She didn't need help, Jane thought morosely. She needed a miracle. "Take him home. Give him an extra hug or two."

More of the same followed. Figi the schnauzer left, and Jane had to laugh at Mckenna's little jig of relief when the big-mouth went home. The two Labs, Mr. Wiggles the mastiff, one of the rat terriers, and both cats were collected by owners who showered Jane with praise and thanks. She didn't feel as if she'd done anything above and beyond what she owed her clients, and she was too tired to patiently recount the nightmare more than once or twice. In fact, the whole awful night was becoming blurred. Details melted together into a jumble of frightening images and horrific possibilities.

But Jane accepted the praise and endured the hyperbole, the tears and the hugs. She knew how she would feel if her animals had been in danger and someone had snatched them from the path of death.

By late afternoon, the barn housed only four dogs, and their anxious owners had all telephoned from out of town after hearing about the fire on national news. The county sheriff had directed them to Mckenna.

So with the animal situation under control, Jane dug out her checkbook and started searching for the most recent payment to her insurance company. It didn't take her long to find it. She had written the check on the fifteenth of April, and the payment had been due May 1.

Jane felt a flush of triumph. Everything would be all right. Mckenna would go to bat for her and force the insurance company to live up to their responsibilities. If they had lost her payment, that wasn't Jane's fault. She had the proof of payment right here in her checkbook. Mckenna crowed in anticipation of yet another victory for the underdog when she saw the register.

Feeling much better, Jane decided she would drive into town to buy some fresh clothing. All she possessed was the clothes she wore, and unless she wanted to launder them every night, a couple of pairs of jeans and several shirts were in order.

Forty-five minutes later, the world was looking brighter than it had all morning. But as Jane threw her bags of Kmart purchases into the backseat of her van, her eye caught a corner of paper sticking out from beneath the plastic drink caddy that fit between the front seats. Ordinarily, she would have ignored it. Her van was full of flotsam and junk—receipts from fast-food drive-throughs, junk mail, discarded shopping lists, and other miscellaneous bits of paper. Daily life was full of bits of paper, and Jane hadn't cleaned out the van in several months.

With a sinking feeling in her stomach, Jane grabbed the corner and pulled. An envelope, wrinkled and dirty, slipped from beneath the caddy. It bore a stamp not franked by the post office. And it was addressed to her insurance company. Even though she knew very well what was inside, Jane opened the envelope anyway.

There it was, her biannual insurance premium. Yes indeed, she had written a check for the insurance payment. Then she had stuck it in an envelope, stamped it, and taken it with other bills to the post office to be mailed. But this little envelope had slipped off the seat of the van and slid beneath the drink caddy.

She was toast.

"I CAN'T believe I did that!" Jane wailed to Mckenna. "How could I do that?" She collapsed into a kitchen chair, nearly sliding under the table in misery.

Mckenna handed her a Bloody Mary. "You didn't do anything. Things like that happen. Envelopes get blown off the seat and hide somewhere where you don't find them until six months later. It's happened to me. It's happened to everyone. The timing sucks, that's all. It's not your fault."

"Explain that to the insurance company."

"Yes, well, it's not their fault either. Legally, you were uninsured when the fire went through your place."

Jane took a healthy swig of her drink.

"Hey, sweetie, go slowly. I put double vodka in that Bloody Mary."

"I need double vodka," Jane replied, then took another gulp. "God, Mckenna. What am I going to do?"

"Things will work out somehow."

Jane thought her assurance lacked conviction.

"Tell you what," Mckenna continued. "We'll talk to Tom tonight when he comes home. Maybe he'll have some bright ideas."

"What bright ideas could there be? Both my home and my business went up in smoke, along with the past week's receipts and everything I own. I have no insurance, and the money in my checking and savings together might last me through the summer if I'm lucky."

As if on cue, the phone on the kitchen wall rang. Mckenna answered, and after listening for a brief moment, put her hand over the mouthpiece and said to Jane, "It's Nell."

"I was going to call, but things have been chaos today," Mckenna said into the phone.

Mckenna waved Jane over. "Of course Jane's all right. It takes more than a wildfire to get our Jane down. And she saved every single dog and cat in her kennel."

She shook her head and handed the phone to Jane. "Mother Nell would like to speak to you."

"I should have called," Jane said when she took the phone.

"No, no," Nell's familiar voice said. "I can understand how you might be overwhelmed right now, but Jane, when I saw the news, I was frantic. They're making a really big deal of the kennel being burned to the ground. Please tell me they exaggerate."

Nell Travis loved the Bark Park almost as much as she did, Jane knew. They had taught obedience classes together for several years before Nell had married and moved away.

Not to mention that the local pet therapy team—Nell's favorite project—had used Jane's home as sort of an unofficial headquarters for meetings, training, social get-togethers, and whatnot.

Jane sighed. "They didn't exaggerate, Nell."

The momentary silence on the line was heavy with distress. "Burned to the ground?" Nell asked quietly.

"That's what the sheriff's office says. I haven't been back to look. When I finally hotfooted it out of there, the place had already caught fire. The way that fire was ripping through everything in its path, I can't imagine that anything survived."

"Oh, Jane!"

The full implications of the disaster welled up anew to choke off Jane's breath. She couldn't utter a word.

"You'll rebuild it even better," Nell comforted her. "And in the meantime, you can live at my place down by the river. Dan and I are coming north for the summer—you know Dan is doing a law internship in Tom's office. But there's the guest room over the garage where you can have plenty of privacy. You can't say no."

Jane swallowed hard, then explained the situation. She couldn't rebuild. She couldn't recoup her losses. God only knew what she could do. Right then she didn't have a clue.

Nell was silent a moment, apparently absorbing Jane's situation. Then she offered to loan Jane the money she needed at zero interest.

Jane shook her head. She should have known this was coming. Ever since Nell had come into a fortune a little over a year earlier, she had worked hard to share it with every Tom, Dick, and Harry who had a need. Only the fact that the trust fund actually belonged to her dog Piggy kept her from splurging on every charity that came calling, and plenty came calling. Nell and Piggy had hit newscasts everywhere when a well-heeled old gentleman had left his fortune to the little Welsh corgi, who had been his favorite pet therapist. Poor Nell, Piggy's official guardian, had endured a deluge from those wanting a part of the old man's largesse.

But Jane was not going to be one of those petitioners, no matter how much she needed money. She could stand on her own two feet. Independence was one of the cornerstones of her life, and a mountain of bad luck wasn't going to make her desperate enough to sponge off her friends.

"Nell, you're choking me up. Really. That is so generous of you. But not necessary. I have a good track record in business, and good credit, too. I should be able to get a business loan from the bank. I was just venting, and I probably made things sound worse than they are. Besides, I swear Piggy nearly has a heart attack every time you find a use for her money that doesn't involve dog treats, dog beds, or dog food."

Nell laughed. "She does, doesn't she? It's amazing how human she seems sometimes. But think about it, please. And I'm reserving our guest room for you at the river house."

When Jane hung up the phone, in spite of Nell's offer of help, she felt worse than ever. Last fall, a car crash had robbed Mckenna of most of her memory, her education, her house, and her means of making a living. Nell had offered Mckenna a place to live and other much-needed assistance. Jane had thought Mckenna a fool for refusing, but now she understood. The prospect of living on someone else's charity, no matter how kind the giver's intentions, left a sour taste in the mouth.

A nudge at her leg drew Jane's attention to Shadow. The golden retriever had dropped a chew toy at her feet in hopes of a game of fetch. Idaho sat a few feet away, watching her with a worried canine frown that echoed the concern on Mckenna's face. Jane had to smile. She certainly had good friends, only some of them human.

"I know what will cheer you up," Mckenna said decisively. "Let's drive over to Jerome and have a beer at the Brewery. That's your favorite place in the world."

When Jane didn't answer immediately, Mckenna added, "My treat."

Another kind offer of charity. It was just a beer, but still, the thought of not paying her own way stuck in Jane's craw. She reached into her fanny pack for her wallet. "No, my treat. I'm still solvent. At least for a while."

She opened her wallet to check just how solvent she was, and a white card sticking out from behind a credit card caught her eye. A faint memory pinged at her brain as she fished the card out.

Angela Gardner, it read in fancy script. *Rising Star Productions.*

A crazy idea, born of desperation, blossomed in Jane's mind.

chapter 4

"SCORE ONE for me!" Cole crowed. "That's seven."

"No fair!" Teri neatly caught the basketball he tossed her.

"Why no fair?"

"No fair 'cause you're tall." She dribbled the ball down the length of the driveway toward the basket, never missing a beat.

"Well, no fair because you're young and agile," her father countered, making little feints in a pretty good pretense—he thought—of guarding the basket.

"No fair because you're old and tall." She danced lightly around his guard, still dribbling steadily.

"When you're thirty-three, I'm going to remind you that when you were an eight-year-old pipsqueak, you said that thirty-three is old."

"When I'm thirty-three," Teri shot back, "I'll be rich and have my own house and I won't care that I'm old."

She darted this way and that, light on her feet as only an eight-year-old pixie can be. Cole feinted, held up his arms in a great show, then quickly circled around to lift the little girl by her waist. Hooting with victory, she slam-dunked the ball.

"That's twelve for me! I win!"

He laughed. "So you do. How about we celebrate with a drink?"

"Yeah!" she crowed as he swept her back to ground level. "I could use a cold one!"

A cold one for Teri, sometimes known as Teri the Terrible, other times Teri the Terrific, consisted of a lemonade, extra sour—the way she liked it—accompanied by a Granny Smith apple, also sour. How such a sweet kid possessed such a sour craving her father didn't understand. But then, there were lots of things he didn't understand about his eight-year-old daughter.

He sat at their kitchen table in the old farmhouse—soon to be someone else's old farmhouse, he hoped—and regarded Teri with paternal bafflement.

"Why do you like your lemonade to taste like pure lemon juice?" he asked.

"Because it's good that way."

"I add sweetener to mine, and it's better that way."

"Nah. It's yucky with sweetener."

He gave up. "Okay. You know, the way you're growing, pretty soon I won't be able to lift you up. You'll have to make your own baskets."

"That's okay. I'll still beat you."

"Probably you will."

"Are we going to have a basketball hoop when we move?"

"Yup. I guarantee it. This very same one."

"Maybe we should get one that's shorter."

"You don't need one that's shorter, because you're growing to be taller."

She shrugged.

"Are you going to help me pack the motor home this afternoon?"

"I guess."

"We'll be leaving in a couple of days."

"Can I take my television?"

"The motor home already has a television, sweet pea, and I think there's only room for one."

She groaned. "Then I have to watch *your* yucky shows?"

"We'll compromise and watch some of your yucky shows, too."

Teri answered with a roll of her thickly lashed brown eyes, a gesture she had perfected to maximum effect in the last few months, accompanied by a long-suffering sigh. "I guess."

He ignored the drama, knowing that Teri could and would dramatize the fall of a pin if she saw it. "Seriously, sweetheart, do you mind us taking this summer to be dog-show bums with Dobby?"

"No," she said casually. "I like dog shows. And there's nothing to do around here now that school is out."

That was true enough for Teri. She didn't have many friends, and the mere suggestion of organized summer activities such as swim lessons, soccer, or ballet school brought on a sulk.

Cole didn't know how to make his daughter happy. Since his wife Mandy's death from cancer two years before, Teri had retreated to a place inside herself where only she knew what she felt and thought. To all outward appearances, she was fine. Her schoolwork was good—too good, in fact. Though she had mastered the fine art of sulking, she never threw tantrums, never raised her voice to her father, never indulged in the brattiness that most children thrived on.

At least it was Cole's understanding that most children Teri's age thrived on brattiness. He didn't have hard data from experience to back that up. During Teri's first six years, Mandy had been the kid person, the nurturer, the one who read child-rearing books and subscribed to the parenting magazines. Cole had been the breadwinner. When he was home, he had dandled Teri on his knee, taught her to play basketball (at the tender age of three), and helped tuck her into bed.

But Mandy had been the one who worried about programming the little brain and avoiding glitches that might build into fatal errors in the internal software. From a very early age Cole had known what made computers tick, but understanding the programming of children involved a much more complicated set of factors.

Now Mandy was gone, bless her, and her death had broken not only his heart, but Teri's as well. She had been very close to her mom, and she didn't understand why that loving, lovely soul, the solid cornerstone of her young life, had been taken from her. Cole, at least, was a grown-up, and he supposedly understood about death and disease and could somehow come to terms with Mandy's leaving. But what did a trusting six-year-old do when the mother she adored left for the hospital one night and never returned?

That was one of the reasons Cole intended to use this summer to get to know his daughter better. He had bought a used motor home that would be their version of a gypsy's wagon. In it they would travel around the country, seeing the sights, stopping at agility trials along the way to let Dobby do her thing. Teri adored Dobby, and she always got so excited watching the little dog compete—either in obedience or agility. At dog shows she truly seemed to step out of that quiet, sad place she had made for herself.

Maybe a summer full of travel, of her dog, and of her father would wipe away the solemn cast to that little pixie face. And when the summer was over, they would set down new roots in whichever little burg could support Cole with a college teaching position and an opportunity to reboot his computer business. Maybe Teri would like small-town life, a new school, new kids to befriend.

Maybe.

• • •

SIX DAYS after the fire had wiped out the Bark Park, Jane found herself in the driveway of Angela Gardner's house in Chandler, Arizona, standing in 110-degree heat, looking at her new home. Painted cream and tan, the buslike vehicle was six feet wide, thirty-four feet long, and came with a diesel engine and six tires. And it was air-conditioned, thank heaven. Too big for Angela's driveway, it was parked on the street in front of her house.

"What do you think?" Angela prodded. "Pretty slick, no?"

"Very nice." Jane tried to imagine living with Angela, Idaho, and Shadow in this tin can for the whole summer, much of it at sixty-five miles per hour. Idaho and Shadow would be no problem. Angela... well, the jury was still out on that. Still, Jane had gotten herself into this. She should try to be a good sport.

"I've never really done the RV thing before," she told Angela. "What kind is this?"

"It's a Challenger. Appropriate, yes? We're going out to challenge the world of dog agility in a Challenger. It's a good sign."

Jane responded with a noncommittal grunt.

"You'll love it, really, once you get used to living on wheels. It has all the conveniences of home."

Except breathing room, Jane thought.

"We'll be modern adventurers, roaming the country like knights of old who traveled from tourney to tourney."

The woman's enthusiasm was downright tiring. And putting the label "adventure" on a ramble along the country's superhighways was a stretch. After all, they had their own portable bathroom, refrigerator, and air-conditioning.

Be nice, Jane reminded herself.

"Come look inside," Angela offered. "Bring the dogs. After all, they'll be living in here, too. I'm just going to love spending a whole summer with your dogs. I've always wanted a dog. Absolutely love them. All animals, actually..."

She rambled on as she opened the motor home door and climbed up the steps. Jane followed, only half listening. The interior of the "tin can" gave the impression of more space than the streamlined exterior. Two big captain's chairs occupied the cockpit, and mounted above and behind the driver's-side chair was an entertainment center, including a seventeen-inch television, a CD/DVD player, and a stereo. The living area had a full-sized sofa, a dinette that seated four, and a fully equipped kitchen.

"The bedroom is back here." Angela led the way. "You can sleep here with me in the queen-size bed, or on the sofa. It folds out to queen-size, also, and really is very comfortable."

"I'll take the sofa," Jane said. "I'm sort of a solitary sleeper."

Angela shrugged. "That's fine. The bathroom is here. We even have a bathtub."

More of a large-scale sink, Jane noted. The tub might hold six inches of water. The bathroom was efficiently designed so that you could sit on the john and brush your teeth over the sink at the same time. In fact, you just about had to. Interesting, Jane noted with a mental sigh.

"It doesn't look like the space is wide enough for that sofa to fold out," Jane said.

Angela gave her a confused look, then chuckled. "You really haven't done the RV thing, have you? When we're parked, that whole section slides out about four feet to create a really roomy space. And there's a slide-out here in the bedroom, too. I have them both drawn in for driving, since we'll be leaving as soon as you can get your stuff on board."

"That'll take about five minutes," Jane told her. "My stuff is mostly dog food. I have to do some clothes shopping between here and the first trial we hit."

"No problem," Angela said cheerfully. "There's a big Wal-Mart in Lakeside, not that far from the trial site."

At least Angela knew where the best shopping was.

Angela helped Jane unload her van and stow her luggage in the surprisingly spacious storage compartments of the motor home. Mckenna and Nell had replaced her shade canopy, exercise pen, and ground mats as a going-away gift, and Jane had worried about fitting these bulky but necessary items in Angela's modern covered wagon, but they slid nicely into the "basement" storage below the floor, as did the fifty-pound bag of dog food. Jane's own personal items—what few of them she had left—took only one drawer of the built-in dresser in the bedroom.

The dogs helped these final arrangements by getting underfoot. Neither Idaho nor Shadow intended to get left behind.

"I'm absolutely beside myself that this worked out for you," Angela chirped merrily. "This series is going to be such a success! Don't be surprised if the dog food companies start pursuing you to endorse their product, and other pet products as well. You and Shadow are going to be famous. Maybe you'll get on some TV talk shows, too. You know, those daytime shows aimed at retired folks and stay-at-home moms.

"In the meantime, we'll have great fun. The network is going to die for this miniseries—a canine sports reality show. What could be better than that? The agony of defeat and ecstasy of victory, and all that. Made better by the athletes being cute and fuzzy."

Jane opened the fridge to put in a six-pack of diet soda. The blast of cold air momentarily cooled her mounting claustrophobia at being locked in such a small space with someone who talked every time she breathed. Jane more than ever appreciated the virtues of canine roommates. One of the best things about dogs was that they didn't talk, at least not with such irritating patter. Idaho could say more with a wave of his tail than most people could say in a ten-minute speech.

Fortunately, the bubbling flow of Angela's one-sided

conversation stopped at the sound of a vehicle pulling into the driveway. She looked out the window and smiled in delight. "Wonderful! Ernesto is here. Ernesto is our cameraman. You're going to adore him. Come out and meet."

Angela literally bounced out of the motor home. The woman did everything in the superlative, Jane noted. Optimism, energy, enthusiasm. She wasn't just glad that Jane had called her, she was beside herself. The network wasn't going to be happy with the series, it was going to die for it. Jane wouldn't like Ernesto, she would adore him.

All the enthusiasm made Jane tired. Or perhaps she was cranky, uncertain that she had done the right thing in calling Angela. Too late now.

Nell had thought the idea rocked. "You'll have such fun!" she'd enthused, almost as over-the-top as Angela.

Even Mckenna had approved. "You've got some big decisions ahead of you," she had said. "It's just as well you take some time to think about them, and getting away for a while will give you some perspective. Besides," she had continued with a twinkle in her eye, "you've been wanting to show the world what a star Shadow is. This is your chance. Go for it."

So Jane was going for it, putting her troubles on the shelf and buying some time to think of solutions. In the meantime, Rising Star Productions, in the person of Angela Gardner, had promised to pick up the tab for food and gas. Jane had only to pay for entries and her own incidentals.

She would learn to like Angela, Jane told herself. The twinkly little blonde wasn't really a bad sort, once you got past all the talk and the excess energy. And no doubt she would just *adore* Ernesto.

Jane sighed and climbed down the motor home steps.

In spite of a certain negativity in her mood, Jane did like Ernesto. A short, square brick of a man, he gave the impression of quiet competence. Neatly trimmed steel-gray hair lay close to his head in tight waves and accentuated the olive cast of his skin. The square, phlegmatic face gave no hint of age, but a certain wisdom in his eyes led Jane to guess his age at around sixty.

"Happy to meet you," he said when Angela introduced them. His handshake was firm and dry. "So your dogs are our new stars, eh?"

"Fabulous, no?" Angela enthused.

Ernesto just smiled. "Better than working with boa constrictors."

Ah, yes, Jane remembered. *Putting the Squeeze on Boa Constrictors.* One of Angela's previous efforts.

Ernesto had brought his own workstation/living quarters with him in the form of a stretch van that included a folding cot, a bedroll, portable toilet, and Coleman stove along with very complicated-looking video equipment.

"You live in this?"

"Only when we're on the road. It's plenty big enough for me, and I value my privacy."

So the camper van was his refuge from Angela. Jane was envious.

"So, Ernesto," Angela said, "are we ready?"

"Ready as ever."

"Jane? Everything in the motor home?"

"Yes. Are you sure my van will be all right parked here in your driveway so long?"

"It'll be fine."

Jane grimaced. "You're right. Who would take this beat-up heap of metal?"

"We're ready, then."

Ernesto led out in his big van, and off they rolled. Idaho and Shadow settled happily on the motor home sofa and grinned their approval of the expedition. Jane would rather have them ride in their kennels, as they did in her van. It was far safer. But the motor home had no room for the large kennels, so they had been taken apart and stored in the basement storage compartment along with the dog equipment, dog food, tools, hoses, folding chairs, gas grill, and other accessories that were necessities of the expedition.

"Lakeside, here we come," Angela said cheerfully as they pulled out onto the highway. "And another Rising Star adventure begins."

Jane suppressed a sigh.

COLE SHUT the back door of the motor home and gave it a satisfied slap. The thing was old and a bit shoddy, a glorified camper mounted on a van chassis, but for just him and Teri, it would be downright cozy.

"There we are," he told his daughter. "We've got enough food to stock a small restaurant—sodas, clothes, books, an RV travel guide..."

"Dog food?" Teri reminded him.

"Of course dog food. Dobby's got to eat, too."

Perched securely in Teri's arms, the tiny black and white dog gave him a smirk. Of course they had packed the dog food. Was she not the most important member of this summer's expedition?

"You could let Dobby stand on her own four paws," Cole suggested to Teri, which earned him another look from the dog, something close to a glare. Sometimes he swore that the little furball understood English.

"She likes to be carried," Teri replied.

Which was true enough. The only time Dobby deigned to put her feet on the ground, if she could help it, was in the agility or obedience ring, where she could garner praise from her admirers.

"And I don't mind," Teri continued.

Teri treated Dobby more like a favorite doll than a pet. And lately she had turned the little dog into a security blanket. For the hundredth time, Cole wondered if leaving their home was more trauma than adventure for his daughter. Change could be cleansing, but it could also be frightening.

Was he doing the right thing dragging Teri off on a summer full of new experiences, then to a new home in a place not even decided upon yet?

Damn, but kids should come with operating manuals. Not those thirty-dollar psychobabble books written by people with alphabets after their names instead of kids in their homes. No, what he needed was the cookbook approach, written by someone who had at least twelve kids. *Parenting for Dummies.* Mix two cups of this, a quarter cup of that, and a teaspoon of something else, let it rise, and you end up with a happy, well-adjusted college honors student who didn't drink, snort, or smoke, and who planned to save herself for marriage. Whoever published something like that would make themselves a fortune, and well worth it.

Until then, though, he would simply have to muddle through.

Cole took a fortifying breath. "Ready, sweet pea?"

Teri shrugged. "I guess."

"Climb in, then. Unless you want to drive."

She snorted. "Daddy, you're so lame."

Cole climbed into the driver's seat and took a look back into the body of the motor home. A tiny kitchen took up the back half, along with a closet-sized bathroom. In the middle was a built-in booth-style dinette that seated two full-sized people or four skinny amputees, and across from that was a foldout couch (you could fold it out, that is, if you didn't want to get to the dinette). The supposedly queen-sized bed was above the cab. Motor home people used a different definition of "queen-sized" than ordinary folks. Lying on the bed, Cole's head touched one wall and his feet were planted firmly on the other wall, and that was with his knees bent.

Still, the little motor home was cute and efficient, and it would be home until September.

He ran through a mental checklist. The house was

closed. The extra set of keys was in the realtor's lockbox. The place was relatively clean, the beds made, the stove off.

So this was it. Good-bye to the old farmhouse which was now surrounded by housing developments. Good-bye to Albuquerque with its traffic and freeways and pollution and drug runners coming up from the border. Good-bye for the summer, at least. And hello to the open road.

"Are we going?" Teri asked impatiently. Dobby had jumped from her lap and made herself comfortable on the special pillow between the seats.

"We're going," Cole said. "Wave good-bye to the house."

Catching a little of her father's enthusiasm, Teri smiled and waved as they pulled out of the driveway and onto the feeder road that would lead them to Interstate 40. "Good-bye, house. Good-bye, yard. Good-bye, tree. We're going to . . . Daddy, where are we going?"

"We're going to Lakeside, Arizona. Lakeside, and beyond that, anywhere in the country where you, Dobby, and I can have some fun."

In the tradition of Buzz Lightyear, Teri confirmed: "To infinity and beyond! Here we go!"

chapter 5

THE GATE steward bellowed, "Shadow next on the line, Murphy on deck, and Max in the hole!"

"The line" in an agility trial was the invisible start line to a competition course. Marked by two orange cones, it was guarded by unseen electronics that automatically recorded a competitor crossing its path. The team next slated to run the course waited behind the line, ready to enter as soon as the gate steward gave them the go-ahead. The team following waited in the gate area, "on deck," and the third in line held themselves ready nearby, "in the hole."

Running an Excellent level agility course generally took less than sixty seconds—when things went right. When things went wrong, the time could seem like an eternity. Still, things moved very fast, and a competitor had to be alert and ready to go into the ring. In a trial with between three and four hundred entries, judges did not like to be kept waiting.

But at the Lakeside agility trial, Shadow and Jane didn't need to be prodded. They both waited at the gate to the ring, ready to move. The sun beat down on Jane's head, birds flew overhead, and a freshening breeze played games with loose strands of her hair. But she didn't notice any of that. Her entire attention focused on the course laid out before her.

"Go to the line when the Doberman's on the dog-walk," the woman acting as ring steward told Jane.

At that point the Doberman would have only the weave poles, a triple jump, and two single jumps to negotiate before the finish—about five seconds' worth of running at the speed he was working. Jane would have just enough time to get Shadow steady on the start line.

So she stood at the ring gate, trying to breathe, trying to slow her heart's nervous tattoo. No matter how many trials she ran, waiting always gave her the jitters. She worried about forgetting the complex sequence of obstacles. She worried about a moment of klutziness that might send her tail over teacup. She worried about Shadow deciding to visit the kid who munched on a hamburger at ringside.

Mostly she worried about not making a clean, fast run. About seeing people at ringside shake their heads, about hearing the comments that Jane and Shadow certainly weren't on form today.

It happened. It happened to every team of dog and handler. It didn't happen often to Jane, and she hated it when it did. Jane didn't know why it mattered so. Maybe because being a dog trainer was what she was all about. She wasn't beautiful or particularly clever, but put her with a dog and she could walk on water. Usually. Some days she sank, and that wasn't fun.

Today Jane's pre-run jitters were worse than usual. The past ten days of her life hadn't exactly been reassuring. The last two nights she had tossed and turned on the motor home's foldout sofa well into the early hours of the morning. Her restlessness had driven both Shadow and Idaho to sleep on the floor. Adjusting to the constant presence of two noncanine companions in such close quarters made her jumpy and irritable, even though both Angela and Ernesto were, on the whole, agreeable people. And then there was the nagging worry that she no longer had a home, no longer had a business, or even a job. For this summer she was an agility gypsy. Worse, she was an agility gypsy permitting tens of thousands of viewers to witness her every stumble and bobble.

And after this summer—what? What would she be then?

But now, standing on the line with Shadow, waiting to run her first course with the camera rolling, was not the time to let her problems turn her knees to jelly. *Think about something else*, Jane chided herself. *Think about the course you're going to run.*

She tried to focus on the team currently running the course. They ran fast, and smooth, the Doberman well in front of the handler but obviously attuned to the handler's every word and signal.

But the entrance to the first tunnel could have been smoother, Jane thought critically, and the dog almost missed the yellow-painted contact zone—which at least one foot was required to touch—on the down side of the A-frame. She would handle the tunnel differently, Jane decided. And Shadow had never yet missed a contact zone.

The Doberman reached the home stretch of the course, sprinted double-time up the long, narrow ramp of the dog-walk, and hit the level middle section at a downright dangerous run while his handler shouted at him, "Easy, there! Easy."

Jane tore her eyes away and stepped into the ring, up to the all-important line, making sure that Shadow didn't break the plane guarded by the invisible electronic beam. She could step over the line without consequence, but the minute Shadow put as much as one toenail over the start, they were running the course, ready or not. Quickly she reviewed in her mind the complex, twisting sequence of eighteen obstacles that constituted today's course. Excellent was the highest level of the American Kennel Club's version of agility competition. It was fast, with wicked turns, side-switches, and temptations for the dog to take the wrong obstacle. One error meant a nonqualifying run. One fraction of a second could mean the difference between first place and no place at all.

The Doberman and his handler had cleared the exit. The timer sitting at ringside gave Jane a thumbs-up. "Go whenever you're ready."

Jane glanced down at Shadow, who looked up with a relaxed doggy grin. "Ready?" she asked the dog.

Silly question. Shadow was always ready. Always paying attention. Always on the ball. He was a dynamite competitor, and he deserved the best run Jane could give him.

"Okay," she said to the dog. "We're ready."

She told Shadow to stay, walked past the first three jumps, then turned and gave the dog the signal to go.

ANGELA DANCED from foot to foot in excitement, trying to restrain herself from disturbing Ernesto, who stood close by, focused entirely on following Jane and Shadow with his shoulder-mounted camera. Ernesto was pure professional. He certainly could do his work without help or comments from Angela. In fact, help and comments from Angela would likely get Angela a lecture on keeping her nose out of his business. But if she didn't express her excitement, she would just burst.

"Oooh! Look at that gorgeous front cross that she did in front of the A-frame! Did you get a good angle on that, Ernie? And look at Shadow fly over the spread jump! Wow! He's like a streak of gold. Spectacular! Oh, man! An audience is going to eat this up."

Ernesto kept filming.

"Look at him go! Is he ever fast! Oops! Dammit! Judge,

get out of the way! She's right between Jane and the camera! Can you move to . . . oh, you did. Good work."

She heard Ernesto's long-suffering sigh and clenched her jaw. Her commentary irritated him. But she was, after all, the producer and director here. Still, it wasn't wise to annoy the cameraman, especially this early in the job.

But before she could squelch another exclamation, out it jumped. "Oh, look! Did you see that wonderful control on the teeter-totter? And Shadow didn't lose a second. What a team! The viewers are going to love them. And here's the dog-walk—beautiful. Now to the weaves, sharp turn, take the triple jump—very nice! And jump, jump to the finish line, and—ouch! Oh, get that, Ernie! Comedy is always good, especially when it isn't staged. Who is that? Nice looking! Hope she didn't hurt him."

A man standing nearby with an Australian shepherd mistook the object of Angela's inquiry. "That's Jane Connor and Shadow. Great team, aren't they? Top competitors. I'm kind of surprised to see Jane here this weekend."

Angela had been about to say she knew perfectly well who Jane was. She had been referring to the man Jane had just mowed down outside the exit gate. But her instinct for a good story perked up her ears and shut down her mouth—except to prod the man on. "Why are you surprised to see her here?"

"You didn't see the news, eh?"

"I never watch the news. Too depressing."

"I hear you there! That poor woman was wiped out by a wildfire up by Cornville. She had a kennel there—boarding and training dogs. The fire burned it to the ground. She managed to get out all the animals just ahead of the flames. And I mean *just* ahead. Risked her life."

Angela felt her creative juices begin to flow. This story had a ton of possibilities.

"There's a lot of grateful folks. The news made her out to be quite the heroine. And she is, you know? I'd like to think that I would have done the same thing—think of the animals even with the fire sending cinders into my hair and onto my clothes. I hope I would have done the same thing. But I don't know."

"Interesting," was all Angela said.

"Wonder what she's going to do now?"

Angela knew exactly what Jane was going to do, at least for the summer. So that was why she had changed her mind, and why she had expanded Angela's idea from a few weekends of filming to an entire summer agility tour in pursuit of Shadow's agility championship. Clever girl.

But why hadn't Jane told her about the fire? Modest? Or maybe Jane was the sort who liked to hold everything close to the chest. Whatever, Angela wouldn't hold her secrecy against her. Actually, she felt a lift of inspiration, heard a knock of opportunity. This whole situation just got better and better. A wealth of human interest could be milked from Jane's heroism. Animal lovers would be brought to tears by the story. Jane would become the viewing public's new favorite daughter, and Shadow could rival Lassie and Rin Tin Tin.

"You have that look on your face," Ernesto told Angela, shifting the camera to a more comfortable position on his shoulder.

"What look?"

"The look that means your brain is turbocharged."

"My brain is always turbocharged. That's why I make the big bucks."

He chuckled and shook his head.

"Okay, the semi-big bucks. Did you get good video of Jane's run?"

"We'll see when we do the editing."

"We need to concentrate on getting some personal stuff, too."

"What do you mean, personal?"

"You know, Jane just hanging out. For instance, she's

still lying on the ground with that hunky guy over there—the one she ran into. Hm. She'd better not be hurt. Get your camera working again. We need to show stuff like this. Did you get the collision?"

"Yeah. Quite a crash."

"Great, wasn't it? Those are the things that make a person real, that will make the audience love her. We need to show Jane up close and personal, all her stumbles and embarrassing moments as well as her blue-ribbon agility runs. Did you know that our girl Jane is a local heroine? People are going to adore her, Ernie. This series is going to be such a hit."

Ernesto squinted at her suspiciously. "Your brain *is* cooking."

"Always." A good filmmaker had to stay flexible, had to go with the flow and adjust the focus to take advantage of new data. She had conceived of this project as a miniseries to showcase a beautiful canine athlete and take advantage of the public's growing fascination with the sport of dog agility. But suddenly, the flow had diverted a bit. Jane had become the more interesting member of the Jane/Shadow team.

And Angela had every intention of going with the flow.

JANE'S FACE was redder from mortification than from exertion as she looked up into Cole Forrest's face. Over three hundred people at this agility trial, and she had to plow into *him?*

"I am *so* sorry," she apologized.

"Are you okay?"

Jane could feel every freckle on her face deepening to a hue of embarrassed crimson. She and Shadow had run a beautiful course and then spoiled the whole thing by cruising out of the ring, arms raised in victory, and smacking full speed into the papillon guy. He had the consistency of brick, and was no more yielding. Jane had ended up on her backside, looking up at an anxious Shadow and an equally concerned Cole Forrest.

As if her clumsiness weren't bad enough, Jane and her victim were tangled in a way that was hardly decent, sending unexpected streamers of heat trickling down to body parts she would rather not think about just then.

What did one say to a guy whose thigh pressed against something it definitely shouldn't be pressing against, and whose arm—a nicely brawny arm, by the way—lay across her right breast? What clever comment would make this less than terminally awkward? Jane had no idea, so she merely indulged in a faint groan.

"Are you hurt?" Cole asked anxiously.

"No. I'm fine. Just fine." Mortally embarrassed, but fine. But maybe he was hurt. Certainly he didn't seem in any hurry to move. "Are you okay?"

A certain slant to his smile hinted that he was very okay. Jane's breast burned where his arm was wedged against it. Clenching her teeth, she squirmed, trying to be discreet and at the same time get free. One of his brows arched upward a fraction of an inch, and his smile broadened. Gingerly he started to untangle the knot of their bodies.

When he had his arms free, he experimentally waggled his fingers. "Seems to be in working order. Good thing. If I couldn't work on a computer keyboard, I'd have to go to work flipping burgers somewhere."

He offered her a hand up, and Jane accepted. While she was no fragile feminine flower who couldn't pick herself up off the grass, ignoring the offer of help would have been rude, especially after knocking the guy over like a bowling pin.

He had a good grip, Jane noted as he pulled her to her feet. His hand was strong, square, and well formed, with neatly trimmed nails and just enough calluses to show that the guy used them for something other than typing on a keyboard. Jane was a hand woman. Some women focused in on shoulders. Others spied out a guy's abs, or biceps, or legs. Jane liked hands. Hands told you a lot about a person.

"You're sure you're all right?" he asked.

He hadn't let go of her hand. And she didn't pull it away.

"I'm all right. Really. You?"

"Me?"

"I knocked into you pretty hard, and no one has ever called me petite."

He laughed—the same combustible laugh she had heard before. "You were the one who landed on your... uh..."

She cut him off with an embarrassed chuckle. "I did, didn't I?"

Jane wished she could think of something clever to say, something that would make him laugh again. She liked his laugh. But she just stood there like a big ox, dumbstruck. And he wasn't saying much either, just standing there looking at her with a curious smile tugging at the corners of his mouth.

"Hey, you two!" came a call from the gate steward. "Move away from the exit!"

They both came to life. Cole dropped her hand. Jane jumped back. "She's right," Jane said. "We're going to cause another pileup unless we move."

Shadow barked in agreement.

"You could have reminded us earlier," Jane told the dog.

Cole laughed again and, as if it were the most natural thing in the world, took Jane's arm as they moved away from the danger zone.

"Here I thought I was the only one who talked to dogs as if they were people," he said.

Jane didn't bother to pull her arm free. "Haven't been around the dog world much, have you?"

"Not long enough, I guess."

"Most of the dogs here are a good deal more human than the people. Smarter, too."

"Well, Dobby certainly is."

"Good thing Dobby wasn't with you when I made like a bulldozer. Poor little thing would have been squashed flat."

"She's off with my daughter, getting psyched for our run. By the way, that was a beautiful course you did in there. Totally clean as far as I could see. And fast, too."

"Shadow is a wonderful—"

A high, insistent voice interrupted. "Daddy! There you are!"

Up bounced a ponytailed youngster. The annoyingly perfect little papillon perched in her arms, gazing down upon the world like a queen on her throne. The girl's cinnamon-colored hair was held back by an elastic sporting pink plastic flowers. Purple barrettes shaped like daisies tried valiantly to pin back stray, baby-fine wisps.

"Teri," Cole said, "say hello to Jane Connor."

He remembered her name. No doubt he would shortly be writing it down on his list of people to keep a safe distance from.

Teri gave Jane a sharp once-over. "Hello."

"Hello, what?" Cole prompted.

"Hello, Miss Connor."

"Hello, Teri." So this little imp was Cole's daughter. Jane had never fancied herself to be much good with children. She tended to treat them like people, which they weren't, really, at least until they were fifteen or sixteen. But this one had surprisingly unchildlike eyes looking out from her little elfin face. Jane had the impression that something fairly unchildish resided inside that little-girl exterior. "You can call me Jane," she told the girl, then glanced at Cole. "If your father doesn't mind, that is."

Teri's little bow mouth pursed as she considered the name. "Jane. Okay," she agreed without seeking her father's reaction. Then she turned to Cole. "I warmed up Dobby.

Took her over the eight-inch jump four times, just like you said." The girl's face lit with animation when she started talking about the dog.

"Good," Cole told her. "Thank you."

"You have a run coming up," Jane remembered. "I'm sorry. Here I am bothering you while you need to get ready."

"You weren't bothering me." He grinned. "Except maybe when you bulldozed into my ribs."

Jane winced.

"But that might have been a good warm-up in itself. I've been known to take a header while running a course."

"How soon do you go in?"

"We have a few minutes. There's still about ten dogs or so ahead of us in Excellent Jumpers class."

The Jumpers class consisted of only jumps, tunnels, and weave poles. Unlike the Standard class, which Jane had just run, Jumpers had no dog-walk, table, or A-frame to slow the run, and the times clocked were very fast. Ten dogs wasn't much time at all.

"Teri warms up Dobby before I go into the ring," Cole said proudly. "She's going to be a great little handler when she's old enough to compete."

"It's five dogs now," Teri told him primly, plainly of the opinion that she should be the one running Jumpers instead of her father.

"Ah. Five dogs, is it? I guess we'd better get over there." He took Dobby from Teri's arms and set the little toy-sized dog on the ground. "Come on, Dobby. Feet on the ground, Your Highness. Showtime." Flashing a smile at Jane, he said, "If you have time to stick around and watch, I could always use some pointers from a pro like you."

Father and daughter walked off toward the ring with the little dog prancing beside them. Grimacing, Jane told Shadow, "Judging from what that little furry pipsqueak did in obedience the other day, we're probably the ones who could use the pointers."

Shadow looked insulted.

"I agree," Jane told the dog. "Humiliating. But I calls 'em as I sees 'em."

She found a spot at Jumpers ringside where she could get a good view, telling herself she wanted only to see the tiny black-and-white phenom. Watching Cole Forrest sprint through the course had nothing to do with it. On the other side of the ring, Ernesto had his camera ready, Jane noted. So Angela and crew were including performances other than Jane's in their grand documentary. The combination of virile man and toy-sized fluffy dog would capture the viewer's attention, Jane guessed. It seemed to have captured hers.

Once Cole was at the gate, Teri wandered over and stood beside Jane, giving her a speculative look that seemed too old for her childish face. "Are you going to watch my dad?"

"I thought I would. Who knows? I might learn something."

"This is a good place to watch from," the child said wisely. "You can see pretty much everything, and there's a good angle to see the weave poles."

Obviously the kid had spent a lot of time at agility trials. She reminded Jane of herself at that age, only back then, obedience had been the dog sport of choice. Agility hadn't yet come on the scene. And there was certainly no such thing as Animal World to bring dog sports into the public interest.

Like Teri, Jane had talked knowledgeably about all things canine long before she had been old enough to compete, and she had done so incessantly, much to the confusion of her parents and the boredom of her friends.

"Do you want to go in the ring when you're old enough?" Jane asked.

"Of course," Teri said. "I'm going to have a dog of my own really soon. A dog like yours."

The girl eyed Shadow with longing, and Shadow gave her the look of special adoration he reserved for children.

"What's your dog's name?"

"Shadow."

"He did very well in the ring," Teri complimented in a very adult fashion. "He's not as quick as Dobby, but then, he's kind of big."

Sensing the possibility of attention, Shadow shifted so that he sat next to Teri instead of Jane.

"Shadow's a good boy," Jane said, giving the dog a fond look. "By the end of the summer, he should have his agility championship."

"Dobby will have one, too," Teri declared. "Dobby and my father are very good."

Even while she praised Dobby, Teri lowered herself to the ground and sat cross-legged beside the golden retriever. She stroked Shadow's soft ears and found the exact spot on his chin where he loved to be scratched, all the while regarding him with an intent look that Shadow returned full measure. "You're a very good dog," Teri told him. "Someday you'll be just as good as Dobby."

Shadow didn't seem offended. His tongue shot out to give the girl a quick kiss. Teri seemed startled, her eyes growing wide. Then she laughed, a sound of pure joy that only children can master. "You're a very smart dog!" she exclaimed, giving him a hug. Then she turned her attention to Jane. "Dobby's not as big as Shadow, but she's smart, too. My dad says she makes him look better than he is."

Interesting that he would admit it, Jane mused. Most men, in Jane's experience, needed to think that they were the important member of the team, and the dog just followed orders.

"But I want a dog like Shadow." The kid and Shadow leaned into each other, and Teri draped one arm over the dog's withers. Shadow sighed in pure ecstasy. "He really likes me," Teri said confidently.

Jane didn't point out that Shadow adored all children. Let the kid think she was special.

"Does your mom come to watch Dobby at the trials?" Jane asked pointedly. If she were Teri's mother, she certainly wouldn't let such a trusting kid wander free in a crowd like this one. Dog people, generally speaking, were the salt of the earth. But one never knew who might wander in.

If she were Teri's mother, Jane mused wryly, she wouldn't let Teri's father wander free either.

Teri pursed her mouth. "My dad says that my mom goes everywhere with us. But I think maybe he says that so I won't miss her so much."

Uh-oh. Jane had stumbled into deep water.

"Your mom is..."

"Dead," Teri stated flatly. "Do you think a person can be with you after you die? Or is my dad just telling a story?"

"I...uh..." *Okay, bigmouth, get out of this one.* Then she remembered Frank Cramer, the crotchety old gent who had left Nell's fat Welsh corgi an equally fat trust fund. Nell had sworn she had seen the old man's spirit at his own funeral, and Nell was a sensible woman who seldom indulged in flights of fancy. "I do think it's possible," Jane told the little girl. "And if your dad says it, then it must be so."

Teri shrugged. "Dad's a cool guy. But sometimes he treats me like I'm a baby. Grown-ups think it's okay to tell stories to kids to make them feel better. Dogs don't do that." She glanced down adoringly at Shadow. "Dogs always tell the truth. You can always trust them."

Jane didn't have time to contemplate the strangeness of that particular observation, because a Welsh corgi entered the ring—speaking of corgis. The little dog's strutting entrance was a welcome distraction. A sable female who surveyed the course as if she owned it, the corgi reminded Jane of Nell's rich little Piggy. Piggy was a good deal bigger than this little dog—the size difference composed mostly of fat—and for certain Piggy would have turned up her little wet nose at anything as energetic as agility. The attitude was the same, though. Piggy also strutted along as though everything in the world was made just for her.

"I've seen this dog run before," Teri confided in a whisper. "She's out of control."

Typical corgi, Jane thought.

"Dobby will beat her really easy."

Jane cocked an eyebrow toward the girl, grateful they were off the subject of dead mothers and lingering spirits. "Very confident, aren't you?"

"Dobby's the best."

The corgi's handler left the dog at the start line and walked to a point past the third jump. When she said "Go!" the little dog shot off the line like a furry brown torpedo, sped over the three jumps, then made the required sharp left turn to the tire jump.

"So far so good," Jane commented.

"She'll mess up. Just wait."

From the tire jump she flew on her short little legs to four jumps arranged in a pinwheel, then into the weave poles without missing a beat.

"Dobby's going to have trouble beating this one," Jane said.

Teri gave a very unchildlike snort.

The handler smoothly switched from the dog's right to the left after the weave poles, and they entered a difficult series of in-and-out jumps. It was there that the little corgi proved Teri a prophet. She jumped the first two so fast that she couldn't make the approach to the third, which sat at an awkward angle to the other two. Off course now, she spied an enticing double jump and took off for that one, ignoring her handler's call.

"Told ya," Teri crowed.

Is there anything more annoying than a cocky kid?

"Out of control," Teri smirked.

The embarrassed handler managed to chase down her

cavorting dog and carry the grinning corgi out of the ring. Cole and Dobby were ready on the line. Jane saw Cole glance at the timer. The timer nodded. In a bold move, instead of placing himself behind the third jump, as the other handlers had done, he abandoned the first series of jumps altogether and stationed himself beside the tire jump.

Jane scowled. "He's expecting Dobby to take the first jumps by herself while he stands over there by the tire?"

"She'll do it," Teri declared confidently. "Just watch."

Cole pointed in the direction of the third jump and told Dobby to go. The little dog instantly streaked forward, a black and white blur, doing exactly as he'd ordered. She bounced over the first three jumps, effortlessly clearing the eight-inch crossbars, then curved toward Cole and sailed through the tire jump. Cole had probably saved a full second of time by taking such a chance, and in agility competition, a second was enormous.

"Good job!" Jane couldn't help but mutter.

"Told ya," Teri crowed for the second time.

Jane decided that she could get tired of this particular kid real fast.

"He'll switch sides in front of the weave poles," Teri explained, just as Cole bore out her prediction. "Not many handlers can do that without confusing their dog, but my dad can."

Jane gritted her teeth.

"And watch here—he's going to walk straight through those twisty jumps and just tell her to go out and in."

This was where the little corgi had misjudged, then split. Not so Dobby. She bounced and turned, bounced and turned to meet each challenging angle head-on. Cole's commands were so soft the onlookers couldn't hear them, but Jane knew he was telling the little dust bunny exactly what to do and where to go. The toy-sized dog was tuned to him and no other, ignoring the crowd noise, enticing odors on the ground, interesting birds flying overhead, and the host of other distractions that could have made her lose focus.

"Now watch him send her out to the triple jump and then cross behind her!" By now Teri had gotten to her feet and was jumping up and down in excitement. "Isn't he wonderful? Isn't my dad wonderful?"

Jane couldn't help but smile. "He is. And Dobby, too."

Teri gave Shadow a spontaneous hug. "You're wonderful, too, Shadow. And I'll bet you do great when you run that course. Just remember not to go too fast on those twisty jumps," she warned, shaking a finger at him, "or you'll run right over them."

"Shadow thanks you for the advice," said Jane.

"I know."

Then Teri abandoned Shadow and transferred her hug to Jane, just for an instant before she backed off, looking embarrassed. "I'm excited," she explained.

"That's all right," Jane told her. "I like to be hugged as much as Shadow does." Certainly a lie. Jane had always had an enormous personal space where she didn't like people intruding. But the feel of little arms around her, unique and strangely gratifying, had almost offset the intrusion.

"I have to go see my dad," Teri said. "He always likes me to tell him what he did wrong."

"I'll bet," Jane said wryly. "I didn't see him do much wrong, though."

"Don't tell him that," Teri cautioned soberly, "or he'll get a big head. Dobby, too."

"What Dobby too?" Cole asked as he walked up to them. While Teri and Jane had hugged and talked, he had calmly exited the performance ring with Dobby and walked over to collect his daughter.

Jane jumped, startled. "Get a big head if we told you how good you looked . . . uh, well you did."

His face split in a grin. "We did, didn't we?"

Teri rolled her eyes. "Told ya." That had to be the kid's favorite comment.

"You did look good," Jane admitted. "Smooth, fast, very coordinated between you and the dog. Apparently my mowing you down didn't do any damage."

He laughed. "If we hadn't run well, you can be sure that I would have blamed you for it."

"Well, you did great."

Yes, great. Smart, good-looking, loved dogs, and the only females in his life were apparently an eight-year-old and a six-pound overgrown mouse. Why was it that an unmarried man was so much scarier than a safely married one? And why did she care? Jane wondered.

chapter 6

"YOU REALLY think it looked good?" Cole prodded. "I thought Dobby got a bit distracted at the weave poles. And the grass is a bit high to let her really show her speed."

His heart still pounded from his run, and a sheen of sweat made the cool, pine-laden breeze feel pleasantly cool against his skin. It was also pleasant seeing Teri so chatty and comfortable with Jane Connor. Teri didn't take to strangers, usually, but Jane had somehow brought his daughter out of her shell, at least momentarily. Perhaps because she was a straightforward, no-nonsense woman who obviously said what she meant and didn't put on a polite act. Children appreciated that in a person, Cole believed. He appreciated it also. Few people came at face value any more.

"Dobby didn't look distracted to me," Jane replied. "And the grass didn't bother her. You just want to hear again how good you were. Teri was right. You do get a big head."

He laughed. "She said that, did she?"

Teri gave him an arch look that she had started to employ after she had seen an episode of *Friends*, a program he normally didn't let her watch. Cole suspected she was trying to look like Jennifer Aniston.

"Did you say such a thing about your father?" he queried.

"Yes," she said primly. "Because it's true."

He grinned. "It *is* true. But cut me some slack, ladies. This is the only sport I can brag about. At basketball and softball I get regularly trounced. And I'd hardly make it in agility if I weren't supported by a six-pound dog."

Jane smiled. "Well, at least you admit it."

Jane had a nice smile, Cole noted. It made her rather unremarkable face light up. Though that wasn't the only thing she had that was nice. He had noticed several nice things when they had tangled together in the grass. He wouldn't have been a man if he hadn't noticed.

He coughed, trying to bring his thoughts back into line.

"He has to admit it," Teri told Jane.

"Admit what? Oh, Dobby. Sure. Her Highness wouldn't let me get away with claiming credit for *her* efforts. She works hard to keep me in line. And so does Teri, as you can see." He reached out and gently yanked the end of the little girl's ponytail.

"Daddy!" She brushed him away with an indignant little moue, but she couldn't hide the hint of a smile.

"And what did *you* think of our run?" he asked his daughter.

"It was okay," she conceded. "But your side-switch at the weave poles looked choppy."

"Choppy?"

"You know. Like your feet were going to get mixed up."

Jane smiled. "Maybe you were the one distracted at the weaves, not Dobby."

"Yes," Teri agreed with a firm nod of her head.

"That might be." For sure he was a bit distracted right now. A few years had passed since a woman had distracted him, for good or ill.

"Daddy!" Teri demanded his attention. "You promised to buy me a hot dog."

"So I did. What's an agility trial without a big, sloppy hot dog?"

"I'm hungry," she told him. "And Dobby wants a hot dog, too."

"Well then, Dobby can have a few bites of mine as a reward for running such a fine course."

Dobby, who had endured the conversation sitting primly at Cole's side, only occasionally sliding a flirtatious look toward Shadow, heard "hot dog" and pricked up her elegantly fringed ears.

"Hungry, are you?" Cole asked.

"I don't think there's much doubt about that," Jane said. "That's a pretty good starving-dog expression she has there."

Her voice warmed considerably, Cole noted, when the subject of discussion was a dog.

"She's a drama queen," Cole told her, then brushed Teri's cheek with his finger. "Just like her girl here. But I can relate. I could eat a whole cow, myself." After a beat of hesitation, he asked, "Would you like to join us for lunch at the roach coach, Jane?"

Teri liked her, Cole told himself. The invitation had nothing to do with him. Nothing to do with the way his arm still seemed warm where it had not too long ago pressed against her breast.

She looked startled, chewed on her lower lip for a few seconds, then nodded. "Sure. I guess. Even a greasy hot dog or hamburger would be better than going back to the RV for lunch. My roomie insists on fixing the meals, and her idea of lunch is a spare salad followed by a candy bar followed by a half hour of running in place to work off the chocolate calories."

"Does she make you run in place with her?" Cole inquired wryly.

Jane chuckled. "I'd like to see her try."

"What's running in place?" Teri asked.

"Running without going anywhere," Jane told her.

Teri screwed up her face. "Why would anyone do that?"

"To keep from getting fat."

The girl pondered a moment, then shook her head. "I don't understand."

"Neither do I," Cole agreed. "I think it's a female thing, so you'll probably understand when you grow up."

"It's not a female thing," Jane denied. "Because I don't understand it either. Actually, Angela spends more time talking about running than doing it. I don't think I've ever seen her actually break a sweat."

"My dad runs," Teri informed Jane, "but he goes somewhere."

"That's the way to do it," Jane agreed with a smile.

They moved away from the Jumpers ring toward the food concession area. Cole noted a barrel-shaped fellow pointing a professional-looking video camera at them and following them instead of the competitor currently running the course. Strange, he thought, but then his daughter distracted him by sidling up to Jane and falling into step beside her. Usually Teri clung to him so closely they might as well have been glued together.

"Can I take Shadow's leash?" she asked the woman.

Jane gave her an assessing look. "Will you be very careful?"

"I promise."

"There's quite a crowd up here in the vendor area."

"I know how to watch out for a dog," Teri declared with a hint of pride. "Besides, Shadow likes me. He'll listen to me."

"Okay, then."

Jane handed Shadow's leash to the eight-year-old, which Cole thought was quite generous of her, considering that the dog clearly meant just about everything to her.

"You be careful, Teri," Cole warned.

Teri heaved a huge sigh, which Cole guessed was

accompanied by an eye-roll. Walking behind his daughter, he couldn't see. But the sigh and the eye-roll generally came as a two-for-one bargain.

The food concession, of course, was positioned so that exhibitors and spectators had to walk past the vendors to get from the competition rings to the food and drink. The Lakeside trial had managed to attract quite a few vendors, more than most agility trials. Vendors swarmed to the big "breed" shows, where canine beauty queens battled for blue ribbons and their owners spent money on grooming aides and squeaky toys. But the agility trial set was a less spendy group, and usually only two or three—if any at all—purveyors of fine dog goods took the trouble to show up. Today, however, two rows of canopies sheltered everything from dog food to racks of collars to holistic remedies for canine stress. The crowd there was thicker than around the rings, especially in front of the booth where some enterprising soul proudly showed off photos and models of the tunnels, weave poles, and jumps he built to order in his garage.

Cole picked Dobby up and tucked the little dog beneath his arm, where she looked over the crowd with aristocratic condescension. Walking ahead with Teri and Shadow, Jane caught his action from the corner of her eye.

She laughed. "Not many men would feel comfortable in public carrying around a little sissy dog like that."

"Sissy dog? Shows what you know. Dobby here is a Rottweiler in disguise. We only let her off her chain to win agility trials. Isn't that right, Teri?"

Teri turned so that this time Cole could see the eye-roll. "Daddy! Dobby's not a Rottweiler." Then, with a little smile playing around her mouth, "She's a black and white dragon with big scaly wings and eyes that turn purple and blue and green. And an evil witch turned her into a tiny little dog who can't even fly."

"Ah!" Cole said. "That's why her ears are so big. They used to be wings."

"That's right!" Teri agreed.

Jane laughed again. She ought to copyright that laugh, Cole thought. It was liquid and gentle, all of a set with her beautiful smile.

"You guys both have way overactive imaginations," Jane pronounced.

"And Shadow is a beautiful good witch who will turn Dobby back into a powerful dragon," Teri continued. "A good witch all dressed in gold. So she disguised herself as a golden retriever."

Jane got sucked into the game. "Shadow can't be a good witch dressed in gold. He's a boy."

"Oh." Teri thought a moment. "That's part of the disguise, see? No one would suspect a boy golden retriever of being a beautiful golden witch."

"You got me there," Jane admitted. "Though myself, I always fancied Shadow as sort of an angel. A boy angel, of course. An angel who can make people smile just by looking at him."

"Well," Teri conceded. "Okay. Maybe he's an angel. But he could still turn Dobby back into a dragon."

Cole enjoyed the exchange. Who would have thought that Jane Connor the super-competitor could trade fantasies with an eight-year-old? And surprisingly, Teri seemed to be having the time of her life. Maybe Jane just had a magic touch with kids. Or maybe it was the golden retriever that made Teri smile so easily. It didn't matter to Cole. He just enjoyed watching his daughter relax and have fun for a change.

And Jane Connor herself, well, she was an equation that didn't quite add up. Trouble was, Cole had never been able to resist a puzzle. That addiction made him a good hand at computer software, Rubik's Cubes, and complicated card games. It also drew him to Jane for reasons that had little to do with her quiet laugh and beautiful smile. In some ways, Jane seemed tough and aggressive, yet another side surfaced often enough to tantalize.

An interesting woman, Cole decided.

They emerged from the vendor area with their wallets intact, which was no small miracle, as Teri always wanted to buy Dobby a new toy—she loved the plush dog toys as much as Dobby did. The picnic tables were crowded. Set in the shade of tall pine trees that bordered the park, the tables were the only place to sit as well as the coolest refuge from temperatures climbing into the eighties. Nevertheless, they lucked out. A trio of ladies, all with Australian shepherds, vacated a table just as they walked up.

"Grab the table," Cole told Teri and Jane. "And I'll get lunch." He handed Dobby to Jane. Woman and dog regarded each other with equal skepticism. "Jane, what do you want?" Cole asked.

She wanted a double hamburger with fries—a woman after his own heart. In Cole's opinion, life was too short to not indulge in junk food.

When Cole returned from the hamburger stand laden with a smothered hot dog for Teri, a double burger and fries for Jane, and the same for himself, Teri and Jane were deep in discussion. Dobby was on the ground—probably not of her own volition—leaning against Shadow's sturdy foreleg as if that pillar of strength might be the only thing holding her upright.

"Food!" he announced, putting the flimsy cardboard tray onto the table. "Dig in. No, dogs, not you. This is people food."

"There's a difference?" Jane asked with a chuckle.

"If the princess there ate everything she wanted, she'd look like a basketball with legs."

"More like a baseball," Jane corrected.

"Good things come in—"

"Small packages," Jane finished with a slightly wicked smile. "And better things come in large packages, don't they, Shadow?"

Cole laughed at the barb. "Good thing these dogs are in different size classes, or we'd just have to lay out a bet on who might come out on top."

"Oh, no." Jane shook her head, but that smile curved her mouth again. "I'd hate to take your money. That would be just too easy."

Teri added her two cents. "Golden retrievers are very hard to beat. But Dobby's a special dog."

"The kid's going to be a politician when she grows up," Jane remarked.

"Lord help us, no. Not that."

Teri look from one to the other. "You mean like President of the United States?"

"Yes," Cole told her. "That's definitely a politician."

Teri thought a moment, then declined. "I don't think I want to be a politician. Living in the White House would be fun, but I want to be a dog trainer when I grow up. When I get my own dog"—she gave Cole a meaningful look—"like Shadow, I can start learning to be a dog trainer."

Cole just smiled. "Last week she wanted to follow in her father's footsteps and work with computers, but I guess I've been replaced as a role model."

"Oh, I don't know," Jane said. "From what I've seen your Dobby do in competition, I'd say you qualify as a dog trainer."

"He never had a dog before Dobby," Teri supplied.

"That's right, I remember your saying that Dobby's your first dog. That's just downright unfair, you know? A novice should have to go through at least one or two also-rans before getting a performer like that little firecracker."

"I had a collie when I was a kid," Cole offered.

"Unfortunately, the poor dog didn't last long. My mother had a thing about dog hair in the house."

Jane shook her head. "Your entire experience is with a collie when you were . . . how old?"

"Three."

"That's just plain disgusting."

"What's disgusting?" Teri asked around a bite of hot dog.

"It's disgusting that your dad is doing so well with no experience to back him up. That makes old hands like me turn green with envy."

"I can't take credit for Dobby," Cole admitted. "She's incredibly easy."

As if knowing she was the subject of conversation, Dobby let loose a miniature howl, then jumped up on the seat of the picnic table and eyed Cole's hamburger, which he had just prepared to perfection with the ideal amount of mustard and ketchup.

Jane laughed. "Apparently she thinks *you're* the one who's easy."

"Not in this lifetime, dog. Get back down with your golden friend. You don't see him taking a seat at the table and begging for someone else's food."

"That," Teri said primly, "is because Jane is a dog trainer."

Cole lifted Dobby from the seat and put her down beside Shadow, who sat quietly, politely, his eyes on the food and only a single drop of drool betraying his discipline.

"Shadow," Jane said, "lie down. And quit drooling."

Shadow settled to the ground, and Dobby followed suit. Teri nodded her approval.

"Yep," Cole said. "I've definitely been replaced as a role model."

Jane chewed thoughtfully on a bite of hamburger. "You might want to rethink your career choice," she told Teri. "Being a dog trainer can be more work than fun. And you'll never be rich. I work twelve- to fourteen-hour days. Sometimes more. Lift fifty-pound bags of dog food until my arms ache. Clean kennels until poop is coming out my ears."

Teri giggled. "Poop comes out your ears?"

"Well, not really. But sometimes it feels that way."

Cole was surprised. "You really are a dog trainer? Full-time? Not just a hobby?"

"I have a kennel in Cornville, over in the central part of the state. I give classes and private lessons in obedience, agility, tracking, and search and rescue training, and I run a boarding kennel at the same time to make ends meet."

"Amazing. I don't think I've ever met someone who works with dogs full-time, without some kind of backup to actually earn a living."

A shadow crossed Jane's expression, and some thought arrested her mid-chew. "Yes, well, I've been doing that for years. But right now, you might say I'm between jobs. My kennel got caught in a wildfire a couple of weeks ago. Everything's ash now."

Teri looked alarmed. "Were the dogs hurt?"

"No. The dogs weren't hurt. And neither were the cats. We were really lucky that way."

Cole didn't know what to say. He suspected that more than luck had kept those animals safe and sound.

"That's terrible about your kennel." The words sounded inadequate. "Are you going to rebuild?"

She shrugged, and her smile seemed forced. "Don't know yet. I'm spending the summer with the dogs. Then I'll decide. But what about you?"

"My daddy's a computer nerd," Teri said proudly. "And a teacher."

Cole gave her a look. "Nerd?"

"Cory Brinks at school says you're a nerd, and that is very uncool. But I told him that you have to be really smart to know about computers, so being a nerd must be good."

"So you're a computer whiz, eh?" Jane said. From the

tone of her voice, Cole figured her opinion might fall in line with that of the little Brinks boy.

"Mostly I teach math and computer science at the community college level, but I also have a consulting company," he confessed. "Or did have one. Teri and I are pulling up roots and moving this fall. And this summer I'm taking sort of an extended vacation."

"Ah. Well, welcome to the extended-vacation set. Where are you moving?"

"We don't know yet," Teri supplied, and Cole thought he detected a trace of annoyance in her voice.

He shrugged. "Arizona, maybe. Colorado. Or somewhere in the Four Corners area. Depends on where I get the best job offer."

"So you're just up in the air for the whole summer?" Jane asked.

"We're going to do agility for the whole summer," Teri answered for him. "Daddy says we're going to be dog gypsies."

Cole hadn't seen his daughter so loquacious since her mother died. He was amazed.

"The whole summer?" Jane asked.

"The whole summer," Cole confirmed. "Since Teri likes dogs and dog shows so much, we're going to hop from trial to trial, stopping at all the tourist traps along the way. You know that old ad jingle"—he sang an off-tune "See the U.S.A. in your Chevrolet . . ."

Jane and Teri both grimaced. "Okay, I can't carry a tune. But you know the one. Only we're going to see the U.S.A. in our motor home."

"And get Dobby's agility championship along the way?"

At her name, Dobby looked up from where she had stretched out against Shadow's front leg.

"Nah," Cole said. "We don't need a championship. What we're really aiming for is the Solid Gold Invitational trial in August. We don't have a prayer of winning that enormous purse, but working toward a goal is more fun than just fooling around. Isn't that so, Teri?"

Teri told him huffily, "Dobby could win. I think Dobby will win."

"The Solid Gold Invitational..." Jane's eyes had suddenly blurred, focused somewhere far away.

"It's new this year," Cole told her. "But you knew that, of course. I hear the hundred-thousand-dollar purse is just a first-year promotion. They want the whole agility world crawling over each other to qualify."

"A hundred thousand?" Her eyes widened, then grew speculative.

"I figure just getting invited would be our goal for the summer. Or maybe"—he winked at Teri—"it's just an excuse to say we're not entirely wasting our time."

Jane suddenly snapped back into focus. "That's great, Cole. It would be a real kick if you could go to such a thing with something that has to jump up and down on the teeter-totter to get it to tip."

Yep, she was back in focus.

"This has been great, you guys," Jane continued, "but I can see they're on the twenty-inch division over there in Jumpers, and that means the twenty-four-inch is next. I should get Shadow warmed up. Gotta run."

And they did run, the golden retriever bouncing happily at Jane's side as they headed for the ring.

"Dobby doesn't jump up and down on the teeter," Teri objected with a small pout.

Cole explained. "Jane was just using an image to say that Dobby's very small, and because she's small, she has to work harder to do some stuff that bigger dogs do just as a matter of course."

"Dogs like Shadow," Teri said.

"That's right."

"Shadow's really pretty. And smart."

Shadow's mom wasn't bad herself, Cole thought, still watching the duo weave through the crowds. Their hips seemed to move in rhythm, with the same jaunty, confident little swing. If Jane had a tail, Cole mused, it would probably wag in perfect synchronicity with Shadow's.

It was interesting that when he'd first seen Jane last winter at an obedience trial, his eye had passed right over her and caught on the dog—not Shadow, but a border collie she had been showing. There was really nothing about Jane, with her mop of red hair and ordinary face, that made a man sit up and take notice—at least not until he got close enough to notice the stamp of character on her face. Not until a man tried to figure out where Jane fit among the usual female categories: easy, cold, flirty, hard-to-get, desperate, man-trap, dog meat...and so on. Men had a million categories to pigeonhole women, most of them rude and sexist, some of them complimentary. Jane didn't really fit into any of them. Not beautiful by a long road, she was a woman who grew on a man. Too sturdy by far to grace any magazine cover, too outspoken and sharp to win Miss Congeniality even in a pageant of spear-toting Amazons, Jane Connor still grew on a man.

She grew on him even faster when he spent a few minutes lying with her in the grass tied in an intimate knot like some sailor's bowline.

Woman and dog disappeared in the throng of people, and the interest index of the day dropped a couple of points. A very definite couple of points.

"Eat your hot dog," Cole told Teri. "Then we'll go watch Jane and Shadow run."

A sudden smile lit Teri's face, bright as the sunlight filtering through the pine trees. And Cole couldn't deny he felt a similar lift of spirits.

.   .   .

JANE AND Shadow did not have a stellar run in Jumpers class. Or rather, Jane did not have a stellar run. Shadow gave her a reproachful look as they exited the ring.

"I know, I know! It wasn't your fault that you knocked off that bar. I got you into that jump entirely wrong."

The golden retriever huffed out a breath of complete agreement.

"And I got my commands out too late, and the front cross at the pinwheel nearly sent us both head over tail. I know. I'm sorry, Shadow. My mind just wasn't on the course today."

And of course Ernesto would have recorded every inglorious moment, but even the thought of thousands of avid television viewers witnessing her every mistake couldn't take the starch out of Jane's newborn excitement.

"Come on, Shadow. Back to the motor home we go. We have work to do."

Across the ring, Cole and Teri waved to her. Jane's heart did an unexpected backflip, and for just a moment, she was tempted to make a detour and chat. But she had work to do, ideas to consider, decisions to make. Though spending time with the man and his kid had been less painful than she had expected. In spite of having questionable taste in dogs, Cole Forrest seemed to be a nice guy. Nice guy, nice hands, nice smile, and a set of shoulders that might not be linebacker material but still made it clear that, nerd or not, he didn't spend his whole life sitting at a desk.

Kathy Harris had been right when she had drooled over him at the Flagstaff shows. Cole was a catch, if one was fishing. Jane wondered how Kathy had done in her pursuit. Kathy was a one-night-stand kind of woman. She liked a fast thrill with no strings. Was Cole Forrest, Jane wondered, a one-night-stand kind of guy?

Not that it was any of her business, Jane told herself. And not that she cared. She didn't have time for a guy in her life right now. Besides, Jane wasn't romance material.

Men required too much effort and too much pretense. Definitely not worth the effort.

Back at the motor home, Jane took Idaho out for a fast potty walk and then dug through her few belongings to find the copy of *Clean Run* that had been in her mailbox the day after the fire. *Clean Run* was a magazine devoted solely to the sport of dog agility. It was bound to have information about the Solid Gold Invitational.

Idaho and Shadow both lounged on the couch, watching with interest as she dug through her still-unpacked suitcase.

"I know I brought it," Jane told them. "It's in here somewhere. If I'd taken the time to read it I would have thought of this before . . . ah! Here it is!"

The dogs cocked their heads.

"Last week in August," Jane told them after she'd leafed through the pages and found the two-page ad. "At Argus Ranch Facility for Dogs in Washington. Nice place."

Idaho responded with a low growl.

"No, really, you would like it. Lots of grass. Brand-new arena building. They're going to invite the top 150 dogs in the sport. Minimum average score in qualifying runs is 195. Harsh, eh? Rank in the sport determined by points based on placements in size division as well as number of dogs defeated overall, both score and time. Um. Very complicated. Eligible scores go back through March."

She sent a stern look toward Shadow. "If you want to go, that means you have to run circles around that silly papillon at every trial where you're both entered. Got it?"

Shadow wuffed quietly.

"And don't you forget it, either. Not to put the pressure on, boys, but one hundred thousand dollars would go a long way toward rebuilding the Bark Park and putting us back in business again."

Jane thought back. She would have to look up Shadow's

scores and placements this past spring on the AKC website, but they might have a fighting chance. Idaho hadn't competed since last autumn, putting him out of the running entirely, which was just as well. At eight years old, the border collie deserved retirement, not frenetic competition.

A little whine from Idaho reminded Jane that the dogs had always been able to read her mind.

"You'll go along as chief canine coach," Jane assured him. "We wouldn't think of leaving you behind."

The door to the motor home opened, and in breezed Angela, her perpetually perfect blonde curls bouncing from the energy of her stride. "Hey there, Jane. Who you talking to?"

"The dogs, of course."

Angela smiled wryly. "Of course. Why didn't I know that? Everyone holds conversations with their dogs. Talking about world affairs? New flea products? Agility strategies?"

"We were talking about a great idea that you're just going to love." Jane smiled. "Sit down, Angela. We have a proposition for you."

chapter 7

"THIS IS *sooo* terrific," Angela gushed. "You are a treasure, Jane. You truly are. Following your bid for an agility championship would have been good. Very good. But this! The Solid Gold Invitational! I love the sound of it! Do they call it Solid Gold because of the money, do you think?"

Jane let a little sigh escape. "Solid Gold is the dog food company who is sponsoring the trial, Angela. And putting up the purse."

"Oh! Well, of course." A certain calculation lit Angela's blue eyes. "I'm sure they'll be thrilled that their event will be featured in our series. They couldn't buy better advertising, so they'll probably want to donate something toward our expenses. I'll have to fire off an e-mail or two and discover how the wind blows there."

They sat in Ernesto's extended van, crowded in with his cameras and a wealth of equipment whose purpose Jane could only guess at. Stuffed beneath the driver's seat was a bedroll, and a folding cot peeked from behind what looked like computer paraphernalia. Jane wondered where the poor man found room to sleep.

"All right!" Angela said. "To business. Our first day's take. Let's see what we have."

The screen directly in front of them was for editing, Angela had told her when she had dragged Jane into the van. And there in full living color was Jane's run in the Standard course.

"You looked very good here," Angela said happily. "Together, you and Shadow simply shine. The network is going to love you. We've almost got a contract sewed up. They absolutely adore this whole 'summer of agility' idea."

Jane had to give the woman credit. "You work fast, don't you?"

"Not as fast as you do," Angela said, watching as the video progressed, making notes for narration and editing. "My god, Shadow is so fast through those weave poles that he's almost a blur. How do you get him to do that?"

"Training." Jane remembered the hours spent perfecting the details, because the details could really trip you up— quite literally trip you up—in agility competition. Shadow was always willing to learn, always quick to please. "Training and talent. The dog's talent. Not mine." Jane was a good trainer, but Shadow was an exceptional dog.

Angela gave Jane a sharp-eyed look. "Do you think you have a chance at this invitational thing? A real chance?"

"Of getting there? Definitely. Of winning? Well, Shadow's a top dog. Young, but very good. It's not impossible."

"Yes, well, for our purposes, your getting there and sharing the experience with millions of viewers will serve very nicely. You don't need to pressure yourself to win."

Jane smiled wryly. "Thank you, Angela. Ouch!" She winced as the recording showed her barreling into Cole at the end of the run. "Speaking of the competition . . ."

"What?" Angela stared at the screen. "Him?"

"Him," Jane confirmed. "Cole Forrest. He has a tiny little papillon named Dobby, but that dog should be named

Dynamite. Cole and Dobby are shooting for the Invitational, too. In fact, Cole was the one who told me about the event."

"Cole Forrest..." Once again Angela's eyes narrowed in calculation.

"You're going to take out that last part, right? The part where I ran into the poor man?"

Angela blinked. "Hm? Oh, uh, no, probably not. It's humor, Jane. The audience loves humor."

"That's not humor. It's disaster. I really flattened the guy."

Remembering that collision made her grow warm, from embarrassment and other things as well. Just Jane's luck that Ernesto had caught the moment on camera so the whole world, or at least the television-viewing part of it, could share that roll in the grass.

"There's your boyfriend again," Angela said. "In Jumpers class."

"Angela! He is not my boyfriend!"

Angela grinned. "Just a figure of speech, kiddo. Don't get your knickers in a knot. He's a photogenic hunk, isn't he? And that little dog is a hoot. Not bad."

Jane huffed. "Well, I'm glad Ernesto is filming more than just me."

Jane watched over Angela's shoulder. She had already seen Cole's Jumpers run, of course, standing at ringside with Teri. But the camera had caught the action from another angle. She followed closely, looking for handling errors on Cole's part and any missteps that Dobby might have taken. She hadn't seen many flaws when she had watched the live performance, but the trainer in Jane couldn't help but analyze.

"He looks good," Jane said.

Angela smiled slyly. "He certainly does. I love the juxtaposition of all that masculinity with that feminine little fluff of a dog. So this is your competition, eh?"

"Certainly not the only competition."

"Maybe the most interesting, though." Angela darted a glance at Jane. "Interesting from a filmmaker's point of view, that is."

Cole's performance ended. The camera swung to Jane and Teri at ringside. "The little girl is his daughter," Jane explained. "I was standing there watching because Cole had asked for some pointers."

Angela lifted one brow. "Did he, now? And did you give him pointers?"

"I didn't see anything to criticize about the run. But oh, man, you should see the guy in obedience. The dog is a wonder, and Cole's a klutz. You want comedy, then you should film that!"

"So you two have known each other a while?" Angela probed.

"Not really. Whoa! What is this?"

There on the screen they all walked away from the ring together, Jane and Shadow and Teri in front, Cole and Dobby bringing up the rear. She saw herself cocking her head to listen to the little girl, then laugh at whatever it was Teri had said. Jane didn't remember the conversation, only that Teri had chattered without stopping. The kid definitely was in danger of growing up to be another Angela. There she was handing Shadow's leash to the kid. Behind them, Cole smiled in a way difficult to interpret, but something in the smile sent a curious little tingle down Jane's spine.

"Why did Ernesto film this?"

"This what?" Angela said casually. "Oh, yes. You walking off with Mr. Competition. Human interest, you know. We can't do a series filled with run after run in the agility ring. People want to know the social stuff, too. The friendships, rivalries, hopes, and disappointments. The drama behind the drama. We film everything that looks like a story, sort it out in editing, then put it together to be something wonderful.

"Haven't you ever watched coverage of sports events with all that personal stuff thrown in on the athletes? Ice skating, football, the Olympics—the broadcasters always have to get the skinny on... hey!" Angela's voice rose to an excited pitch. "I just thought of a great angle! This is like the canine version of *Survivor*! All these dogs and their super-competitive people striving to be the last one standing on the island! We'll use that as a hook! I am brilliant, if I do say so myself. This is going to put you and Shadow and the whole agility world in a spotlight so bright that the sport will never be the same!"

Jane stifled a sigh. She was getting an uneasy feeling that this summer wasn't going to be the simple getaway she'd hoped for.

Angela rolled on, her eyes still glued to the editing screen. "The whole country will be cheering for you to get to the Invitational, then to the finals, then to win. Or cheering for Cole Forrest. Or somebody else. It doesn't matter, as long as they're watching the series and cheering. They'll be taking bets at the local watering holes. Office pools will circulate in every workplace. You'll be the subject of every lunchroom conversation. Oh, man! This could be great! With the right promotion, the right look... hmmm."

She frowned at a close-up shot of Jane waiting to enter the Jumpers' ring.

"Jane, have you ever thought of doing something with your hair?"

Self-consciously, Jane put a hand to her ponytail. "What's wrong with my hair?"

"Nothing's *wrong* with it, if you like a burning bush on your head."

"Hey!"

Angela turned to face her. "And speaking of burning bushes, why didn't you tell me about your fire?"

"*My* fire?"

"Yes, your fire. The one that has the news media labeling

you the heroine of the moment. We can really use that in promoting this series, you know."

Jane's temper flashed and she stood. "That fire wiped out my entire life. And you think it's good for business?"

Angela motioned with her hands for Jane to sit back down. "Don't erupt. I didn't mean anything by it. My mouth always runs off without checking first with my brain. But it's true. Some guy at ringside filled me in about the news coverage of how you saved all those animals, and then I looked it up on the network websites. That's what made you change your mind about getting involved in my project, right? Suddenly your place is ash, and you need some time to regroup."

"You might put it that way," Jane agreed warily.

"So why didn't you tell me?"

Jane shrugged. "It seemed sort of . . . private."

Angela smiled and shook her head. "Jane, Jane, Jane. We're friends, aren't we?"

Jane wasn't sure she would call Angela a friend. A business acquaintance, maybe, but it took more than living together in a motor home and working together on a television series to bring a friendship into bloom. A friend was someone like Mckenna or Nell, who could sit quietly while she spilled her guts and know instinctively if she wanted advice or just a shoulder to cry on. Friends were rare and precious, and Angela hadn't yet qualified.

"Angela, I don't want you blathering on about the fire in this series. It's about agility, remember?"

Angela's lower lip slid out into a pout. Jane suspected she'd hurt her feelings by not immediately proclaiming their friendship.

"I won't blather," the producer promised. "I never blather. Just a mention here and there. It's already been on the network news, you know, so it's not exactly a secret. Now!" The pout dissolved into her usual sunny smile. "Back to your hair."

The woman skipped from subject to subject like a flea jumping from dog to dog. "What do you have against my hair? I like it. It's easy, and I can tie it back out of my face."

Angela heaved a sigh. "Jane, you're going to be a star. The whole country will be watching you. And audiences are more interested in terrific-looking people than in people whose biggest concern with their hair is keeping it out of their faces."

Jane felt her stubborn streak rising to the surface. "Forget it, Angela. I'm not some Barbie doll you can dress to fit the part."

"What a thing to say! The part I want you to fit is simply a terrific version of Jane. And by the way, do you never wear makeup? With a little eyeliner and shadow, and maybe some blush, you could be a stunner."

Right now the only one Jane wanted to stun was Angela. "No, I do not wear makeup. I don't have time to spend an hour in front of the mirror every morning."

"But see how washed out you look on screen!"

Jane looked, reluctantly, at the image Angela froze on the screen. She never enjoyed seeing photos of herself, and she used a mirror only to check that her hair was in place and her smile free of food particles. Not that she hated her looks. She could have been handed worse in that department. True, her hair had a mind of its own, and the color could set off a fire alarm. But her nose fit her face, her teeth were straight, her eyes were a rather nice shade of green, and her skin was clear—clear, that is, of everything but a herd of freckles.

Still, Angela had a point. The camera washed out everything about her except the blaze of her hair.

Jane looked away from the screen. "You knew when you picked me for this project that I wasn't some *Cosmo* model."

Angela laughed. "Even *Cosmo* models don't look like *Cosmo* models without the aid of a professional makeup artist and a bit of computer retouching. Trust me. Besides, we don't want you looking like some slinky model. We want you looking like a lovely athlete who can be strong and competitive without giving up her femininity. It's what you are, girlfriend. We'll just bring it out so the camera can see it."

This all was happening too fast for Jane. First she'd lost her home and her business. Then she had to surrender her privacy. Now she had to work on a new version of her looks? No. No more. She liked herself the way she was, and she had lost too much of herself already.

"I don't like it," she said stubbornly. "I need to concentrate on high scores and fast agility runs, and I don't have time for hair and makeup nonsense."

Angela smiled in a way that reminded Jane of Mckenna's cat Titi, who always got what she wanted, one way or another. "I'll bet that hundred-thousand-dollar prize would go a long way toward rebuilding a bigger and better kennel, wouldn't it?" Angela said with deceptive sweetness.

"Oh, please, Angela! Dolling myself up isn't going to win me the Solid Gold Invitational."

"No, but a contract with Animal World would certainly help you get there. And even if you don't get the big prize, the fans you'll collect along the way might very well lead to advertising and spokesperson contracts. Big bucks there, sweetie."

Caught like a rat in a trap, Jane thought. A redheaded, less-than-photogenic rat in need of a makeover. She sighed. "I get the picture. Become a Barbie doll or get dumped."

"Oh, Jane! I would never dump you. We're friends, right? In this together, striving toward a common goal. Besides, you're going to just adore the ideas I have for the new, improved Jane Connor. Just see if you don't!"

WHEN ANGELA took on a project, Jane learned, she dove into the deep end without hesitation, whether that project was filming a television series or transforming plain Jane

Connor into someone fit to be filmed. The Lakeside trials were over; the handlers and dogs—some elated, some discouraged, all tired and dusty—had climbed in their cars, SUVs, and motor homes and headed home.

Likewise, Jane longed for nothing more than to take her dogs and go home, if she'd had a home to go to. Instead, she found herself sitting in a chair in a beauty salon, aptly named "The New You," being squinted at by both Angela and a twenty-something hairstylist by the name of Kandi.

Kandi's hair was coal black streaked with violet. Her T-shirt was black. Her very short shorts were black. And so were her fingernails. This fashion ensemble did not inspire Jane's confidence.

"Is that color natural?" Kandi asked, giving Jane's hair the evil eye.

"Of course it is," Angela replied, without consulting Jane. "You think Clairol or L'Oréal would market something like that? Call it Fire Engine, maybe?"

"True." Kandi fingered a thick, bushy lock that fell past Jane's shoulder. "And I don't suppose this is a bad perm?"

"Bad luck is more like it," Angela commented. "Unfortunate genes."

Jane gritted her teeth. She felt like a dog being discussed by disdainful judges, a dog obviously not in line for Best of Breed.

"Hey, ladies. I'm sitting right here, you know, and I still have my hearing. And I do *not* have unfortunate genes, by the way. They're strong Irish genes passed down from a long line of strong Irishmen. Could we get on with this silly nonsense?"

Kandi nodded sympathetically, but her sympathy appeared to be for Angela, not Jane. "A real challenge," she said in a solemn voice. "You're going to have a lot of work to do."

"But I recognize potential when I see it," Angela claimed confidently. "Now let's get to work."

Jane had very little to say about what that work entailed.

Angela commanded like a general. Kandi carried out orders like a good little trooper. Jane felt like Mission Impossible.

First a thorough wash and a dousing in some sort of cream that smelled of roses. Then they brought out the shears.

"Longish but in layers, do you think?" Kandi speculated.

Angela hastened to shoot that idea from the sky. "Like she needs more volume? No, no, no! We need to tame the beast. Smooth it. Soothe it. Make it bouncy. Make it cute, carefree, flirty."

Jane made a face. Bouncy, cute, carefree, flirty—four words no one had ever before tried to stick on any part of her. She did not bounce. She was not cute or carefree, and she was about as far from flirty as a woman could get and still be above ground. If these fashion commandos succeeded, there was going to be a major disconnect between Jane and her own hair.

"Shorter, I think. A lot shorter." Angela paged through a book of hairstyles, brows puckered in serious concentration. "We need something that takes advantage of all that volume. Something with just a touch of sophistication but that still shouts smart and confident and go-getter."

That was a lot to ask of anyone's hair, Jane thought. Especially her tangle of fire-engine red.

"Ah!" Kandi declared. "I have just the thing. Let me show you this do that I cut out of the last issue of Us. It might be just the thing."

Kandi whipped a folded magazine page out of a drawer and showed it to Angela. The two huddled together, scrutinizing the photo and Jane in turn.

"How about showing it to me?" Jane asked.

"What?" The request seemed to take Angela by surprise.

"It is still my hair, you know."

"Of course it is," Angela admitted. "You're going to love this. It's just right."

"It's very cute," Kandi assured Jane.

"Bouncy," Angela added.

"Carefree," from Kandi.

"Breezy," Angela said with a satisfied nod.

Jane gritted her teeth. But when Kandi started to snip away with her shears, Jane still hadn't seen the photo.

Why did she put up with this? Jane wondered. Where was the independent, forceful Jane who could face down an ornery Rottweiler without flinching and whip a class of obedience school students into shape with one hand tied behind her back? Why was she sitting passively in this chair and letting these two crazies have their way with her own very personal hair?

Money, of course, though it hurt to admit it. Jane needed her chance at that hundred-thousand-dollar purse, and she needed Angela's help to get there. If she had to endure a certain amount of indignity and embarrassment, if she had to bite her tongue to keep from getting thrown off Angela's project and out of Angela's motor home, then so be it.

It grated, though. Jane had never been one to bite her tongue, or to cede leadership to someone other than herself, or to practice the fine art of accommodation. When this summer was over and she was once again on her own, for better or worse, never again would she give up her precious independence. Not for anything. She swore it.

But the summer wasn't over, and her independence was regrettably on hold, so she watched in silence as clippings of red hair fell to the floor and grew into a pile, and then the pile grew into what looked like a mountain. And though she feared she was going to end up bald as a Mexican hairless, she held her silence.

But of course, Angela didn't. Angela didn't know what silence was.

"Oh, Jane!" she enthused. "This is going to make such a difference! You're not going to recognize yourself!"

And this was a good thing?

"This new look is so good that I may just cut the footage we've taken so far and introduce you in this new version. You are going to look so terrific!"

Jane doubted it. But if this got her bumbling collision with Cole Forrest edited out, that would be a good thing. Possibly the only good thing to come out of this humiliation.

Cole Forrest... She wondered how he would react to the new Jane, then squashed the speculation. If she had any luck at all, Cole would meet up with some unavoidable obstacle and drop out of the agility tour. Jane absolutely did not care if she never saw him again. Him or Teri either. Absolutely not.

The pile of hair on the floor grew to rival Mount Everest before Kandi finally declared "mission accomplished." At least the first part of the mission.

"How cute is that!" she exclaimed, standing back and studying Jane as she might a work of art. "Do you love it? You must feel as if a ton of weight just lifted from your head."

Jane dared to glance in the mirror, something she hadn't yet had the courage to do. Her jaw dropped. The only comment she could get out was a horrified "Gaaaak!" Hair that had hung to the middle of her back now barely brushed her chin. The absence of weight gave her unruly curls the freedom to run truly amok, and somehow the thick mane looked even redder than before.

"Do you feel liberated?" Kandi asked happily.

"Aaargh!"

"So happy she can't express it," Angela said, a wicked little smile curving her lips. "And now we need to discuss color."

"Absolutely," Kandi agreed.

"Color?" Jane choked out.

"Just something to calm down the fire a bit. You'll love it," Angela assured her.

"But..."

Angela raised one eyebrow a half inch, and that half inch conveyed a wealth of meaning. How far was Jane willing to go for a chance at that hundred thousand? Pretty far, Jane decided with a resigned sigh. After all, most of her hair was gone. Whatever they did to the rest of it didn't really make that much difference.

"No ifs, ands, or buts!" Angela declared. "You're going to love it. Guaranteed."

At the end of another two hours of torture, Kandi presented her masterpiece.

"Ta-dah!" she said, making a grand gesture toward the new Jane. "I am a miracle worker."

"You certainly are!" Angela agreed. "Jane! To think you've been hiding your candle under a basket all this time."

Jane didn't exactly love it. But after all that time sitting in an uncomfortable chair, enduring shears and razors, dunkings and dousings, smelly chemicals and, finally, a blast of hot air to rival Hurricane Andrew, Jane wasn't sure she would love anything. The woman who stared at her from the beauty salon mirror was nearly unrecognizable. Her hair lived up to every goal the Mission Impossible team had set—cute, bouncy, and breezy, it framed her face with lighthearted waves and curls. Smooth curls, not the untamed frizz that had plagued Jane since puberty. The color still was red, but it was a red with highlights of gold and auburn, the red of rich silk instead of the red of an angry blaze. And the transformed hair had a domino effect, changing other features until Jane scarcely recognized her own face. Her eyes seemed bigger, her nose shorter, her cheeks higher, and her chin more sharply defined.

Jane supposed this version was an improvement over the old, if one coveted good looks. But she already felt nostalgia for the old plain Jane.

Angela grinned, obviously delighted. "Are you absolutely astounded by the transformation?"

"Absolutely," Jane said without much enthusiasm. "Quite a change. My own dogs won't recognize me."

"Sure they will, and they'll think you're gorgeous. And now! Now we work on the wardrobe!"

"Right." Jane could go along with that. "I do need some more jeans."

Angela just smiled.

A half hour later, Jane was grateful that Angela had paid for the new hairstyle, because even though the town of Lakeside boasted a huge Wal-Mart, Angela insisted on shopping for clothes in the trendier, more expensive stores.

"But I'm not a trendy sort of person," Jane objected. "Besides, I have a very finite bank account right now, with no money coming in for the foreseeable future, and Wal-Mart fits my budget just fine."

"Buying good-quality clothes is less expensive in the long run than buying the cheap stuff."

"Wal-Mart has good-quality clothes," Jane insisted. "I always shop there."

"And it shows, girlfriend. Just humor me and try to expand your horizons a bit. Look here! American Outfitter! Practical, sturdy clothing for the outdoor enthusiast. Just what you need."

Jane followed her through the door. It was either that or be left standing on the sidewalk. "I still don't see what could be better than jeans and T-shirts."

What could be better, Angela declared finally, were the two pairs of khaki trousers, three camp shirts that promised to "wick moisture away from the skin," and a set of cargo shorts.

"I never wear shorts," Jane insisted.

"You should. Anyone with legs as good as yours should wear shorts."

"My legs are good?"

"I wish mine were so good. It's genes, I tell you. I exercise and walk and stretch and exercise some more, and my thighs still rub together. It's not fair."

Jane snorted.

"You definitely need to wear shorts, Jane. Take my word for it."

"If I fall during an agility run, I'm going to trash my knees."

Angela smiled blithely. "Then don't fall." She piled a second set of shorts on top of the first.

All that was bad enough, Jane thought, but at least the slacks, shirts, and even the shorts were practical enough. But when Angela set her eye on a green shift with a braided leather belt, Jane dug in her heels. "No dresses. I don't need a dress."

"But that shade of green will look terrific on you! It'll bring out your eyes."

"Eyes, schmeyes. I never wear dresses. No reason to."

"I'm sure we'll find some occasion when you would want to look nice and feminine."

"Forget it."

"Hm." Angela pulled the dress off the rack and looked at the tag. "You would be a size . . . what? Eight? Or a tall six?"

"In dresses I don't have a size, Angela. Oh! Look at these cool shoes over here. Cross-trainers."

But Angela refused to be distracted, and inevitably, a size-eight forest-green shift with a braided leather belt was added to the pile. Jane felt like she had been run over by a bulldozer. A fashion bulldozer. Who would think, looking at blonde, twinkly Angela, that the woman could turn into such a pit bull to get her way.

After what Angela was putting her through, Jane figured she deserved that hundred-thousand-dollar prize.

chapter 8

"CRIMINY, NELL! You oughta see me. I look like something out of a magazine. My hair barely covers my ears, for cripes sake! And they colored it. Or rinsed it in some concoction called Sunset Gold. Would you believe? Sunset Gold!"

Jane complained into her cell phone while sitting on the motor home sofa, knees pulled to her chest and bare feet tucked beneath her. Next to her curled Idaho and Shadow, peaceful except for an occasional ear twitch, and in the driver's seat, steering them down the road toward Carson City, Nevada, sat Angela. Angela sat in the driver's seat in more ways than one, Jane mused with a certain amount of chagrin. But hey! Jane had asked for it. When someone needed something really badly, like Jane needed the Solid Gold Invitational, then that someone had to keep the ultimate goal in sight and ignore some of the small stuff—like the fact that her current benefactor was a tyrant of the worst kind. A fashion tyrant.

"I think that sounds lovely," Nell replied.

Jane snorted. She should have known that Nell would

try to find the positive side. Nell could be annoyingly optimistic.

"It isn't lovely. It's . . . well, it's going to be a hell of a lot of trouble to keep it this color."

"Then you do like it," Nell concluded cheerfully.

"No! Yes. Maybe. I don't know. It's just so different. I don't look like myself. I mean, I might not have been beauty queen potential before they got me in that salon, but at least I looked like myself. You know?"

"You still look like yourself, I'm sure. There's nothing wrong with looking good."

"Well, it feels like a lie. Did I tell you that Angela pinned me down last night and *plucked my brows?*"

"Horrors!" Nell said with a laugh. "I'll bet you look beautiful."

"Ha! Dyed hair, plucked brows! I'm a living, walking piece of fakery."

Nell laughed again. "No more than I am. Do you think my hair is naturally this shade of blonde?"

"It isn't?"

"Butterscotch Banana."

"Butterscotch Banana? Oh, that's just obscene. Do you eat it or put it on your hair?"

"And twice a month someone pins me down and does my brows, not with tweezers, but worse. With wax. And I pay her to do it!"

"Holy cripes!"

"You thought I was born with perfect brows?"

"Well, gee, Nell," Jane said with a touch of annoyance. "I've never given your brows much thought. Or your hair color. Or my brows or hair color either." Nell had never been a good person to complain to. She always played the part of Little Miss Sunshine.

"But Jane, if you really don't like these changes that Angela wants you to make, why don't you just dig in and say no? You've never before had any trouble standing up for yourself. At least, not that I've noticed."

Jane sighed. "You're right. It's just...well...there's this thing that's come up."

"Thing?"

"A thing worth a lot of money. You remember I've always said that I competed with my dogs just to have fun, and for the rush I get from doing the very best possible?"

"Yes?"

"Well...uh, for this summer, at least, that's changed a bit." With a twinge of something like guilt, Jane told Nell about the Invitational. Mckenna and Nell both loved animals. They had to. After all, they were Jane's two best friends (aside from her dogs, of course), and Jane's whole life was animals. But they didn't understand about showing and competing. Nell's scruffy little Welsh corgi had never seen the inside of any kind of show ring, and Mckenna's uppity cat was so sure that she was queen of the world, she didn't need a cat-show judge to verify her superiority.

So Nell and Mckenna couldn't truly understand animal competitions, but they would understand a hundred thousand dollars.

"One hundred grand?" Nell gasped when Jane explained. "You're kidding."

"Would I kid about something like that? One hundred thousand to the winner. One hundred fifty of the top competitors invited, based on some complicated formula they came up with. Basically, to get an invitation, we have to be one of the winningest teams around. And we're going for it. Me and Shadow, with Idaho along for good luck. We're going to hit every agility trial we can until we've kicked enough butt to be in that top one-fifty."

"What fun!"

"The catch is, Angela and company are making this docu-series, or something, out of it. They're already talking contract with a cable network. And since Angela doesn't want me cracking her camera out of sheer cussed ordinariness, she got this notion to beautify me. And when that woman gets a notion, she's worse than a terrier with a rat in its jaws."

"I heard that!" Angela called back from the driver's seat. "And I never called you a rat. I never said you would crack the camera, either."

"You shouldn't listen in on private conversations."

"When you're living with someone in a motor home, nothing is private. How do you think I found out you have great legs?"

"What did she say?" Nell asked with a little gasp.

"She said I have great legs. You have to get used to Angela. She just says whatever comes into her mouth without giving it a thought."

Nell laughed. "Kind of like someone else I know. Someone named Jane."

Jane couldn't deny that. She could impose discipline on the unruliest dog, but not on her own runaway mouth.

"Remind me to never again call you on the phone and expect sympathy," Jane growled.

"I have loads of sympathy," Nell objected. "But most of it is for that poor baby dog you're working so hard."

Jane snorted and looked down at the snoozing Shadow. "Baby indeed. Anyway, you hard-hearted woman, you'll let Mckenna know, won't you, because I'll need everybody's good thoughts coming my way. I tried to call her, but no one answered."

"She and Tom decided to go to Lake Powell for the weekend. They're not back yet. Their animals are staying with me and Dan and Piggy. Sweet old Clara is no trouble at all, but Her Majesty Titi struts around as if she owns the place. It's so funny watching her and Piggy play their little games of one-upmanship."

"Lucky you. Make sure Titi gets her tuna treats, or she'll take Piggy hostage."

Nell laughed. "Piggy can hold her own with Titi. You hang in there, Jane. We miss you. Give Idaho and Shadow a hug for me. And keep us posted on how things are going."

"Sure thing. Right now we're headed to Carson City for two trials. I'll call you next Monday and let you know how we did."

They said their good-byes, and Jane snapped shut her cell phone with a sigh. Her mood was nearly as bleak as the landscape that flew by outside the motor home window. Was there any country more barren than the stretch of Interstate 40 between Seligman and Kingman, Arizona? Rock, sand, dust, and scrub brush stretched as far as the eye could see. Mountains rose in the distance, but they were simply higher rock, sand, dust, and scrub brush. The June sun beat down like a hammer, and Jane's eyes hurt just from gazing out the tinted motor home window.

Not that her home—her ex-home, that is—in Cornville was that much more pleasant during the dry summer months, but at least mesquite and cottonwood trees relieved the monotony in the Verde Valley, and nearby, the cool pines of Flagstaff and swimming holes in Oak Creek Canyon provided refuge.

"Hey back there!" Angela said. "How about you fix us some sandwiches so we can eat lunch? Call Ernesto on his cell phone and tell him to pull over somewhere in Kingman."

"Is there anything to see in Kingman?"

"Heck no. We'll stop in Laughlin tonight. There's a nice RV park right on the Colorado River, and we can get a shuttle into the casinos for dinner. I'll bet Ernesto can win enough at blackjack to buy us all steak dinners. He has a system. That guy never loses. Last time through here we feasted on lobster dinners on his winnings. Now that's what I call useful gambling."

"Don't you ever think about anything besides food?" Jane asked.

"Thinking and talking about food never put an inch on any woman's hips. It's a poor substitute for eating everything I want to eat. Of course, if I went low carb, I could eat a big, juicy steak without worrying about the fat. Lobster too. Hm. Maybe I'll try that."

"Low carb, eh? So you want your sandwich without bread?"

"Heavens no! I'll wait until we get to the steakhouse, then I'll go low carb. Make my sandwich on one of those nice submarine rolls. And remind me to exercise an extra ten minutes tomorrow before we hit the road."

"Whatever you say."

Jane went to the tiny motor home bathroom to wash her hands before fixing lunch, and the sight of the "new Jane" in the mirror startled her yet again. She had looked pretty much the same since age twenty, if one didn't count the deepening laugh lines around her eyes. Ten years of seeing the same reflection in the mirror led to expectations of continuing to see the same image. Those expectations didn't fade in a day, even though she had witnessed the changes herself. In fact, had practically been chained to the chair while those changes were made.

She fingered the chin-length "Sunset Gold" curls that she had pulled back from her face with two clips. The clips made her look like a twelve-year-old, she thought. On impulse, she stuck out her tongue at her mirror image, then turned on heel and went to make sandwiches.

TERI READ aloud from the travel guide on her lap. "Carson City, capital city of Nevada. Population 52,457. That's not nearly as big as Albuquerque."

"Nope," her dad agreed. "Not nearly."

She read on. It was more fun than looking out the motor home window at the dry, boring desert along the highway. This place where they were now was ugly, brown, and hot, but the book said Carson City had trees and grass, like Albuquerque. Only a lot smaller.

"When are we going to get there?" she asked.

"Not until tomorrow, sweet pea. It's a long way from eastern Arizona to western Nevada. When we get there, we'll be almost in California."

"Oh."

"Then we'll get to play around for a few days and see the sights before the trial. Would you like that?"

Teri shrugged. "I guess." At least it wouldn't be as boring as driving through the middle of nowhere in their creaky old motor home, listening to her dad's boring old music and listening to Dobby snore on her little bed between the seats. For a tiny dog, Dobby had a big snore.

Teri sighed and returned to the travel guide. "Elevation 4,687 feet. What's elevation?"

"How high the land is above the sea. I'm real impressed you can read all that."

Her dad impressed easily, Teri decided. He saw her report cards, so he should know how smart she was. There were still a few things she had to ask him about, though. That was all right. It made him feel smarter.

"What's lat...uh...this word." She turned the book toward him and pointed to the word.

"Latitude. Carson City's latitude tells you how far north of the equator it is."

"Why would we want to know that?"

"It goes along with longitude, which is how far east or west it is from an imaginaary line in England. If we know latitude and longitude, we can find any place on a map."

She made a face. Sometimes grown-ups made the world a lot more complicated than it had to be. "Are we lost?"

"No. Of course not."

"Then why do we need the latitude and long—whatever it is?"

Her dad laughed. "We don't. Not right now. Not as long as you're sitting in that seat keeping me on the right road."

"Okay." Wanting to do the job right, she unfolded the map. If her dad depended on her to keep them from getting lost, then she had better do the job right. "Carson City is real close to a big lake. Can we go see the lake while we're there?"

"That would be Lake Tahoe. Yes, we can go see the lake."

"Can we swim?"

"Maybe. If it's not too cold."

"I'll bet Shadow would like to swim in the lake."

Her dad's brow crinkled. It crinkled a lot during their conversations, which just went to show how easily grown-ups got confused. "What was that?" he asked.

"Jane told me that golden retrievers really like to swim. So maybe she'll take him to swim in the lake."

"Sweet pea, Jane and Shadow were back at Lakeside. You don't know that they'll be at Carson City." A peculiar smile twitched his mouth as he slid her an inquiring glance. "Do you?"

"I'll bet."

His eyes turned back to the road, but the hint of a smile remained. Her dad liked Shadow, too, Teri noted, because he only got that look on his face when he thought about something nice. Maybe now, while he thought good thoughts, was the time to ask him the Big Question.

"Daddy?" She made her tone as adult as she could, so he could tell she was really serious about this very important subject.

"Yes, sweetheart?"

"Can I get a dog like Shadow?"

He nodded. Her heart fluttered with hope. "Certainly you can, someday."

The fluttering died. Grown-ups used "someday" to mean the same thing as never. But she couldn't give up like she usually did when her dad wanted to put her off. This was too important to give up.

"When is someday?" she demanded.

He glanced at her in surprise. "You're really sold on this golden retriever business, are you?"

"I really want a dog like Shadow. I would train him at Jane."

"And look at me like Shadow looks—"

"Like you're the only person in the world."

"Yeah. That's it."

His smile turned kind of sad. "Well, then, we need to pay attention to this. Maybe next fall, when we get settled in our new place, then we'll find a good breeder and get you a nice golden retriever."

Teri felt like sticking out her lower lip, but that would only get her a dark look and a lecture on sulking. She knew that from experience. But fall seemed forever away. A whole dogless summer stretched ahead of her. (Dobby was great, but she was too little to be considered a real dog.) And at the end of summer they had to find a new place to live. And then she had to start a new school with all new teachers and kids. And then her dad would be really busy with a new job, and he wouldn't find time to help her get a golden retriever like Shadow.

Her lower lip inched out even though she knew it wouldn't do any good. And her dad sent her a look, but not a bad one.

"I'll bet you're getting bored, eh, sweet pea?"

She was bored because she needed a dog of her own to play with. Dobby didn't play. She just sat on her pillow and looked snotty, and she didn't do anything Teri told her to do. Teri loved Dobby, but she really wanted a dog who understood her. A dog like Shadow.

"How about we stay in a really nice RV park tonight—one with a swimming pool?" her dad said.

Her lower lip slid in just a bit, and her dad smiled, which

made it slide in the rest of the way. He reached over and placed a big hand on her knee.

"Everything's going to be all right, Teri. You know that, don't you? We're going to live in a great new place, and you'll meet lots of nice kids, and you'll get that puppy, when you're ready. But this summer is just for us. You, me and Dobby. We're an unbeatable team, right—"

"I suppose."

Then, like a bolt from the blue, an idea struck her. Jane—Shadow's mom. She was a nice person, and she talked to Teri as if Teri was a grown-up instead of a kid. Her dad liked Jane. He thought she was a good trainer, because he'd said so a couple of times. Jane maybe could talk to her dad, and her dad might listen. Because Jane was a grown-up, just like her dad.

Teri crossed her fingers that Jane would be in Carson City, that Teri could get on her good side so that Jane could persuade her dad. Jane was a dog trainer, so she would know how important it was for a girl to have a dog of her own.

Teri smiled to herself. This was a really wonderful plan.

"That's the face I like to see," her dad told her. "So the thought of a nice cool swimming pool perks you up a bit, eh?"

"That would be nice," Teri replied. "A swimming pool."

Just too bad she didn't have a golden retriever to swim with her, but she would. Jane would help, Teri told herself. Jane would help.

MIDDAY FRIDAY, the Challenger and Ernesto's van pulled into the Comstock Country RV Resort in Carson City. Jane was more than ready to be in a place that wasn't moving. The motor home was comfortable, even when on the road, but the constant hum of the tires and sway of the chassis wore a person out. Not only a person. Shadow and Idaho had a dog door at home—their ex-home, rather. They had been able to go into the big fenced yard whenever they pleased, to take care of dog business, or just lie on the patio to keep an eye on the local families of quails and bunnies. In the motor home all they could do was lie on the sofa, or get beneath everyone's feet, which got them shooed into the bedroom. Life in a motor home was tough for a dog.

But now they were in Carson City—finally! Tuesday night they had spent in Laughlin, and Ernesto had won five hundred dollars at blackjack. Over a sumptuous steak dinner in the restaurant, paid for by the big winner, the cameraman had persuaded Angela to spend the next night in Las Vegas. He knew a winning streak when he saw one, Ernesto had claimed, and he was on one. Such things couldn't be wasted.

Wednesday night in Las Vegas he dropped nearly a thousand dollars at the roulette wheel. That night they had eaten cheese sandwiches in the RV and listened to Ernesto complain that the wheel was rigged. But at least he wasn't urging Angela to stay another night.

Except for joining her traveling companions for the steak dinner in Laughlin, Jane had stayed in the motor home with the dogs, taking them out to stretch their legs, doing a bit of laundry at the RV park facilities, trying to concentrate on a mystery novel that just couldn't catch her interest. She wanted to hurry to Carson City and return to where she was most comfortable, the competition ring. She wanted to score her wins and have that invitation to Solid Gold in her hand. Get it over with. Get the whole summer over with, so she could get back to Cornville and repair her life.

"Wow!" Angela exclaimed as they pulled up to the park office. "This is a nice park. Now I'm glad we decided not to stay at the trial site. Look! A swimming pool."

They pulled into a parking site with a shade tree and room for Ernesto to park his van. Together the three of them made short work of setting up—leveling the motor home, pulling out the awning, and connecting the hookups for water, electricity, and sewer. Angela, who had driven most of the way, immediately turned in for a nap. Ernesto took off to film some shots at the trial site, and Jane snapped leashes onto Idaho and Shadow and took them out for a walk.

She could like Carson City, Jane decided as they strolled among the other trailers and motor homes. At three o'clock on a June afternoon, the temperature had only climbed a little above eighty degrees. To the west rose the impressive escarpment of the Sierra Nevada, and on the east, the horizon lifted to more mountains, less impressive but still picturesque. The high desert here was far from barren. Trees and grass proved relief from much of the country they had driven through since leaving Lakeside on Tuesday.

"What do you think, guys?" she asked the dogs. "Nice, eh?"

Idaho expressed his opinion by choosing that moment to stop and decorate the road. Jane pulled a plastic bag from her pocket and did her civic duty.

"That's what you think, eh? You're just jealous because Shadow is going to get all the glory this summer instead of you."

Idaho gave her a look of pure border collie superiority.

Jane chuckled at the dog's almost human expression. "Don't worry, old man. We all know that you taught the kid everything he knows. If he wins that prize money, we'll split it three ways. Then we'll all get busy building us a new home."

Visions of the new Bark Park rose in Jane's mind. This time the grooming area would be attached to the main kennel, so she wouldn't have to take the dogs across the yard to bathe and brush. And maybe an indoor training area—the height of luxury. Cool in the summer, warm in the winter. Lovely idea. And for herself, Idaho, and Shadow, a real stick-built house with a wraparound porch. With a garden out back, and a fenced yard for the dogs in the front.

Shadow's tug on the leash brought her back to reality.

That lovely dream would take more than a hundred thousand to build. But then, she didn't have to have it all right away. A kennel would be enough to get her back on track. She could buy a used trailer to live in temporarily, and the indoor training facility would come much later.

Just thinking about it gave Jane's spirits a lift. She was going to take her life back. But first, she had to win the Invitational. Not just get there, but win it. She glanced at Shadow, who looked up at her with a slightly goofy smile.

"It's a lot on your young shoulders, my lad. But you'll come through for us, won't you?"

Something in Jane's tone made the goofy canine grin fade into a worried frown. Jane gave him a slap on the shoulder. "We're up to it, Shadow. Just see if we aren't."

Back at the motor home, Angela still snoozed, and Ernesto hadn't returned from searching for photo ops. Enjoying the rare privacy, Jane donned the bathing suit she had gotten in Laughlin, grabbed a towel from the bathroom, and headed for the pool.

So much for privacy! The pool was crowded—kids, mostly. A few adults occupied lounge chairs and watched their children enjoy the water.

Jane wasn't about to let a herd of kids keep her from cooling off, so she found a relatively unpopulated spot in the deep end and slid into the water. It was almost shockingly cold.

But more shocking was the high-pitched child's voice that squealed out a greeting. "Jane!"

Thirty feet away, in the shallow end, a slender little arm waved furiously to get her attention. Teri. So Cole would no doubt be one of the adults sitting on dry land. Jane fought a sudden urge to sink beneath the surface of the water.

Jane didn't understand herself. She'd never been the shy sort. Why did this man make her want to blush, to catch her breath, even to hide whenever she encountered him?

But it was too late to hide. Cole, hearing his daughter's

voice, unfolded himself from a chair and stood up. He'd had his face buried in a book, or Jane would have recognized him right away. And there went her breath, right out of her lungs. Who would have thought the obedience trial klutz, the easygoing guy with the little sissy toy dog, the computer nerd, would look so good in a bathing suit?

It was just too much. Jane grabbed her nose and dunked herself. She imagined the cool water turning to steam next to her overheated skin. Shame on her for reacting like a hormonal teenager to the sight of all that sleek male muscle. Then she remembered the amount of skin she had on display (the Target store at Laughlin didn't sell what she considered modest swimsuits). She wondered if she could manage to hold her breath until Cole and Teri left.

Apparently not, because something thrashed through the water, coming in Jane's direction, and that something turned out to be Teri, her strong little legs kicking furiously. The little girl dove beneath the surface, looked around, spotted Jane, grinned, and waved. Jane surrendered and surfaced—just as Teri's father executed a clean, graceful dive into the pool to discover what his daughter was up to.

Teri bobbed to the surface beside Jane. "I can hold my breath a really long time," she boasted. "Just like you."

Cole came up beside the little girl, water streaming from his hair and an exasperated look on his face. "Teri, what did I tell you about the deep end?"

Teri rolled her eyes. "Don't go in the deep end unless you're with me." She gave Cole an impish grin. "But you're with me, so it's okay, right?"

"Don't split hairs with me, young lady. You know what I meant."

Teri tried to look chagrined, but her acting skills needed work. Cole's sigh made Jane want to chuckle, but she refrained, figuring the scene was humorous only to a nonparent.

"Hi, Jane," Cole said with a wry smile. "I see Teri has already said hello."

"I'm afraid that I'm what lured her into forbidden territory." Jane self-consciously pushed her wet hair out of her face. "I see you decided to stay someplace other than the trial site."

"I've discovered that when you're traveling with a child, it's a good idea to have water and sewer hookups. And a swimming pool doesn't hurt, either."

"We went to Lake Tahoe!" Teri informed Jane. "And rented a boat. And I got to swim in a life jacket. And the water was really cold. But Dobby wouldn't go in the water, because she was too sissy. I'll bet Shadow would have gone swimming with me if he had been there."

"He probably would have," Jane agreed. "I see you swim pretty well."

"She does," Cole said. "But not well enough to be in the deep end without her father. Sweet pea, you're turning blue. I think it's time you got out and warmed up for a while."

Teri's lower lip started to slip out, but before she could voice her objection, Cole gently pushed her toward the ladder. "Out with you. Go get a towel and wrap up."

Teri reluctantly climbed up the ladder, then brightened. "Can I have a soda?"

"They're in the cooler."

Cheered by the prospect of a soft drink, she trotted off, leaving a trail of water as she went.

"You're a brave man," Jane said with a smile. "It's not every father who would spend an entire summer alone in a motor home with an eight-year-old."

"She's the joy of my life," Cole admitted, then grinned. "And sometimes the bane of my life as well." He grabbed the ladder, climbed from the water, and turned to ask, "Want a cola? I've got plenty in the cooler."

Jane tried not to stare, but she couldn't help it. The water streaming over Cole's body outlined every sinew, starting at broad shoulders, flowing over solid pecs, tumbling and dripping down a chest ridged with muscle, and converging in a rivulet that followed the dark line of hair that disappeared beneath the waistband of his swim trunks. The swim trunks fit him very well, Jane noted, especially when they were wet. In spite of the cool water covering her up to her neck, her face insisted upon heating.

Jane could hear Mckenna's voice mocking her, because if she were standing here, her friend would be laughing at her discomposure.

What, Mckenna would have said, *like you've never seen a nearly naked man before?*

Mckenna was a world-class mocker, in a good-natured sort of way.

Of course I have, Jane replied in her imaginary conversation. *Just not one so close, or so ... so ...*

Hot? This time it was Kathy Harris's voice. What had Kathy said about Cole back in Flagstaff, where Jane had first seen him? *A hottie. Good biceps, nice tush.*

Oh, yes. All of that. If the real Kathy were treading water in this pool, as Jane was, she would be foaming at the mouth. A hunk indeed.

"Jane?" Cole inquired, giving her a curious look. "Coke? Root beer?"

No way she was getting out of this pool with Cole watching, not in a bathing suit that wasn't much more than three scraps of spandex and assorted strings. "Thanks." Her voice shivered a bit with the cold, but her face still burned. "But I think I'll swim a bit more."

"Okay. Nice seeing you here. Good luck with Shadow at the trials this weekend."

"Thanks. Same to you and Dobby."

Jane watched him walk around the pool toward his daughter. So much for hoping the competition wouldn't come to Carson City. The competition was here, and so was the distraction.

.   .   .

"HEY, BOY. Put those eyeballs back in your head," Greta Holbrook said to Cole. "She's about the least likely female west of the Mississippi to want to distract herself with a man."

Cole could hardly tear his eyes away from Jane's retreating figure. The woman had an athlete's muscular figure, but all that trim muscle did nothing to detract from her feminine curves.

"Cole?"

"Huh?"

Greta chuckled. "I said, pull in your horns, my friend. Jane Connor would be as tough to scale as Mount Everest. Maybe tougher."

Greta, who had hauled her fifth-wheel trailer from Phoenix, was in her forties and about sixty pounds overweight. She competed in agility with a very fast Australian shepherd, and somehow managed to keep up with the dog, so she knew about scaling difficult obstacles. Cole gave her a guilty grin. "What? Me? Jane?"

" 'Me?' " Greta mimicked. " 'Jane?' Come on, boy, I have eyes in my head, and I'm old enough to recognize that look in your eye."

Cole laughed. "You have to admit she looks mighty good in that swimsuit."

Greta glanced toward the woman, who was striding off between rows of RVs. "True, though I'm the wrong gender to really appreciate it. Who would have thought that Plain Jane Connor had such a figure? She usually dresses in T-shirts big enough to double as a nightgown." A twinkle came into Greta's eyes. "You be careful now, you hear? Jane's a nice girl, but she's headstrong as a bulldog and single-minded as that border collie of hers. Tough, too. I once saw her take down a hundred-pound malamute who ran amok at an obedience trial and attacked the judge. And the malamute didn't come out on top, let me tell you."

Cole was impressed. "No kidding?"

"No kidding." She laughed. "There's a bunch of agility people going to carpool into Reno tonight for dinner. Why don't you come?"

He shook his head and jabbed his thumb toward Teri, who had resigned herself to the shallow end of the pool.

"Bring your little girl." Greta's smile took on a wicked slant. "I'm going to stop by and invite Jane and her friends. It'll be a good time. And we'll get you home in time for the little one's bedtime. You'd better have your fun tonight, my boy, because you won't be having fun tomorrow when my Strider runs away with all the points toward Solid Gold."

Cole laughed. Greta was one of the friendliest souls you could meet. But she made it a point to remind one and all that she and her Aussie weren't out of the competition just because Strider was no youngster and she was no lightweight. "Okay, Greta. You got yourself a date."

chapter 9

"I THINK I'll take a pass on tonight," Jane told Angela. She lounged on the motor home sofa, leafing through the pages of *Dog Fancy* magazine while Angela stood in front of the bathroom mirror, using a curling iron to torture her blonde hair into tight curls.

"Coward," Angela tossed back without hesitation.

"What do you mean, 'coward'?" Jane huffed.

Keeping an eye on the process in the mirror, Angela raised a brow in Jane's direction. "You're afraid to show off the new you."

"No, I'm not." Jane insisted. Just because the thought of sashaying into a restaurant looking "breezy and bouncy" made her nervous, that didn't mean she was afraid. "Afraid" was not a word that Jane associated with herself. Old acquaintances might tease her about the new look. They might think she was trying to be something that she wasn't. But that didn't mean she was afraid.

"I have a headache," Jane claimed. The age-old female excuse.

"And I have a bottle of aspirin," Angela told her.

"Everybody's going to see the new, improved Jane tomorrow, anyway. You might as well give them a preview. Besides, I want to get some footage. Social stuff, you know. We need to bring the audience into the whole agility world, not just the trials. Plus, other competitors will be there. We need to put a personal face on the competition."

Jane gritted her teeth.

"Come on. You'll have fun."

There was no resisting Angela when she was determined. And she *was* determined. Protests notwithstanding, a few minutes later Jane found herself in the bedroom, clad only in her underwear, with Angela dangling the forest-green dress in front of her.

"I told you we'd find an occasion for the dress!" Angela gloated. "You are going to look so hot in this!"

Only her face was going to be hot, Jane suspected, when her friends got a load of her trying to pass herself off as some kind of fashion plate.

"Now the makeup," Angela insisted once Jane had slipped the dress over her head.

Jane's stomach cramped. "Makeup?"

"Makeup," Angela said emphatically. "I can't believe you made it past the age of twelve without getting hooked on makeup like the rest of the world's females."

"I really have no talent with makeup."

"Well, relax, kiddo, because in the makeup department, I am world-class."

What followed was a ten-minute torture session, with Jane squirming helplessly on the sofa while Angela sat beside her, armed with an entire arsenal of cosmetics.

"You're going to poke out my eye with that thing!" Jane complained when Angela took a kohl pencil to her eyelids.

"I won't if you'll hold still! You need to practice with this until you can do it yourself. I don't believe a grown woman exists in this country who doesn't know how to put on eye makeup."

"Why should I wear eye makeup? The dogs don't care."

"You're not in the kennel right now. You're a star, re-member? And the camera always finds the worst flaws in our appearance, so let's make sure the dog world's answer to *American Idol* looks as good as we can make her."

By the time Angela got through with eyeliner, eye shadow, foundation, highlighter, blush, and a dusting of powder, Jane had thought she would see a clown's face in the mirror. To her surprise, the makeup looked quite sub-tle. Her eyes looked bigger, her cheeks and chin more de-fined. But the effect wasn't brash enough to make her a candidate for Barnum and Bailey.

"See!" Angela exclaimed. "You're gorgeous! Is that so bad?"

Jane made a face at herself in the mirror. "I could never do that."

"You'll learn. I'll teach you."

"It'll never last through a sweaty session in the agility ring." Still, she couldn't resist another look in the mirror as they were leaving. Thirty years of living with herself, and she hadn't known until now that her eyes were quite that deep shade of green.

RENO WAS a downsized version of Las Vegas. But small as the town was, the glitter was just as bright, the casinos just as lush, the high life just as high. Unlike Vegas, Reno of-fered more than bright lights, shows, and gambling. Close by were mountains and fresh air for those who cared for the great outdoors, Lake Tahoe for water sports enthusiasts, and historic Virginia City for Old West buffs.

The Peppermill rated as one of the top resorts in town. It boasted luxurious rooms, a lively casino, and eight res-taurants ranging from very swank to low budget. Greta's group, with Jane, Angela, Ernesto, and several others in tow, decided to eat dinner in the International Food Court, which fit everyone's budget with minimum strain.

As the group settled around a table, Jane had to admit this was more fun than spending the evening in the motor home with the dogs. No insult to Idaho and Shadow. In their own way they were better conversationalists than most people of Jane's acquaintance. But once in a while a person had to branch out and socialize with her own species.

Other than Angela and Ernesto, Jane didn't know anyone at the table well. She and Greta went back about five years, ever since Jane had added agility to her list of canine endeavors. But they saw each other only at trials, and their conversations had always centered on the competition rather than the personal. Greta's traveling companion, Sybil, was a newcomer to the sport. Jane had seen her once or twice running a sheltie in novice class, but had never had occasion to talk to her.

The two other people in their group were a forty-something married couple from San Bernardino—Frank and Sheila Metzer, who competed with border terriers. They drove a huge van that had a generator-driven evaporative cooler on top so their dogs could lounge about in cool comfort when the van was parked. A beeper let Frank and Sheila know if the temperature in the van rose above eighty-five degrees, so they could safely leave their dogs in the heat of the day while traveling or at a trial. If the cooler failed, they could get back to the dogs before serious heat set in.

Jane figured that anyone willing to spend that much money for the comfort of their dogs had to be okay.

The waitress had just brought their drinks when two latecomers arrived at the table. Jane's heart jumped when she saw that it was Cole and Teri.

"Hey, slowpokes," Greta greeted them. "It's about time you got here. I thought you were right behind us."

"We got caught at a stoplight."

"Everyone here know Cole Forrest and his daughter Teri?" Greta asked. "Cole and his papillon are aiming to beat the pants off the rest of us this weekend, and Teri's going to help, aren't you, honey?"

"Yes, ma'am."

Jane was surprised that Cole had been included in the group, but then, Greta knew everyone who was anyone in the sport of agility, and Cole and Dobby were rapidly becoming a team to be reckoned with.

Once everyone had settled in with menus and drinks, Jane felt eyes start to turn her way, followed by curious smiles and a few raised brows. Greta wasn't shy about making a comment. But then, Greta always said exactly what she thought. Sort of like Jane herself. "Jane, you're positively glowing. I've never seen you look so good."

"Uh . . . well."

"You changed your hair, didn't you?"

Jane felt like pulling a napkin over her head. "Uh . . . yes. I got tired of wearing it the old way, so I decided to splurge."

"Wow! What a difference!"

"She's gorgeous, isn't she?" Angela chimed in, rather smugly, Jane thought.

"She is," Greta agreed. "You look five years younger, Jane."

Jane could feel herself turn red. Worse, she could feel Cole's eyes on her. Was that an amused smile playing around his mouth?

Sybil laughed. "I think we're boring Cole and Ernesto to tears. That's what you guys get for going out to dinner with a bunch of females."

"Don't worry about it," Ernesto said with a smile. "Cole and I will start talking about the Arizona Diamondbacks any minute, and then you ladies will be the ones yawning."

Teri objected. "What about me? Who are the Diamondbacks, anyway?"

Ernesto gasped dramatically. "Cole, you've neglected your daughter's education."

Cole shrugged. "Not my fault. The only sports that Teri likes are the ones that include dogs. Although she is a terror at basketball, aren't you, sweet pea?"

"I beat my dad a lot," Teri confirmed.

"Well, if the choice is between basketball and dogs, then we should talk about dogs," Greta decided. "I don't know a thing about basketball."

"Speaking of dogs," Sybil said to Jane, "aren't you the Jane Connor who pulled all those dogs and cats out of the fire up in Cornville?"

Angela answered for Jane. "She is. The very one."

"I saw the story on Channel 5. Omigod, it nearly brought me to tears. To think of all those dogs and cats burning to death, trapped in their kennels—what a nightmare. But I'm not sure that I would have had the guts to stay until the fire was licking at my heels. God, Jane, you must have nerves of steel."

"It wasn't that big of a deal," Jane muttered, more embarrassed than ever.

Cole smiled at her, but his eyes were very serious. "It is a big deal. All of us would like to think that we would've done the same. But how many of us would have, when push came to shove?"

Jane couldn't imagine doing anything else, and didn't believe that any adult sitting at the table, anyone who loved animals, wouldn't have pulled those dogs and cats out of their kennels the same as she had done. She wished everyone wouldn't make such a fuss.

The waitress came to take their food order, and the talk moved on to other things. Jane ordered a smothered enchilada. Cole also chose Mexican—the chimichanga. Teri couldn't make up her mind between a cheeseburger and

pizza, so Ernesto suggested that she order the cheeseburger and let him order pizza.

"That way I can give her a couple of slices."

Teri liked the idea. Cole expressed his gratitude.

"I have five daughters," Ernesto explained. "And eight
grandchildren. I've learned a thing or two."

Cole laughed and nodded.

The server arrived with appetizers. Angela ordered three
bottles of wine for the table, then inveigled everyone sitting
there to give permission for Ernesto to film them at dinner.
So the story of Angela's project leapt out of the bag. Angela
gushed about the possibilities, as only Angela could gush.
Teri's eyes grew round with excitement. Frank Metzler, who
worked in the film industry in California, asked about
Angela's other film credits and nodded knowledgeably
when she spun off a list.

"Jane's going to be a television star!" Sybil declared. "Oh
my gosh, Jane! Will we be able to talk to you when you're
front-page news in *The National Enquirer?*"

"And living the high life with bodyguards to keep the
fans away?" Cole added, a teasing twinkle in his eye.

Jane took a gulp of wine. Unaccustomed to drinking
anything harder than iced tea or soda, she nearly choked,
but the chardonnay lost its bite as it slid down her throat.
The warm glow of alcohol took the edge off her embarrassment. She could even smile smugly at Cole. "When I'm living the high life and enormously rich from advertising
contracts, maybe I'll buy Cole a real dog so he can try his
hand at running something that isn't a wind-up toy."

The whole table laughed.

"Me too," Sybil said, sounding pathetic. "Would you get
me a dog who doesn't make up his own agility course instead of running the one the judge set?" For which crime
her sheltie was in the doghouse after flunking both days at
the Lakeside trials.

Everyone had suggestions for what Jane could do for

them once she was rich and famous. Ernesto filmed for a few minutes, hardly noticed by the group, who by now had polished off enough wine to be feeling quite good about themselves. Sybil flirted with Cole, and so did Sheila Metzer, despite her husband sitting right beside her. Jane surprised herself by feeling a twinge of resentment toward both women. Where that came from she couldn't imagine. She certainly didn't care who made eyes at the guy. They scarcely knew each other. And Jane didn't care about men or dating or any of that nonsense, anyway.

Let Sybil and Sheila knock themselves out, just like Kathy.

Except that the poor guy didn't seem comfortable with all the female attention, Jane noted. He even made a silent plea to his daughter to save him, if Jane interpreted the glance correctly, but Teri could spare no attention for anyone but Ernesto, who had finished doing his duty with the camera and had taken it upon himself to explain the game of blackjack to the kid. Frank was deep in discussion with Greta about differing methods of training weave poles, paying no mind at all to his wife Sheila's wandering eye.

"I think it's just so exciting that you know all about computers," Sheila said for about the third time. "You know, I think nerds are just terribly sexy. Give me a man who can think, not some stud who can bench-press the world." She laid a hand on Cole's arm, oh so casually. "Not that you're stringy like some other computer jocks I know."

Sheila giggled for some reason. Jane couldn't figure out what was supposed to be funny. But at least Sybil had retreated to join Frank and Greta's weave pole discussion, which by now had become a bit heated.

Suddenly Cole turned to Jane. "I see you've finished dinner. Maybe we could go out now and take a look at Dobby."

"What?" Jane said, confused.

He gave her a meaningful look, but Jane didn't have a clue what the meaning might be.

A muscle twitched at the hinge of Cole's jaw, and with a tight smile, he put his napkin on the table and gently took Jane's arm. "Excuse us for a few minutes, folks. Jane promised that she'd take a look at Dobby, out in my RV. She's looking a bit peaked to me, and I'm presuming on Jane's good nature to give me some advice. Teri, you stay here, and don't let Ernesto take you into the casino to demonstrate that blackjack strategy. We'll be back in a few minutes."

Feeling as though she'd skipped a page somewhere, Jane followed docilely as he led the way out. Maybe she'd had too much wine. "What do you mean Dobby's feeling peaked?" she demanded as they emerged from the casino into the huge parking lot. "Is she sick? Vomiting? Diarrhea? You're not going to make her run tomorrow, then, are you?"

He shook his head and sighed. "Nothing's wrong with Dobby. That was just an excuse to escape. Sheila was getting out of hand. I figured that you're such an acknowledged dog expert that the others would believe me if I said I wanted you to look at Dobby."

So she was just a diversion. She wasn't sure she liked that.

They walked in silence toward Cole's motor home, which was in the parking lot a good hike from the casino.

"We might as well go in," Cole said. "We can have a cup of coffee, then go back. By that time Sheila will either have passed out or at least gotten interested in something else."

As they climbed into the motor home, Dobby—who did not look at all "peaked"—greeted them with a wave of her tail. She was curled comfortably in the folds of a plush dog bed on the narrow sofa.

The tiny dog looked as if she were specially designed for such a small living area. In fact, the Forrest motor home made Angela's vehicle look like a palace. This one was not much more than a glorified camper with a miniature kitchen, a cramped eating area, and a bed stuck high over the cab. But it was tidy—a surprise, considering an eight-year-old and her single father lived in it.

The space seemed even smaller with Cole moving around inside it, fixing coffee in the tiny kitchen. Dobby didn't bother to get up from her pillow, so Jane wedged herself onto the sofa beside her, ignoring the little dog's withering look.

"I guess I could use some coffee," Jane said.

"You, me, and everyone else, too. Poor Sheila has downed a glass too many, that's for sure. She's going to wake up tomorrow morning wishing that she couldn't remember the night before."

Jane thought Cole was being amazingly charitable with Sheila's behavior. Jane had wanted to turn the plate of stuffed mushrooms over the woman's head. Not because she was jealous, Jane told herself, but because the woman was making such a cake of herself.

Cole handed her a steaming mug, and the sharp aroma of coffee made Jane very aware of the wine-induced fuzz on her brain.

"Sorry I dragged you away from the party like that. But it was either find a plausible excuse to leave or use one of those fancy linen napkins to gag the woman."

That was more like it. Jane like that image. "Won't Teri worry, hearing you say Dobby is under the weather?"

Cole chuckled. "Teri was so intent on listening to Ernesto's stories of how to win a fortune that I doubt she heard anything I said. Eight-year-olds have big ears, but those ears are seldom tuned to their parents. Though Teri is better than most."

"Teri seems to be a really nice kid." She took a sip of coffee, hoping the caffeine would dispel the goosey feeling that made her stomach flutter and her heart pick up speed. It was the wine that made her feel that way, of course. Being alone with Cole in a cramped space had nothing to do with it.

But goodness, were the man's shoulders really that broad, or did the smallness of everything around him just make them seem so?

She dragged her eyes away from Cole and stared into her cup. "Thanks for the coffee. I think we all had a bit too much wine in there."

He squeezed himself sideways into the tiny dinette booth. The aisle between the sofa and dinette was narrow enough that their knees touched. His gaze rested upon her, strangely intent. Or perhaps the intentness was Jane's imagination, inspired by the wine. Or maybe not, because his next comment jumped right into personal territory.

"I like your hair."

Surprised, she said, "What?"

"The new do. Not to get too personal." He smiled. "My wife used to tell me that we guys ought to tell women when we think they look nice. It lifts us out of the caveman category, she used to say."

"Oh." Jane bit her lower lip. "Well, thanks. Angela made me do it, actually. She thought I might break the lens of Ernesto's camera, otherwise. She has very definite ideas about what looks good and what doesn't look good on the tiny silver screen."

"Ah, yes, the Big Show. Where is this going to play?"

"Angela's aiming for Animal World. Frankly, I don't care to watch myself on television, and I'm not real keen on having the rest of America watch me, either. But it's a way to get to the Invitational."

"You've decided to make a bid for it, eh?"

She smiled. "Shadow and I are going to clean your clock. But we'll be glad to have your support at the Invitational from the spectator seats."

He laughed. "A challenge. I guess we'll be seeing a lot of each other this summer, then."

He didn't look displeased by the prospect, which gave Jane an unexpected feeling of satisfaction, and also produced a glimmer of uneasiness. It was almost as if the guy was flirting. Jane had so little experience with such things that she couldn't be sure.

Abruptly, she put down her empty coffee cup. "I'd better go," she said, standing.

"Yeah, we'd better get back." He put the cups in the sink and gave Dobby a brief scratch on the head. The dog acknowledged him with a twitch of her tail. "I think I'll collect Teri and go back to the RV park. I'm glad I brought my own vehicle instead of riding with Greta and her crew, in spite of the trouble of unhooking everything at the park and then hooking it back tonight. I suspected that those ladies would want to do a lot more partying than I do."

"Not much into partying, eh?" Jane preceded him out of the motor home. In the parking lot, bright lights held back the night. "I guess being a parent takes away some of those privileges."

"Never have been much for late nights." He smiled wryly. "Unless I'm working on some mathematical or computer puzzle. I'm afraid Sheila got it right on a couple of counts. I really am a bit of a nerd. I've been known to get so involved unraveling some complex program that I forget to sleep. More than once I've looked out my office window to see the sun rising, only to realize I forgot to go to bed."

Jane laughed. "Your wife must not have liked that!" She instantly regretted her thoughtless words. "I'm sorry. I shouldn't have said that."

"It's all right," he said with a smile. "Mandy's been gone for two years. I can talk about her now and be grateful for what we had together. And you're right. She hated it when I pulled all-nighters."

He took Jane's arm to guide her over a curb—entirely unnecessary, but Jane thought it was kind of sweet.

"I'm not sure that Teri has made that adjustment, though," he continued. "She pretty much retreated into a shell when her mother died. I think finally, maybe, she's coming out of it. That was one of the reasons I decided to sell the house and business and move, and to take this summer to just be with her and have fun."

"And it's working, you think?"

"I think," he said with the crooked beginnings of a smile. "And by the way, I want to thank you for being so nice to Teri. She adores Shadow. And you're one of the few women I've seen her warm to. Thank you for that."

Jane didn't know what to say. She hadn't treated the kid differently than she treated any other person.

"She's a good kid," was the only thing she could think of. "I admire anyone who has the guts to be a parent. Kids are so much harder to train than dogs."

They paused at the casino entrance, both a bit reluctant to go back in. He raised a hand, almost as if he intended to touch her cheek, but then dropped it again, self-consciously. "Thanks, Jane, for going along with my little deception."

"Any time. It's the least I can do for someone I'm going to flatten on the field of competition." She flashed him a grin. "But wait! I did that already, didn't I? Flattened you clear to the ground."

He laughed. "And I've still got the bruises to show it." The laughter faded to silence. He looked down, then up again, and the lines around his eyes had deepened with a lingering smile. "By the way, I didn't mean to imply that I didn't like the way you looked before Angela's makeover. Really."

Jane felt her face begin to heat, and Cole looked as if he regretted his little foray into paying women compliments. Impulsively, she leaned forward and gave Cole a quick hug. "I know you didn't." She quickly drew back, amazed at herself. She never got physical even with her close friends. And with a man, almost a stranger? Unthinkable.

Still, Cole grinned. He captured one of her hands, and a

certain light came into his eye. For a moment they just looked at each other, both faintly embarrassed.

Then he shook his head, and his smile twisted upward into amusement. "Good luck tomorrow, you and Shadow."

"Same to you."

The strange intimacy of the moment sputtered to an end. But Cole didn't surrender her hand until they had walked through the casino and found the entrance of the restaurant.

"How is Dobby?" Greta asked when Jane and Cole returned to the table.

Jane detected the sparkle in Greta's eye. If Cole's ploy had deceived anyone, it hadn't fooled sharp-eyed Greta.

"Dobby is fine," Jane replied evenly. "She's just being a whiny little princess. As far as I can tell, she's ready to beat the pants off of all our dogs tomorrow."

Everyone nodded and made appropriate noises, going along with the story that Cole had left the room to consult about his dog. Sheila looked mildly embarrassed. Apparently some of the wine effects had worn off.

Teri, however, drilled Jane with her eyes, with an intensity that no eight-year-old should possess. Her expression took Jane by surprise.

"Hate to break up the party," Greta said, "but I should turn in if I don't want my dog to be leaving me behind tomorrow. Excellent class starts at seven, and oh my, that comes very early in the morning."

Murmurs around the table agreed with her.

"Ditto to that," Cole said, and tweaked Teri's nose. "Sweet pea, you ready to leave?"

His daughter gave him a speculative look, then shifted her attention to Jane, who was looping her fanny pack over her shoulder and preparing to follow Angela and Ernesto toward the door. "I have to pee," Teri informed them in no uncertain terms.

"You can use the bathroom in the motor home," Cole reminded her.

"I want to use the one here, where there's lots of water." Her focus on Jane spoke plainly about who she expected to take her to the potty.

Cole gave Jane an apologetic look. "Would you mind, Jane? She's really too old to go into the men's, and I don't think the ladies would appreciate my presence in the women's."

"No problem," Jane said. "If you would catch Angela and tell her I'll be right out."

Teri held out her hand. Jane did the expected and took it. "My daddy doesn't like me to go to the bathroom alone," the child informed her solemnly. "Except at home. Then I can go alone. But not with strangers around."

"Your daddy is a smart man," Jane conceded.

As they made their way to the bathroom, Jane felt as though she'd stepped out of her world and into someone else's. The child's hand felt strange in hers—alien, and at the same time warm and sweet. Jane had never felt the need to dote on children. She had always regarded them as miniature adults, to be treated in the same manner as adults. Some were worth having a conversation with. Most were simply annoying.

But that little girl's hand in hers ignited something odd inside her. Perhaps all women had a primitive weakness for children. Either that, or the wine was making Jane maudlin. She remembered what Cole had said about Teri's struggle, and it made her want to see a smile on that pixie face. The kid could visit with Shadow as much as she liked, Jane decided. Enough time spent with a sympathetic dog could make almost any dark cloud seem lighter.

The bathroom was as much a ladies' withdrawing room as a potty, with a marble counter below a huge mirror, plush pink chairs, a pink and lavender flower arrangement in one corner, and every convenience a woman might need—including facial tissues, hair spray, and hand lotion. Teri took her time doing her business, and when she came out of the stall, her face was set and determined, as if she'd been pondering serious matters and had made momentous decisions.

She gave Jane a considering look. "I like your new hair and face," the little girl said. "You look much prettier than before."

Always check your ego at the door, Jane reminded herself, when dealing with a kid. "Thank you, I think."

"You're welcome." Teri plunked herself down on one of the plush chairs and sat like a little queen interviewing a subject. Right then it occurred to Jane that Teri and Dobby had quite a few traits in common, personality-wise.

"Did you fix up your hair and stuff because you like my dad?" Teri asked primly.

"What?" Jane didn't know whether to laugh or cuss. "Why would you ask a thing like that?"

Teri sighed. "Since my mom went up to heaven, all sorts of ladies have liked my dad and tried to get him to pay attention to them."

"What a thing for an eight-year-old to say!" Jane leaned against the marble counter, folded her arms, and regarded the little wiseacre with a gimlet eye. "Are you really a fourteen-year-old in disguise?"

Teri screwed up her face. "What?"

"Never mind. It's just that eight-year-olds generally aren't that familiar with their parents' love lives."

"You don't know that many eight-year-olds, do you?"

The kid had her there.

"My dad thinks I don't notice stuff, but I do. He doesn't pay any attention to the ladies, because he still loves my mother. I know he does. Everyone loved my mother."

"I'm sure they did."

"I just didn't want you to be like those other ladies who

make moony eyes at him, because you're different and nicer. Maybe you could just aim to be my dad's friend instead of his squeeze."

"Squeeze?" Jane tried not to laugh. "Where did you hear that word?"

"Television."

It could have been much worse, Jane admitted silently. "Teri, I don't think you have to worry about me becoming your dad's squeeze. I don't have any ambition in that direction, okay? Your dad is safe."

"I wasn't worried about my dad. I told you he never pays attention to the ladies."

Teri might get a rude awakening someday, Jane thought, but certainly Jane Connor wouldn't be the one moving in on the private world the girl shared with her dad.

Then she remembered the little glow deep inside when she had sat in that motor home having coffee with Cole. And her idiot behavior giving the poor man that hug.

Such silliness! She *didn't* have any ambition in that direction.

Did she?

"I was worried about you getting your feelings hurt," Teri clarified.

"That's very sweet of you, Teri, but you don't have to worry. I'm made of pure steel. My feelings don't get hurt easily."

"Shadow thinks they do."

It took a minute for that comment to fully register. "What?" she asked cautiously.

"Shadow thinks your feelings get hurt a lot, and he doesn't like it when they do. So I decided to warn you about my dad. 'Specially after you guys went out together, you know, and when you came in, you looked all moony."

Jane was instantly defensive. "I certainly did not look moony!" Then she remembered the extraordinary thing the kid had said. "Shadow thinks my feelings get hurt? Did he tell you that?"

"Yes." Teri regarded her with a speculative look. "You don't believe me, do you?"

"Well..." Never had Jane felt her lack of finesse with children more than now. "I don't know. Shadow talks to me all the time, but not in so many words."

Teri shrugged. "Maybe you just don't listen well enough."

"Uh-huh." What *was* this? "Uh...if Shadow tells you anything else, especially about me and my feelings, you let me know, okay?"

"Maybe. Sometimes it's not nice to tell something someone tells you."

"Well, right."

"But I'll tell you something Dobby told me."

It got worse and worse. "What did Dobby tell you?"

"She said I should warn you."

"Yes?"

"That she and my dad always win. I didn't tell that to Shadow, because, you know, he might feel bad. But it's true. My dad and Dobby always, always win."

Jane had to smile. Here she was on more familiar ground. "You tell Dobby that she'd better get used to losing."

"She wouldn't like losing," Teri replied.

As they walked out together, Teri offered a hand for Jane to hold. "Can I ask you something personal?" the girl requested.

As if the kid hadn't gotten personal already. Jane sighed. "Shoot."

"What?"

"Shoot. Go ahead. Ask away."

"You think dogs are important, don't you?"

"Dogs are very important."

"Dogs are really good for people, right?"

"That's what I think."

"They're even good for kids, right?"

Jane agreed. "Especially good for kids."

Teri gave her a beatific smile, leaving Jane thoroughly confused. Anyone who claimed to understand kids, she decided, was full of bull.

chapter 10

THE NEXT morning dawned a bit chilly, just a hint of dew on the grass of Fuji Park, where a big banner at the park's entrance welcomed spectators and competitors alike to the Truckee Meadow Dog Training Club agility trials. Jane, Angela, and Ernesto arrived even before the banner went up, all three of them plus Shadow and Idaho crowded into Ernesto's van with the video equipment.

Because they arrived so early, they had their choice of locations for Jane's canopy, which would shelter both dogs and people from the sun. They chose a spot well away from the busy highway that bordered the park, under trees that would provide extra shade. The canopy went up, the woven plastic floor mats went down, and by the time the sun had risen over the mountains, Shadow and Idaho were wrestling happily in a shaded exercise pen while Ernesto and Angela relaxed in folding chairs and sipped coffee.

Jane could indulge in no such relaxation. The gate steward was already hollering from the Excellent ring that the course was open for walk-throughs. Handlers had ten minutes to walk the course, memorize the order of obstacles, and think of strategies to handle the "challenges" that the judge had concocted for them.

Jane took a quick sip of caffeine from the steaming Styrofoam cup Angela handed her. A thermos jug of hot coffee sat on top of the cooler that held their lunches. "Thanks," she said to the producer. "I'll finish it when I get back. Gotta go."

"Guess I'd better get busy, too," Ernesto said. "You dog people certainly do believe in getting up early."

Jane left them behind to talk about what Angela wanted to be filmed today. If she thought about Ernesto recording her every step to be broadcast into thousands of homes, she would give them a show more laughable than admirable.

Handlers were already making the rounds when she got into the ring. A couple of people waved—people that Jane saw at nearly every trial. She didn't know their names, but she knew the names of their dogs. She started searching for the course start line, finding it just as someone came from behind and touched her arm. It was Greta.

"Hey, kid. Ready to kick everybody's ass?"

"Going to try."

"Well, you won't have trouble wiping up the course with me this morning. I should know better than to drink the night before a trial."

Jane just laughed, and Greta responded with a pained grimace. Her eyes were pinkish and set in dark circles.

"You look perky enough," Greta said, "even though you seemed to be having a good time last night. With Mr. . . . uh . . . what's his name?"

"You know very well what his name is, and don't go spreading tales concocted from your overly ripe imagination."

Greta chuckled. "A wee bit sensitive, are we? Speaking of the devil, there he is, puzzling over the tunnel/A-frame trap. Maybe you should go help him."

"Greta, get lost. The only thing I want to do with Cole today is leave him in my dust."

Greta laughed. "Go get 'em, tiger. And watch out for the triple jump. The approach is about as blind as can be. It'll kill you."

Jane tried to forget Greta's teasing, ignore Cole's presence, and concentrate on the course. If she wanted an invitation to Solid Gold, she needed to win from here on out. She needed to work on her dog handling and forget the distractions—distractions like how Cole's eyes got that warm crinkle when he smiled, and how he had almost touched her cheek with his hand outside the casino the night before. Such a simple gesture, but in a way so intimate. How would she have reacted to such a caress?

Someone bumped her, and Jane blinked, startled to find herself standing like a statue, daydreaming. *Focus!* she commanded herself. *Focus, focus, focus!*

She had walked the entire course three times, looking at distances, angles, footing, and flow, when she inevitably ran into Cole. Inevitably, she mused with a bit of resignation, because whenever the two of them were on a field together, she somehow always ended up nose to nose with the man.

She was not, definitely *not*, seeking him out. No. It was just bad luck that he was squatting a short distance in front of the triple jump, looking for a good angle of approach (which Jane had already decided didn't exist), when Jane almost stumbled over him.

"Oops!" She changed course just in time. "Cole! What are you? A speed bump? You're asking to get trampled."

He straightened up, still puzzling over the jump. "I guess I am, aren't I? Can't figure this triple, though. Coming out of the tunnel, Dobby's going to be looking straight ahead to the dog-walk. She won't even be able to see the triple jump until the very last minute."

"Yup. It's a devil."

"I think I'll let her go out a bit before I call her, to get a better angle."

"It might be better to get her attention the minute she sets paw out of the tunnel," Jane suggested.

"That makes the angle really bad."

"Letting her go out could get you an off-course penalty if she doesn't turn immediately when you call her."

He smiled. "Guess I'm just a risk taker."

Jane snorted. "Better not take too many risks, or I won't be seeing you at Solid Gold."

"What's the fun in playing it safe, when just a little boldness might produce a far better result?"

Jane was pondering the possible meaning of that statement when the steward bellowed out that the first dog should be at the line in two minutes.

"That's me," Cole said. "We're first today."

Jane chuckled. "First to run, not necessarily first in the ribbons."

"We'll see about that," he replied with a wicked grin.

They headed for the gate together.

"By the way," he said. "Thanks again for the help last night. With . . . well, you know. And with Teri, too. I had no idea she would keep you in the bathroom that long. What the heck was she doing, anyway?"

Jane teased. "It's not polite to ask us ladies what we do in our more private moments, Cole. As the father of a girl, you need to learn that."

He gave her a look. "As the father of a girl, my goal is that she have as few private moments as possible. Especially when she gets to be a teenager."

"Ah. Well, it was just girl talk. Better get that little fuzzy toy of yours. You'll need some time to wind her up before expecting her to run."

Whatever Cole did to wind up little Dobby, it worked, because he and the little dog ran a flawless Excellent course and crossed the finish line five seconds under time. That would chalk up a few points toward a Solid Gold invitation. Two hours later, third from the last to run, Jane and Shadow ran an equally flawless course, two seconds under time. Both Dobby and Shadow won their size divisions, but Dobby would chalk up the points for the overall best run.

"Cripes!" Jane complained to Angela as they stood in the officials' tent looking through the pages of score sheets. "How does he do that with that itsy-bitsy dog? And it's the first dog he's ever trained. Talk about there being no justice!"

"You won your class hands down," Angela pointed out. "Or should I say paws down. That'll move you forward."

"One step behind Cole and Dobby."

Angela shrugged. "We got some great shots today. And I want you to look extremely pleasant when they hand out awards."

"I'll smile until my teeth ache," Jane promised facetiously, then shook her head in frustration. "There's just no justice."

TERI SAT cross-legged beside Ernesto as he filmed the very informal process of handing out the awards for Excellent Standard class. Teri had always found the awards boring. Boring and long. The first four placements earned ribbons in five different size divisions, and the scores of the dogs qualifying but not placing were read also. The process took a while. And there was no suspense to make things more interesting. Her dad and Dobby always won their size division, and today Dobby had clocked the fastest time in the whole class. No surprise there. Dobby was superdog. Just as Teri had told Jane the night before, Dobby always won.

Dobby hadn't really told Teri to say that, of course. Dogs didn't usually talk. Except for Shadow. Shadow's communication had come as quite a surprise to Teri. At first she had thought the images and feelings that formed in her head when she got close to the golden retriever were from her own mind. Her mind did that sometimes. Sometimes she talked to her mom, even though her mom had been in heaven for a long time. Teri didn't know if her conversations with her mother were a trick that her mind played on her—something that seemed real but was pretend, like special effects in the movies—or if those comforting words and almost-felt touches were real. She hoped they were real. Maybe angels like her mom could come back to earth sometimes to give their little girls an angelic hug. Teri wanted to think that was so.

Teri had less trouble believing that her mom really spoke to her than accepting that Shadow could do the same thing. Unless her mom had maybe touched Shadow in some special way, because she knew that Teri really needed a special friend. Maybe that was what had happened. She didn't have too much trouble believing that.

Her mom had chosen well, because Shadow was a wonderful special friend. Whenever the dog looked at her with those soft brown eyes, wave after wave of warmth and love came Teri's way. Shadow loved Jane best, of course, because dogs have to love the people who own them. That was dog rules. But he loved Teri, too. The golden retriever had enough love in him to spread around, and he knew that Teri needed all the love she could get.

Not that Teri's dad didn't love her a lot. He did. But he was her dad, and parents just naturally loved their kids. He didn't love her because she was special. Shadow thought she was special.

Someday Teri would have a dog just like Shadow, and that dog would love her more than anyone else.

"Teri, *chica*, do you see that lawn chair over there?" Ernesto asked, snagging her attention away from someday. He squatted beside her, camera balanced on his shoulder, about fifteen feet from the canopy where people were receiving their ribbons.

"The green one?"

"Yeah. Would you go move it for me? Just a little ways. I just found a good camera angle and the chair's in the way."

"Okay." She unfolded herself from the ground and ran to do his bidding. When she returned to his side, she asked, "Did you film my dad and Dobby getting first place?"

"I sure did. I got their run this morning, too. They make quite a pair, your dad and that little dog."

"My dad says that he and Dobby are a team."

Sometimes when her dad said that, Teri felt left out. She always got stuck watching from the sidelines while her dad and Dobby ran around the agility course. She wanted to be part of their team, but in this sport, teams had only two. One person and one dog.

Teri needed a team of her own.

"That little Dobby of yours is cute enough to make the camera smile," Ernesto said. He took his eye from the eyepiece for an instant and gave Teri a grin. "Just like you are. Do you want to be in our television show?"

"No." Teri didn't want to offend Ernesto, because he was a nice old guy, but she couldn't imagine that being in the television could be half as fun as watching it.

"You don't, eh? I thought all little girls wanted to be stars like Britney Spears."

"Britney Spears doesn't have a dog," Teri said, assuming Ernesto would understand the significance of that. "Are my dad and Dobby going to be on television?"

"Most likely, if Angela gets this series sold. And she will. She's a go-getter, that girl."

"She's not a girl. She's as old as my dad."

"Honeybunch, to an old man like me, Angela and your dad seem like spring chickens, and you're practically still in the egg."

Teri gave him a puzzled look. Sometimes old folks spoke a different language than normal people.

"Look," he told her while squinting through the eyepiece

of the camera. "There's Jane. She got first place in the twenty-four-inch division."

"My dad's time was better."

Ernesto chuckled. "You don't miss a thing, do you, kid?"

"Nope. My dad says that paying attention to details keeps a person from making mistakes."

"So maybe that's why your dad is so smart, eh?"

"I'm smart, too."

"No doubt about it. If I were as smart as you, I'd win at cards all the time."

"Are you going to play blackjack with me?"

He followed Jane with the camera for a short distance as she and Shadow walked back toward the canopy, then shut down and slung the camera from his shoulder. Teri gave him a few beats more, then figured he was ignoring her. Grown-ups were good at pretending they hadn't heard a question they didn't want to answer.

"When are we going to play, Mr. Ernie?"

Ernesto squinched his eyes as if something pained him. "Now, why would a nice little girl like you want to learn blackjack?"

"Because you said you would teach me."

"I did?" He looked suspicious. "When did I say that?"

"Last night, when we were eating."

"Oh. I guess I remember that. But you have to ask your dad first."

"He likes for me to learn new things."

Ernesto chuckled. "Well, some new things are different than other new things."

He started back toward the canopy, and Teri tagged along. She liked Ernesto. For an old guy, he knew a lot. And he didn't treat her as if she didn't know anything. "If my dad says yes, will you play blackjack with me?"

Ernesto stopped and looked down at her, a resigned smile on his face. "Okay, Miss Cardsharp. Tell you what. I'll teach you a game that's more fun than blackjack. Cribbage.

Your dad will be cool with it, because it teaches you to count. And it's not a game found in dens of iniquity."

"What's iniquity?"

"Something fathers don't want for their daughters. Trust me. I have five daughters, and I know."

"You have five daughters?"

"Yup. Five. Amelia. Sophia. Carmen. Soledad. Annamaria."

"But I already know how to count."

"Well, cribbage will teach you to count better. And it'll get me out of hot water with your dad."

She took Ernesto's word for it. She was willing to give this cribbage game a try, even if it did sound like an arithmetic lesson.

When Ernesto started walking again, Teri followed. He didn't object, so she figured she was invited. When they got to Jane's canopy, the first thing Teri saw was Shadow alone in the exercise pen. Idaho and Jane were both absent. Probably Jane had taken Idaho off to spend some alone time with the border collie. Teri's dad said that dogs were like kids. They didn't like it if they thought someone else was getting most of the attention.

Teri knew what he meant. Sometimes she was jealous of Dobby, even though she knew feeling jealous of a dog was silly. Still, sometimes Teri caught herself wishing that she were a cute, fuzzy dog who won blue ribbons and curled up every night next to her dad's pillow.

"Can I say hi to Shadow?" she asked Ernesto.

"Sure you can. Don't take him out of the exercise pen, though. He might take it in his head to go looking for Jane and Idaho."

So Teri crawled into the pen with the dog. "Hi, Shadow. You did great today. You're a very smart dog."

The golden retriever answered with a wave of his tail, but no images or feelings in Teri's head. She supposed that he had to be in the mood to have a conversation. Just like people. Sometimes her dad didn't talk much, either.

She sat cross-legged on the mat and leaned against the dog when he came to sit beside her. Ernesto had disappeared into the van, and Teri felt safe enough to let Shadow know what was on her mind.

"Someday, Shadow, I'm going to have a dog just like you. I can't have you, because you belong to Jane. But someone just like you. Because you are way cool."

Shadow gave her a canine grin.

"You know what an awesome dude you are, don't you? Dobby is a super dog, and I love her a lot, but I love you, too, and not just because you think I'm special and talk to me."

A wave of warmth washed over her, and she knew it didn't come from the midday breeze or from her imagination. She put her arms around the dog and hugged, inhaling the clean aroma of his golden coat. If she closed her eyes, she could see herself in the agility ring with a golden retriever that looked just like Shadow. They shot off the start line like a pair of rockets, flew over two jumps, then a triple jump, then made an almost impossible turn to the A-frame. The dog—she would name him Dash, Teri decided—had eyes only for Teri as she nimbly executed a perfect side-switch in front of the A-frame. And then they were off together again, weaving, jumping, diving through tunnels, and finally crossing the finish line a full ten seconds under time. The crowd watching at ringside roared with approval. No one had thought the course could be run so perfectly and so fast. Her father lifts her up into the air, a proud smile on his face. And Jane is there as well, telling her what a super job she and Dash had done. The applause is thunderous.

A swipe from Shadow's tongue brought Teri back to reality. She wasn't riding high on victory, and the swell of applause was coming from the Novice ring, where a tiny little sheltie had just earned a qualifying score.

Teri sighed. Shadow sighed with her, as if sensing her daydream. But someday it would all come true.

In the distance, she saw Jane throwing a ball for Idaho on the other side of the rings, far from the crowd. If she were Jane's little girl, Teri thought, she would have a dog of her own, because Jane knew that dogs were the most important thing in the world. If she were Jane's little girl . . .

The thought slammed against Teri like a brick wall. Instant guilt turned the day downward, made a rock grow somewhere in the vicinity of Teri's stomach. How could she think such thoughts? How could she daydream about having another mom? Jane was nice, and she had Shadow, which made her special. But wanting to belong to someone other than her mother just wasn't right. She would hurt her real mother's feelings as she looked down from heaven.

Teri's mom had probably been just as nice as Jane. Maybe she had liked dogs, too. Maybe she had talked to kids just like they were people and not babies, like Jane did. Teri didn't remember very well.

And that in itself made Teri ashamed. She had a perfectly nice mother, a very special lady that her father had loved, still loved, in fact. And Teri didn't remember much about her at all.

Suddenly she felt like crying, because she was bad to not remember, but she didn't know how to fix it. She hugged Shadow tighter, burying her face in the soft golden ruff. Even though she was bad and thought bad thoughts, Shadow still thought she was special.

"If you were my dog," Teri told the golden retriever, "I would let you be with me all the time. I would never leave you alone in an old pen while I pay attention to another dog. You would be my only dog, and we would be best friends."

Shadow swiped her face with his warm tongue. The tears that had been pushing at the back of her eyes receded a bit.

"You want to go for a walk? We could go sit under the trees over there and watch the Novice class. Just you and me."

Shadow didn't say anything, but he did grin. Teri took

that as a yes. There was a leash clipped to the exercise pen. Teri unclipped it and fastened it to his collar. Then she opened the pen and invited the dog to come out.

Shadow pranced happily at her side as they headed for the shade of a little copse of trees that would give them a good view of the ring. Having the big dog on the end of a leash felt very different than taking little Dobby for a walk. While Dobby came up to Teri's ankle, the top of Shadow's head nearly reached her shoulder.

It was okay, though, Teri told herself, because Shadow never pulled on the leash or got wild like Dobby sometimes did. Dobby seldom paid attention to Teri, but Shadow always had her in the corner of his eye, even when he was looking somewhere else. He did this even though he was Jane's dog, not Teri's. That was because he thought Teri was special. So Teri began to feel special, and she began to forget that the world was far from a fairy-tale place with happy endings.

Feeling more peaceful than she had in a long, long time, she settled down in the shade of the trees and leaned against the big golden dog to watch the entertainment in the agility ring.

WHEN JANE returned to her canopy with Idaho, an empty exercise pen awaited her. An instant flash of panic almost made her heart stop, then speed to double time as a sick, helpless feeling began to roil in her stomach. A dozen questions flew through her mind. Had Shadow been stolen? Had some rival maliciously opened the pen? Or were the animal rights terrorists infiltrating agility trials now as well as dog shows? For years such misguided souls had set show dogs free from their kennels—freeing the "slaves" to be killed on the highway or suffer some other fate that awaited the wandering dog.

Frantically she turned in a circle, eyes sweeping over

every part of the park she could see. No golden retriever ran free. No dog of any kind wandered loose without a handler.

Just then Ernesto came out of the van. "Hi, Jane. That was a great run for you and Shadow this morning. And I got good video of the awards. You look great with the new—"

"Ernesto! Where is Shadow?"

He glanced toward the pen. "Shadow?" He let loose an intense volley of Spanish Jane didn't understand. "He was here when I came back with the camera, only fifteen minutes ago! Teri asked me if she could—Teri! I told her she could pet him. I warned her not to take him out."

Jane's panic dropped a notch. Better the dog be with someone, even an eight-year-old, than running free.

"His leash is gone," Ernesto said. "Jane, I'm sorry. I didn't think there was any harm in her petting him."

Just then Cole walked up, his face reflecting a panic similar to Jane's. "Has either of you seen Teri? She was supposed to wait for me by the ring, but I can't find her anywhere. She's not where she was supposed to be, not at the motor home—"

"She's somewhere with my dog," Jane said tersely. "She came back here with Ernesto, and when he went in the van, she took Shadow on an unauthorized walk."

Cole's eyes narrowed, but his breath came visibly easier.

Ernesto said guiltily, "I didn't think there was any harm in her tagging along with me. I told her she couldn't take Shadow out of the pen."

Cole's lips compressed to a pale, thin line. "Wait until I catch up to her, the little scoundrel. She will be so sorry...."

"First we have to find them."

"We'll find them."

Cole wrapped one arm around Jane's shoulders and squeezed. Without thinking about it she leaned into him, instinctively seeking comfort. Even when she realized how that might look, she didn't withdraw. She didn't care how it looked. Right now she needed the solid strength that seemed to flow from him to her.

"We'll find them," he repeated more softly, for her ears alone, and gave her a reassuring smile. Jane couldn't quite return the smile. Right then her hand itched to connect to Teri's little behind. Just the thought of Shadow being under the very dubious protection of a puny eight-year-old made her shudder—almost as much as the thought of that eight-year-old wandering somewhere with nothing but a good-natured golden retriever to keep her from harm.

"Let's spread out," Cole suggested grimly.

They took off in three different directions, each recruiting help along the way. Five minutes later at least twenty people were scouring the park for a cinnamon-haired, dark-eyed urchin wearing a Winnie the Pooh T-shirt and traveling with a golden retriever. Ten minutes later, Jane found the little dognapper sleeping in the shade of an elm tree at the park boundary, her head pillowed on Shadow's flank. Shadow greeted Jane's arrival with a happy thump of his tail, but he chose not to disturb Teri by getting up.

It was all Jane could do to keep from grabbing her dog, wrapping her arms around him, and weeping into his silken coat. The tension drained out of her like water out of a sieve, leaving behind a sludge of anger.

Teri looked like a little freckled angel, sleeping peacefully in childish innocence. Her hair had escaped its pony-tail and lay against Shadow's golden coat in chaotic waves. Her cherub's mouth curved gently upward. The fingers of one hand curled lovingly in Shadow's ruff.

Any woman with half a heart would have forgiven the little imp on the spot, Jane figured. Which just went to show that heaven had known what it was doing in assigning Jane Connor the single life. She wanted to pick up the little trou-blemaker and shake her until her teeth rattled.

But in a civilized world, one couldn't—and shouldn't—use the kind of teaching methods on a kid that one might use on a bulldog, and in fact, Jane didn't even use that kind of "shake and bake" tactic on the dogs she trained. But then, none of her student dogs had ever run off with her star golden retriever.

"Teri!"

Teri's eyes popped open. Not for a moment did Jane feel guilty about the momentary panic she read in those dark brown eyes. Well, maybe for a very short moment.

"Teri," she repeated in a more moderate tone. "What are you doing here with my dog, when you're supposed to be waiting for your father over by the ring?"

Teri yawned and sat up. Now that she saw the intruder was just Jane, the kid was more sure of herself. Obviously, she had never seen Jane crack down on the unruly dogs in her class.

"Well?" Jane demanded.

"Shadow wanted to go for a walk."

"Shadow didn't want to go for a walk, and even if he had, he should have known better than to go off with a half-grown kid who's barely taller than he is."

Shadow took note of Jane's tone, lowered his head to the ground, and regarded her with big brown puppy-dog eyes. He knew he was guilty.

"Ernesto told you specifically not to take Shadow out of the pen, so why did you?"

The girl's lower lip crept outward.

"Teri, you never, ever take someone's dog without permission. And you shouldn't be wandering about the park without telling your dad where you're going. He told you to stay by the ring, and that's what you should have done."

The lower lip started to tremble. Jane got the feeling that the act was just that—a practiced act. So why did she feel as if she was beating on a puppy?

"You can't scold me!" the child declared indignantly. "You're not my mom! You're not my teacher!"

"No. I'm Shadow's mom. And I don't want you to ever again take him out without my permission. Understand?"

A tear dribbled down Teri's freckled cheek. Jane closed her eyes. When the universe had handed out genes for maternal instinct, Jane had been cleaning a kennel somewhere. Fortunately, just then Cole walked up.

"Daddy!" Teri got up and ran to him, hugging him around the legs and throwing Jane a triumphant look. "Jane says I'm bad."

Jane rolled her eyes. "I didn't say she was bad."

But Cole didn't toss his daughter the lifesaver she wanted. "You were very foolish, taking Shadow without permission. All sorts of terrible things could have happened to both you and the dog. Now apologize to Jane. Right now."

Teri gave him a hurt look. "But . . . Shadow wanted to go for a walk."

"Shadow can't always do everything he wants. Just like you."

The lower lip became a veritable shelf.

"You heard me, Teri. Apologize."

Shadow sat two feet away, looking curiously from Cole to Teri to Jane. With an expression of having made up his mind, he contributed his two cents with a soft "Wuff!"

Teri sagged, all the rebellion drained. Without looking directly at Jane, she muttered, "I'm sorry."

"What was that?" Cole inquired firmly.

"I'm sorry!" Then more softly, "We just got to talking, Shadow and me, and I thought it would be fun to come over here and watch the trial. Then I sort of got sleepy. But I wouldn't have let anything happen to Shadow. Honest."

Jane relented. A person could resist those puppy-dog eyes for only so long. And she wasn't thinking of Shadow's puppy-dog eyes. "I know you didn't mean any harm, Teri.

But you scared your father and me half to death. And Ernesto, too. Don't do it again, ever. Okay?"

The little girl swiped at her eyes, wiping away tears. "Okay."

Cole gave Jane a private smile over Teri's tousled head, and Jane felt a bond click into place between them, two adults equally bemused by the incomprehensible behavior of a child. But Cole certainly had handled the situation better than Jane had.

Of course, he was the father, and Jane was single, childless, and lacking the least bit of maternal instinct.

And liking it that way, Jane thought as Cole marched Teri off for a promised lecture and discussion on just what sort of punishment she deserved.

God help her, Jane mused, if she ever fell in love with a man who had a kid. God help her if she ever fell in love at all.

chapter 11

THE DRAMA and frights were over for the weekend, Jane figured the next morning as she stood in the line ready to go into the ring. Having a dog go missing was scare enough to last her the whole year. Lucky for her the incident had ended well. Her dogs were her children. When something happened to one of them, it stabbed her right in the heart and stuck there. She still had bad dreams about the herding trial where a young, clueless Idaho had taken off after a coyote—a wild cousin who had watched the event from a nearby hill. She had thought for sure the dog would be lured into the pack and killed.

Scares like the one yesterday always opened up her mental file of close calls, and each one of them still inspired a shudder down her spine.

But Shadow's escapade with Teri had been relatively minor. Cole had come over to Angela's motor home after dinner and added his apology to Teri's somewhat-less-than-sincere one.

"I guess I need to put her on a leash," he had said as

they'd sat together in the fast-fading dusk. "She's less pre-dictable than Dobby and doesn't listen half as well."

Jane had invited him to sit under the motor home's awning in their rickety lawn chairs and drink a glass of iced tea. After all, the man had taken the trouble to come over and apologize. The least Jane could do was try to be polite.

"I don't envy you the task of raising a kid in today's world."

He had shaken his head, but his love for his daughter was written plainly on his face.

"It's a lot like training a dog, only kids are tougher to communicate with." He'd chuckled. "And they expect to be accorded the rights of a human being. Things might be a lot easier if I could lure her into good behavior with a treat or two, or give her a time-out in a kennel when she acts up." His voice had grown sad. "I don't know if this is working. Like I told you, this summer is supposed to be a sort of bonding experience for me and Teri. I thought if she wasn't banging around our big old family house where memories of her mom haunt every room, she might get her smile back. Memories are precious, but a person can't let them be a barrier to moving on." Jane had wondered if Cole was talking about Teri or himself, or maybe both.

A gasp from the spectators jerked her back to the present. The border collie in the ring had lost his footing on the up-ramp of the dog-walk and had jumped off, uninjured, but now out of the running. The handler shook her head and asked the judge to be excused rather than have her dog finish the course.

Jane firmly pushed the night before from her mind. Focus, she told herself. In only moments the timer would signal her to go. Every run counted, Jane reminded herself. Every run had to be spectacular if she wanted a chance at that Solid Gold purse, and the chance to rebuild her life.

She remembered a time when waiting to enter the ring gave her a thrill. The anticipation of running the course, of achieving a state of mind where she and her dog were perfectly in tune, of crossing the finish line knowing they had done the best they could—all that had never failed to put a big grin on Jane's face. This summer she had lost that sharp thrill. Now, agility wasn't just fun; it was serious business.

But Jane didn't have time to brood on the loss, because the team ahead were clear of the ring and the timer was signaling Jane to go.

Go they did, and got off to a great start on a difficult course, sailing through a pinwheel of jumps and negotiating a dog-walk/tunnel trap without Shadow batting an eyelash. From the corner of her eye, Jane saw Cole and Teri standing at ringside, watching. A split second of distraction made her almost stumble, and she pulled her mind firmly back to the matter at hand. Somewhere outside the ring, Ernesto's camera ground away, she knew. But she couldn't think of that. If she let stage fright throw off her timing, she would provide the audience with some unintended comedy—such as tripping over her own feet.

About halfway through the course, things started to go wrong. Right beside the triple jump sat a young woman holding a toddler. Just as Shadow approached the jump, the toddler shrieked. Shadow, like most golden retrievers, had a partiality for kids, an almost irresistible drive to protect and comfort. At the little boy's piercing objection, Shadow's attention wavered. A mere glance toward the toddler was enough to throw him off balance. He cleared the triple but landed badly. The kid screeched again. This time Shadow ignored him, and the toddler's mother, with a guilty grimace of apology, stood and took the little noisemaker away from the ring.

But Shadow's usually flawless timing and concentration had been shaken. At Jane's call, he veered right to take the tire jump, launched himself into the air a split second too early, and caught the bottom of the "tire" ring with his front paws. As he continued on through, the lightweight jump came with him, toppling over, tangling his rear legs just as his front feet hit the ground.

An older, more experienced dog might have simply untangled himself and gone on. But Shadow was young, and young dogs often react rather than think. An instant of panic made the dog try to run away from the mess that held him. But when he tried to sprint away, the enemy pursued, creating true alarm.

Jane commanded him to stop, to stay, but Shadow ignored her. He pulled free of the tangle and took off. Jane made a grab for him, but he wore no collar. He ran naked, as the agility folks put it, free of anything that might catch on a jump or obstacle. But no collar meant nothing to grab, and his silky fur slipped through her fingers as he sought to escape the thing that seemed determined to eat him. He jumped the ring barrier—in beautiful form—and headed away from the crowd. Away from the crowd and the noise, straight toward the highway that bordered the park.

Jane heard her own voice raised in panic, using language that could get her barred from many an AKC event. Inside her chest, a sick and frozen stillness sucked at her heart. This couldn't be happening. Her mind screamed, *No, no, no!*

She ran, even though she knew that chasing a fleeing dog was the exact wrong thing to do. She shouted Shadow's name, but the imagined monsters pursuing him allowed the dog to hear only his own panic, see only freedom and safety in front of him, not a highway where cars sped by at sixty miles per hour. Jane had lectured her students for years: *Condition your dogs to a whistle or a sound that always means treats, and they'll come to you ninety-five percent of the time. Or sit on the ground and weep. Hardly a dog alive can resist investigating a wailing human being.*

But her semi-foolproof methods wouldn't work here, Jane knew. This was that five percent when nothing would work. Shadow was lost to panic. Deaf to recall. Blind to anything but his own fear. Jane's dread choked her as she ran.

Then someone faster than her entered the scene from stage right, in front of the fleeing retriever. Cole. He tackled the dog broadside and held on for dear life.

"Oh God thank you thank you thank you," Jane panted as she ran. She slid to her knees beside Shadow, snapped a collar around his neck, and gave thanks to every power in the universe that she could think of.

Shadow looked up at her, shamefaced. Then his wide jaws parted in his usual goofy grin. *Wasn't this fun?* he seemed to ask.

Tears stung Jane's eye. To hide them, she buried her face in Shadow's soft ruff. Jane Connor, Superwoman of Cornville, tougher than any pit bull, simply did not cry in public. She could hear cars whizzing by on the road, almost feel the wind of their passing. The unfenced park boundary was only feet away, and beyond that lay the highway—a four-lane strip of death for an unwary dog. She had been frighteningly close to losing one of her dearest friends.

When Jane looked up, Cole's face was only inches from hers. He still had one hand on Shadow. The other hand reached out and touched her cheek, which was hot and wet.

"Are you all right?" he whispered.

A small crowd had gathered. Beyond the edges of the crowd, Ernesto wielded his camera, and beside him, Angela's mouth moved at the speed of light. But all that seemed to be in another world. She, Cole, and Shadow seemed somehow to be encased in their own private bubble. Nothing beyond the three of them mattered just then.

Tears renewed their assault on Jane's dignity, overflowing to dribble down her cheeks.

Cole's hand slipped to her shoulder, squeezing gently. His breath ruffled her hair. "Jane . . ."

"I'm okay," she assured him—a lie, of course. Her heart continued to thunder, her stomach cramped, and panic still had a grip on her voice. "You . . . I . . . Cole . . ." She paused to take a breath, dropped her head briefly to rest on Shadow's solid shoulder, then looked up again. Funny how panic shredded every inhibition and turned the heart to mush. She couldn't help herself. Without a single thought for what she did, Jane leaned toward him and placed a brief kiss on his cheek. A jolt hit her, traveling from her lips clear down to her toes, stealing what little breath she had left. Her lips burned, along with her face, and a more insidious warmth spread from the pit of her stomach into places she didn't even want to think about.

She struggled to breathe as she pulled back and looked into bemused chocolate eyes. She couldn't believe she had kissed the man, even on the cheek, even under such extreme circumstances—and with people looking on! Not to mention the camera! And what was with the bolt-of-lightning reaction? It had been a simple peck on the cheek, for cripes sake!

She squeezed her eyes shut, embarrassment seeping over her. "Sorry. I shouldn't have done that. I'm sorry. I plead insanity."

That didn't sound right either, as if a woman would have to be out of her mind to let her lips get that close to Cole Forrest.

"Not insanity! I meant...oh, hell! You know what I meant! I've never been more scared in my life. There's no way I can thank you."

He grinned. "I think you thanked me quite well."

If possible, her face now burned even hotter.

He squeezed her shoulder again. Actually, it was more of a caress than a squeeze. "Jane, it's all right. It's fine. Shadow's fine."

She took a couple of deep breaths. "He is now, thanks to you. I never would have caught him, and he for sure wasn't going to stop on his own. Thank you, thank you, thank you!"

Cole patted Shadow's ribs. "My pleasure." He seemed unaware of their audience, lying on the grass beside a now-calm, tail-thumping dog and a not-so-calm Jane. If she'd had a tail, it would have been tucked between her legs.

Cole relaxed, propping his head on one elbow and regarding Jane with a steady gaze. "So does this make up in some small measure for my kid absconding with your dog?"

Jane smiled weakly. The blood pumping through her veins felt thin as water. "More than makes up. If we're keeping score, I'd say that I just dove deep into the debit side of the ledger."

She got unsteadily to her feet. Shadow came with her, shaking the grass from his coat and commenting on the adventure with a happy bark. Their bubble of privacy seemed to burst as everyone crowded in to help. Cole accepted a hand up from a helpful fellow and came off the grass like a football player who'd taken one too many hits.

Alarmed, Jane asked, "Are you all right?"

"Oh, yeah. That tackle just reminded me why I became a computer jock instead of a football jock. A little Ben-Gay will fix me up just fine."

"Are you sure?"

"I'm sure. A few pulled muscles and grass stains on the elbows never hurt anyone. Is Shadow okay?"

"Move him out, Jane," a woman onlooker advised. "Is he limping?"

Jane speculated that there might have been a hint of hopefulness in the question. Not that anyone at the trial would wish Shadow serious injury, but if he couldn't compete for the next few weeks, that would certainly leave room at the top for someone else.

"He's okay," Jane said, but thought silently, *He'd better be.*

"Rick Tolleson is here with his chiropractic booth," someone suggested. "He's by the food concession."

"Thanks. I'll probably drop in on him." Jane smiled knowingly. "But don't get your hopes up, people. I'm betting that Shadow's fit enough to give you all a run for your

money at the next set of trials." Pure bravado, but necessary. If you're down, never show it.

The crowd drifted away in search of other entertainment, and Jane found herself alone with Shadow and Cole.
Shadow was wagging his tail happily, oblivious to how close
he'd come to being roadkill. But the incident still had Jane's
heart pounding.

"Well," Cole said, brushing the grass from his jeans, "I
think that's enough excitement for my day. How about
yours?"

Jane let out a long, shaky breath. "Maybe a bit too much
excitement. Cole, I'll never be able to thank you enough."

He grinned. "Good. I love having a pretty woman in-
debted to me."

It was a joke, but in truth, Jane hated to be in debt to
anyone—friends, family, mortgage companies, it didn't
matter. Obligations made her uneasy.

And then his words registered in quite a different way.
Had the man called her pretty?

She herself? Jane Connor? Plain Jane with the burning-
bush hair, the swarm of freckles, and the too-wide mouth?
Straight-up-and-down Jane, too-tall Jane? Pretty?

Another joke, she was sure.

"Hey there. Something wrong? You look as if someone
hit you with a bat."

"What? Oh, no. I...uh...why don't you come over to
the motor home tonight for a nice juicy steak? I owe you a
lot more than a meal, but it's a start."

Where had that come from? Wasn't she getting to be the
bold one?

Cole hesitated, and suddenly Jane wanted desperately
for him to say yes.

"Teri, too, of course. Tell her she's officially forgiven for
kidnapping Shadow."

"She'll be glad to hear that. She was afraid that you
would put Shadow off-limits to her."

"I would never deprive a kid of the company of a dog."

"She is crazy about that dog." He scratched Shadow's ear, and Shadow's tail accelerated to takeoff speed. "I guess that just shows she has good taste, eh, Shadow?"

Shadow obviously agreed. Jane resisted the sappy warmth that threatened to envelope her. The way to a woman's heart was most certainly through her dog.

AN HOUR later, Jane, Angela, and Shadow walked toward Dr. Rick Tolleson's booth, where the unconventional vet sold everything from miracle cures from the Amazon rain forest to freeze-dried raw food diets that promised to turn fat, lazy dogs into world-class athletes. Angela's mind churned as they walked. Shadow seemed fine, but what if this dog doctor proclaimed him unfit to compete? Suppose her canine star had pulled a tendon, strained a foot, cracked a rib? Where would her project be then? Where would *she* be then? She had invested a great deal of time, money, and energy into making this canine "reality show" happen. Animal World was absolutely drooling over the idea. And if they didn't give her the terms she wanted, a couple of other cable networks waited in the wings.

But all her effort could be trashed because the stupid tire jump had spooked her star into running like the demons of hell were chasing him. Of course, Ernesto had gotten some great footage of the drama. But all that would be just so many useless pixels if their star golden retriever couldn't continue to compete.

Beside Angela, Jane moved with her usual purposeful, ground-eating stride. Angela envied Jane her unflappable composure, her ability not to care what other people thought about her, how she looked, what she said. If it was just an act, then it was a good act. But Angela didn't think it was an act. Any woman who had to be dragged into a free makeover had to have too much self-confidence. And didn't Angela just wish she had some of *that* precious commodity!

Not a moment of any day went by without Angela worrying about how she looked, how she sounded, how other people saw her. Not because she was self-absorbed, though she confessed to a certain amount of that. But mostly because she had to impress the stuffed suits who controlled network purse strings. They expected sophistication, savvy, originality, creativity, and vision, and it never hurt if all that was packaged together with a face and figure pleasing to their cold, stingy hearts. Angela's life was entertaining people, but without money, she couldn't entertain anyone, or pay her rent, for that matter.

Of course she had to be self-conscious. She didn't have the luxury of hiding out in a kennel in the middle of Hicksville, Arizona, as Jane did.

Still, she couldn't help but envy Jane, who seemed unconscious of the impression she made, unneedful of maintaining a facade, and unconcerned about the opinion of anyone besides herself and her dogs.

"Do you think Shadow's all right?" she asked Jane for the tenth time.

"Yes, Angela," Jane replied, strained patience fraying her voice. "I think he's fine. I'm just being cautious. Cole tackled him pretty hard."

"He should have been more careful."

Jane actually bristled. "He saved Shadow's life! Pretty much at the expense of his own body, I might add."

Angela picked up on Jane's high color, and wondered. Cole Forrest and Jane . . .

"He *was* sort of amazing," Angela said, prodding a bit.

"I could have kissed his feet, I swear."

Not the part of the man that Jane had kissed, Angela remembered, and smiled. She hadn't thought much about it at the time, but maybe there was something there that could add a bit of spice to this odyssey.

"It was quite a feat. Looked terrific on film."

Jane darted an uneasy glance her way. "You're going to make that part of the show?"

"Of course! It was great. Drama! Excitement! Tension! I can hear gasps all over America."

Funny thing about Jane, Angela reflected, that for all her self-confidence, she seemed remarkably queasy when it came to letting the eyes of America's dog lovers follow this tiny segment of her life. She was shy, almost. Hard to believe, but there it was.

No matter. Angela had dealt with shy stars before. Hadn't she once persuaded a mama wombat to come out and be photographed with her baby wombat? One of these days, Jane would look at her reflection in a mirror and realize that she was a knockout. And like any woman with a full set of X chromosomes, she would like being a knockout. Then Angela wouldn't have to persuade her to experiment with cosmetics, or to use the curling iron to tame her hair, or to think about the colors she wore. Then Jane wouldn't regard Ernesto's camera as an intrusion. The camera would be her friend, and she'd be only too anxious to show her face to the world. It was only a matter of time.

"Here we are," Jane declared. "Are you going to go wandering around the other booths while the doc looks at Shadow?"

Angela was about to say yes, but instantly changed her mind, because there, half-seated on a table cluttered with a cash box, credit card machine, a jumble of brochures, receipt books, and a couple of thick catalogs, stood the world's most gorgeous male.

Maybe other women wouldn't have seen him that way, but to Angela's eye, he looked as good as a maple-walnut biscotti from Starbucks. Tall and broad—the breadth coming as much from a healthy appetite as an exercise regimen—the guy wore his dark blond hair long enough to touch his shoulders, clean looking, but sufficiently messy to save him from an accusation of having an unmanly concern for appearance. A slight brownish stubble, darker than his hair, shadowed his cheeks and chin—very fashionable in a grunge sort of way, as was the tarnished gold ring dangling from one pierced ear.

His attire was as casual as the rest of him—a Hawaiian print shirt revealed enough of his chest to prove that the fellow had more muscle than flab. Cargo shorts ended mid-thigh on legs like tree trunks. He was big, and his size certainly wasn't all lard.

The man was talking to a frowsy middle-aged woman with a standard poodle, pointing out something on the label of a bottled product. He didn't immediately look up when Jane and Angela stepped beneath the canopy of his booth, which gave Angela time to admire the sight of him. When Poodle Woman left, he turned his attention to Jane, giving her an expansive smile that made him look like a merry pirate, all shaggy hair, stubble, and flashing white teeth.

Absolutely to die for, Angela thought. Any notion of cruising the other vendors while Jane visited the doggy chiropractor flew out of her mind.

"Jane!" Dr. Gorgeous said. "How goes it? I saw your runs yesterday. That youngster of yours is coming right along, isn't he? And here he is in person. How are you, young Shadow?"

Jane seemed oblivious to the man's sex appeal. She was all business. "That's for you to say, Rick. We had a bit of an incident this morning."

"Oh, yeah. I heard about it. Got tackled just in time is how I hear it."

"Too right. A friend..."

There was that peculiar catch to Jane's voice, Angela observed. She might be oblivious to the good doctor, but not to that other fellow. Wonderful prospect for drama. Truly wonderful.

"...a friend got him for me. Thank heaven. But they both went down pretty hard. I just want to be sure that Shadow's sound. I wouldn't want to put him in the ring if he's hiding some injury."

Dr. Gorgeous chuckled, a deep, warm sound that sent a pleasant thrill through Angela's veins. How she did love a man who rumbled when he laughed!

"What about your friend?"

"What?" Jane looked puzzled. "Oh. Rick Tolleson, this is Angela Gardner. She's in television."

With slightly raised brows, he turned his attention to Angela. Her heart picked up its beat when his eyes fell on her—eyes the color of new spring leaves, she noted. Softened by his smile, his jawline still spoke of a stubborn streak beneath his amiability. Stubborn and strong. Angela suddenly wished she hadn't eaten two pieces of pizza for lunch. Each piece had probably added an inch to her hips, plus she hadn't done a minute of calisthenics this last week.

But a certain look in those spring-green eyes told Angela that Doc Gorgeous liked what he saw. She knew that look, had seen it more than a time or two in several journeys around the proverbial block.

"Don't tell me *she's* the one who tackled him," Rick scoffed.

"Who? Me?"

"Lord no!" Jane said with a laugh. "Cole Forrest tackled him. The guy with the papillon prodigy."

"Ah." Rick winked at Angela. "And here I was going to offer free treatment for the heroine. Too bad."

Angela caught her breath as the image of herself on the treatment table flashed into her mind. And the doc's smile made that breath disappear almost completely.

A wry observer to the byplay, Jane cleared her throat. "I'll tell Cole about the offer. He got up from the ground looking a lot less sound than Shadow."

"Send him over, then. Just don't tell anyone. I'm a vet,

not a doctor. The suits on the licensing board get attitude about us extending our practice to the human animal."

Angela knew one human animal who wouldn't mind getting a treatment. As the vet lifted Shadow to the exam table, part of his smile was aimed at her.

While the doc and Jane went over Shadow muscle by muscle, sinew by sinew, Angela wandered through the stall. Portable shelves displayed everything from herbal relaxants to energy-boosting nutritional supplements, for dogs and horses both. Mixed in were remedies for everything from arthritis to bad breath, digestive boosters to herbal flea products. A table along one canvas wall was piled high with books for sale—books on canine health, canine massage, canine chiropractic, homemade dog diets, homeopathic treatment of canine disorders, and so on and so forth. Endlessly.

"Can I help you find something?" a stringy teenaged boy asked. He sported hair as long as Rick's, and the same color. Here was a son, Angela thought ruefully. And a wife probably lurked just around the corner.

"You work here?" she asked.

"Yeah," the boy said, then jerked his thumb toward Rick. "He's my uncle. My mom said either I work for Uncle Rick for the summer or work in my dad's nursery." He grinned. "All those plants make me sneeze. So I opted for the dogs. They make me sneeze, too, but they're more fun."

"You know about all this stuff?" Angela waved a hand at the displayed products.

"Oh, yeah. Sure. But not as good as Rick. He's, like, an encyclopedia. If you want to wait around, he shouldn't be too long over there."

"Oh, no. Actually, I'm just waiting for Jane, the lady with the golden retriever."

"Sure. I know Jane. Everybody does."

Soon that would be true, Angela mused with a certain

satisfaction. "So your uncle Rick doesn't have kids of his own to help him run his business, hm?" Angela tried to make the question sound innocent, but the string bean gave her a knowing look.

"Rick? Have kids? That's a major laugh. He's never stayed in one place long enough for any of the ladies to catch him. My mom is his sister, and she keeps nagging him to settle down. But he likes the road, you know? A real road warrior."

Angela nodded. It sounded as if the doc was another version of herself. Except that she had tried to settle down once, with disastrous results. That was something she wouldn't try again.

She wandered back toward the table where Shadow stood having his limbs stretched this way and that, enduring it with typical golden retriever patience. In spite of his size, Doc Gorgeous had a gentle way about him, Angela noted.

"He seems very sound to me," Rick told Jane. "You know, these youngsters can take a beating and spring back like new. Comes from having elastic bones and supple muscles." He grinned. "Unlike us old folks."

Jane replied with a smile. "Speak for yourself, Methuselah. I'm not getting older, just better. Or so I tell myself."

Rick chuckled. "It's all downhill from thirty, lady. Soon enough, you'll be coming in for a bit of therapy after a couple of hard agility runs." He lifted Shadow off the table as if the eighty-pound dog was a featherweight.

Jane instantly dispensed with the kidding. "You're certain he's fine to go in the ring?"

"Certain as I can be. Besides, you have what—five days?—before the next trial. He'll have a chance to rest between now and then. If he shows any stiffness, give him a few drops of this." He handed her a bottle.

"Arnica," Jane read from the label.

"Great stuff," Angela chimed in. "I've used it myself."

Rick turned her way with friendly interest. "You're into herbals, then?"

She certainly could be, if being into herbals would draw the man's attention. "Absolutely. I'd really like to come back sometime when you're not busy, to talk about some of the products. In fact, I might want to talk to you about an idea I have for a documentary on alternative health strategies for animals."

Rick beamed. "That would be great."

Jane gave Angela a suspicious look. The woman was way too perceptive, Angela decided. "We'll talk," Angela told Rick. "I'm sure our paths will cross again soon."

"Nice to meet you, Angie," Rick called after them as they left the stall.

Angela almost choked. The only person who had ever shortened her name to Angie had been her ex-husband. Definitely not a good sign. On the other hand, to hell with signs. Rick Tolleson, DVM, was just too delicious to pass up.

JANE LOOKED at herself in the bathroom mirror for the third time in the last half hour—quite a change for a woman who had been known to go all day without one glance. What she saw made her frown. Her designer fancy-free curls were a bit limp this evening, and her brows, plucked into elegance in Lakeside just a week past, were making a comeback. Soon she would have a forest spanning the bridge of her nose.

"Do something about it, Jane," she told her reflection. "Don't just stand and look. Do something."

At the sound of her voice, Shadow's tail thumped on the motor home floor and Idaho raised his head to give her an inquiring look. Both dogs had squeezed into the tight little hallway next to the bathroom to keep her company.

"This is just silly," Jane told her furry friends. "I have spent the last thirty years of my life without obsessing about eyebrows. Or hairstyles. Or clothes." She stared at her reflection. "Does this yellow shirt make me look like I have jaundice?"

Both dogs waved their tails. Shadow whined.

"Yes, I agree," Jane replied. "It does." She reached across the hall, grabbed a green sleeveless shell from the open closet, and held it up against her face. "Better. Much better." She peeled off the yellow shirt and pulled the green over her head, combed the limp curls with her fingers, and gave her image a bright, artificial smile. "That'll have to do," she told herself.

Both dogs sat up, hearing the prelude to action in Jane's voice.

"What do you think?" she asked them, and turned a full circle so they could take in her khaki shorts and green shell. "Casual, yet neat. Practical, but feminine." Her mouth pulled sideways in thought. "Are these shorts too short?"

Idaho cocked his head.

"Yes, I think so, too. But Angela made me buy them. Angela can be a real alpha bitch when she gets a burr up her butt."

"Jane!" came Angela's voice from just outside on the "patio"—the cement slab between the motor home and Ernesto's van. "Who are you talking to in there?"

"The dogs," Jane admitted.

Angela's head popped in the motor home doorway. "Are they talking back?"

"Of course they are." Jane remembered suddenly what Teri Forrest had said about Shadow talking to her. Crazy kid. Didn't she know that a dog talked only to its owner?

Angela shook her head. "There are so many documentaries I could do on you."

"One is enough," Jane told her with a smile.

While Jane hung the rejected yellow shirt in the closet, she heard Angela query Ernesto, "Do you remember where we put the charcoal?"

Jane didn't hear the answer, but Angela sounded perturbed. "We do have charcoal, don't we?"

She wished she hadn't invited Cole and Teri for steaks. What a production this had become. Angela was obsessing on charcoal, Jane had doffed her usual after-trial sweatpants for the formality of tailored shorts, Ernesto had gone to the grocery store twice because the first time he'd gotten distracted by slot machines and forgotten what Jane had asked him to get, and Jane was becoming overly intimate with a mirror. Her stomach felt as though a herd of butterflies were using it as an exercise room.

"Oh, crap!" Jane heard Angela say. "Here they come, and I still can't find the charcoal. Jane! Get out here and help me, or I'll have Ernesto film you primping in front of the mirror."

Jane hastily switched off the bathroom light. "I was not primping," she lied. "And if Ernesto steps foot in here with his camera, I'll break it."

"You were too primping, and I'm thrilled, but do you know what we did with the charcoal?"

"Got me," Jane said as she descended the steps.

"Damn! It must be somewhere."

"Did you look in the basement?" Jane opened the underthe-floor storage compartment and dug through the hoses, extra lawn chairs, ground mats, a toolbox, and a huge box of paper plates. Not until she heard Cole's amused hello did she realize that she was greeting her guests with her top half swallowed by the motor home and her backside pointing toward the sky.

"Can I help?" Cole asked when Jane emerged, red faced and flustered. His eyes crinkled in a silent laugh. "With whatever you're doing?"

Jane squared her jaw and managed to give him a polite refusal, at the same time vowing that Angela would pay for the little smirk on her face. And she definitely was going to find a way to break Ernesto's camera.

chapter 12

THEY NEVER did find the bag of charcoal. The steaks went back into the freezer, and the little group decided that dinner at Denny's would be the best solution for their growling stomachs.

Except that Angela pleaded a headache and decided to stay at the motor home for chicken noodle soup. And then Teri declared that she wanted soup also, and she wanted Ernesto to teach her to play cribbage as he had apparently promised to do.

"You and Cole go on to Denny's," Angela suggested casually—a little too casually for Jane's comfort. "Ernesto and I can watch Teri."

It was a good thing for Angela that her ambitions lay behind the camera, Jane thought, not in front of it. The woman's acting left something to be desired.

"We could stay here and eat ham sandwiches," Jane suggested.

"This is how you repay Cole for saving Shadow's life? Go to Denny's, you ungrateful woman, and buy the man a good meal."

"She doesn't have to buy me a meal," Cole insisted.

"Yes, she does. You both deserve a break. So go. Oops!" Dobby chose that moment to hide from Shadow, who was whining an invitation to play. Her chosen hiding place was behind Angela's legs. Angela almost tripped as the little dog dashed between her ankles.

"Dobby!" Cole chided. "Quit taunting Shadow."

The papillon danced from behind Angela, bounded toward Shadow with a high-pitched yap, and took off at full speed toward the bedroom.

"Listens well, doesn't she?" Jane couldn't resist the dig.

"Only in the ring," Cole confessed.

"Isn't that cute?" Angela cooed. "The dogs just want to have a good time. It's the people who get uptight about who gets the blue ribbon."

"I don't get uptight," Jane declared. "Shadow and I make the competition uptight." She sent Cole a challenging smile. Best to set the tone right away. She owed him. But first and foremost they were competition. Jane was good at being competition. At anything else, especially regarding the opposite sex . . . well, she gave new depth of meaning to the word "novice."

Cole answered mildly. "That's the nice thing about competition. On any particular weekend, anything can happen. Nobody gets to count on their eggs hatching into live chickens."

So much for Mr. Nice Guy. The blue ribbon bug had bitten him just as hard as it bit anyone else.

But Jane had a debt to pay off, so she and Cole headed to Denny's on their own, leaving Angela to her headache, Teri to her cribbage lessons, Dobby pouting in her little portable kennel beneath the dinette, and Shadow with his nose up against the kennel door, casting woeful looks at his tiny playmate. As they walked out the door, Angela was heating soup on the stove, Ernesto was breaking out the cribbage board, and Idaho had assumed charge of the whole group, stationing himself in the middle of the kitchen where he could watch everyone, just in case border collie expertise was needed.

"You really don't need to buy me dinner," Cole reminded Jane as they climbed into Ernesto's van.

Jane gave him a crooked smile. "Never let it be said that you didn't get what was coming to you."

He met the challenge of her grin. "All right. One steak dinner, then. And pie."

They arrived at Denny's in the middle of a thunderstorm. Between exiting the van and dashing through the restaurant door, they both got soaked with rain and pummeled with pea-sized hail. So much, Jane thought, for all the time spent primping.

"Some party this is!" Jane complained as they slid into a booth at the restaurant. "Though it looks like our steak fry would have gotten rained out anyway."

Cole reached across the table and plucked something green from her hair. The wind and rain had decorated her new hairdo with the storm's debris.

"Lovely," she said.

"Actually, it is. You look very nice tonight, even after a bit of rain."

Oh, he was smooth. She didn't want to think about the little thrill she got from his casual touch.

"You like the wet, tangled look, do you? Or maybe the earlier presentation of my backside sticking out of the motor home basement?"

"I'd say it was a very nice backside," Cole offered with a smile, "but you'd probably flatten me."

"Damn straight I would." But she softened the words with a laugh. "You don't have to be charming to me, Cole. I'm not as sensitive as most women about looking like hell."

He gave her a quizzical look. "You're a long way from looking like hell," he said generously.

When had she started feeling sensitive about how she

looked? Jane wondered. Probably the same time she had started wasting so much time in front of a stupid mirror. Self-consciously, she touched her hair, no longer sensibly tied back and out of her way, as it had been for years, but "breezy" and curling every which direction in wild, wet abandon. Not to mention adorned with leaves.

Cole shook his head. "You are way too hard on yourself. You know that?"

"Not true. I have a very realistic view of myself. I try to make the most of my strong points and not obsess about my weak points. More folks should do that, and we'd have fewer people in jails and loony bins."

"Loony bins?" He chuckled.

"One of my weak points is a disregard for political correctness," Jane admitted with a grin. "Or maybe it's one of my strong points. That one's sort of on the boundary. What about you? As long as we're sitting here cataloging *my* flaws..."

"Flaws? You think I have flaws?" he demanded with mock indignation.

"I'll bet you could name one or two if you thought about it really hard." Jane liked this sort of sparring much better than talking about her appearance.

Just then a waitress came with water and the table setting. "You know what you want?" she asked, pulling out her pad and pen.

One hundred thousand dollars, Jane thought. But she ordered a cheese omelet. Cole ordered a patty melt.

"That's not a dinner I would order if someone owed me big-time and was trying to pay down the debt with food."

"I like patty melts."

Jane smiled. "Restraint must be one of your strong points. Or in this situation, it could be considered a weak point. That's the complicating thing about life. Good and bad, strong and weak—it all has a way of switching around on a person."

"You're a philosopher."

"I took a minor in philosophy at Northern Arizona University. Major in business."

"No kidding?"

She raised a brow. "Thought I was the sort of person lucky to graduate from high school?"

"Not at all. A bit defensive, are we?"

"No," she said stiffly. "And weren't we talking about *your* weak points when we were interrupted?"

"I told you, I don't have any."

"Liar."

He chuckled. "Okay. Coming out second best at matching wits with a philosopher from NAU. That's a weak point."

"Har, har."

"And I'm not very mechanically inclined. Put a hammer in my hand and I'll pound my thumb every time."

"Okay, that would be annoying."

"And I'd sure like to be better at this parenting thing. I don't suppose any of your philosophy courses covered stuff like that, did they?"

"If there had been a Philosophy of Parenting course, I wouldn't have taken it. Not my thing. But you seem to be doing all right. Teri's a good kid."

A good kid who had conversations with dogs. Maybe Cole had a point in thinking he could use some help in that area. But then, Jane talked to dogs also. The difference was, she didn't really expect them to answer, at least not in so many words.

Still, Teri was sweet, and when she looked at her father, the look in her eyes was similar to the one in the eyes of a dog looking at his master. A headstrong, independent-minded dog, that is.

"Teri is a good kid," Cole admitted. "That's mostly due to her mom. Mandy quit her job to become a full-time mother, read all the books you're supposed to read, never ran short on patience or creativity." He sighed. "Losing Mandy was hard on both of us, but especially hard on Teri."

Their food came, and between bites they continued to talk about Teri, her occasional moods and withdrawal, Cole's worries about her. Jane wondered if she should tell him that his daughter fancied she was conversant with canines, but decided against it. Chances were the kid had been pulling Jane's leg, and there was no reason to add another brick to the load Cole already carried.

Usually conversations about kids bored Jane to tears, but not tonight. She admired Cole's devotion to his daughter, and Teri sort of reminded Jane of herself as a small girl. Jane also had been precocious and rather withdrawn from the normal world of school and friends. She also had been obsessed with animals. She had been lucky to have two parents, where Teri was left with only one. But Jane's dad, a Wisconsin dairyman, had been distant and rather forbidding, more absent than present when it came to providing affection and nurturing. Her mother had tried to fill in the gaps, just as Cole was doing for his daughter.

"I think you're a pretty good dad," she told him. "I have to admire anyone with guts enough to raise a kid in this world. Dogs are much easier, and you don't have to worry about college tuition."

Cole laughed, and Jane had to smile. She did like the bright sound of his laugh. But no good could come of that—liking his laugh, his smile, his kid. And liking the feel of her lips against his skin. Couldn't forget that little detail. A lot of no good could come from liking too much about Cole Forrest. This summer was certainly the worst time for Jane to try to dabble in romance.

She shouldn't have let Angela maneuver her into this silly tête-à-tête. But Jane did owe the man. She could feed him a dozen dinners and not settle the debt, especially if all he ate were patty melts.

At least she was able to persuade him to get dessert. Cole ordered apple pie, and Jane got a chocolate sundae.

"So what made you get a papillon, of all dogs?" Jane asked. As long as they were going to talk about kids, they might as well talk about the kind of kids she could relate to.

"I found her at the animal shelter right after Mandy died. I wanted a Labrador retriever, but Dobby looked so pathetic that I just couldn't resist."

Jane snorted. "At least you *wanted* a real dog."

The humiliation got worse and worse. Their nemesis wasn't some dog bred carefully for performance ability. Oh, no. Dobby was a pound puppy. And she was such a phenom that Cole had adopted her only two years ago and already was competing in the highest levels of obedience and agility.

Of course, Shadow was only eighteen months old and had similar accomplishments to his credit, but he was a golden retriever, a top performance breed, and Jane was a professional trainer.

Not that she didn't respect Cole for adopting from the shelter. She wished all dogs in every shelter in the country could find an equally good home. But being shown up by a shelter dog was almost as embarrassing as losing to an animated six-pound hairball.

"I'm glad now that I got Dobby instead of going with a Labrador. She's got more smarts per ounce than any dog I've ever met."

A bite of chocolate sundae stopped halfway to Jane's mouth. If that wasn't a direct challenge, then she'd never heard one. "You haven't met many golden retrievers and border collies, have you, then?"

"Never met one to top Dobby," he claimed with a wicked smile.

Jane knew he was egging her on, but she rose to the bait anyway. After all, it was her family the man was dissing.

"Border collies," she declared, "are smarter than most kids I know."

"And how many kids do you know?" he asked, a twinkle in his eye.

"Enough to know that most of them are untrainable. And golden retrievers will turn themselves inside out to please you. Most toy breeds, papillons included, prefer to sit on a pillow and have their owner wait upon them."

"I'll confess that Dobby does like her pillow, and if she doesn't get a cookie at the appointed time each evening, she puts on an act worthy of an Academy Award. You would swear she was on death's door from abuse and starvation."

Jane smirked. "I rest my case."

"And then she goes into the ring and kicks butt."

Including Jane's, more often than not. But Cole was polite enough not to point that out, at least not aloud.

"Okay. Dobby's an exceptional little toy dog," she admitted. "And kicking butt in an artificial competition like obedience or agility is all very well and good. But I'd like to see a papillon herd sheep, or retrieve a duck."

"Geniuses often excel at only one thing," Cole said smugly.

Jane snorted. "Not that I don't think Dobby's a sweet little thing, but she's a dust bunny with legs. Hardly a dog at all. More of a smart mouse with long hair."

Cole just smiled, but the light of battle was in his eyes. "A smart mouse who's going to Solid Gold."

"And get her little toy butt beat by the real dogs who were bred for such things."

"Like Shadow?"

"Of course like Shadow. Shadow is eighty pounds of muscle and staying power, and he doesn't lie on a pillow every night and demand to be served cookies. If he had hands, he'd be serving me cookies."

Cole stabbed the air with a forkful of apple pie. "You are a woman of confidence. I like that."

Jane didn't trust the shine in his eyes.

"But I feel obligated to defend Dobby's honor. After all, she has her pride. She would probably stop right in the middle of the next agility course if she thought I didn't have the guts to stand up for her."

"Which just goes to show what a little prima donna she is."

"She knows her own worth. Nothing wrong with that. Tell you what"—Cole smiled archly—"just to prove how sure I am that my dog is as good as yours, maybe better, how about we make a small wager about which dog gets invited to Solid Gold?"

Jane's first instinct was to laugh. "Being in Nevada has corrupted you."

"Don't tell me you're reluctant to stand behind your dog. A confident woman like you?"

The challenge started to itch in Jane's blood. "Just what kind of a wager are you talking about? Not money, I hope, because I don't have any."

"Something more interesting than money." He thought a moment, then sent her a speculative look. "Okay, here's the deal. The loser takes the winner out on the town, in the town of the winner's choice, to the dining establishment of the winner's choice, at the time of the winner's choosing."

Jane scoffed. "No fair! You could choose New York City! Or Anchorage, Alaska."

He lifted a brow. "Do you expect to lose?"

"Hell no."

"Well then . . ."

She nailed him with what she hoped was a confident glare. "Well then, won't you be surprised when I choose some ritzy place in Hawaii?"

"Do I look nervous?"

"You should. Can you afford to take me to Bangladesh?"

He shook his head chidingly. "Tch, tch. We agreed that this isn't about money. Maybe we should limit the distance to within a two-hour drive from wherever we are when the winner is declared."

"Which will be when . . . ?"

"When one of us drops out of the race."

"Not going to happen," Jane declared confidently. "Not unless you and Dobby drop out, that is."

Cole just smiled.

Jane snorted. "What if we both get invited to Solid Gold?"

"No problem," he said with a shrug. "Then the winner will be the dog who goes farthest in the competition."

"And if neither one of us makes it?"

He laughed. "That's not going to happen, and you know it. But in that case, I guess we console ourselves with a hamburger at McDonald's, and all bets are off."

She couldn't suppress an eye-roll. "That is really insane. You're doomed to lose, you know. Dobby's a phenomenal dog, for a toy, but she'll never keep up the pace with the real dogs."

Cole just grinned.

Suddenly, Jane felt a bubble of delight rising inside her. Competition always lit a fire in her gut. Going for broke in the obedience or agility ring was something she could deal with—so much better than trying to deal with fires, unpaid insurance bills, and a camera following her around to record her every move.

This could put things back into perspective.

"Okay," she said, and put her hand out to seal the wager. He clasped her hand in his. His hand was warm and surprisingly callused for a computer jock, and the firm clasp made her heart jump. But she managed to grin. "Winner take all."

"Winner take all," he confirmed.

• • •

RICK TOLLESON hadn't planned to spend the night in Carson City. At the end of Sunday's trial, he had packed his displays, products, and equipment into his utility trailer, checked out of his motel, and prepared to hit the road, back to the small apartment he maintained in Denver and then almost immediately on to Aspen to work an all-breed dog show in that elevated, very exclusive town. But while eating at a diner on the way out of town, he got to thinking, thinking about Shadow, Jane Connor's beautiful golden retriever who had been the center of that morning's excitement. The dog had seemed perfectly all right when Jane had brought him in for examination, but sometimes a muscle injury or skeletal misalignment didn't show up until quite a while after the animal was stressed. Maybe he should check on the dog, just to be sure he was sound. Jane, after all, had been his friend since he had first taken to the road with his practice. And Shadow was her rising star. Rich owed it to Jane to make very sure of his evaluation, and a follow-up visit would take practically no time at all. If, that is, Jane was parked in the RV park she had told him about earlier.

Rick looked down at his French fries and had to laugh at himself. "Come on, Rick, old man," he said out loud, "you don't need to see that dog again. Or Jane. You just want to take another peek at the hot blonde with the twinkly eyes."

The waitress gave him a wary look as she passed the table with her coffeepot, and Rick mused that he'd been traveling alone too long. Talking to himself was a bad habit he'd acquired during long hours alone on the road, alone in motels, and alone in his apartment. He didn't think it was that strange, frankly, but it could freak out other folks.

He paid the check, asked directions to the Comstock Country RV Park, and continued his conversation in his truck.

"This is a pretty lame excuse to get another chance to gawk at what's-her-name."

Shit. He didn't even remember the blonde's name. But he surely did remember that figure—full and curvy, just as a woman's figure should be. And her skin—it had seemed to glow in the muted light of his vendor's stall.

"Okay, so I'm using the dog as an excuse. I'm a man who wants one more look at a pretty woman. I don't really need an excuse. I'm a man. Men like to look at pretty women, okay?" he shot at an imaginary critic.

Rick continued down the road, wondering if he really *had* been alone too long.

When he got to the RV park, he cruised the rows of trailers and motor homes, searching for a setup that looked like dog people—exercise pens, grooming tables, bumper stickers boasting about one breed or another. He passed a noisy group of terriers scrapping in their pen, and a sad-looking bloodhound tied to the steps of a Winnebago. Then he hit pay dirt. At a big tan bus of a motor home, Shadow sat alertly in his exercise pen, watching a man and a little girl who played cards on a grooming table, and also keeping an eye on a tiny papillon curled nonchalantly in a canvas chair.

Rick parked his truck crosswise to the motor home. His trailer blocked the neighboring fifth-wheel's parking spot, but he figured he wouldn't be here long enough to be a nuisance.

"Hey there!" he said, slamming the truck door behind him. "Jane around?" As if Jane were the person he wanted to see.

The man, a barrel-shaped Latino on the gray side of middle age, looked up. The kid just kept frowning at her cards. Now that he was closer, Rick saw they were playing cribbage.

"Nope," the man told him. "You missed her. She went into town for dinner."

Disappointment stabbed at him. Jane's sexy friend was probably wherever Jane was. "Oh. Well, I...uh...just stopped by to see if Shadow had developed any stiffness or lameness. I'm Dr. Tolleson. I examined the dog today after his little incident."

"Oh," the man said. "Yeah. I think Shadow's fine, but if you want to look at him again, I'm sure Jane would appreciate it. She surely does dote on that dog."

The kid looked up and fastened on Rick with suspicious eyes. "Jane doesn't let anyone take Shadow out of his pen unless she's right there watching. She'll really yell at you if she finds out."

As if in agreement, the papillon uncurled and let out an emphatic squeak.

"Well, now," Rick replied, "I can understand why Jane made that rule. So I won't take Shadow out of the pen. I'll just climb in with him and say hello. Shadow and I are old friends, aren't we, fella?" he asked the dog, whose tail wagged back and forth in delighted greeting.

The kid still looked suspicious. The papillon danced back and forth on her chair, barking—if you could call that squeak a bark. Then the door to the motor home opened to reveal a very curvy blonde backlit against the interior. "Who are you guys talking to? And does Dobby really have to make that racket?"

Rick's spirits rose. And they rose even higher when the blonde spotted him and smiled brightly. "Well, hello. You're Dr....uh..."

"Tolleson," he supplied, and refused to be deflated because she didn't remember his name. After all, he hadn't remembered hers. He had remembered her face and that spectacular figure, though. "Rick Tolleson. And you're Jane's friend..."

"Angela."

"Right. Angie. Who's in television. You're an actress?"

She laughed. The sound of music, Rick decided.

"Not an actress, God forbid. A producer. Didn't Jane tell you that she and Shadow are the subject of my new documentary series?"

"No. She's been keeping secrets from me, apparently. She and Shadow are going to be television stars, are they?"

"Absolutely."

A television producer. Very hip. Probably out of his league. But then, he was just looking, not buying. Still, he tried to see if her left hand sported a gold band, but the fading light was too dim.

"Are you looking for Jane?" Angela asked. "She's in town."

"I already told him," Ernesto said.

"He wants to see Shadow," Teri informed her in a slightly miffed voice. "But I told him that no one can take Shadow out without Jane saying so."

Angela undulated down the motor home steps. "Undulated" was the only way to describe it, but her descent was more a matter of grace than exhibitionism. Still, the way she moved was nothing short of an exhibit, and Rick enjoyed every second.

"It's nice to see you again," Angela said politely. But her tone purred. Or was his deprived, womanless life making him imagine things? "I think what you do is so interesting."

"Really? I mean, yes, uh, I've always been amazed at how much chiropractic adjustment can contribute to a dog's overall health, not to mention keeping the animal fit and flexible to give his very best possible performance. Even though some of my veterinary colleagues dismiss animal chiropractic as a scam, I've found—" He checked himself before he launched into a dissertation, which he was prone to do at any hint that someone might be interested in his profession. "Sorry. Don't get me started."

But Angela's eyes hadn't yet glazed over, which was unusual. Most women started yawning after the first sentence.

"No, really," she protested. "I'm fascinated. But you

came to see Shadow, didn't you? I'm sure Jane would appreciate your taking another look at him, even though she's not here. She told me how much good you do for the dogs you treat, and she worries about her dogs like they were kids. In fact, why don't we bring Shadow into the motor home where the light is better?"

"Jane's gonna yell," Teri warned.

"Jane's not going to mind," Angela told the girl. "You'd better start paying attention to your cards, or Ernesto is going to trounce you. You have to watch him. He's sneaky."

"I am," Ernesto confirmed.

Shadow was only too glad to come into the motor home and be made the center of attention, and Dobby protested the retriever's absence so loudly that the papillon had to come inside also. Idaho, who had been sprawled in the kitchen, promptly came alert at the sound of activity and paced between Angela and Rick, looking for some way to help. The motor home, large as it was, seemed to be wall-to-wall canine, with two large dogs vying for attention and one tiny dog bouncing from sofa to floor to chair to floor to sofa and back again.

Rick was used to working amid canine chaos, however, and Angela didn't seem to mind the dogs underfoot—a definite asset for any woman, in Rick's opinion. She sat on the sofa, ignoring Dobby, who periodically ricocheted off her lap, and watched while Rick gave Shadow a once-over.

Shadow was fine. Sound as solid rock. Rick had known the dog was fine when he had left the diner and headed out in search of the RV park. Shadow had merely been an excuse. And what a good excuse he was, because here Rick sat within the close confines of a cozy motor home with gorgeous Angela, and her watching his every move as if she were really interested.

"You're really a licensed vet, right?" she asked as he manipulated Shadow's neck.

"That's right."

"Did you have to take additional training for the chiropractic?"

"Sure did. Can't start playing around with the body without knowing what you're doing."

She smiled at that, taking, he hoped, an entirely different meaning than what was on the surface.

"And you still do regular veterinary treatment?"

"If it's needed."

She continued to grill him, asking intelligent questions about his practice, how he combined standard veterinary, chiropractic, acupuncture, and holistic techniques. After he finished looking at Shadow, they sat on the sofa with mugs of coffee, and he turned the tables and grilled her about her profession. Very convenient. This way they could talk, show interest, and yet not get too personal. Not that Rick wouldn't like to get personal. Getting to know Angela—know her very well—would be a treat any man would look forward to.

Rick should get so lucky.

Finally Angela asked, "Where are you headed now? Up to the trials in Casper? That's where we're going."

Her expectant look held as much invitation as question, or so Rick wanted to think. He had vendor space reserved at an all-breed show and obedience trial in Aspen, where he would have an opportunity to make a lot more money than at an agility trial. But he didn't tell Angela that.

"I haven't quite decided where I'm headed. I like to keep my life flexible. Sometimes too flexible."

She nodded. "I know exactly what you mean. I'm kind of a 'don't fence me in' woman myself."

Then, just as the conversation started to turn nicely personal, Teri and Ernesto blew through the door, Teri giggling and Ernesto griping about mosquitoes.

"Getting eaten alive," he complained. "And this little cardsharp was cleaning me out."

Teri giggled again, attracting attention from the dogs, who promptly converged on her in hairy, tail-wagging glee.

Rick took his cue to leave. But something in the scene—the kid, the dogs, the easy camaraderie between Angela and Ernesto—pulled a few strings in his heart that he hadn't known were there.

And later, turning from the RV park onto the highway, he wondered if he could reserve last-minute vendor space at Casper.

chapter 13

INTERSTATE 80 through Nevada and Wyoming was a long, straight asphalt ribbon over barren deserts and plains. Occasionally a rugged mountain range or water-starved river broke the monotony, but mostly the road consisted of mile after burning mile of sand, scrub brush, and a whole lot of nothing. An adult traveling alone in a good, fast car might be able to drive the distance between Carson City, Nevada, and Casper, Wyoming, in one very long day, though the drive would be a stretch of endurance. But in a motor home bearing the burden of two hundred thousand road miles and an eight-year-old kid sitting in the passenger seat, the effective distance seemed to at least triple. The tried-and-true mathematical formula no longer applied.

The savant who quantified the relationship between distance, velocity, and time, Cole thought, staring through the motor home windshield at the empty highway in front of him, obviously didn't have kids. Neither had he traveled in a geriatric vehicle. The kid had to eat/pee/drink a soda/explore a tourist trap at least every sixty miles. And the vehicle demanded fuel every hundred or so. Not to mention oil. Cole began to wonder if he should have forked over more money to buy a motor home that wasn't quite as over the hill as the one that now chugged along the freeway, carrying them toward Elko, Nevada. Though saying that old Rumblestiltskin, as Teri had named the thing, was over the hill was an exaggeration. Rumblestiltskin could barely get up the hill, much less over it.

"Daddy, that sign says there's a McDonald's at the next exit."

"Trust Mickey D's to put up a restaurant in the middle of nowhere," Cole replied.

"Is this the middle of nowhere?"

"Just about. Nevada is noted for having a lot of nowhere." And that was the geography lesson for the day. "I suppose you want to stop at the McDonald's?"

"I have to pee," Teri confirmed. "And I want a Happy Meal."

"Okay, kiddo. One potty stop and Happy Meal coming up."

Cole didn't really resent the frequent stops along the way. After all, he occasionally needed a potty stop himself, not to mention a Big Mac, or Whopper, or the specialty of whichever roadside eatery was handy. And he wasn't trying to break any speed records getting from one place to another. This summer was supposed to be a laid-back vacation where he could reconnect with his daughter, where his daughter could rediscover happiness, and where they could both have a bit of fun with Dobby. He and Teri were footloose and fancy free, not a care in the world except having fun at the agility trials and seeing the country in between.

It was just too bad that this particular countryside held so little to entertain an eight-year-old. If Cole had to listen to one more Disney movie blaring from Teri's portable DVD player, he was going to round up the Little Mermaid, Mulan, the Beauty, the Beast, Pocahontas, and Aladdin, and shoot them all. And oh yes, Nemo the fish would meet the same fate.

"We're here, Daddy. Hadn't you better slow down?"

"Okay. That's right. When you learn to drive, in a decade or so, you'll have to remember not to drive as fast as your daddy does."

"I won't drive fast. Ernesto says that Angela burns up the road, and that she's a menace. You don't think Angela really burns up the road, do you? How could other cars go on the road if she did?"

Cole chuckled. "Why don't you ask her when we see her at the trials this coming weekend?"

"I will," Teri said decisively.

This McDonald's, it turned out, was not quite in the middle of nowhere. Next door was a Texaco gas station, and across the road was a stucco tepee with a sign out front advertising moccasins, kachina dolls, and Apache tears, along with gems, minerals, and rocks.

Teri eyed the tepee as she hopped down from the motor home cab. Hands on her hips, she cocked her head and said, "I think I need some moccasins."

"I thought you had to visit the little girls' room and eat a Happy Meal," Cole reminded her.

"Uh-huh. But then could we look at the moccasins?"

"At the last pit stop you bought a can of rattlesnake eggs." Which were actually egg-shaped chocolates with hard sugar shells, Cole had been grateful to learn. "I thought that was supposed to be your souvenir for the week."

"Well," Teri said, screwing up her face. "Moccasins would be better. Besides, we ate the eggs, and they're gone."

Cole smiled. He hoped his new job, wherever it was, came attached to a whopping salary. His quiet little daughter, who for two years had barely shown interest in anything outside plodding back and forth to school, watching television, and going to see an occasional movie, was on her way to becoming a shopaholic.

The observation made Cole ridiculously happy.

An hour later, they were on the road again. Their stomachs were full, bladders empty, and new Teri-size moccasins were safely stashed in the back closet where Dobby couldn't get to them. Dobby absolutely loved leather. The papillon was a bit miffed, because Teri had modeled the moccasins for the little dog before Cole told her to put them away. Now Dobby was curled on the sofa, keeping a hopeful eye on the closet. Sometimes doors could swing open on their own, after all, especially when the motor home was moving. A dog could always hope.

They stopped for gas at Elko, which didn't offer a lot to attract a little girl's attention, so soon they were on their way. The motor home's air-conditioning labored to keep out the scorching heat, and the road ahead shimmered in the burning sun. Dobby snoozed, curled on her pillow between the seats, and Teri's usual talkativeness had run down. The DVD player lay idle on her lap, and she stared at the passing landscape, leaving her father to his own thoughts.

Inevitably, those thoughts drifted toward the night before, and Cole wondered what had possessed him to bait Jane Connor into making that bet. He had flirted with her all evening, from the time they had left the others behind at Angela's motor home until the moment he had issued a challenge that she couldn't resist.

Why? Why the bet? Cole really didn't care if Dobby was the best at anything. He, Teri, and the dog were doing the agility tour as an excuse to see the country. He didn't care if they won. Well, okay, maybe he did get a kick out of winning, but he wasn't so hooked that he would pit his little squeak-toy dog against a natural canine athlete like Shadow, especially when that natural athlete was trained and handled by a kick-ass professional like Jane.

So why the bet? It was out of character. Not to mention the flirting. Cole wasn't a guy who came on to women. He was a guy who had lost a beloved wife, worried about a beloved daughter, and up until a couple of weeks ago had held down two jobs that left a social life, not to mention a sex life, pretty much a memory.

Yet whenever Jane came within sight, he itched to get her attention. He liked the way she looked, with or without Angela's makeover. He liked the way her smile spread from her lips to her eyes. And he damned well liked the way her lips had felt on his cheek when he'd put a stop to Shadow's flight. Too bad she hadn't missed his cheek and planted that kiss on his mouth. He would have liked that even better.

And bless her, she had turned red as a beet when she had realized what she'd done. How many women in the world today were that unaffected, that spontaneous?

Damn, but he liked the woman! He even liked her combativeness.

Since Cole had lost Mandy, too many women of his acquaintance turned themselves inside out to please him. They hastened to make sure their hair and lipstick were straight when they saw him coming. They sent him come-hither smiles, trapped him into oh-you-poor-lonely-man conversations. Single women, it seemed, and some married women as well, just couldn't resist setting the bait for any widower still young enough to have brain and bladder function.

Most annoying of all, some weren't above using Teri as a route to his attention. One perky blonde soccer coach had taught him that. Good thing that Teri hadn't wanted to play soccer anymore.

But Jane was an entirely different breed. Jane had attitude with a capital *A*. She spoke whatever came into her mind without a thought for who might get huffy or misunderstand. She didn't flirt. She didn't pander for favor. And he couldn't imagine her primping to impress anyone.

Jane glowed with a kind of attractiveness that didn't need primping to improve, even before Angela had spruced her up. The glow was there when she looked at one of her dogs—her kids—with such affection in her eyes. It was there when she labored to be a good sport over losing to Dobby. It was there when she tried to figure out how to talk to an eight-year-old who had kidnapped her dog.

Angela's makeover had put the sheen on someone who was already twenty-four-carat gold.

That was why the flirting. And that was why the bet. Ironic, Cole mused, that when he finally got a hankering again for the opposite gender, his interest fell on a woman who didn't care to do cartwheels to get his attention. He was the one doing cartwheels—throwing a dare in her face, making the competition between them personal. Jane couldn't resist a challenge. A guy didn't have to be a genius to know that.

Cole smiled at himself, admitting that the tactic was truly worthy of a junior high brat. He should put a leash on his inner adolescent and give that leash a firm yank. He was a father, after all, and he had no business bringing someone into Teri's life who might slip into the little girl's heart and then leave a hole behind when she hit the road.

And speaking of the road, Cole frowned at a new note in the engine that sounded like the screech of a dying squirrel.

"Daddy?" Teri asked, yawning.

"What, sweet pea?"

"Did I tell you that I skunked Ernesto last night at cards?"

"Skunked him, eh?"

"That's what Ernesto said. He said I was too smart for an itty-bitty kid, and that I was a card shark."

Cole chuckled. "Probably a cardsharp."

"I think he said 'shark.' I told him that I'm not an itty-bitty kid. Do you know that he has bunches of grandkids?"

"How many is bunches?"

"Well, lots. He told me, but I forget."

This summer just might work the miracle Cole had hoped for. New people and new places were making Teri come alive again.

Maybe new people and new places were making Cole come alive again, as well.

They rolled on, and the squirrel in the engine still complained.

JANE PERUSED a road map, sitting in the passenger seat of the Challenger with her feet propped on the dashboard. "There is truly a lot of nothing out here," she commented to Angela.

"Depends on your definition of nothing," Angela said. "I once did a program on snakes. Rattlers, mostly. People love learning about the dangerous snakes, you know, and they ignore anything done on the harmless snakes. There are a lot of snakes that do a bunch of good in the ecology. Not that rattlers don't have their place, but—"

"And your point would be?" Jane interrupted.

"What? Oh, yes. Snakes love this country. Lizards too, and an amazing variety of insects."

"Which is way more than I needed to know. I got an ant bite at the last rest stop."

"Well, the ant probably saw you coming and said, 'Look at that big sloppy-looking giant coming my way. She needs a bite if anyone ever has.'"

Jane made a rude sound. "What? Sloppy-looking giant?"

"A joke."

"Don't give up animal shows for comedy. Sheesh!"

"I just thought I'd give the ant's point of view: being accosted by a scary-looking human without makeup and wearing a baggy sweat suit."

"I'm supposed to look like Julia Roberts even when we're not filming?"

Angela brayed out a laugh. "Julia Roberts you will *never* be. Ha! Oh, my! But hey, I don't want you to be Julia Roberts. We want you to be Jane Connor. The best Jane Connor possible."

Jane sighed. "Come on, Angela. We're not doing anything today except riding this endless road toward Wyoming."

"You never can tell. Besides, you need to get in the habit of looking good. Especially after the program gets on the air and everyone starts looking your way."

"Don't you ever spend a day without makeup, or without color-coordinating your clothes?"

"No," Angela assured her. "My mother told me that a woman should always take pride in her appearance, because appearance is a big part of what you are. Besides, you never know when you might need to marshal the full force of feminine power to overcome some obstacle."

Jane laughed. "You need makeup for feminine power?"

"Of course."

"Cut me some slack. I combed my hair this morning."

"You pinned it back into a stubby little ponytail."

"And I coordinated my wardrobe."

"By putting a gray T-shirt with gray sweats."

"That's coordinated."

"Oh, please!" Angela's expression grew sly. "And by the way, how did your date go last night?"

"Date?" Jane asked incredulously. "Angela, you can change a subject of conversation faster than anyone I know. It's a talent."

Angela grinned. "It's a way of catching people off guard."

"It's a way of confusing people," Jane corrected. "Date? What date? Going to Denny's with Cole after everyone else crapped out on us is not a date."

"Crapped out? Really, Jane, when you're in the public eye, you need to watch your language."

"I'm not in the public eye. I'm sitting in a motor home with a crazy woman and two dogs. And by the way, the dogs are on my side, no matter what we're discussing."

"You didn't answer my question."

"I wasn't on a date. There was no date."

"A bit sensitive on the issue, are we?"

"No," Jane said firmly. "We got rained on, hailed on, had dinner, talked about dogs, mostly, and some about his kid. And agility. We talked about agility." And Cole had somehow made the race for Solid Gold into a personal contest. But Angela didn't need to know about that. She would probably incorporate their silly bet into her silly film.

"Just dogs, eh? And a word or two about Teri?"

"Yes."

"Nothing personal?"

Jane examined a broken nail. "Dogs are personal. So are kids, I guess."

"You know what I mean."

"I tell you, Angela, this wasn't a date. I don't know what you're fishing for here, but forget it."

"So you spent how long in front of the mirror yesterday before he came? Just to talk about dogs?"

Jane studied the scenery.

"And now you're slobbing around to, maybe, prove to yourself that Mr. Hunky isn't having any effect on you whatsoever? That you're not wondering how he likes your new haircut? Your updated face? The new clothes that show off your terrific figure?"

"I have a terrific figure?" Jane asked, surprised.

"Sure you do. And damn it, I wish I had your genes. I look at a chocolate shake and add two inches to my hips. You can eat two supreme burritos for lunch and a double cheeseburger for dinner and take off a pound. You know, I ought to hate you for that, but I don't. Partly because it's hard to envy someone who has so much potential and doesn't know how to use it."

Jane let her head drop back onto the headrest, groaning in frustration. "There you go, changing the subject again. Do you know what 'non sequitur' means?"

"Of course I do. And I think that I employ it brilliantly." She tossed Jane a sidelong look. "Would you rather talk about your date?"

Jane groaned again.

"There's nothing worse on a long trip," Angela said with a sigh, "than someone who refuses to engage in girl talk."

"You're incorrigible. If you were a dog in one of my training classes, I'd tell your owner to take you back to the pound and get a dog with less attitude."

Angela grinned. "Attitude. I like it. I have attitude."

"And Angela," Jane said, serious now, "I warn you. If you even hint in this so-called documentary about some sort of Thing"—and her tone definitely capitalized the Thing—"between me and Cole, anything that you've concocted from your overly busy, way-too-nosy little mind, then we're going to have a huge problem. Understand?"

"Oh, for heaven's sake, Jane. Would I do something like that?"

"In a New York minute."

"Do you ever wonder where that phrase came from?"

Angela was off and running on another tangent, but Jane trusted she had gotten her point across, so she closed her eyes, got more comfortable in her seat, and let the buzz of Angela's voice lull her into a doze.

They stopped in Elko for gas, a couple of doses of caffeine in the form of Diet Cokes, and a potty stop for both women and dogs. Shadow and Idaho bounded about on their leashes, sniffing the ground, the air, the scraggly landscaping, and each other before settling down to business. When a mother and little girl approached with a request to pet the dogs, Idaho's therapy-dog training kicked in and he sat politely for his admirers, enjoying the petting with only a minimum of sloppy kissing. Back in the Verde Valley, he was one of the medical center's most popular pet visitors, and very proud of it.

Not to be bested, Shadow imitated his older kennel-mate, though youth and energy made the task difficult. His whole golden body positively vibrated with the need to lick and jump and wriggle his joy at making a new friend.

"These are big dogs!" the little girl exclaimed, then giggled as Shadow got in a surreptitious kiss.

"So well behaved," Mom said.

Jane thought of Teri, and of course thinking of Teri just naturally led to thinking of Teri's father, with whom she now had the tenuous connection of that silly bet. That was the only connection, Jane told herself, but perversely, she wondered where they were—Cole, Teri, and tiny Dobby. Were they headed straight to Casper for the trial, or perhaps taking a detour up to Yellowstone to do the tourist bit? It didn't matter, Jane told herself. If Cole wanted to blow off the Casper trial and pass up the points available there, all the better. She didn't care if he was there or not. Certainly she didn't.

"Can I give them a hug good-bye?" the little girl asked. "Would they mind?"

"They would love it," Jane assured her. "They think kids are the greatest people on earth."

The little girl grinned and wrapped Shadow in an enthusiastic embrace. Most dogs would object to such familiarity from a stranger, but the big golden retriever simply sighed and closed his eyes in ecstasy. Idaho was a bit more reserved and very conscious of his dignity. But he endured the child's attention politely.

"They're so wonderful," the mom declared.

Out of the corner of her eye, Jane caught a glimpse of Ernesto and his ever-present camera, filming the kid encounter. In a flash of irritation, she wondered if any corner of her life was immune from the camera's prying. The answer was no, she guessed, until she won the dadgummed

Solid Gold, rebuilt her life, and no longer had to sell herself and her pride just to survive.

With that gloomy thought in her mind, she climbed back into the motor home. As they started on the road, Ernesto's big white van following, Jane searched through the refrigerator to find some comfort food. She found it in a frozen chocolate Popsicle.

"Super!" Angela exclaimed when she saw the treat. "Get me one, too."

"You'll have to do an extra fifty push-ups." Not that Jane had ever seen Angela sweat a drop over the exercise program she kept complaining about.

"I don't care. I didn't have much lunch. Just a bologna sandwich. I deserve a Popsicle."

They rolled down the highway, drinking their supersized Diet Cokes and eating chocolate Popsicles. The afternoon stretched ahead down an endless-seeming road, baking and tedious beneath the midsummer sun, until they spotted a vehicle parked on the freeway shoulder.

"That looks like . . ." Angela frowned in speculation.

Cole Forrest instantly popped into Jane's mind.

"What's his name again?" Angela asked, then answered herself. "Cole. That's it. It looks like Cole."

And it was.

TERI SAT at the table in Angela's motor home, eating a green lime Popsicle and feeling sorry for herself. Even the Popsicle didn't make things look brighter.

Shadow and Idaho sat close by, watching the Popsicle with hope in their eyes.

"Dogs don't eat Popsicles," she told them.

Dobby, who was above begging for treats, lay curled on the front passenger seat, looking at the two larger dogs with contempt.

"Told ya!" Teri scolded her audience. "Dobby knows that dogs don't eat Popsicles. The sugar isn't good for you."

The sugar wasn't good for Teri either, but she figured that she needed it. She and her dad and Dobby were going to be stuck back in Elko, another name for Nowhere, until Rumblestiltskin was repaired, and who knew how long that would take? Maybe forever. Maybe it couldn't be fixed. It was pretty old and run down, and the engine had died a noisy, miserable death. Noisier even than her dad's cussing as he'd pulled onto the shoulder of the road. Maybe they would have to rent a car and just go home, except that home wasn't home anymore, because Mrs. Farley the real estate lady had e-mailed her dad that someone wanted to buy it for a bunch of money, and her dad hadn't decided where they were going to live when this summer was over.

Even sugar couldn't make Teri feel better about all that.

"I don't wanna have to rent a car," she told the dogs. "It's not fair. Dobby's still got agility trials to win."

Dobby merely blinked. Idaho looked sympathetic, and Shadow cocked his head as if he understood. None of them answered, though. Actually, the only dog Teri had ever heard in her head was Shadow, and he didn't say much when other dogs or people were around.

It didn't make any difference. What could Shadow say? If her dad couldn't make the motor home run again, a dog certainly couldn't.

Jane's head poked out of the bathroom doorway. "Who are you talking to out there, Teri?"

"The dogs," she admitted.

"Oh." Then, in a cautious voice, "Is Shadow answering you again?"

"He doesn't say anything unless we're alone."

"Ah. That's probably wise of him."

Jane was probably the only grown-up Teri knew who wouldn't shoot off like a rocket at the idea of a dog talking to someone. That was pretty cool. But right now Teri was too depressed to be cheered.

With a sigh, she jumped down from the dinette seat and tossed her Popsicle stick in the kitchen trash. "Can I get in the bathroom?" she asked Jane. "I have to pee."

"Be my guest." Jane came out, carrying the sweatpants and T-shirt she had gone in wearing. Now she was dressed in khaki shorts and a red cotton sweater that made her hair look like it had caught on fire.

"Didn't you get dressed this morning?" Teri asked.

"Of course I did." Her answer had the short, clipped tone that adults used when they were teed off. Teri didn't waste time wondering why Jane was teed off. Grown-ups got irritated at the strangest things. It was impossible to understand them.

"Your eyeliner's crooked," Teri advised.

Jane whipped around to confirm it in the bathroom mirror. "It is! Dammit all! Angela makes this look so easy!" With a disgusted snort, she grabbed the eyeliner pencil from her bag.

"You shouldn't say 'dammit,'" Teri told her. "My dad says it's not ladylike."

"Your dad is right. Don't use me as an example."

"How come you're putting on makeup in the middle of the day? My mom used to put it on first thing in the morning. I used to sit and watch her, and sometimes she put some pink color on my cheeks. I remember."

Jane made a funny sound, kind of like a horse snorting.

"Your cheeks don't need much color," Teri advised. For a grown-up woman, Jane seemed to need a lot of advice in this area. "They're already really pink."

Through the sound of gritting teeth, Jane said, "Thank you, Teri." Then she zipped the eye pencil into a little bag with her other makeup and shoved the bag beneath the sink.

"Can I pee now?" Teri asked. "I really, really gotta go."

"Be my guest. And don't forget to flush."

Teri assured her indignantly, "I'm not a baby!"

When she finished peeing and left the bathroom—after flushing the funny way you had to flush in a motor home— her dad was there, talking to Jane. He was pink all over his face, just like Jane, only her dad was just hot and sweaty. It wasn't as if he had been using makeup. He had a bottle of cold water in his hand and gulped it down just as if it was a really good-tasting soda pop. Then he wiped his mouth and gave Jane a funny smile.

"Did you plant a bomb in old Rumblestiltskin?"

"I beg your pardon?" Jane said in a huffy voice.

"My motor home. That's the name Teri gave it."

"Rumblestiltskin and Dobby. The kid has an imagination when it comes to names."

"Yes, she does, don't you, sweet pea?"

Teri walked over and climbed once again into the dinette booth. "My dad says names are important," she told Jane. "That's why he lets me name stuff. He says that he doesn't have any imagination at all."

Jane looked at her dad with one eyebrow raised. It was a look that Teri's second-grade teacher had used when she knew some kid was trying to get away with something. "No imagination, eh?" Jane said. "Coulda fooled me. Seems I've heard some fairly far-out stuff come out of your mouth."

"Ah, well." Her dad chuckled. "Sometimes I get inspired."

"And for your information, Mr. Forrest, I don't need to sabotage your motor home to win a lobster dinner."

Teri didn't have a clue what they were talking about, but she didn't remember ever seeing her dad grin like he was grinning just then. And his eyes had gotten all crinkly and twinkly. Teri's own eyes narrowed. Something was up, that was for sure.

"I wouldn't count those expensive calories just yet," he said in a voice that sounded almost like a laugh. "Motor homes can be fixed. Or replaced. There's a lot of trials yet to be run."

"You can run as many trials as you can find," Jane said huffily, but her eyes were as twinkly as her dad's. "I'm not sweating who's going to come out on top."

"Keep thinking that way. And I'll start looking forward to a steak dinner with a huge bottle of champagne."

Still laughing, Teri's dad threw his empty water bottle into the trash and opened the motor home door. "Stay cool, Teri," he told her, then winked at Jane. "You too. It's going to be a while yet."

Teri watched as Jane stared after her dad with an expression waffling between exasperation and sort of a funny smile. Teri knew what that meant. She might be just eight years old, but she was no dummy. After all, she watched television. She listened to the other kids in school talk about their single moms and single dads.

Just like the other ladies that got clingy around her dad, Jane thought he was hot. That was what the kids in school said when someone got moony over someone else. Teri wasn't sure exactly what "hot" meant, but she got the general drift. Jane had promised not to be like those other ladies, but she was. That was why she had put on nice clothes and put makeup on her face. She wanted to look nice for Teri's dad.

There was a difference, though. Her dad didn't seem to be ignoring Jane like he did the other ladies who chased him. Maybe he liked Jane. Maybe Jane was going to be her new mother. She heard kids at school talk about that as well. Some of them had had two or three moms or dads, and most of them didn't much like it. Some of them did, though. Her friend Shirley had gotten a new mom just last Christmas, sort of as a Christmas present. And she thought the new mom was cool.

As Teri sat at the table and watched Jane, a thought crept into her mind. If Jane became Teri's new mom, she could for sure talk her dad into getting Teri a dog of her very own just like Shadow, because Jane thought that dogs were more important than breathing, even. A pulse of excitement made little butterflies flutter in her heart, but the butterflies drowned in an instant flood of guilt. She shouldn't be thinking about a new mom, Teri reminded herself. Her real mom up in heaven would get hurt feelings if Teri let a new mom into her life, and into her heart.

Jane had quit her mooning and was starting to fix some snacks. Teri folded her legs up to her chest, gave herself a hug, and sighed. It was too bad, really. She liked Jane. And she really liked Shadow. But no way was Teri ever going to get a new mom.

chapter 14

COLE HAD his head beneath the hood of his motor home, wrinkling his nose at the acrid smell of oil, coolant, and something—heaven knew what—that stunk to high heaven when it got too hot. The motor home's engine had obviously gotten much too hot. But that was the extent of Cole's diagnosis. He was a mathematician and computer jock. Ask him to differentiate or integrate any complicated equation and he would shine. Ask him to distinguish one doohickey from another in a truck engine, and he came up a total dunce.

But the tow truck was taking its own sweet time about rescuing them, and right now there was nothing else to do but examine the engine and try to look intelligent. It was what men did, even if they didn't know jack about engines.

"Doesn't look good," Ernesto said. His head was in the same dark space, inhaling fumes right along with Cole.

"Doesn't smell good, either." Cole coughed and came up for fresh air. Ernesto stayed put a moment longer, but he shook his head when he surfaced.

"I don't know, Cole. Your radiator is shot. That much is

obvious from the coolant splattered all over the pavement. And I think your water pump is definitely dead. But from what you tell me about how this buggy was acting when it finally cratered..." Another ominous shake of the head. "I'd lay a bet that your transmission has ground itself to bits."

Cole winced. "You good with these things?"

"Hell yes. In my neighborhood, a boy wasn't considered a man until he could tear down a V-8 and put it back together blindfolded. You'd have to put this thing on a lift and get your hands dirty to find out exactly how bad it is, but I can tell you that it ain't gonna be pretty."

Cole admitted, "Engines are a mystery to me."

"Well, computers are a mystery to me," Ernesto confessed generously. "I suppose young men these days bury themselves in computers the way my generation buried themselves in hot rods."

"Maybe." All Cole had been interested in when growing up was computers. And that led to math, which led him back to computers. It was a good way to earn a living, both teaching and consulting, but not nearly as manly as being able to stick his head beneath the hood of an ailing vehicle and, like a physician making a life-and-death diagnosis, come up with a verdict. In this case, it looked as if the diagnosis was thumbs down. The patient didn't have much time to live.

"You think it can be fixed?" he asked the expert.

"Anything can be fixed, if you have enough time and money. The real question would be, is it worth getting fixed? You might spend less just getting another used motor home."

Cole felt like cussing, but before he could get a good line of curses strung together, Jane showed up with a bottle of cold water for each of them, along with a plate of Oreos.

"How's it look?" she asked.

Cole was willing to bet that Jane Connor knew one doohickey from another in an engine. She impressed him as that kind of woman—competent in ways both men and women would envy. Mandy hadn't been like that. His wife had been sweet, feminine, and very willing to let men deal with things like wrenches, screwdrivers, cars, and lawn mowing. She never would have dreamed of supporting herself in her own business, and she had met most crises and emergencies with panic.

That was all right. Mandy had been a wonderful wife and mother, and a darned good math teacher. They had had so much in common. Having stuff in common was important in a relationship.

Which made his attraction to Jane less than sensible. But such matters seldom were sensible. Unlike math or physics, neither heart nor hormones followed the rules of logic.

"It doesn't look good," Cole said. Though Jane looked mighty good, especially considering it had to be at least 110 in the shade. If there were any shade. It was oven temperature even in the big motor home with the air-conditioning running. "At least Ernesto tells me it doesn't look good. I don't know about these things."

Jane stuck her head beneath the hood without hesitation. She came up shaking her head. "I'd start playing taps if I had a bugle."

As if choreographed, Ernesto moved away and left them alone with the deceased engine.

"This is really tough luck, Cole." She sounded genuinely sympathetic. "You know, Dobby is a great little dog. She deserves to go to the Invitational. I hate to see any dog drop out of the race just because of rotten luck."

Cole noticed that she regretted poor Dobby getting dumped on by luck, but said nothing about Dobby's owner. Maybe his charm just wasn't what it used to be.

Ernesto had gone to his van and come out bearing a camera. Cole wondered if sometime down the road he'd be watching himself on television.

"It's just an agility trial, Jane. Just a game."

She looked at him as if he'd blasphemed.

"Besides, maybe the buggy can be fixed. Or maybe I can get another one cheap. And you know what? Dobby won't care. She loves agility, but as long as she has her pillow and two square meals a day, she's not going to complain about missing a couple of trials. And to her, the Invitational will be just another trial."

Cole's cell phone played the opening notes to Beethoven's Fifth, which forestalled any reply that Jane might have made. Probably a good thing, Cole thought as he flipped the phone open. He listened, nodded, muttered a "Thank you," and closed it with a satisfied flip.

"Tow truck is about ten minutes away."

"Great," Jane said. "Things are looking up."

Ninety minutes later, it became obvious to Cole that things were not looking up. Things were a long, long way from looking up, in fact.

Jane and her crew had followed the tow truck back to Elko, giving Teri and Dobby a ride in Angela's luxurious (by comparison, at least) motor home. Cole rode in the tow truck with a loquacious driver who seemed to delight in telling him over and over again that his poor crippled motor home was closer to being dead than any vehicle he'd seen. And he'd seen a lot, he boasted.

So the mechanic's verdict didn't come as much of a surprise. Cole stood in the garage with him to receive the bad news while Teri played cribbage with Ernesto in the Challenger. Jane was waiting in the garage waiting room, leafing through back issues of *Popular Mechanics* magazine. Angela sat beside her. They both sucked on Diet Cokes from the vending machine.

"Transmission," the mechanic proclaimed, wiping greasy hands on a rag. "Shot. I'm not surprised, with the mileage you have on this baby. Next to that, the radiator and water pump don't matter, ya know? And oh yeah, you need new valves. But like I say, that don't hardly count."

Cole pinched the bridge of his nose. "Can all that be fixed?"

Horace the mechanic considered solemnly. He was tall, spindly, dour, covered liberally with various lubricants, and smelled almost as bad as Rumblestiltskin's engine. But for all that, he seemed competent in his trade.

Sucking in his lower lip, Horace nodded. "Fix it? Sure. We could put in a rebuilt tyranny—I wouldn't rebuild the one that's in there, though. Not enough left of the thing. New radiator, water pump, hoses, and belts. Fix the oil leaks. Hell yes. But to tell the truth, mister, you'd spend less money getting another motor home."

Cole uttered a single cuss word, but the word was colorful enough that it pretty much covered the situation.

The mechanic continued, "I know a fellow who might take this wreck off your hands. He's a buddy of mine. Likes to tinker with junk like this, ya know. You couldn't get a pile of money for it, but some is better than nothing. Right?"

Cole let out a long, resigned breath.

JANE AND Angela shamelessly eavesdropped from the garage waiting room.

"Poor Cole!" Angela said. "What a pity!"

Jane's feelings were jumbled and confused. On one hand, she ought to be glad that Dobby would be out of the running for Solid Gold. One less rival competing for those 150 spaces increased the odds that one of those spaces would go to Shadow. On the other hand, no true competitor liked to see a good team get a bad rap from luck. And on a third hand, if she'd had one, the immediate future had just become a bit less interesting without the prospect of meeting Cole around every corner. He and Dobby did add a certain sizzle to the competition.

Rather, Cole added a sizzle. Jane forced herself to be honest. Dobby was cute. But Dobby was a dog. That persistent little current of electricity came from the man. Definitely from the man.

So it probably was a very good thing that she wouldn't be meeting Cole Forrest around every corner. He was definitely a distraction.

"Do you hear a thing I'm saying?" Angela whispered.

Jane came back into focus. "What?"

"You can tune out better than anyone I know." Angela's eyes narrowed. "Where were you just now?"

"Nowhere!" Jane scoffed. "Why are we whispering?"

"Because we're talking about Cole, and he's right next door in the garage."

"We are?"

"We would be if you would pay attention."

"Okay." Jane tossed her pop can into a garbage pail and went to the vending machine for another. "What are we saying about Cole?"

"That we should invite Cole and Teri to travel with us, now that they're without transportation."

For a moment Jane was nonplussed, an unusual occurrence, because the direct, uncensored line from her brain to her mouth seldom went down. But the sudden suggestion that she spend the summer in such close quarters with Cole—not to mention an eight-year-old who claimed to talk to Shadow—exploded in her head like a terrorist bomb.

Then she understood. Angela was making a joke. A joke. Of course. Jane laughed.

"Why are you laughing?"

"It's a joke, right?"

"No." Angela rolled her eyes heavenward, as if begging for help to deal with someone so dense.

Jane did not especially like being the target of such an eye-roll. "It has to be a joke. Not even you would suggest squeezing you, me, two and a half dogs, a six-foot man, and an eight-year-old girl into one thirty-four-foot motor home for an entire summer."

"It would be fun," Angela said.

"Angela! Cole is one of our top competitors. It's not a good idea to put two very driven people trying for the same prize in a small space where there's no escape."

"Oh, you're just afraid that you'll fall for the guy if you spend so much time together."

Jane snorted with all the indignation she could muster. "That is so much bull!"

"I've seen the way you look at him."

"I do not look at him! No way do I look at him. To me, he's blank space."

Angela chortled. "It's nothing to be ashamed of. It just shows you're normal, like the rest of us girls."

Jane took a deep breath. Angela could be so...so... persistent!

"Oh, don't look like such a thundercloud," Angela chided. "I was just teasing."

Jane's heart slowed from its double time. "Of course you were teasing. I knew that. Four people and three dogs in your motor home. Ridiculous."

"Not about that. I was serious about that. I meant that I was teasing about you and Cole."

Perversely, Jane wondered, what was so ridiculous about her and Cole?

"Honestly, Jane, it is so easy to get your goat."

Jane gritted her teeth. "Has anyone ever told you that you can be very annoying?"

"Tons of times," Angela admitted blithely.

"You really intend to invite Cole and his daughter to join us?"

"I consider it the only neighborly thing to do. It would probably just be until they can find another motor home. Probably."

"That is such a bad idea. You really know nothing about competition, do you?"

Angela huffed. "I can't believe you're so against the idea. Look what the man did for you. He saved Shadow's life! You owe him, Jane. You owe him big-time."

Jane shut her eyes and sighed. She did owe Cole big-time, just as Angela had reminded her. But spending so much time in close company with that man—with his smile, and his crinkly-eyed laugh, and that look he sometimes gave her that made tingles go up and down her spine—that struck her as a very bad idea. Very bad.

Why? she asked herself. So what if he was attractive? So what if her knees sometimes turned to water when he smiled at her? She was an adult. She could focus on what she needed to focus on and ignore such adolescent giddiness. Couldn't she?

Angela gave her a speculative look. "Okay, listen, Jane. Let's do it this way. I'll invite them to spend the night with us at a park here in Elko, while Cole is thinking over his options, you know? And we'll see how it goes. If it's a disaster, we're out of here tomorrow, and they can make their own way to do whatever they're going to do. But if things go all right, then we'll do the nice thing and suggest they come with us. Okay?"

Mixed feelings battled inside Jane's head. She owed the man. No doubt about it. And having him around for a while, day and night, certainly eliminated the possibility of boredom. But she could feel disaster in the near future.

"It's your motor home," Jane conceded. "But I reserve the right to a huge 'I told you so.' "

COLE SPRAWLED on the sofa of Angela's motor home, which now bore the name Enterprise, compliments of Teri, who was a fan of *Star Trek* reruns on the Sci Fi Channel. Teri wasn't too far off base with the name, Cole mused, looking around him. The Challenger was just about as big as the fictional starship, or so it seemed after traveling endless miles in Rumblestiltskin.

They were hooked into all the amenities at an RV park in Elko. The park had a pool, a shuffleboard court, and a clubhouse with ping-pong and board games, but so far none of them had the energy to take advantage of such luxuries. They simply sat under the blast of the air-conditioning and enjoyed the cool. Angela and Ernesto were in the bedroom with notes and outlines spread over the bed, discussing some point of production for Angela's agility series. Jane sat on the floor with Teri, who had wheedled her into a demonstration of teaching stupid pet tricks. And Cole simply sat on the sofa looking on, contemplating going to the fridge and grabbing some iced tea, but mostly not having enough energy to move.

He'd been grateful when Angela extended an invitation to spend the night in her motor home. She had hinted that a more encompassing invite might be in the offing, but he wasn't sure that accepting Angela's generosity would be a good idea. Mostly because this motor home, big as it seemed now, would quickly become very crowded with such a crew living in it. And also because he sensed resistance from Jane. He didn't blame her. This was her parade, and he had already rained on it a time or two.

Not that she could get rid of him that easily. Rumblestiltskin was gone—sold for peanuts, but still, peanuts was more than the rust bucket was worth. The dust of the day's disaster was beginning to settle, and Cole had time to regroup. He knew that he wouldn't allow their grand adventure to end this way. When he had explained to Teri that Rumblestiltskin had reached the end of the road, her face had fallen so far that he could have picked it up off the ground. He had pulled his daughter away from her home and pointed them both toward an unsettled future—with the best of intentions. But perhaps he hadn't realized how disconcerting so many changes could be for an eight-year-old. He had promised Teri a summer of seeing the country and going to agility trials, and he wasn't going to let a few mechanical problems get in the way of that promise.

It wasn't as if he didn't have plenty of money. They had just received a very good offer on the house in Albuquerque, and his business partner, Henry Mason, had bought him out of Southwest Computer Consulting at a very generous price. He could get another motor home. In fact, he'd already done some looking on the Internet, courtesy of the RV park's cable modem and his laptop computer. This time he would get a motor home that wouldn't strand them in the middle of nowhere. But Elko, Nevada, he had learned, wasn't the place to get the best deal on a good RV. If Angela offered them a chance to trundle on down the road in the Enterprise, then what harm would it do to take her up on the offer, at least until they got to a place where they could do some serious motor home shopping?

All the while these thoughts had occupied his mind, his eyes had been on Jane and Teri. Mostly on Jane. He liked the way her cropped hair shimmered when she leaned forward. "Shimmered" was a strange word, but that was what it did. He liked the freckles that seemed color-coordinated with the hair. He liked the way each fluid movement was a study in economy.

A giggle from Teri drew his attention to his daughter, who dangled a smidgen of hot dog in front of a hopeful Dobby. In her other hand she held out a quarter-inch dowel. "Touch, Dobby. Touch," she commanded.

Dobby squeaked in exasperation. The little furball didn't have a clue what the command meant.

"She doesn't understand you," Cole told Teri.

"I'm teaching her!" Teri explained. "Jane is showing me how to use a clicker."

A clicker was a training device that was all the rage. Cole didn't know how to use one. All he knew was that it was a thumb-sized little plastic box that would make a loud click when pressed.

"You could join us if you like," Jane invited. "New training techniques never hurt when you're trying for a steak and lobster dinner."

She had plenty of sass. Lord, but he did like her sass.

Teri frowned. "What?"

"It's an in-joke," Jane explained. "Just keep holding the dowel where Dobby can see it."

The little dog squeaked again and turned a frustrated little circle.

"She's never going to get it," Teri complained.

"Just let her figure it out. She'll get it."

Idaho lay beneath the dinette, ignoring such basic training with a superior air. But Shadow sat a couple of feet away, taking in the scene with an anxious look on his face. He shifted back and forth on his front paws.

"You stay out of this, Shadow," Jane warned. "Dobby has to do it on her own."

Finally, more by accident than anything else, Dobby's circles and feints brought her nose in contact with the dowel. Jane immediately clicked the clicker, and a delighted Teri gave the papillon the coveted piece of hot dog. Shadow woofed quietly.

"You'll get your turn," Jane promised.

"Now what?" Teri asked.

"Let her think about it. I can see lust for another piece of hot dog in her beady little eyes."

As Teri held out the dowel again, Cole got up from the sofa and moved to get a closer view.

Dobby began to jump up and down. She went to Jane, who ignored her. She bounced over to Cole, who repressed an urge to give the tiny dog a bit of sympathy. And she sidled up to Teri, who simply waved the dowel and commanded, "Touch it!"

Shadow whined, no doubt trying to give his friend a hint. Dobby looked thoughtful. She sniffed the floor. No response. She jumped up and down. No response. She paced back and forth, whining, and again happened to hit the dowel. *Click.* Hot dog.

Cole began to understand. Jane was marking the behavior she wanted with a click.

"Earlier we taught her to associate the click with a treat," Jane told him. "You can encourage any behavior you want with the clicker and put it on command."

"And touching a dowel is going to accomplish . . . ?

"It's just a basic exercise that teaches her the principle."

Dobby was beginning to understand, also. No dummy, that little dog. She pranced deliberately to the dowel and boinked it with her nose, earning another click, another treat.

Jane nodded approval. "The click is faster than a 'good girl' or 'attaboy,' so you can mark the exact moment the dog does what you want. It helps them learn faster."

Another boink. Another click. Another piece of hot dog.

"I'm surprised this hasn't been applied to training other creatures—like husbands."

Jane grinned wickedly. "Don't think it hasn't been. Even fish have been trained with similar methods. And if fish can learn, can men be far behind?"

Boink, click. Boink, click. Boink, click.

Teri giggled in delight. "Can we teach her something else?"

"We'd better," Jane agreed. "She's getting too good at this."

In a matter of minutes, Dobby learned to wave a paw, roll over, bow, pray—

"She's going to have to pray if she's going to make it to Solid Gold," Jane said in an aside to Cole.

"You wish," he replied in a low voice. "What would you think about a nice rack of lamb for my winner's dinner?"

Jane merely snorted. "You think you can afford it?"

Maybe, Cole mused, it was her orneriness that attracted him.

Poor Shadow, literally vibrating with the need to show off golden retriever talent, looked on while Teri applauded Dobby as a dog genius. Finally able to stand it no longer, he started doing each trick that Dobby did, waving when the little dog waved, praying when she prayed, and getting his feet caught beneath the dinette when he tried to roll over. The mouse-sized dog had an advantage when it came to doing tricks in the limited space of a motor home.

"Look at Shadow!" Teri exclaimed, clapping her hands. "We could have a contest!"

"That would hardly be fair to Dobby," Jane said. "Shadow knows tons of tricks. He's been working on his repertoire for a year or so."

Cole gave her a slow smile. "A challenge. Dobby loves a challenge."

Jane gave him a look. She had as many meaningful looks as Shadow had tricks. "Another dinner?" she inquired archly.

"We'll settle for the loser buying pizza."

Teri jumped for joy, rocking the motor home. Shadow barked. Dobby squeaked.

"Can Dobby afford pizza?" Jane asked.

"She'll hit me up for a loan. But she won't have to, because she's not going to lose."

And so the trick wars began. Teri made the rules. They would only use tricks that Shadow hadn't yet learned. Each dog would be timed on learning a new trick with the clicker. At the end of five tricks, the winner would be the dog who learned fastest.

"Papillons are very smart," Teri informed Jane. "I want a supreme pizza with the works."

"Don't count your pepperonis yet, kid," Jane warned.

And they were off. Dobby took ninety seconds to learn

how to turn in a circle on command. Shadow learned the same thing in a minute.

"He was watching Dobby," Cole objected. "Cheater!" But he had to laugh as he made the accusation.

Next round they reversed the order. Shadow learned the two-step in seventy-five seconds. Dobby trailed him with a time of eighty. Then Dobby caught on to counting to three with her paw in a mere forty seconds with the clicker, and Shadow needed a full minute to learn the same trick.

"You can tell her father is a mathematician," Cole said with a laugh.

"And Shadow's mom definitely isn't," Jane admitted.

Next, Shadow learned to pick up a toy and put it in the dog toy-box in the bedroom. Dobby learned just as quickly, but as the toy was almost as big as she was, it took her more time to drag it to the box. And in the final round, they both succeeded at opening one of the kitchen drawers—Shadow pawing open a middle drawer, Dobby pitting her fragile strength against a bottom one.

All through the contest, each dog watched the other with canine disdain, as if they knew their pride was at stake. Or maybe each simply wanted to have the victor's choice of what kind of pizza would be ordered. Idaho, representing the older canine generation, lay on the cool kitchen tile and simply watched, secure in the knowledge that a border collie could best both contestants by a mile.

By the time the fifth and last trick commenced, Angela and Ernesto had left their notes in the bedroom and had crowded around to watch, and Ernesto had fetched his camera. And Cole had laughed as hard as he had in years. Harder, maybe. By then he understood at least one reason he liked Jane. She added zest to his life, and to Teri's. The combination of Jane and Teri, Shadow and Dobby—it would never be easy, but neither would it be dull.

. . .

AS THE evening in Elko wound down, Jane had to admit that she quite unexpectedly was having a good time. Teri, aside from being a troublemaker, a chatterbox, and at times annoyingly perceptive, could get under a person's skin and inspire a kind of warmth. Probably nature designed kids that way as a defense mechanism, because otherwise few of the little pests would survive to adulthood. Plus, the kid had a way with dogs. Saying that Shadow talked to her carried things a bit far, but there was no denying that Teri communicated with the dogs in a way that was almost uncanny. Jane had possessed that ability when she was growing up. She still did, to a degree somewhat diluted by the realities of adulthood. Watching Teri was sometimes like rolling back time.

And then there was Cole. All evening Jane had felt his eyes upon her. When he laughed, bubbles rose inside her chest. When he smiled, her blood warmed. Jane told herself to stop that nonsense. She couldn't let a man distract her from the business at hand. Her priority had to be getting her life back in order. There was no time for any romantic silliness.

But still, the evening had been fun.

Sleeping arrangements, it turned out, were not as much fun. Jane let Cole have the sofa, which pulled out to be a supposedly queen-sized bed. The dining booth converted into a small bed that accommodated Teri, who fell asleep the minute she crawled into her sleeping bag. Dobby snored tiny snores beside Teri's head, and Shadow took whatever foot-room the bed afforded, which the kid didn't seem to mind at all. She curled into a fetal position between the comforting presence of two dogs.

Jane got stuck sleeping with Angela. The bed in the rear bedroom was big enough for both of them, certainly, but Angela, as always, had conversational energy that didn't easily dissipate. Even with lights out and the bedside clock showing hands straight up at midnight, she had to talk.

"This was fun tonight," she declared cheerily.

Though she had just been thinking the same, Jane merely grunted. Encouraging Angela to talk was never a good idea.

But Angela seldom needed encouragement. "I just don't understand what you have against Cole. I think he likes you. His eyes absolutely ate you up tonight."

The image sent an unwelcome tingle down Jane's spine.

"If some hunky, brainy guy like Cole looked at me that way, you can be sure I would look back."

Jane sighed. "I don't have anything against Cole. I like him just fine."

"Then why don't you loosen up and give him a smile or two?"

"I smile."

"You know what I mean. He's a very nice guy. Especially once you get to know him. I love a man who has brains as well as all the other stuff."

"All the other stuff?"

"You know. Pecs, biceps, shoulders, nice teeth."

"You're insane, Angela."

"Maybe, but sometimes a bit of insanity makes living more fun. You know?"

"No, I don't know. Listen, don't try to play matchmaker, okay? I don't have anything against Cole, but I don't have the time or desire to get involved with anyone. My two best friends just recently overdosed on love and romance, and they both got caught up in all sorts of drama and trauma before they got things sorted out. They're both happy enough now, I'll admit, but their priorities have totally changed, and their lives too. I like my priorities and life just the way they are." Jane paused for a single beat of uncertainty. "At least, I like the life I had, and I want to get it back. Which means I need to concentrate on business and win against the best agility dogs in the country. Including

Dobby. So how do you figure I have time to mess around with Dobby's owner?"

"That's got to be about the longest speech I've ever heard you give," Angela said, sounding awestruck. "And here we are supposed to be getting to sleep. Tomorrow's going to be a long day, you know."

Jane gritted her teeth in exasperation.

"So good night," Angela said cheerfully. "See you in the morning."

Finally Angela was silent. Jane lay in the dark, waiting for sleep to come, her mind wandering through the motor home to where Cole slept—or maybe didn't sleep. What did he wear to bed? she wondered. Pajamas? Boxer shorts? Nothing at all? Did he sleep on his back, his side, his stomach? Or perhaps like her, he struggled to bring the solace of sleep to an overactive mind.

Was it possible that he also lay in the dark with his mind wandering toward the bedroom, where Jane lay, thinking about him?

Nah! Jane decided. Give the guy credit for some brains. She was the only one idiot enough to do that.

chapter 15

NEXT MORNING, Jane woke in the gray dawn, wondering what had disturbed her. Idaho was curled on the bed at her feet, but the border collie was awake, his head raised and turned toward the bedroom door.

A small sound caught Jane's attention. A rustling. A little creaking. Alarm chased the fogginess of sleep from her mind, and she remembered that she and Angela no longer had the motor home to themselves at night. Teri was with them. And Teri's father. *Teri's father.*

Jane muttered a soft complaint and buried her head beneath her pillow. She really did not feel up to facing the day. But she was by habit an early riser. She could bury her head beneath ten pillows to insulate herself from the morning, but sleep wouldn't return. So she got up, moving carefully to avoid waking Angela, whose soft snores rumbled from the other side of the bed. Pulling sweatpants over bare legs and straightening the T-shirt that she'd slept in, she opened the bedroom door and stepped quietly into the narrow hallway, Idaho slipping like a black and white shadow behind her. In the dim light, she saw Cole sitting on the sofa tying the laces of his running shoes.

Cole spotted her immediately. He greeted her in a whisper. "Morning, Sunshine."

She made an inarticulate reply, not sounding much like sunshine. Teri still slept soundly, nearly buried in her sleeping bag, one hand fisted in the dark tangle of her hair. She had two dogs in attendance—Dobby on her pillow and Shadow curled on the sleeping bag at her feet.

Far be it from Jane to switch the kid to the on position, so she labored to be silent as she padded barefoot into the kitchen/living room area.

"Want to come jogging with me?" Cole invited in a low voice.

Jane almost said yes. It would feel good to inhale fresh air, enjoy the cool morning breeze, watch the sunrise with the blood pumping warmly through her body. And it wouldn't take all that much exercise to get the blood rushing, because Cole apparently intended to brave the road in nothing more than brief nylon shorts and running shoes. The sight of all that naked lean muscle—the broad shoulders, the nicely defined biceps, the washboard abs—made Jane swallow hard. No way was she going to subject her peace of mind to such a risk.

"Do I look like I jog?" she scoffed.

"You look like you do something to keep fit."

"Genes," she told him. "You go ahead. Are you taking Dobby?"

He laughed softly. "You kidding? Twinkle-toes Dobby?"

At the sound of her name, Dobby opened one disdainful eye, took in Cole's jogging outfit, and closed the eye again—firmly.

"The only exercise she enjoys is agility. Want me to take your dogs?"

Shadow had jumped from the foot of Teri's bed to join

Idaho. Both dogs sat staring at Jane, expectant looks on their faces.

"Will you make them behave?" Jane asked doubtfully.

"They'll be safe with me. I promise."

She hesitated. A self-confessed overprotective dog-mom, she never felt comfortable turning her children over to someone else.

"Come on," he urged. "Just because you're a couch potato doesn't mean they have to be."

"I'm not a couch potato."

He just grinned.

"Okay. Take the dogs. But watch out for broken glass. And snakes. Watch out for snakes."

"Yes, ma'am."

He left, and Jane actually suffered a pang of loneliness. It was the company of her dogs she missed, Jane told herself, not the company of the man.

Everyone else was sleeping, so Jane settled down on the sofa—lately Cole's bed—with a book, a paperback mystery she had bought in the grocery store in Carson City. It was a decent mystery, but Jane couldn't keep track of the plot twists because her attention jumped at any noise that might signal the return of Cole and her children. So what if her kids had fur? That didn't make them any less important.

And speaking of children, Teri didn't sleep long after her father made his exit. A few mumbles and groans led to thrashing, and the thrashing ended with a sleepy-eyed child sitting up and looking around her as if she didn't know where she was. For a moment Jane feared she would cry. She knew nothing about crying kids. Whining, anxiety-ridden dogs, fine. Weeping children, no.

But Teri didn't cry. She just wiped a hand across her face, looked down at a now alert Dobby, and said with a little-kid moan, "Is breakfast ready?"

"Only if you know how to cook," Jane replied.

Teri lifted a lip. Jane assumed that meant the same thing with kids as it did with dogs.

"My dad always makes me toast and oatmeal."

"And you don't know how to make it yourself?"

"I'm only eight years old," Teri reminded her.

"How are you ever going to take care of a dog if you can't fix your own oatmeal?"

The kid considered that for a moment, then compromised. "You could show me how. Then I would know how to do it, and we could surprise my dad."

That sounded reasonable.

"Where *is* my dad?" Teri asked, looking around with a frown.

"Jogging with Shadow and Idaho."

"You didn't go?"

Great. Now she had to explain her laziness to the child as well as the father. Teri made it sound as if jogging with her father was a treat no one should turn down.

"When I turn twelve, I get to go jogging with my dad. He says until then my bones are too little. Your bones aren't too little, though."

Jane sighed. "Let's see if we can find some oatmeal."

By the time Cole and the dogs returned, the dogs panting happily and Cole dripping sweat, Angela and Ernesto were both in the motor home, oatmeal bubbled on the stove, and bacon sizzled noisily in a skillet. Toast and cold orange juice waited on the table.

Cole gave Teri a kiss on top of her still-tousled head.

"I'm learning to cook," she boasted.

"Terrific." He took a deep, satisfied sniff of the inviting aroma. "Did you make enough for your old dad?"

Teri giggled. "Of course we did!"

Jane wondered if there was anything more appealing than a grown man who wore his heart on his sleeve for his kid. Not that Cole had a sleeve right then. Or a shirt. Or trousers either, for that matter. And who knew that sweat could look so sexy?

He grinned at Jane over Teri's head. "Your dogs protected me from every bird, bug, and rabbit along the path."

"Of course they did. They know their job."

Both dogs noisily lapped from the water bowl by the door. Jane was inordinately happy to see them. And maybe her rising spirits owed a bit to Cole, as well.

This just had to end.

Dobby greeted the group's return by jumping up and down, dividing her attention between Cole, Idaho, and Shadow. Idaho was politely aloof, being the self-appointed canine chaperone that he was. Shadow, however, bowed in delight and took off down the length of the motor home in an invitation to play. Dobby squeaked out a bark, then jumped into Cole's arms for shelter, apparently withdrawing her overture.

Cole laughed. "Sorry, big fella," he said to Shadow, who looked back in confusion. "She's a typical female. Giving out the come-hithers and then turning coy."

"That is not typical female," Jane objected. "Some females just know when to be cautious. Dobby knows she's out of her league."

"Dobby's in a league of her own," Cole replied. "Just like some others I could name."

Jane merely sniffed and dished herself out a bowl of oatmeal. Cole laughed and deposited Dobby back on her pillow. "I'm going to shower before I drive everyone out of here," he said. "Then, just because you guys worked so hard cooking, I'll do the dishes."

"Done deal," Angela said. "It's a pleasure to know a man who doesn't expect to be waited upon." She raised a brow in Jane's direction.

Jane simply rolled her eyes.

Teri inhaled two servings of oatmeal and bacon, then wheeled Ernesto into showing her his video equipment.

"It's not the kind of machine you watch rented movies on, if that's what you're thinking," Ernesto warned, then looked thoughtful. "Though I guess you could."

"I have a player to watch movies," Teri informed him. "I want to see how to make a movie. Angela said that's what you do in your van."

"Going to be a producer like Angela?" Ernesto grinned as Teri preceded him down the steps, then flashed a look back at Angela and Jane. "Good thing I stuffed my dirty underwear out of sight under the cot this morning. Didn't know I was going to have a lady visitor."

"Isn't this nice?" Angela commented once Teri was out of earshot. "Such a well-behaved little girl. And Cole couldn't be a nicer guy. Doesn't complain. Willing to help out."

Jane gave her a look. Angela ignored it.

"Last night was fun, wasn't it? Sometimes it's a good thing to have people around. And it makes an interesting twist to the series. Here we are traveling with the very guy who might keep you out of the Invitational."

"Thank you for pointing that out."

"It adds to the drama."

"It adds to the complications," Jane insisted. "Listen, Cole is a nice guy." *Not to mention a hunk.* "And Teri is very cute." *Precocious, sometimes annoying, but cute.* "But this isn't a good idea. There's no reason Cole can't get another vehicle in time to make the Casper trial."

Angela scoffed. "This is no place to get a good deal on a motor home."

"Then he can rent a car and go to Denver."

"But it's much more fun this way," Angela said, spreading her hands wide in a sweeping gesture that took in the crush of luggage, the pile of dirty dishes, Cole's size-twelve—at least!—running shoes parked outside the bathroom door.

Just then the shoes' owner came out of the bathroom,

wearing cutoffs, sandals, and not much more. His damp hair lay in wet, careless waves. White teeth emerged in an engaging grin. If Jane had seen that face, that torso, that heart-softening grin on a movie poster, she would have bought out the theater.

He picked up his shoes—a very unusual gesture for any male, according to Jane's friends—and squeezed himself through the tiny hallway toward the aroma of bacon and oatmeal.

"You saved me the dishes. Good. Did you save me some food as well?"

Jane felt as if a truck were bearing down upon her, so clearly could she see trouble coming down the road. But the Enterprise was Angela's ship, and the captain got to make the calls.

"Sit down, sit down," Angela invited Cole. Her eyes twinkled. "I have a proposition for you."

Some perverse corner of Jane's mind was glad.

FROM THE eastern Nevada border, Interstate 80 ran straight as an arrow across the Great Salt Lake Desert toward the Wasatch Mountains and Salt Lake City. The desert was flat and barren. Only the hardiest plants and animals could survive there. The formidable Wasatch Range, the backbone of Utah, first appeared as a faint shadow on the eastern horizon. Slowly the shadow resolved into serrated peaks stabbing upward into the sky, and the farther east the motor home rolled, the higher the mountains appeared.

"Wow!" was Teri's comment, watching from the front passenger seat. "I thought the mountains at home were really, really big. But these mountains are stupendous."

Fixing sandwiches at the kitchen counter, swaying with the road rhythm, Jane smiled. She had to admit that she also was impressed with the harsh extremes of Utah—the salt flats, blinding white in the sun, the brilliant blue sky, and ahead, the jagged upthrust of mountains. She had never ventured into this part of the West.

"And home is...?" Angela prompted from the driver's seat.

"It was Albuquerque," Teri replied. "And Albuquerque has the big Sandia Mountains. They're nice mountains, but not like these."

"These are big, all right."

"And Albuquerque isn't home anymore," Teri went on. "We don't have a home."

Cole, stretched out on the sofa, looked up from the book he was reading. "Teri, we do so have a home. Wherever you and I are together is home, and come fall, we'll have a house to go with it."

"A big house!" Teri declared.

"Maybe."

"With a swimming pool."

"That's asking a lot."

"And I'll have my own room."

"Of course."

"With my own TV."

"Not in this lifetime."

"And a golden retriever like Shadow."

Cole rolled his eyes heavenward. Not for the first time in this initial day of their combined journey did Jane contemplate the trials of parenthood—twenty-four hours a day, seven days a week, 365 days a year. How Cole kept his patience was beyond her.

Teri accepted the defeat with her own eye-roll, then returned to "entertaining" them all with facts and figures from the travel guide on her lap—something she had been doing since they left Elko early that morning. Jane now knew more about Nevada and Utah than she had ever wanted to know.

"Utah is most famous for the Great Salt Lake," she read,

then frowned. "So why is Utah called the Beehive State, Daddy?"

"Don't know," he said without looking up from his book. "You're the one with the travel brochures."

"Hm," she said noncommittally. "Okay. It says here the Great Salt Lake is really big. But it gets smaller and bigger. Depends on how much water is in it."

Jane couldn't stifle a yawn.

"It used to be named Lake Bonneville, back in pre... pre..." She showed the word to Angela, pointing with a somewhat sticky finger (they all had been eating ice cream sandwiches as a prelude to lunch).

Angela darted a quick look, then turned her attention back to the road. "Prehistoric," she told the little girl. "It means before history."

"You mean in caveman times?"

"Exactly."

"All right, then. The cavemen must have named it Lake Bonneville, and it was ten times bigger then."

"Astounding," Angela said with a grin.

"And now it's really salty. More salty than the ocean. Why is that, Angela?"

"I don't have a clue."

"Jane?"

"You got me, kid."

She appealed to her father as a last resort. "Daddy?"

Cole put down his book. "It's so salty because water comes in but doesn't have a way out. When the water evaporates in the hot sun, it leaves salt behind. And the more that it evaporates, the saltier it gets."

Teri thought on that awhile, then nodded. "Okay."

"You know what 'evaporate' means?" Cole asked.

"Sure I do. Like when a puddle gets smaller, then maybe goes away. Will the lake ever go away?"

"Maybe some day a long time from now."

"Can we go see it first?"

"You'll have to ask Angela, sweet pea. This is her buggy. She says where we go and what we do."

Teri turned pleading eyes on Angela. Jane had to admire the kid's acting ability. The eyes alone would have melted stone, even without the polite "Pretty please, Angela."

Angela groaned. "This is why I'm not a mother. I'm such a sucker."

THE GREAT Salt Lake was great indeed, as they saw when they got close enough to see it from the road. The lake was so big, Teri now informed them in an officious voice, that it had ten whole islands. And on one of those islands—the biggest one—was Antelope Island State Park. The Utah travel guide promised white sand beaches, beautiful sunrises and sunsets, interesting wildlife, and RV camping. It was the last that won over Angela at the end of a long day's drive.

"Just give me a water hookup for the motor home so I can take a decent hot shower," Angela said with a sigh.

Jane silently agreed, except that what she wanted even more than a shower was a long walk with her dogs to stretch her legs and get off by herself. For a person who had always cherished her own private space, she was spending a lot of time cooped up with others.

They discovered later that Antelope Island State Park was a great place for Jane to walk her dogs and for Cole to jog, but not so great in the shower department. The campground had water available, but no water hookups for the motor home. And no electrical hookup or sewer. The motor home was self-contained with a full tank of water, but that tank would only support skimpy camp showers.

Fortunately for Teri, the hour was too late and everyone was too tired to consider going elsewhere. Teri was ecstatic, because just five minutes away was a swimming beach, and from their camping space they could see white sails dotting the lake.

Jane shared Teri's delight. The primitive, sparsely populated surroundings—scarcely anyone was in the campground—were welcome after too many days spent on crowded highways, full-to-the-last-space RV parks, and frantic agility trials. Jane had always enjoyed the crowds and bustle of performance trials, both obedience and agility, but then again, she had always been able to recover in the solitude of her home.

"Can we go to the beach?" Teri begged her father once they had the motor home leveled, the awning unfurled, the chairs and the exercise pens set up. "Please! I want to swim in the salt water."

"Teri, it would be going on dark before you got your suit on and we got down there. Angela said we could spend tomorrow here, and maybe the next day, too. You'll have plenty of time to swim."

Her mutinous whine died almost before it began, killed by a sharp look from Cole.

"Why don't you go help Angela with dinner?" Cole suggested. "Jane and I are going to take the dogs on a walk."

"Can I go?"

"Not this time. We're just going a little way, then we'll be back to help with dinner. Later maybe Ernesto will play cribbage with you. Maybe he would even teach me."

That cheered her up. She trotted away toward the motor home.

Jane smiled and shook her head. "No wonder you're a good dog trainer. You practiced on Teri."

He grinned. "Dobby is a lot easier."

"It's a good thing I never got married. I would have made a lousy mother."

"Why do you think that? I think you would make an excellent mother," he told her. "You'd be the same kind of mother to kids that you are to your dogs."

She made a rude sound. "Kids are harder than dogs. I'd be in a constant state of frustration."

"You'd be joining a big group," he told her. "Frustration's a big part of parenthood."

He bent down to lift Dobby from her exercise pen. Jane remembered being caught in a similar position not too long ago, with her backside presented foremost and the rest of her swallowed by the motor home. She bit down hard to keep from making a comment. Cole's backside topped hers by a mile, in her opinion.

Not that she'd ever really seen her own backside from this point of view. But Cole's backside was fine, superior to most any other backside she'd seen. It must be all that jogging.

He straightened, bringing the little papillon with him, and caught Jane in mid stare. She had the grace to color up, and he gave her a quizzical look. "What?"

"Nothing."

But his smile hinted that he knew exactly what she'd been staring at. To hide her embarrassment, she turned toward her own dogs, opening their pen and snapping a leash on each collar. "You want to stretch your legs, boys? Come on, then. We'll see what this island has to offer."

They strolled together on a path that led away from the campground. Once they had left the few other campsites behind, they unsnapped the leashes and let the dogs bounce through the scrub and sand. Shadow and Dobby chased each other up the path, Dobby yapping, Shadow prancing joyfully. Idaho circled them both, supervising.

"Dobby's not at all intimidated by bigger dogs, is she?" Jane noted.

The papillon feinted toward Shadow to deliver a rebuke for the bigger dog's boisterous advances.

"Dobby isn't intimidated by anything," Cole said. "She thinks she's queen of the world."

"Must be nice to have that kind of confidence."

At the crest of a small hill, they discovered that Antelope Island did indeed have spectacular sunsets. Glowing orange streaked the sky to the west, and to the east, the Wasatch Range basked in the reflected glow. Even the dogs quieted, seeming to appreciate Nature's show.

Cole lowered himself to the ground and sat cross-legged on the sand. "What do you have against marriage?" he asked abruptly.

Cole was almost as good at the non sequitur as Angela, Jane thought.

"If it's not too nosy of me."

Jane shrugged. "I don't have anything against marriage." She gave him a half smile. "Or even against men. But being single has a lot of advantages." Not that she hadn't wondered lately ... No, she definitely wasn't going to go there.

Folding herself to sit beside him, Jane rested her chin on her hands and gazed at the brilliant colors glowing in the sky. This was too different from her normal life. Her home, her normal routine, her everyday habits—all gone. Without them she didn't feel like herself, found her mind straying into strange areas, her heart subject to strange emotions. Nothing seemed set any longer—neither the present nor the future, not her ideas of what she liked and disliked, what she should do and not do. Here she was sitting with a guy watching a sunset, feeling all squishy inside. How unlikely was that? Jane Connor, Amazon of the Bark Park, did not get squishy for anything other than dogs, cats, and maybe an occasional friend or two.

But those friends didn't make her want to lean in close so she could feel the warmth coming off their skin. And those friends didn't make her wonder at the sight of hands so close to hers, splayed in the sand. Cole had nice hands. They made Jane's look almost small and feminine.

"Not every person in the world needs to go the couples route," she insisted.

"Of course not," he agreed.

"It makes life complicated."

"Yeah. Tell me about it."

"Especially when kids get involved . . ."

"You have a point. Kids can be a problem."

Who was she trying to convince? Jane wondered. Cole? Or herself? And why the hell were they having this conversation anyway? Cole Forrest, major hunk, father, competitor, could not be truly interested in Jane Connor. They were as different as oil and water.

The colors of the sunset had deepened. Shadow and Dobby, having worn themselves out pouncing on bugs and chasing after each other, lay panting at Jane's and Cole's feet. Idaho sat watching them all, alert to any need of border collie expertise.

Jane scarcely saw the sunset. Her eyes were on the sky, but her attention was on the man sitting beside her.

"It's been a long day," Cole said, stretching his arms over his head and then letting one arm drop around Jane's shoulders in the classic casual First Move.

It was so staged that Jane had to laugh. "What are you doing?"

"Oops!" he said. But somehow Jane landed on her back in the sand with Cole beside her.

Shadow barked, making Dobby jump from her comfortable nest in the sand. The tiny dog turned circles to get settled again, then chided her big noisy friend with a glare. Idaho watched with indulgent interest, secure in his own sense of superiority.

Jane laughed again, at the dogs this time, but her laughter died away when Cole propped himself on one elbow and leaned above her. His other hand landed on the sand on her other side, effectively caging her, a position that made her heart beat faster and started butterflies winging around her stomach.

"What *are* you doing?"

He seemed to consider thoughtfully. "I was thinking of kissing you."

"You've got to be kidding."

"Why would I be kidding?"

"I . . . I'm . . ." She was about to say that she wasn't exactly kissing material, but suddenly, unexpectedly, she wanted to be kissing material.

Not that Jane had never been kissed. Of course she had. But what little kissing Jane had tried made her suspect that the romance of The Kiss was much ado about nothing. She was curious, though, about how Cole Forrest might compare. In fact, she admitted to herself that she had been curious since she had first laid eyes upon the man.

Still, it was awkward, lying there on the ground with Cole looming over her, the dogs watching avidly, and only the sound of the lakeshore breeze breaking the silence.

"Well, go ahead and get it over with if you're going to!" Jane instantly wished she could kick herself. Would she ever learn to think?

Her embarrassment was cut short by Cole, who did exactly as she'd suggested. Jane stiffened just a bit when his mouth first covered hers, but the unexpectedly pleasant sensation of that intimate touch instantly softened her whole body. Cole's kiss was no sloppy, drooly experiment, no hurried clench behind a school cafeteria. No pawing, grabbing battle on the steps of her college dormitory. No duty peck after a failed blind date.

No indeed. This kiss topped the mark of anything Jane had experienced so far, and she speculated that it might be the apex of her lifetime kissing experience. Cole hit just the right mixture of gentle persuasion and aggressive coercion. His lips performed the miracle of being soft at the same time they were delightfully firm. His weight pressed her against the warm ground, heavy enough to make her feel secure, but not heavy enough to cause discomfort.

Jane felt as though she were melting into the sand, happily oblivious to anything else in the universe except the man whose mouth moved over hers and whose arms held her such willing prisoner. Her own arms moved to wrap around him, at first tentatively, then with more confidence. Beneath her roaming hands, his back was comfortingly broad and solid. The black, crisp hair that feathered along his collar slipped softly through her fingers. The warm skin of his neck, the evening bristles that roughened his cheek—her hands suddenly wanted to explore everywhere as she drowned in wonderful sensation.

Then something wet and cold thrust into her ear, and an indignant, high-pitched yap nearly burst her eardrum. The magic dissolved. Cole's weight lifted, his mouth deserted hers, and cool evening air rushed between them, raising goose bumps on Jane's heated skin. She opened her eyes to a sky gone dusky and Cole's face wearing a half-startled, half-bemused expression that reflected her feelings almost exactly. Except it left out dismay. Dobby continued her jealous yapping, and Jane's two dogs looked curiously embarrassed.

Jane let her head drop back onto the sand, rolled her eyes heavenward, and uttered the phrase that so many women think after being thoroughly and unexpectedly kissed. "Oh, shit!"

SITTING ON the scraggly grass, Cole watched Jane march back toward the campground, Shadow and Idaho in tow, her every footfall digging a little crater of agitation into the sand. She disappeared below the crest of the hill, and he dropped back onto the sand, groaning. Then the groan turned to laughter.

"Great move, Romeo! You really impressed her!"

The laughter died away. He closed his eyes, then opened them again, staring up at the stars that had started to appear in the sky. Spread-eagled on the rapidly cooling ground, with the stars brightening above him and the lake breeze playing over his skin, he felt a smile spread across his face. He couldn't help it. That smile spread all by itself.

The truth was, the kiss—that amazing kiss—had been a doozy. He hadn't felt a jolt like that for . . . well, almost too long to remember.

And, in spite of Jane's less-than-romantic reaction, he had a feeling it had impressed her as well. Knocked the socks right off her, in fact. An expletive wasn't exactly what a man wanted to hear after he'd just made his move, but that choked-out "Oh, shit!" at least meant he'd made an impression. So did the blushing, inarticulate sputtering, the chaotic confusion in those green eyes, and the indignant little huff that had preceded her hurried exit. He'd never before seen Jane Connor at a total loss for words.

That had to be a good sign, he mused. And the smile still didn't go away.

chapter 16

TERI SAT on a towel. Not that sitting on a towel made any difference. Her damp swimsuit was full of sand, and that sand grated and itched in the most uncomfortable places. And that wasn't the worst of it. She felt sticky. And every little scrape and mosquito bite on her skin stung like fire. Everywhere the lake water had touched her, she wore a crust of salt.

The beach was pretty, and so was the lake, but swimming in this big salty lake wasn't anything like swimming in a pool on a hot day in Albuquerque. When they had first gotten to the beach that morning, Teri had thought the salt water was fun, because she floated really well and didn't have to work as hard to keep her head above water. But then she had gotten salt water in her eyes. That wasn't fun. And sand in her suit. Yuk. And when she got out of the water, she felt all sticky.

So she sat on a towel, watching Shadow and Idaho play in the little wavelets at the water's edge. Watching Ernie— he had said that she could call him Ernie if she wanted— point his camera. Watching Angela lie on her towel and do nothing. She just lay there with her eyes shut, not moving or anything. Not even talking, and that was weird for Angela. When Teri had asked her why she was just lying there, Angela had told her she was "soaking up rays, honey." Whatever that was. It looked really boring.

"Hey, sweet pea!" Her dad dropped down beside her on the sand. He didn't seem to care about sand in his suit. "Tired of swimming, eh?"

"Yeah."

"You sound tired."

She wasn't tired. But this whole beach thing was disappointing. She sighed. "I'm not really tired."

"You want to play Frisbee, then? That's tradition on a beach, you know."

She sighed. "No."

He pointed to Jane, who had started to play a game with Shadow and Idaho. "Jane's playing Frisbee. It looks like she's having fun."

The Frisbee sailed upward on the breeze, curving in a graceful arc above the ground—until Idaho made a spectacular leap to snatch it from its flight. Shadow looked puzzled, the question plain on his face: *How did he do that?*

"That's a dog game," Teri pointed out.

"People can play Frisbee, too. I could teach you how to throw it."

"No, thank you," Teri said in a polite voice. "I'll just watch for a while."

Her dad looked disappointed. "Okay. You stay where I can see you. We'll be going back to the campground pretty soon."

He left. Teri was sorry he was unhappy about her not wanting to play that dumb game with him, but it looked pretty lame, unless you were a dog. She wasn't real pleased with her dad right then, anyway. He and Jane were both acting funny. Funny peculiar, not funny ha-ha. Ever since they had come back from walking the dogs before last night's dinner, they were acting like weirdos. They gave each other strange looks, real quick like, and if one of them caught the other looking, they both looked as if somebody had pinched them. And they weren't saying much to each other, but you could feel something really odd in the air when they were both in the same place.

Teri knew that something was going on between Jane and her dad. After all, she wasn't born yesterday. Plus she knew that people got real peculiar right before they started smooching and mooning over each other and all that stuff. All the TV shows and movies showed that.

The thought of her dad maybe getting moony over Jane gave Teri a stomachache. Her dad still loved her mom, even if she was up in heaven. She didn't want her mom's feelings hurt. Yet the thought kept returning, the thought that having Jane around might be fun. Jane and Shadow and Idaho. And Jane would get Teri a dog like Shadow. A real dog. Not like Dobby, who had insisted upon staying in the motor home to nap on her pillow. Real dogs played Frisbee and chased waves at the lakeshore.

But Teri couldn't have another mother. And her dad shouldn't be liking any ladies other than Teri's mom. That's what Teri had decided. So when she saw Jane and her dad acting funny, she felt as if someone was playing tug inside her tummy. Even right then her dad had this strange look on his face as he watched Jane play with the dogs. It didn't matter that Jane looked every direction but at her dad. Romantic ladies always got huffy and standoffish before falling into their lover's arms. That was just how things worked.

Teri wondered if she could manage to get Jane on her side about getting her very own golden retriever, even while she had to show both Jane and her dad that she didn't like them acting this way. Probably not, she decided. She didn't think she could manage to sulk and suck up at the same time. That's what the boys at school called it when a kid acted nice to a grown-up in order to get something. Suck up. It sounded nasty. And with her dad, sucking up didn't really work.

It might with Jane, though. But there was still the problem of really needing to sulk about Jane and her dad getting ready to fall in love.

Life certainly was complicated.

JANE FLIPPED the Frisbee high in air and enjoyed the thrill of watching her dogs take off at a dead run, racing to be the first to grab it. Idaho would win, of course. Built for speed and agility, he painted a black and white streak down the beach, speeding to get under his target as it began to drop. Shadow had the advantage of youth, but fit as he was, his build was heavier, his stride shorter. He was fast, but not nearly as fast as Idaho.

Idaho launched himself into the air, snatched the Frisbee, and landed on his feet with the grace of a dancer. Casting a triumphant look toward Shadow, he trotted back to Jane and presented her with his prize.

How many weeks had passed, Jane wondered, since she had played with her dogs? Since she had seen them run and leap with the joy of being alive? Too many weeks, she decided. Too long. How had she forgotten the delight of being together like this?

Both dogs looked up at her expectantly, tongues lolling, bodies vibrating with anticipation. "Aren't you tired yet?" she asked, laughing.

Shadow whined, a clear answer that he was never too tired to play chase.

"Okay. Here goes." She launched the Frisbee into the air, and both dogs raced off.

The only thing that kept this morning from being perfect was the feel of Cole's eyes upon her. Jane had felt his gentle perusal every moment since the night before, even when he wasn't really looking at her. He must be sending out some kind of radar, she mused. Because even now, when he was swimming in the lake and couldn't possibly be watching her, Jane still felt the weight of his regard.

She could hardly complain, though, because her eyes kept straying his way as well, as much as Jane tried to keep them to herself. Even late last night when she had diligently tried to sleep, that kiss had glowed in her mind, keeping her awake, keeping her wondering, speculating, remembering. She had felt his presence on the sofa, fifteen feet away, as if he were lying next to her. As if she could reach out and touch him with her hand instead of just with her thoughts.

Criminy! Could this get more awkward?

They were acting like thirteen-year-old hormonal idiots, Jane admitted. Mostly, *she* was acting like a hormonal idiot. Last night's kiss had simply plowed through her senses and erased any pretensions she had to maturity.

Idaho strutted up to her with the Frisbee in his mouth. Shadow followed behind, soft brown eyes telling Jane that he really would like a head start next time the Frisbee flew.

"Got to be a level playing field, buddy," Jane told the golden retriever. "Winner take all." Just like the Solid Gold Invitational.

She flipped the toy into the air, and the dogs took off yet again.

Winner take all. Wasn't that what she and Cole had agreed in making that stupid bet? An instant of suspicion made her scowl. What were the odds that the man was trying to sabotage her game? Maybe he just wanted her so distracted and brain-fried that she would stumble all over herself in the agility ring.

A split second after the thought entered her head, she dismissed it. Cole wasn't the type to win by cheating. *Grow up*, she told herself. Her preoccupation with one little kiss was just plain silly. Cole had probably all but forgotten it by now. Most likely her overheated imagination made him seem to be following her with his eyes, regarding her with something more than his usual amiable warmth.

With sudden determination to act like a mature adult, Jane turned on her heel and walked in Cole's direction, trying to make her stride casual and unhurried, as if she just happened to be wandering his way as he emerged from the lake and reached for the towel he'd hung over the back of a folding chair.

"Hi," she said, using every ounce of courage.

He looked up, pausing in the process of drying himself. "Hi," he replied with a smile. "Idaho is quite a Frisbee player."

"Yeah. He's great at it."

He finished toweling the salt water from his torso. Jane tried not to stare as the towel caressed firm muscles, broad shoulders, trim abs. The only way she could manage it was to shift her gaze down to the white, glaring sand—not nearly as interesting a view. But she was trying to reestablish a normal relationship here, and that wasn't going to happen if she started drooling over the guy.

"Have a seat," he offered, nodding toward the chair.

"Nah. I just came over to...to..." Damn! Why hadn't she thought of a plausible reason to come over here?

But Cole didn't seem the least self-conscious. With a grin he spread the damp towel on the sand, sat down on it, and patted the towel beside him. It wouldn't do to be rude, Jane told herself, so she sat, gingerly, as far away from temptation as possible without sitting on the sand.

"Jane. About last night..."

She braced herself.

"If I stepped over the line, I apologize. I didn't mean to go where I wasn't welcome, and maybe I wasn't reading the signals right. I sure didn't mean any offense."

Jane tried for a bland answer, but her tongue tied itself in knots. She grimaced, clenched her teeth, looked at the sky, and labored to get a grip. Honesty, she reminded herself, was always the easiest.

"You didn't...there wasn't any..." She sighed, closed her eyes, and shook her head. "There wasn't any offense. That...well, that..."

"Kiss?" The dark chocolate eyes crinkled, with what? Amusement? Damn him!

"Kiss," she agreed, her voice growing more firm. "That kiss was...well...I didn't exactly fight you off, did I?"

A smile twitched his mouth. "Not that I remember, no."

That mouth. Cripes! She was never going to forget that mouth.

"It wasn't all your fault," she conceded.

His laugh lines deepened. "Good to know."

"Maybe...I guess I might have been a little bit curious about how it would feel to kiss you."

He nodded understanding. But damned if he didn't look as if he was going to break out laughing. "Did I satisfy your curiosity?"

"Sure thing."

"Well, good then."

"Two adults can kiss without it being a big deal, right?"

"I suppose that can happen," he said. "Then again, sometimes when two adults kiss, it does turn out to be a big deal."

Intriguing. Did Cole think their kiss was something more than a casual, almost accidental encounter? But that particular ground was full of pitfalls. "Teri's over there shooting black looks our way," she said, attempting to steer away from dangerous territory.

Cole glanced toward his daughter. "Teri has some kind of burr under her saddle today. Indulging in the classic sulk. She generally gets over it on her own."

A moment of silence, an inaudible shift of conversational gears.

"But back to last night," Cole began.

Jane didn't want to go back to last night.

But he continued, "I have to confess that I'd been plotting and strategizing about that kiss for a while before it happened."

"Really?" That caught her off guard.

"Yup. I confess. Guilty of plotting and careful consideration. When a guy has a family to consider, casual playing around just isn't an option. You have to be careful who you might bring into the mix."

Jane's heartbeat started to speed with a strange mixture of dismay and elation. Was she getting seriously hit on? Her? Plain Jane Connor?

No. Cole couldn't be serious. Besides, she didn't have time to get involved. And she didn't have the know-how to do romance. Give her a pissed-off Doberman pinscher to handle, and she would be fine. Sit her down with a man who was looking at her like Cole Forrest was looking at her, and she was going to get mangled.

Jane had to put an end to this before she got really tempted.

"Listen, Cole."

He leaned back, resting on his elbows in the sand and regarding her seriously. "I'm listening."

"I'll bet you have women panting for your attention."

He didn't deny it, which inspired a totally irrational twist of jealousy in Jane's stomach.

"Because," she continued, "look at you. You're a hunk."

"I am?" He grinned, as if the compliment took him unaware.

"Like you don't know. Give me a break. You're a major hunk, smart, nice, single, and a great kisser. What woman could resist?"

"A great kisser? I'll have to put that on my resumé." The laugh lines around his eyes were deepening again.

"Be serious, will you?" Jane couldn't look at him, or she might falter. So she stared at the sand. "Cole, before anything else gets said here, I have to tell you: you're out of my league. I've always been rotten at dating and all that. On the shelf, so to speak, and liking it there."

He was silent for a moment, staring out over the lake. Then, still looking into the distance, he said, "You know, I was happily married for seven years, and since Mandy died, I haven't gotten into the singles scene. Jane, I don't want to play games. I simply like you. I think you're intriguing, attractive, not to mention kind, smart, funny, and courageous. And oh yeah, you're not a bad kisser yourself."

Such a list of unexpected virtues dumbfounded her. "I'm a good kisser?"

"We could try again," he said with a grin, "and I could prove my point."

A totally out-of-control thrill vibrated through Jane at the thought. She struggled to retrieve her resolve. "You didn't hear a thing I said."

"Sure I did. You think I'm a major hunk and a good kisser. I think you're terrific and a good kisser. From the sound of that, this relationship has gotten off to a great start."

"I don't have time for these games!"

"Jane, I'm not playing games."

"That's what scares me! I don't have time for the distraction. And let me tell you, Cole, you're one major distraction. Any other time...maybe, well..." She refused to think about maybes. "I *have* to get to Solid Gold. I *have* to deal with Angela and her stupid canine version of *Survivor*. I *have* to concentrate! And you're the competition, dammit! How can I be kissing the competition one minute and wiping up the agility ring with him the next?"

"Jane, you and I are not a game. Agility is a game, a

hobby. It's not the most important thing in life. It's not something that should determine the course of a relationship between a man and a woman."

A relationship? He was talking relationship? He didn't understand. Of course he didn't. She had never told him that she needed the Invitational purse to rebuild her life. He would have assumed that insurance would be taking care of the damage she had suffered.

And she wasn't about to tell him now. If she did, how would she know if the next time she beat him, he hadn't pulled up just a little short to give her an advantage?

So she simply reiterated. "I don't have time for this. My relationships with my dogs can be complicated enough. I can't handle a relationship with a guy."

He was silent for a moment. His smile had faded, but the corner of his mouth twitched wryly. "Okay. I guess I can understand that. For now, we'll be friends. A person can't have too many friends."

Jane stifled a bit of disappointment. He could have fought harder.

"Right," she agreed, pasting a smile on her lips. "We'll be friends. You're a great guy, Cole. Questionable taste in dogs," she said, with a slightly quavering grin. "But a great guy."

Before he could reply, she pushed herself to her feet and made a hasty exit. She felt the weight of his eyes on her back, but she didn't turn around. Teri watched also, Jane noted from the corner of her eye. That kid sometimes looked years older than eight.

THREE DAYS later, Angela sat in a folding chair at ringside, watching her star get ready to do her thing. She should get a dog, Angela mused. She could have Jane train it in agility, and Angela would take it through its paces in the ring and gather all the kudos. That would surely be enough exercise to take a few inches off her hips and let her fit into a size eight. So many styles looked cute in size eight and frumpy in size twelve.

An Airedale and his disgustingly petite handler exited the ring. Angela made a face. That Airedale woman had to tip her scales at no more than one-ten. Some women just had all the right genes. Jane had her head turned toward the timer, waiting for the go-ahead. Ernesto already had his camera grinding away. On the other side of the ring, Cole never took his eyes from Jane. And Teri's face looked like she'd just eaten a sour pickle.

There was a story—Teri, the motherless little girl who was watching her dad fall for another woman. Too bad Angela drew the line at exploiting children. She didn't cavil at using Jane and Cole, but someone had to give a kid a break.

"Hello there! I wondered if you and Jane would be here."

Angela's heart jumped into her throat as she recognized the voice. She turned, smiling. "Well, if it isn't our Doctor of Dog."

"The very same," Rick Tolleson acknowledged.

"I didn't see your booth in with the other vendors."

"I just got set up. Got here late because I had to swing by Denver and smooth things over for my nephew."

"The young man who was working in your booth in Carson City?"

"Yeah. The string bean. Nice kid, but not great with customers. And after I had to set a bone on a Great Dane, he decided he couldn't take it any longer."

"The Dane's pain and misery really got to him, eh?"

"Hell no. The Dane was anaesthetized. The handler's pain and misery was what bothered him. The boy's got no stomach for veterinary work, not to mention he couldn't sell water to a man dying of thirst. He took a bus back home before Sunday's trial was over. My sister wasn't pleased."

"Didn't want him back, eh?"

"Wants him to learn to stick with things. What she doesn't realize is that boys that age don't. Their minds are as scattered as their hormones."

Angela raised a brow. "That's a fair description of most men I know."

Rick laughed. "Glory be, a woman with attitude!"

She gave him a smile. "Present company excepted, of course. You must be lonely now, without your nephew for company."

"Sweetheart, believe me, good company is not exactly what I'd call a restless seventeen-year-old boy." He gave her a look that sent a pulse of warmth into her veins. "Not that I don't get a craving for company now and then. My idea of perfect company runs more to"—he gave her a quick but thorough once-over—"female, thirtyish, five foot three and maybe—"

"Stop!" Angela warned him. "If you even guess at the weight, you're toast."

"Angie, sweetheart, tell me right now that you're not one of those anorexic model wannabes who live on lettuce and obsess over the scale, because you're much too gorgeous to not appreciate yourself just the way you are."

For once in her life, Angela was stunned into silence. Rick looked down at her with a smile that was positively lustful, and it started her heart pumping double-time and made her knees turn to water.

The rush of sensation pulled her up short. At the ripe age of thirty-five, Angela knew her own weaknesses, chief among them a weakness for a good-looking hunk of man. All her life she had darted from man to man on impulse, and the results had been predictably disastrous. Especially with her rat-bastard ex-husband. Big Rick Tolleson, with his tousled jungle-man hair, beefy shoulders, and come-get-me smile, was more tempting than a double dip of maple walnut in a waffle cone. She could slip between the man's sheets as easy as breathing.

And then what? She'd made a pact with herself the day her divorce had become final, a year ago. No more impulsive hunk-jumping. When she decided to settle down and stay in one place—if that sort of dullness ever overtook her—then she could think about men again. But no more drive-by relationships. It was too wearing on a girl's psyche.

On the other hand, Rick Tolleson might just be more temptation than she could resist.

She gave him a worldly, you-can't-impress-me-with-that-crap smile. "A flatterer as well as a canine bone-cracker. Do your talents never end?"

"Actually," he admitted with a grin, "no. How about dinner tonight?"

Temptation, Angela pleaded, *get thee behind me.* But temptation wouldn't comply. He just stood there looking irresistible. "Are you expecting me to cook for you?"

"Nope. Would I be that rude? There's a cowboy bar I know that's just down the road. Good country western, great barbecue ribs. You can't help but love it."

Angela was afraid that she couldn't help but do the same to Rick. She really ought to say no. Tonight there would be editing to do, Jane and Cole to observe, story sidelines to develop in her mind. So much work to keep her busy. She really couldn't go out.

"Sure," she said. "What time?"

And just then, she realized that she had missed Jane's entire run.

PANTING, JANE doubled over just outside the course exit, bracing her hands on her knees, laboring to catch her breath. What a glorious run! Shadow had been perfect. Jane's timing had been right on. Her communication with the dog had been next to telepathic. Finally—finally!—she felt as if she and Shadow had both hit their stride.

"Great run, Jane!"

She glanced up. There stood Cole, looking down at her, grinning. Shadow greeted the man with a happy wave of his tail, and Jane's unruly libido greeted him just as happily. Damn, but her heart didn't need to beat any harder than it was.

"Thanks," she choked out, still panting.

"Clean and fast," he said. "A thing of beauty."

She assumed he was talking about the run.

"You seem a bit winded, though."

She straightened and took a deep breath. "Long course."

He shrugged, eyes twinkling. "No longer than others."

"Your point would be?" she prompted warily.

"You're an athlete," he said. "You tell me. Come on. The food concession over there is selling bottled water. You look as if you could use some."

"Oh, thank you," she said wryly. But it was embarrassing that a desk jockey like Cole could finish this long, challenging course with a grin on his face and air still in his lungs—she had watched his beautiful run with Dobby an hour earlier—and Jane, who spent her life on her feet getting physical with big dogs and heavy bags of dog food, finished it looking like a deflated balloon. A sweaty deflated balloon. Maybe she needed to pay attention to that, Jane acknowledged to herself.

She let Shadow take a cooling drink from the bucket of water set by the ring for the dogs. At the same time, the ring runner delivered the timer's sheet to the officials' tent, and she just happened to be able to see her time on the last run. Fifty seconds. A full six seconds under the set course time. Excellent.

Cole had walked ahead toward the food concession. Jane hastened to catch up, Shadow bouncing happily beside her. "What time did you run?" she asked when she caught up.

"Fifty-four," he told her.

Little dogs were allowed more time to run the course,

leveling the playing field in consideration of their shorter stride. But even allowing for the adjustment, Shadow had beat the clock by a greater margin.

"Ah," Jane replied smugly.

He gave her an inquiring look, and she smiled. "Finally beat you."

chapter 17

THE NEXT morning, Jane woke while the sun was a mere promise in the east. All her life she had been an early riser, but this morning, she had a new reason to climb out of bed.

She nudged the black and white lump of fur at the foot of the bed. "Wake up, old man. New day arisin'."

Idaho raised his head, yawned, then put his head back down, showing every intention of going back to sleep. But when Jane threw back the covers and got out of bed, he followed.

They left Angela snoring in the bedroom and tiptoed into the narrow hallway—just as Cole exited the bathroom, face and hair dripping, in his standard jogging costume of nylon shorts and running shoes.

He looked startled to see her. "Morning, Early Bird. Out to catch up with the worm?"

"Don't be so hard on yourself," she advised. "I wouldn't go so far as to call you a worm."

He chuckled quietly. "Thank you."

She opened the hall closet and took out her battered

athletic shoes, Wal-Mart specials that had cost her all of twenty-five dollars. Cole observed with interest.

"You going jogging with me this morning?"

"Well, I'm going. And if you're going, I suppose you could say I might be with you."

He grinned knowingly. "Took my words to heart, eh?"

Her face heated a bit. "I'm not above listening to good advice. I've been living the soft life the last few weeks, and it's showing in my runs."

"Smart woman."

"Though I'm not *that* out of shape."

"I think your shape is just fine."

That earned him a scowl, which inspired an even wider grin.

Jane sat down on the floor to put on her shoes. Teri, Dobby, and Shadow occupied the converted dinette, and the sofa bed was still pulled out, sheets and blankets rumpled from cradling Cole's body. No way would she sit there, at least not with Cole looking on wearing that wicked grin.

Shadow's tail wagged gently in greeting for both Jane and Idaho, but he didn't leave his guard post at Teri's feet. The golden retriever spent every night curled at the foot of the girl's bed. He seemed to have adopted the kid, a behavior Jane would have expected more from Idaho than Shadow. Border collies lived to supervise, to direct, to protect, and assuming kid-sitting chores with Teri should have been right up Idaho's alley. But the border collie seemed to sense that Shadow felt something special for this particular kid, so he had ceded his duties where Teri was concerned.

When Jane motioned to Shadow, the retriever gave his charge a concerned glance, then stepped off the bed, careful not to disturb the little girl, and padded over to greet Jane with a lick on the cheek.

"Thanks, buddy," she said, ruffling his ears. "Want to go for a run?"

His ears picked up, but his expression grew worried.

"Don't look as if I've never before gotten off my duff and taken you running."

"Dogs never lie," Cole reminded her.

"Ha!"

The early-morning Wyoming air was bracing even in early July. The sun was only a glowing sliver on the eastern horizon when Cole and Jane started down the dirt road that ran alongside the fairgrounds, where the trials were being held. The road was empty of traffic, so Jane allowed the dogs to run without leashes. They bounded happily ahead, sniffing the road, the roadside ditches, the scrubby vegetation, and the air. Shadow was momentarily transfixed by a flock of birds that winged overhead, then ran ahead to try to keep up with them. Idaho gave the younger dog a look that was the canine equivalent of an eye-roll.

For the first quarter mile, Jane enjoyed herself enormously. The air was crisp and refreshing. The dogs were having a great time. And adrenaline pumped energy into body and mind alike. Not to mention that running beside her, Cole looked great. She couldn't resist letting her eyes rest on the play of muscles in legs and arms, the smooth slide of sinew in his bare back. Soon, a sheen of sweat made all that muscle glisten.

Jane gave herself a mental slap. After all, she'd been the one who had poured cold water on their relationship. She'd been the one who'd denied she wanted anything more than simple friendship. She'd been the one who'd told Cole that she didn't have time for the distraction of romance.

So put your eyeballs back in your head, Jane scolded herself. She'd made her bed, and now she had to lie in it. But that thought inspired unfortunate images of a bed for two, and just what those two might do in that bed. Damn! Jane wanted to eliminate distractions, and here she was panting after the biggest distraction of all. Never in her life had she been so wishy-washy.

And speaking of panting, after a half mile, some of the

ecstasy of that initial adrenaline was turning into agony. Breathing was becoming a chore, and the muscles in her legs had traded exhilaration for pain. To make matters seem worse, Cole, jogging slightly ahead of her, turned to face her, running backward with amazing agility.

"Great morning, isn't it?"

"Yeah." Jane managed—just—to sound as if she weren't fighting for every breath.

He turned to face forward and dropped back a few feet so that they were jogging side by side. "I love these wide open spaces. Wyoming isn't everyone's cup of tea, I guess, but all this fresh air and empty space makes me feel great. Just great."

Jane bit back a sarcastic comment. *Great. Just great.* In Casper, the wind blew constantly. All one had to do was cross the Wyoming state line to get blown off the map. And here nothing distracted the eye from the endless plains or the mind from the ever-present wind. The Rocky Mountains were a distant fantasy, far to the west.

Yes, the sheer scope of the rolling grasslands could take a person's breath away—as in when a person jogged down a stupid dirt road that continued forever toward an ever-receding horizon. If she didn't stop soon, Jane thought, she wasn't going to be able to fill her lungs or move her legs to make her agility runs that day.

"You okay?" Cole asked.

A certain knowing glint in his eyes made Jane nod her head yes. She was not going to admit that he was in that much better shape than she was. Damn! How far had they gone, anyway? Ten miles?

Cole glanced at the watch on his wrist. "This curve up here should mark about a mile and a half. Ready to turn around?"

Was she ready to turn around? Would she even make it to the curve? Air whistled painfully in and out of her chest. In spite of the cool air, sweat dripped into her eyes and trickled between her breasts. The dogs still bounced along, pictures of canine energy. Cole continued to run easily, sporting a sheen of perspiration more cosmetic than drippy.

When they reached the curve in the road, Cole jogged in place, waiting for Jane to catch up. Then he stopped. "Time for a rest," he said.

Jane knew very well that Cole didn't need a rest, but if he wanted to be nice and pretend, then she'd take him up on it.

"Feels good to get some exercise." She choked out the lie and stumbled gratefully to a stop. Leaning over, hands braced on her knees, she took deep breaths of air.

"You shouldn't overdo it the first day out," Cole advised cautiously.

"Overdo it? Me? Nah." Gasp, heave, gasp. "Oh, shoot! Is that Ernesto's van over there on that road?" Gasp. "It is! I'd recognize that damned camera anywhere." She groaned and hung her head.

Cole deliberately moved to block the camera's view of Jane. "They don't let you have much peace, do they?"

"No peace at all. None." She straightened. Air was flowing into her lungs again. "And you've become a part of this as well. I hope Angela explained that to you."

"I don't have an issue with that."

"Shit! Smart, good-looking, and well adjusted, too."

"Think I could be a star?" he said with a wry grin.

"You're welcome to it." Feeling a spark come back into her spirit, she added, "As long as I get to be the one going to the Invitational."

"And then I get to buy you steak and lobster?"

"Or maybe crab with drawn butter." She laughed, then realized he'd managed to take her mind off the persistent camera. "Thanks."

"For what?"

She shrugged. "Just thanks."

"Shall we walk back?"

"What? You think I can't jog another lousy mile and a half?"

He glanced down at her legs, which were admittedly a bit shaky. The glance lit the competitive fire in her blood.

"I'll race you," she challenged.

He shook his head. "You never give up, do you?"

"Not yet."

"Winner makes breakfast?"

"You're on."

"I'll be nice and give you a ten-yard lead. Because you have shorter legs."

She wasn't too proud to take advantage. Off she went, both dogs racing alongside her, the need to win overriding the burn in her lungs and the ache in her legs.

TERI WATCHED her dad leave the motor home with Jane and the dogs through one narrowly slitted eye. Dobby's little snores rattled gently in her ear, and louder snores coming from the bedroom indicated that Angela was still sleeping.

Teri sighed and wrinkled her nose. It was really early. The window over the sink showed a sky barely lit by the first rays of sunrise. She could snuggle into her sleeping bag and go back to sleep, knowing her dad and Jane wouldn't return for just about forever.

But Teri wasn't sure she approved of her dad jogging with Jane. Running down a road and getting all sweaty wasn't a very romantic thing, but the more time her dad spent with Jane, Teri figured, the more likely it was that he would forget about her mom. And that just wasn't right. And now all the thinking about Jane and her dad made her mind whirl, so she couldn't go to sleep again.

Quietly, so as not to disturb Dobby, Teri climbed out of her sleeping bag and pulled on yesterday's clothes. Once

Dobby woke up, she would start jumping around and barking for her breakfast, then Angela would wake up, and Teri would have to do whatever Angela told her to do. So Teri didn't want either Dobby or Angela to wake up for a while. She climbed onto the kitchen counter so that she could open the cupboard where the breakfast stuff was kept. In the cupboard was a choice of Pop-Tarts or instant oatmeal. She chose the Pop-Tarts, taking two out of the box. A cup of milk completed her breakfast.

It took her only a few moments to eat. When she slipped out of the motor home, Dobby still snored on Teri's pillow. The sun had risen halfway above the horizon, and people were beginning to stir in the RV parking area of the fairgrounds. Since there was nothing much to do until her dad got back, Teri decided to stroll down the row of motor homes and trailers to see what she could see. The day before, she had noticed a litter of golden retriever puppies. Or maybe they were Labrador puppies. Sometimes Labradors were yellow, so it was hard to tell. But the puppies were very cute, and maybe they would be out in their pen already, because puppies needed to pee a lot in the early morning.

She found the puppies ten motor homes down and two rows over. It had taken quite a search, but the puppies were worth it. The little golden babies slept, piled together on a fleece blanket in their exercise pen beside a big fifth-wheel trailer. Most of them wore smears of oatmeal-like puppy gruel on their muzzles and feet, and a big communal feeding pan in the middle of the pen had been licked down to its shiny stainless-steel finish.

Fascinated, Teri hunkered down beside the pen and stared, her heart swelling in her chest. For some reason, her eyeballs started to ache with the pressure of rising tears.

One of the puppies squirmed about, trying to find a more comfortable bed on its brothers and sisters, muttering little puppy noises as it tried to settle. Then it spied Teri. Dark puppy eyes met dark little girl eyes. The puppy yawned mightily, got to its feet, stretched, and ambled toward Teri. Teri stuck a finger through the wire panel and wriggled it. Immediately the puppy pounced.

Sensing the activity, the other puppies began to stir. One by one they untangled themselves from the pile and trotted over to discover what new thing the world had delivered for their entertainment. Soon Teri had six baby golden retrievers nibbling and sucking at her fingers. She didn't mind the needle-sharp milk teeth or the wet tongues. She didn't even mind when one of the babies excused himself from the pack to make a smelly poop in the middle of the pen, or when most of the others decided that pooping was a pretty good idea and deposited their own little messes nearby. After tending to business, they all hurried back to Teri's fingers.

Teri couldn't help but laugh. The puppy nibbles made her heart swell. The puppy yips and cries warmed her, even though the morning air was cool. She'd never before seen anything that made her feel so soft and squishy inside.

"Like those puppies, do you?"

The man's voice made Teri jump. Like a kid caught with a hand in the cookie jar, she quickly drew her hand back from the pen. The puppies protested loudly.

The man stood on the steps of the trailer, the door open behind him. His hair stuck up all over his head, as if he'd forgotten to comb it, and his eyes sagged like an old man's eyes. The rest of him didn't look as old as his saggy, puffy eyes.

Teri tried to think of something smart to say. She knew very well that she shouldn't have been messing with someone else's puppies. How did she explain to an adult that staying away from puppies, especially golden retriever puppies, was more than any kid could resist?

"I didn't hurt them," she told the man.

He started to smile, but the smile died early. The man's mouth drooped down as if weights were attached to the corners. He didn't look mad as much as sad.

"Of course you didn't hurt them. Aren't you Cole Forrest's little girl? With the papillon?"

"I'm Teri. Cole is my daddy."

He nodded. "I thought so. Do you want to go into the pen with the puppies so you can play with them?"

Teri's mouth fell open at her good luck. "Can I?"

"Sure. Just let me clean up those messes first. They just ate, and that's what happens."

For the next twenty minutes Teri experienced heaven. She sat in the middle of the exercise pen with puppies climbing on her lap, chewing on her hands and fingers, pulling on the laces of her sneakers. Sometimes the man came out and watched, but mostly he stayed in his trailer, so she had the puppies all to herself. In just a few minutes she could tell one puppy from another. They were alike and yet different. Some were light gold; others were darker. Some were fatter; some thinner. One puppy had enormous ears that had dipped liberally into the food pan.

She lost track of time, all her attention taken up with little ears, noses, paws, and wagging tails. When the puppies got tired, they fell into piles around the pen. A pile of three here, a duo snuggling together there. And in Teri's lap, one fat puppy curled up contentedly and went to sleep, eyes closed peacefully, soft fur rising and falling with its slow breathing.

Teri's heart swelled so big that it hurt.

"Tuckered them out, I see."

Teri looked up to the man watching her. "They were playing a lot."

A smile twitched his mouth. "Puppies do that."

"This one likes me," Teri said, stroking the puppy curled in her lap. "Someday I'm going to have a golden retriever of my own, and I'm going to take him into agility and obedience."

The man didn't answer, but he looked at her a long time, his eyes shifting back and forth between Teri's face and the happily sleeping puppy. Finally he asked, in a soft voice, "Would you like to have that puppy?"

Teri caught her breath. "You're selling them?"

His head shook no. "I'm not selling them. I'm finding them very, very good homes, and then I'm giving them."

Teri almost couldn't believe it. "You're not keeping even one?"

"I can't." His voice cracked. "They all have to go. Every last one of them."

THE TRIP home took Jane and Cole a lot longer than the trip out, because they ended up walking most of the way. Jane sprinted about a hundred yards, jogged another fifty, then doubled over, grimacing with the pain of a leg cramp. Shadow and Idaho circled her, whining with concern.

Cole caught up within seconds. He could have caught up any time he wanted, Jane knew. Damned humiliating. She was going to have to start taking this exercising business more seriously.

"You okay?" Cole asked, jogging in place beside her.

"Sure thing. Be quiet, boys," she told the dogs. "I'm fine."

"Let's walk a bit, then."

"I suppose you're tired." She chuckled weakly.

"Don't want to strain anything important before today's runs."

"Right you are." But as Jane took her first step, she yelped and bent down to grab her right calf.

"Leg cramp?"

She answered with an inarticulate groan.

"Sit down," Cole directed. "Sometimes these things will go away with a little massage."

"Ow, ow, ow!" Her leg didn't want to bend, so she dropped gracelessly to the hard dirt of the road. Cole slipped off her shoe, then gently brushed aside her hand, which was gripping the offending muscle. He cradled her calf in both hands as she tried to fend off the dogs, who wanted to help by climbing into her lap. Finally she persuaded them to back off.

"Try to flex your foot upward," Cole directed.

"Ow."

"Concentrate on relaxing the muscles in your leg."

"Ow!"

With strong but gentle pressure, he kneaded her leg. Jane tried to breathe, tried to relax as he'd told her to do. Slowly the spasms eased. The pain faded enough to make her wish she had shaved her legs before starting out on this run. And to make her appreciate the feel of his hands on her leg for more than just relief of a leg cramp. Her face heated, and she knew every bright freckle telegraphed impure thoughts.

"Better?" he asked.

If he only knew. She sighed. "Lots better, thanks."

He let her go and stood up. Her calf still tingled from the warm pressure of his hands.

"Up?" He extended a hand. Since her pride had already been trampled, she took it.

They walked the rest of the way home. When they got to the motor home, the sun was well up. Ernesto was doing something to his camera beside his van (did Jane dare hope a lens or something else vital was broken?). When he saw Jane and Cole, he nodded toward the motor home.

"Those slugabeds in there are still asleep. Don't you guys run the course first thing this morning?"

Cole glanced at his watch. "We have about forty-five minutes."

"Well, if anyone's going to have breakfast, you'd better get those girls to rise and shine."

Jane wasn't that surprised that Angela had slept in. She had gone out the night before with none other than Rick Tolleson, and Jane had been in bed well before she came in. In fact, she had cranked open one eye to see the hands of the bedside clock pointing to two A.M. when Angela had slipped into bed. The party girl had mumbled to herself sourly and banged around the bedroom in a huff. So the date, apparently, hadn't gone that well. Poor Rick, Jane had thought, wondering what Angela had done to the man.

Jane allowed the door to bang open as she climbed into the motor home. "Wake up, you slugs! The sun got up a half hour ago."

The first thing she noticed was that Teri's bed was empty, though Dobby still snored on the kid's pillow. Thinking the little girl must have joined Angela in bed, she peeked into the bedroom. No Teri. Angela was just then twitching awake.

"Angela! Where's Teri?"

"Huh?"

"Teri. Where's Teri?"

"How should I know?"

The beginnings of panic stirred as Jane opened the door to the tiny bathroom, the only other place the kid might be. Teri's pajamas lay on the floor. She had a habit of dropping clothes wherever she took them off. But no Teri. Cuss words started ricocheting inside Jane's head.

Cole still lingered outside, talking to Ernesto. Jane flew out the motor home door, almost missing the steps.

"Teri's gone—again."

He actually uttered the words that Jane had only thought, ending with "Goddammit! Where's Angela?"

"Sawing logs, up until just a moment ago."

The three of them—Cole, Ernesto, and Jane—fanned out to comb the overnight parking area, a maze of motor homes, trailers, exercise pens, and trucks. Jane trotted from motor home to trailer to van, forgetting the ache in her recently abused legs. And in only a few minutes, she spotted the little fugitive sitting in an exercise pen surrounded by—what else?—golden retriever puppies. Talking to her was

George Cahill, a top-flight agility competitor who three months ago had lost his wife to a tragic car accident.

The moment Teri spotted Jane, the little girl carefully set aside the little golden furball curled on her lap, then literally bounced out of the puppy pen and ran over to Jane.

"Jane! Jane! This man wants to give me a puppy! He said I could have the fat one with the big ears, and it wouldn't cost anything! I can have him if my dad says it's okay!"

Oh, great! Just what we need. With Teri hanging on one leg, still chattering about "her" puppy, Jane looked at George.

"Hi, George." She didn't bother with a polite "How's it going?" because everyone in the agility community knew that the man was devastated. No one had expected to see him on the agility tour, but he claimed that doing something—anything!—was better than sitting around his house sorting through memories. Apparently, diving back into competition hadn't provided the needed distraction, because he looked haggard from grief, with a lost look in his eyes that made Jane's heart hurt.

"Hey there, Jane," he said. "Nice run yesterday with Shadow."

"Thanks." She turned her attention to the puppies. Teri's choice, after being ejected from the girl's lap, had gone to sleep on his back, tiny legs splayed, one ear covering his face. The others lay in two piles of tangled puppy parts. "These are Maizey's babies?"

"Yeah. Born a month after . . . after . . ." He bit down on a lip to regain control.

"They're beautiful, George." Jane picked up a snoozing puppy and cuddled it against her face. The puppy didn't wake. "So precious."

"I've got to place them all, Jane. I can't look at them without thinking of Marla. She . . . she looked forward to this special litter so much, and . . ."

"You don't have to explain to me, George."

"I wouldn't do justice to any of them. I'm getting out of the game, for a while at least. I can't concentrate, can't think. My son wants me to move to Ohio, be closer to their family, get involved in the business again. Maybe in a year or so, I'll come back." He sighed. "Who knows?"

"You serious about giving Teri one of these little guys?"

"Jumbo over there really took to her. And he's going to be a dynamite performance dog, I think. The kid would have fun with him."

"Yes, yes, yes, yes, yes, yes ..." Teri kept repeating. Jane gave her a look, and she reduced the volume to just under her breath.

"I'm sure Teri will talk to her dad about it, and he might want to talk to you."

"I'll be here," George said. "And so will the puppies. I'm not going to run the course today. I'm just ... a little under the weather. I think yesterday was maybe my last run for a while."

As they walked back toward their own motor home, Teri jumped up and down, tugging on Jane's hand. Jane quelled her with a firm look. "Young lady, your dad is not going to be happy with you for wandering off on your own. You know how he feels about that."

Teri's expression instantly transformed into dread. "You think he'll really be mad?"

"We'll find out."

"Mad enough to not let me have the puppy?"

"Didn't he tell you that you could get a puppy this fall, after you got settled into your new place?"

"But this puppy is here now!" Teri declared, trotting along at Jane's side. "And he likes me. This puppy really, really likes me. Did you see him go to sleep on my lap? He wants to be my dog."

"Kid," Jane said, "I'm not the one you have to convince."

"But ... but I'll die if I can't have that puppy. He's the sweetest puppy in the world. And the man said he would be a good agility dog someday. I'll...I'll...I just really need him."

The words were a typical childish whine, but something in Teri's tone made Jane stop and look seriously at the little girl's face. The kid's eyes held a deep need that Jane recognized, because that need was part of her own soul as well. How often in her life had she thought she couldn't survive without the steady and loving support of her dogs? Since before she was Teri's age, Jane had always had a special dog at her side, sometimes two.

Teri had Dobby, but Jane had seen the way the kid looked at Cole and Dobby when they worked together in the ring. The big man and the tiny dog had a special bond, and while Dobby loved Teri, too, the relationship wasn't the same.

Teri grabbed onto Jane's shorts, as if grabbing on to some part of her would make Jane listen to her pleas. "You could tell my dad that I need the puppy. If you told him that, he would say yes, because he likes you a lot. You could make him say yes. He would listen to you. Please? Please, please, please?"

"Teri, I don't have any influence over your dad."

"Yes you do! He likes you a lot! A really, really lot! Please, Jane. Just ask him. Please?" Tears started to dribble down Teri's cheeks, and her dark eyes grew even darker with misery.

Jane sighed. She really wasn't cut out to deal with kids. And she didn't think she had any special influence over Cole, didn't even want to entertain the possibility.

On the other hand, instinct told her that Teri's distress was real, and so was her need. Another adult might have dismissed it as a childish yearning that would pass and be forgotten, but not Jane.

"Okay, I'll tell you what. Let's go talk to your dad. He's real worried because you weren't at the motor home when we got back from jogging, so he's bound to be cranky, but

we'll see what he says about the puppy. Maybe he'll understand."

Teri sniffed loudly and wiped her nose with her hand.
"Okay," she quavered.

"And if you're brave enough and grown-up enough to
apologize to your dad for worrying him, and if you ask him
about the puppy without sulking, without crying, and without being a snot, then I'll put in a good word for your
puppy. Okay?"

Teri brightened. "Really?"

"Yeah, really. But I don't guarantee anything. It's your
dad's decision. Agreed?"

"You can make him say yes," the kid said confidently.

When they got back to the motor home, both Cole and
Ernesto were still out kid-searching. Jane used Angela's cell
phone to call with the good news that the wanderer was
home. As Jane had feared, Cole returned with a thundercloud over his head and lightning shooting from his eyes.

"Jane, I can't thank you enough," he said, all the while
glaring at his daughter, who began to wilt. "Teri, you and I
are going into the motor home to have a talk."

Teri asked in a meek voice, "Can we talk out here?"

"I'll leave," Jane gladly volunteered, "and give you guys
some privacy."

"Jane!" Teri wailed in supplication. "Stay."

Jane gave Cole a helpless look.

"Jane isn't going to save you," Cole told his daughter.

"I want her to stay," she said, and implored Jane with her
eyes. "You promised. We had a deal."

Cole raised an eyebrow in Jane's direction, looking so
stern that he made even her nervous. She shrugged helplessly. A deal was a deal.

chapter 18

THE MORNING quickly slid downhill for Teri. Her dad was really, really mad. She'd hoped that if Jane stood there listening, her dad wouldn't yell so much. But he yelled anyway. Her dad didn't yell very often, but when he yelled, he really did a good job of it. Not that he was loud about it. Not like Jimmy Crocker's dad, who made a room shake when he yelled. At least that was how Jimmy described it. She'd heard Jimmy's dad yell at him once when he'd picked him up from school, and Teri had thought their car was going to burst apart from the volume.

She was glad her dad wasn't loud like Mr. Crocker, but even at a lower volume, the yelling made her feel awful, like maybe she was going to throw up. She hadn't meant to worry him. When her dad was mad like this, Teri knew it was her fault, and that made her feel even worse. She hadn't even gotten to ask him about the puppy yet, because he just kept scolding her.

"Why can't you do as I tell you?" he demanded, but didn't give her a chance to answer. "How many times have I told you not to go wandering off alone, to keep in sight of me, or Jane, or Angela, or Ernesto? Don't you realize that bad things can happen to little girls who wander off alone? That you need to be careful about where you go and who you talk to? Wasn't it part of the rules when we started this trip that you stay where I can see and hear you?"

Hot tears scalded Teri's eyes.

"Well?" he demanded.

"I . . . I didn't mean to. I just woke up, and you were gone, and . . . and . . ." The tears spilled over, wetting her cheeks and dribbling off her chin. "I didn't mean to be bad."

Her dad sighed and shook his head. "I know you don't mean to be bad. You're not *bad*, Teri. You're still my sweet girl. But sometimes you just don't think. This is the second time this has happened."

"I'm sorry," she whimpered.

"Jane and I spent a lot of time this morning looking for you. I missed my Standard run with Dobby because I was looking for you. And more important, you scared all of us to death."

Teri hung her head. "I'm sorry."

"What were you thinking, if you were thinking at all?"

Here was her chance, Teri knew. This might not be a good time to ask her dad for a puppy, but it might be her only chance. At the end of today, they would leave, and the man with the puppies might leave anytime. He had told Jane that he wasn't going to run in the trial today.

She balled her fists and took a deep breath. "I went looking for puppies, 'cause I saw them yesterday, a whole litter, and I wanted to look at them. And I found them. And the man there said I could have one, if you said yes. And they're golden retrievers. And one of them liked me a lot. And the man there said he was going to be a really good dog. And I can have him for free if you say yes."

There. She had gotten it all out. Her dad looked at her with a peculiar expression on his face.

"You went looking for . . . puppies?"

"Jane saw them, too. They're wonderful puppies. And the man said I could have the one with big ears. That puppy likes me a lot."

"The puppies belong to George Cahill, Cole," Jane chimed in, and that moment, Teri liked her more than ever. It was true that she couldn't have another mother, but Jane was special. Jane was going to help her, because she knew how much Teri needed this puppy. Hooray for Jane. "They're Maizey's babies. You probably don't know Maizey, because she's taken some time off for motherhood. But she's a wonderful dog, and she was bred to a top-winning golden. George is placing the whole litter. His wife died in a car accident three months ago, and right now he's in over his head. These are really nice puppies."

Teri held her breath, praying to God to bless Jane, praying to her mother to speak to her dad from heaven and tell him to let her have the puppy.

But her dad scowled. "You think a puppy is a suitable reward for bad behavior?"

That was what Teri had feared he would say. In a small voice, she reminded him, "I didn't mean to be bad."

"I know you didn't, but you have to learn to think, sweet pea. And you have to learn to do what I say."

"But . . ." More tears flooded into her eyes. "This puppy likes me! He wants to be my own very special dog! And if we don't get him today, we'll never get him!"

"I told you that I would get you a golden retriever when we get in our new place."

"But I need this one!"

"Don't use that tone with me, young lady. You go into the motor home, eat your breakfast, and don't set one foot outside until I tell you that you can."

Her heart was ripping apart. Teri was sure that the pain in her chest was going to make her die. Then her dad would be sorry. She would go into the motor home, eat her breakfast, and die.

• • •

COLE SAT down heavily in the canvas folding chair beneath the motor home awning and dropped his head into his hands. Their morning run hadn't tired him, but the encounter with his daughter certainly had.

Jane's heart went out to him. For about the hundredth time since meeting Cole and Teri, she wondered how any parent held up. But she sympathized with Teri as well. That little girl had a hole in her life that her dad alone couldn't fill. Maybe a mother could have filled it, but the kid didn't have a mother. That puppy might set a bad precedent as a reward for irresponsible behavior but, on the other hand, the little furball might be just the thing to give solace to a heart still hurting from a terrible loss.

Not that any of this was her business. Of all the women in the world, she certainly knew the least about children. But she had promised Teri. And now, for some reason, her own heart was engaged. Because of Cole? Because of the kid? Or maybe both. Jane had never been accomplished at self-analysis. She only knew that with Cole and Teri both hurting, she hurt also.

She sighed, dropped her backside onto the motor home step, and propped her elbows on her knees. "You think you might have been a little hard on the kid?"

Cole looked up with a scowl. "How so?"

"Teri didn't think about what she was doing, and she conveniently forgot that you didn't want her wandering around alone, but she's a kid. Eight years old."

"You think I don't know that?"

Jane felt herself getting into deep water, but she plowed ahead. "It's not like she set out to worry you into a heart attack. Doesn't that just go along with having a kid?"

He snorted. "The little imp has been driving me crazy since we hit Salt Lake City—sulking, whining, giving me lip. I thought this summer trip was helping her. I thought she was coming out of herself and starting to enjoy life again. But suddenly, she's a snot. What the hell is going on here? Dammit! You know I missed the Standard class run with Dobby. We were supposed to be first in the ring."

Jane shook her head and smiled. "Come on, Cole. Agility doesn't mean that much to you, as you've told me more than once. What's one score more or less?"

He groaned, pinching the bridge of his nose.

"You know what the truth is? You're just like every other mom or dad that I know. You're scared to death of your own kid, and you don't have a clue how to make things right."

She expected a sarcastic put-down, because she probably deserved one. After all, what did she know about raising kids?

But Cole merely looked up and gave her a rueful smile. "You got that right."

He looked so miserable that, without thinking, Jane reached out to put a comforting hand on his arm. And before she could withdraw it, he covered her hand with his own, a gesture that sent a thrill of pleasure clear down to her toes.

"You ought to have kids, Jane. You've got good perspective."

She laughed. "Not me. But maybe I'm just a little more objective about Teri than you are. You love her so much... it's got to be hard not to lose it when she does something like this."

"That's the truth." He squeezed her hand, then let it go. Jane felt the loss.

"Can you bear with a little more objectivity?" she asked softly.

"Maybe I need a shot of objectivity. It's hard to come by when you're a parent."

"About the puppy..."

"Geez! Don't tell me you think she should have that puppy after the way she's been behaving."

"Well..."

"She got to you, didn't she, Jane? The sad brown eyes. The quivering lip? Oh, she's good."

Jane thought about it. "No. I don't know that much about kids, Cole, but I think this was real. Either that or you should get her an agent and send her to Hollywood. I think she really needs that puppy."

He made a rude sound.

Jane sighed. "I know. You think I have a dog addiction." She paused. "I do have a dog addiction. It's true. But you yourself told me that Teri was withdrawn, sad, doing battle with feelings that a kid shouldn't have to endure. Idaho is a certified therapy dog, and I've taken him to see countless hospital patients and nursing home residents, and even to a school for troubled kids. You wouldn't believe the miracles a dog can work, with kids, old folks, and everyone in between."

Cole was silent.

"Maybe Teri needs her own personal little therapy dog."

"She has Dobby," he reminded her.

"Who is *your* special dog, not hers. There's a difference."

He made a face, so she tried another tack. "I figure that raising a kid is a lot like training a dog."

She half expected him to object to the comparison, but he gave her a wry smile. "I suppose there are certain similarities."

"Most of us train using treats or toys as a motivator, and we've found that it's a good idea to sometimes surprise the dog with a bonus—more treats than expected, or way better treats. Understand?"

He raised a brow. "You're saying that a puppy would be a hell of a bonus."

Jane rested her case. This wasn't her business, and she

probably should have kept her mouth zipped. But when Cole's broad shoulders squared, as if a weight had been lifted from them, she was glad she had butted in.

"Okay. This is against my better judgment, but let's go see this special puppy."

Fifteen minutes later, Cole climbed into the motor home with a big-eared golden furball in his arms. Beside him, Jane wore a wide smile.

Angela, spiffed and polished as usual, was putting scrambled eggs and bacon on the dinette table. "There you are, Cole. Ernesto said they were looking for you at the ring a while back. Aren't you running today?"

"Family matters got in the way," he told her, smiling ruefully. "I'll have to cede this day to Jane."

"Ah," Angela said. "The little tiff with Teri. I heard it even though I was taking a shower. And Teri is flooding the bedroom with tears." Angela seemed more concerned with Jane than with Teri, though, scowling at her dirt-streaked shorts, flyaway hair, and wrinkled T-shirt.

"You look like you just climbed out of bed," she commented sourly. "Ernesto says the classes are moving pretty fast. Shouldn't you consider maybe taking a shower and getting dressed?"

"Sure, sure. I'll get there. I won't miss my run." But Jane didn't intend to miss Teri's first look at her new dog. Neither did she want to miss the eggs and bacon. "In a minute."

It was then that Angela took a closer look at Cole. Her eyes narrowed. "Is that a dog?"

"Baby version of Shadow," he said, stroking the little head.

Jane's heart swelled just a bit. Was there anything more appealing than a man who was such a softie?

"Teri's in the bedroom, you say?"

"Sulking, as far as I know. Wouldn't eat breakfast. Not even a Pop-Tart. I tried."

"Teri!" Cole called.

An inarticulate objection sounded from behind the closed bedroom door.

"I think you'd better come out," Jane called to her.

The sound of a theatrical sigh carried the length of the motor home. The door opened, and Teri emerged. Her mouth drooped. Her eyes were red. She dragged her feet down the narrow hallway—until she saw what her father cradled in the crook of his elbow.

Magic couldn't have made a more startling transformation, Jane thought as she watched Teri's reaction. The kid's mouth dropped open. Her eyes lit with a glow that made the whole motor home seem brighter. Words seemed beyond her. Only inarticulate sounds of rapture escaped her throat.

Jane's own throat closed with emotion.

Cole stopped Teri before she could reach out for the puppy. "Listen to me, young lady. This puppy is not a toy. He is a living creature, a baby who will be totally dependent on you to care for him. It's a very serious responsibility."

Teri immediately grew somber. "I'll take good care of him! I promise! I'll feed him, and train him, and brush him, and talk to him, and . . . and everything!"

Cole lowered the puppy into Teri's waiting arms. "That's good," he told her. "Because you're going to have to do that for a very long time. This dog will be with you for many, many years, and he's your responsibility for as long as he lives, even if he gets into trouble, or if he's not as smart as you think he should be, or if he gets sick and you have to take care of him. He's still your responsibility."

"I'll take care of him forever," Teri promised in a voice grown small with the awesome nature of her new duties.

"And Jane here will help you train it."

Jane's mouth fell open.

"Won't you, Jane?" Cole asked, turning toward her with a twinkle in his eye. "After you persuaded me to let her have the dog, don't you think it's only right that you have a hand in the work? Besides, we wouldn't want someone like me, a mere novice handler with a wind-up toy dog, to mess up the training of a real performance dog. Would we?"

Jane chuckled, giving Cole credit for a very neat flanking strike. "You got me there," she admitted.

THE NEXT morning they hit the road. The next set of trials were in Washington state, near Tacoma, at the Argus Ranch Facility for Dogs—the site where, in August, the Solid Gold Invitational would be held. Angela was looking forward to checking out the place where she hoped Jane would provide a riveting finale to the series, which she had tentatively titled *Winner Take All*. She and Ernesto could preview camera angles, lighting problems, sound difficulties. Angela expected an enclosed arena to be nothing short of an echo chamber, with the sounds of barking dogs and human conversation bouncing around the big building to interfere with the mike on the camera.

Argus Ranch would be the first indoor trial they filmed. Jane had assured her that it was the Cadillac of dog-show sites. Supposedly it had a gorgeous house where judges stayed, RV hookups for motor homes and trailers, and even a comfortable dormitory for exhibitors. This would be quite a change from the usual agility trial held at a park or a fairground, where if they wanted to park the motor home on site, they had to do without electric or water hookups.

They took off with Cole driving the motor home, Jane riding shotgun, and Angela in back with Teri and the dogs. Ernesto's van led the way out of Casper and north on Interstate 25, and the long trip through the windswept plains of northern Wyoming toward the equally windswept plains of eastern Montana began.

Angela was glad enough to be shed of driving responsibilities for once. It gave her a chance to get some shots of life on the road. She had commandeered one of Ernesto's smaller cameras for that very purpose—and what more engaging scene to shoot than cute little Teri with her puppy?

Teri was happy to show off her new friend, hoisting the puppy up so that the camera could get a good view.

"What did you name him?" Angela prompted.

"His name is Dash," Teri told the camera. "That's because he dashes here and dashes there. That's when he's awake. Usually he's asleep. Because he's just a baby. But when he grows up, he's going to be a great agility dog. And obedience, too. And we'll have our picture in all the dog magazines."

"Good for you!" Angela exclaimed. She had been delighted at the addition of yet another dog to their traveling menagerie. Nothing could win over an audience like the combination of kid and puppy. Ernesto had already gotten good footage of the pup being introduced to the older dogs. What delicious comedy! Little Dobby had turned up an indignant nose. Shadow had immediately wanted to play with the small newcomer. In fact, he had touchingly presented the baby with one of his own toys as a welcome gift. And Idaho had appointed himself guardian, herding the puppy away from the motor home steps and other places where he shouldn't be.

This series was going to have it all—competition, drama, tears, heartbreak, pathos, joy, romance, a cute kid, an even cuter puppy, heartwarming dogs. This series, in fact, was going to put Rising Star Productions on the map.

And speaking of romance . . . With a satisfied smile, she pointed the camera toward the front of the motor home, where Cole drove and Jane, legs propped on the dashboard, gesticulated with long-fingered, graceful hands to stab home points in their discussion. Angela envied Jane those hands. Her own hands were short and stubby—kind of like the rest of her—with oversized knuckles that made it almost impossible to wear rings. Jane didn't appreciate her good features, even after Angela had dragged her, kicking and screaming, into good hair, good makeup, and better clothes. Neither did she appreciate how lucky she was to have caught the attention of Cole, a guy who had looks and smarts as well as being very nice. They were made for each other, it was obvious. Take just now, for instance, when they seemed totally involved in each other, deep in discussion. Eavesdropping, Angela couldn't decide if they were talking about dog-training techniques or kid-training techniques. Whatever, the two of them so often shut out the rest of the world when they were together. They seemed to connect on so many levels—and Angela intended to document their connection down to the last smile, the last scowl—hell, the last kiss, if she could catch it. So far, if they were kissing, they'd managed to slip it by both her and Ernesto.

Angela made a mental note to put Ernesto on alert for any romantic tidbits. Only that morning the two potential lovebirds had slipped out to jog in the early dawn, for the second day in a row. The only reason Angela knew this—dawn was not an hour she normally saw—was their return together, sweating and red-faced (at least Jane had been red-faced) just in time for breakfast. The jogging thing was becoming a habit, and Angela suspected Jane didn't go along just for fitness.

"Hey there!" Jane turned around in her seat and gave Angela a quelling look. Angela was growing accustomed to such looks. "Are you filming back there?" She self-consciously straightened an errant curl that fell across her face. (Angela did appreciate Jane's increased attention to grooming since Cole had come aboard.) "Angela! Do you have to film everything? All the time?"

"Relax," Angela told her. "I'm just getting filler material. It's not like you two are doing anything embarrassing up there. Are you?"

Jane muttered, "Give Angela a camera, and she can make your whole life embarrassing."

"I heard that!" Angela said with a grin. "If you must know, right now the puppy's antics are much more interesting than yours. So there." She turned the camera back toward Dash, who had squirmed out of Teri's arms and now entertained himself by pouncing on Shadow's paws. Shadow, who had been napping, joined in the game, moving his feet to make the puppy chase them. Idaho watched the two youngsters with benevolent condescension, and Dobby, curled on her pillow between the two front seats, opened one eye, sniffed disdainfully, and closed it again.

"You know, Angela," Teri said in a serious voice, "when Dash is the best agility dog in the whole world, maybe you should make a show about him."

"Maybe I will," Angela agreed as she watched little Dash change tactics and go after Shadow's waving tail. "Maybe this series will be such a hit that the public will demand a sequel."

"Me and Dash!" Teri grinned from ear to ear. Then the grin faded, and she wrinkled her nose.

Angela did the same. "Eeeww! What is that?"

That was Dash, looking very proud of himself, standing over a brown deposit he'd just made on the carpet.

"Time for a housebreaking lesson," Angela called up to the front.

"Your dog," Jane told Cole.

"You're the official trainer," Cole responded. "Of both kid and puppy." He grinned. "See ya later, sucker."

With a groan, Jane clambered out of her seat and headed for the mess.

"Good timing," Jane told Dash. "It was time to stop for lunch, anyway."

They stopped at a McDonald's in Sheridan that offered parking for RVs. They could have fixed sandwiches in the Enterprise, but everyone agreed that a Big Mac and fries would be more fun. Wind and dust greeted them when they piled out of the motor home. The wind had to be blowing, of course, because they were still within the boundaries of Wyoming.

Wind, dust, and all, Angela was glad enough to escape while Jane helped Teri clean up Dash's contribution to the motor home's ambiance.

"Who knew that puppy poop could be so fragrant?" Cole commented to Angela as they went into the restaurant.

"What? You never changed diapers when Teri was a baby?"

"I changed plenty of diapers. You just forget, after a while, what uncivilized little creatures infants are—human and canine."

Angela barely heard him, because sitting alone at a table in the restaurant, enjoying a burger, fries, and gigantic soft drink, was none other than Rick Tolleson. Her heart started doing calisthenics.

Angela had tried very hard not to think about Rick since their dinner together Saturday night. Dinner itself had been wonderful—a country-western experience that Willie Nelson himself could have sung about. The cowboy bar Rick had taken her to was little more than a hole in the wall, but it had great sloppy barbecued ribs and a wonderful band. She hadn't danced so much in years. And she'd learned to line dance, of all things! The bar had one of those fake bulls that let people pretend they were hotshot rodeo stars as well. That experience she had gladly passed up. But watching others make fools of themselves, while drinking beer and enjoying the feel of Rick's arm around her, had been downright delicious.

Rick had proved to be an old-fashioned gentleman—attentive, entertaining, a great dancer (both line dancing and the better sort, where moving to a sad, slow, country-western song was little more than an excuse for close-contact foreplay). Angela had enjoyed the dancing even more than eating the sloppy ribs. Rick made her blood steam, her knees turn to water, and her resistance melt like butter on hot toast.

Yes indeed, an ideal date. Until they had gone back to his motel room. Angela had decided her vow to forgo drive-by relationships could be broken just this once, because Rick was a hunk too tempting to pass up. She had been ready for a hot and raunchy finale to the evening, but after just a little bit of kiss and tickle, the man had gotten much too gentlemanly. He had actually declined to take the evening to its natural conclusion. She was much too special a woman for a one-night stand, he had told her. They should aim for more, he had said.

More? What more could two people like Angela Gardner and Rick Tolleson possibly have? The high-sounding words had been an excuse. He just hadn't wanted to make love to her. She was too fat, too short, too old, or hell, maybe her deodorant had failed her after all that dancing.

She'd put a good face on it, of course. He had tried to be a gentleman, and she couldn't force the man to think she was hot. Still, during that little bit of kiss and tickle, she could have sworn that fireworks had shot off in both of them.

And now here he was—following her? Or were their itineraries simply running a parallel path? Dog shows and performance trials were where the man made his living, after all, and right now she traveled the same road.

As she and Cole joined the line to order lunch, Cole spotted Rick. "Hey! Isn't that our traveling vet over there? Tolliver, Tolman, something like that?"

"Tolleson," Angela said. "Rick Tolleson."

"That's right." He paused to place his order, then returned to the subject. "He's a nice guy," Cole said. "Sort of unconventional, but he seems to know what he's doing."

Not with women, Angela thought morosely.

"He gave Dobby a massage last Saturday that worked out a bit of stiffness she had in her shoulder. Would you believe? A dog massage!"

Angela wouldn't mind having a similar massage from the good doctor, and not for her shoulder. But she shouldn't think about what she had missed. That just wasn't her style. If a girl obsessed about things like that, she would drive herself stark staring crazy.

"We should say hello," Cole proposed as he paid the cashier. And before Angela could stop him, he took his tray and headed for Rick's table.

They ended up all having lunch together—Angela, Jane, Cole, Teri, Ernesto, and Rick—laughing together like old friends, telling dog stories, talking about the upcoming trials in Washington. Rick greeted Angela with a wide smile and a hug, just as though he hadn't slapped her in the face by turning down his chance for maybe the best sex of his life. Or maybe it would have been the best sex of *her* life. There she went, obsessing again.

After lunch Rick came to the motor home to admire Teri's new puppy. He checked him over with gentle, practiced hands and declared him to be a picture of health. Those gentle, practiced hands...Oops! Obsessing. She just was not going to take this, Angela decided.

"Got to check the tire pressure," she said stiffly, and headed for the motor home door.

Jane caught her as she squatted beside the first tire. "Hey, Angie..."

Angela straightened and regarded Jane with narrowed eyes. Jane never called her Angie. Rick called her Angie. So Jane had mischief in mind.

"Has Rick ever got the hots for you!"

Angela snorted.

"Absolutely drooling."

Rick had definitely not been drooling, either on their

date or here at this impromptu lunch party. "There's not a hint of drool," Angela replied archly.

"It's all there in his eyes. I've known Rick for years, but I've never seen him smitten. Until now."

Jane was getting revenge for Angela's maneuverings with Cole. Sometimes, Angela thought, the woman's cheek could be very annoying.

"He is not smitten. How ridiculous. We went to dinner one time, and if you must know, we didn't hit it off that well."

That was a lie. They had hit it off great until Rick had decided that she wasn't good enough to sleep with. Obviously, the big lug had no taste in women. Or maybe...She squeezed her eyes shut, as if darkness would nip that thought in the bud. The notion was just too painful. She wouldn't even consider it.

"Well," Jane said, a "gotcha" in her tone, "here he comes, and that big smile on his face sure isn't for me."

Angela's eyes popped open, and she couldn't tear them away from the big blond bear who came lumbering down the motor home steps. What had she ever done to deserve this?

Jane chuckled wickedly. "See ya."

"Where the hell are you going?"

"I need to see a little girl about a puppy dog. Have fun."

Yes indeed, Angela thought sourly as Jane strode away. The woman could be very, very annoying. She quickly returned her attention to the motor home tire. If she ignored the man, maybe he would go away.

"Hi there," Rick greeted her.

"Hi." She concentrated on the tire as if it held the solution to all her problems.

"Something wrong with the tire?"

"No," she replied sharply. "I'm checking the pressure."

"I think you're supposed to use that gauge thingy that's

in your hand. Staring at the tire usually doesn't tell you much."

Angela sighed and stood up. "Smart-ass."

"It's one of my more endearing qualities."

She put a hand on one hip. "You're headed to Tacoma for the trials," she said, accusation in her sharp tone.

"That's the plan."

"Funny how our paths seem to be on a parallel course. Especially when you'd make a lot more money setting up at one of the big all-breed conformation shows instead of an agility trial. Lots more people there."

"Maybe I like to follow the dog athletes. They need my attention more than the beauty queens."

She tried to freeze his geniality with a chilly glare. "You're not becoming a stalker, are you, Rick?"

He chuckled. "I could be a stalker if that's what turns you on."

That was just the limit! Turn her on? As if he wanted to turn her on, the louse! "You sure sang a different tune the other night, didn't you? You have a nerve . . ." Damn! What the hell was Ernesto doing with that camera. Taking video? Of her? "Oh for God's sake! Ernesto!" she yelled. "Cut it out." She grabbed Rick's arm and pulled him to the other side of the motor home, where she could kill him in private. "I'm the producer of this goddamned show, and these people give me no respect." She backed Rick up against the side of the Challenger, noting that he was amazingly willing to cooperate in being slung around like a big, burly teddy bear. The least he could do was put up a fight. What was the use in being a bitch if you couldn't piss off the person you were being bitchy to?

But those killer blue eyes simply crinkled in amusement, and the twitch of that sensuous mouth hinted at a smile rather than alarm.

"Listen, Rick. You had your chance, okay? I'm not one of

these women who keeps coming back to let a guy slap her down again and again. Okay? Got it?"

"Angie, the last thing I want to do is slap you down. I'm just trying to give you the respect you deserve."

"Ha! Good try, buster."

"Like I told you, you deserve more than a one-night stand."

"That's a bit nineteenth century, isn't it?"

He shrugged, not fazed in the least by the scowl that usually made underlings flee. "I guess maybe I'm a nineteenth-century kind of guy."

Like she would believe that? Her eyes narrowed, and a dreadful possibility pushed into her mind. She didn't want to think it; she didn't want to say it. But she had to know. With a set jaw, she asked, "Are you gay?"

One of his bushy brows shot upward.

"Not that I have anything against gays. And not that it's any of my business. But in your case, I'd kind of like to know. Just call me nosy."

He sighed and shook his head. Then, without knowing quite how it happened, Angela found her own back pressed against the motor home and Rick's impressive bulk blocking out the sun.

"Does this make it seem like I'm gay?" His mouth captured hers in a kiss that held as much conquest as passion. His big hands took possession of her—one curled warmly around her neck, the other cradling her head, fingers woven through her hair.

Angela couldn't do anything but surrender. This man was so delicious, even though he was a pain in the ass. Delicious, confusing, nineteenth century. But oh, could he kiss!

When he finally released her, she could scarcely breathe.

"Well?" he asked archly.

"Nope," she sighed contentedly. "Not gay."

"When something is worth doing, Angie babe, I believe

it's worth doing right. You and I are destined for something a lot more right than a fast one-night grope and then good-bye."

She tried to glare, but couldn't quite manage it, tried to deny his conviction, but the words wouldn't come.

WHEN THEY got back on the road, somehow Rick had been invited to tag along. The best that Angela could remember, Jane had extended the invitation, spouting some nonsense about safety in numbers. The devil had danced in her eyes, for sure. Annoying woman. But turnabout was fair play. Angela had insisted on bringing Cole along to add some spice to the mix, and now she was getting slapped with some spice of her own.

But Angela hadn't been able to muster the energy to object. That kiss had sucked out all the energy she had. That didn't mean she was falling for Rick, Angela told herself. It just meant she was a sucker for a good kiss.

So now they headed north again, the tires humming along the asphalt, and a CD blaring a George Strait song from the motor home speakers. Up front, Cole sat in the driver's seat. Jane rode shotgun. Ahead of them, Rick's truck chugged along, towing the trailer that held his booth setup. And in front of Rick, Ernesto's van led the way.

Quite a procession, Angela thought wryly.

Apparently Cole agreed. Because he turned to Jane with a grin on his face. "Breaker, breaker, good buddy! I do believe we have us a convoy!"

chapter 19

THE RISING Star convoy crossed the border into Montana and turned west on Interstate 90. When they reached Billings, Rick got himself a motel room, but after dropping off his trailer and suitcase, he joined the rest of the group at the RV park, where they took advantage of the swimming pool to cool off from a long day on the road.

Teri was torn between wanting to go to the pool and at the same time stay in the motor home with her puppy. Jane could relate to her dilemma, because she also hated to go anywhere without a dog in attendance.

"Can't I bring Dash with us to the pool?" she asked her father.

Cole displayed admirable patience. "Swimming pools are not good places for puppies. They get in even more trouble than eight-year-old girls."

Teri scoffed. "I don't get into trouble." Then, at her father's skeptical look, she added, "Much."

"It wouldn't be safe for him, Teri. And besides, it isn't allowed."

The girl's bottom lip crept out, and Jane decided to give Cole a helping hand.

"Teri, Dash needs to learn that he can't always be with you. He'll be safe and comfortable in his kennel, and he'll have Dobby and Shadow and Idaho to keep him company."

"But—"

"It's part of his training, kid."

And since Teri was absolutely determined to raise Dash to be the perfect dog, that was a line of reasoning she swallowed.

So as the sun went down, the human members of the convoy gathered around the pool. Jane still felt self-conscious in her rather scant—at least by her standards—bathing suit, but she did feel flattered by the look in Cole's eyes when he dropped his lean body into the lounge chair beside her. Jane reminded herself that Cole's admiration was a thing of total unconcern to her. They were friends, and that was all. She had made that clear to him. And to herself. If that slow burn in his expression started a sizzle in her lower regions, she could ignore it as inappropriate and irrelevant. They were friends. And friends didn't sizzle just because they showed an unusual expanse of skin. And on his part, muscle.

Cole refrained from comment when he sat, and Jane accepted his silence as the comfortable thing it was. Most silences between people, especially between a man and a woman, turned the air heavy with tension. Amazing, Jane mused, that she could feel the same ease with a man that she felt with her closest friends. Especially considering how good he looked in swim trunks.

Still, sitting there beside Cole, watching Teri paddle around in the pool, Jane got an inkling of how it might feel to have a family of her own. Not that she needed one. A husband would be more of a bother than he was worth, and dealing with a kid like Teri went way beyond Jane's ambition. Dogs were much easier.

Still, she had dealt with Teri fairly well so far, Jane thought, then scolded herself. She needed to stick with dogs, who were more loyal than kids, and seldom talked back.

And speaking of dogs—Jane had a new ace in her game of one-upmanship with Cole. She might as well rub it in.

"So, Cole, how long is it going to take you to admit that my advice about that puppy was right?"

He raised a brow in her direction. "Right?"

"The kid seems to be a much happier camper."

"And I'm a much busier dad," he commented. "I feel as though I've added another child to the family—a child who isn't potty trained."

"Think of the housekeeping skills you're learning. You're now an expert on miracle products that remove urine stains from carpeting."

"Like that was my ambition in life."

Jane laughed. And suddenly, she wished she were the kind of woman who could fit into family life. If she were, Cole certainly—but no, she wasn't going to think about that. Her life was just fine the way it was, or it would be, once she got that life back.

"Now that you talked me into that puppy, you're Teri's hero, you know. Every other sentence out of her mouth is Jane does this and Jane says that. Are you going to allow her to come when we go out to celebrate my winning our bet?"

"You mean when we go out to celebrate *my* winning our bet, don't you? And maybe she can come. It'll keep you from being too nasty about losing."

"Sometimes nasty can be a good thing."

Jane's heart jumped at an unbidden image of just how delectable nasty might be, with Cole. But she wasn't going to think about that. So she moved to another subject. "Look at that. Ernesto's got his camera on this little scene, too. I swear."

"Ernesto gets everyone and everything on that camera."

"That doesn't bother you?"

He grinned. "Hell no. Who's going to notice me when they can look at you?"

"You are so full of bull," she tossed back.

For a while they watched Teri splash in the shallow end of the pool. The kid targeted Rick as her victim, insisting that he show her how to squirt a lethal stream of water from her hand, just like he did. She learned fast, then challenged him to a duel. Angela watched, her eyes on Rick, her expression half sullen, half wistful.

And that was the point when a wicked thought pushed its way into Jane's head. "Excuse me," she said, climbing out of the lounger and wrapping a towel around her hips. "I hear an idea calling."

Casually, she walked over to Ernesto, who had a camera glued to his shoulder, as usual. "Ernie . . ."

"Huh? Oh, hi, Jane."

"I think you're missing the best part of the action here."

He looked uneasy. "Listen, Jane, I know you don't like the camera pointed at you a lot of the time, but Angela knows what she's doing—usually. Viewers like the personal stuff, and—"

She put a firm finger on one of his shoulders and turned him in the direction where Rick and Angela sat on the edge of the pool in animated conversation. At least Rick was animated. Angela might be better described as fuming. Teri had finally left them alone and had gone to demonstrate her new water-squirting technique to her father.

"There's something personal you could get on camera."

Ernesto's mouth flickered in a brief, wry smile. "That's a thought. They look as if they're pretty deep in some kind of significant discussion. Look at that. When Angela gets that expression on her face, someone's in trouble. Wonder what poor Rick did to get under her skin."

Jane wondered also. Whatever it was, Rick was giving as

good as he was getting. "I think Angela should be a part of this little reality series," she said. "Don't you think?"

The smile grew into a full-fledged grin. "You're going to get me fired."

"Nah. We're just giving Angela a reality check of her own. We'll see how she likes a minute-by-minute video commentary on *her* life."

Ernesto shook his head. "You're bad." But as Jane walked away, his camera swung toward Angela and Rick.

TRAVELING WESTWARD, they left the plains behind and climbed through the mountains of western Montana and northern Idaho, driving through scenery so spectacular that Teri was too awestruck to bother reading to them from her travel book. Angela drove the Enterprise, Teri kept her company in the shotgun seat, Dash curled in her lap, and Cole and Jane battled through a game of Monopoly in the back.

When they rolled through Coeur d'Alene in Idaho, Cole mentioned that his family lived up ahead in Spokane. Angela, who was succumbing to road weariness, brightened.

"What kind of family?" she asked.

"A sister and her fiancé."

"Excellent. Let's stop there for the night."

Caught off guard, Cole barely got out an uncertain "Uh ..." before Angela plowed ahead.

"Does your sister have room for a motor home in her driveway?"

"Well ... yeah. She has a huge new house on two acres."

"I'll bet she would love a visit from her brother and niece, right?"

"Don't fall for it, Cole," Jane warned. "She's just after fodder for her viewing audience."

But Teri was already singing out "Yippee!" at the prospect

of a visit to her aunt, so Cole dug out his cell phone and informed his sister that she would have guests for the evening.

Nancy Forrest's house on the outskirts of Spokane was a rambling ranch with six bedrooms, a four-car garage, and an attached studio where Nancy created her nationally syndicated cartoon strip *Slugnuts*, which had transformed her from a financially struggling high school art teacher to someone who could afford such a house and have enough money left over to require the attention of a financial manager. Nancy welcomed her younger brother and niece with open arms and treated the rest of the convoy as if they were family as well, pooh-poohing the idea that Angela, Jane, and Ernesto should sleep in the motor home and van or that Rick should get a motel room.

"This place has six bedrooms!" she declared, throwing her arms wide to encompass such luxury. "Would you believe that anyone would build a house this big?"

"What I don't believe," her brother gibed, "is that you bought a house this big."

"Well," Nancy said, looking a bit embarrassed, "I wanted the studio. The studio is absolutely superior. And besides, Mark wants lots of kids. Kids just like Teri," she said, tugging her niece's ear and laughing. Turning to Jane, she explained. "Mark and I are getting married in two weeks. Can you tell I'm in a tizzy?"

"Two weeks?" Cole exclaimed. "I thought you were getting married in October."

"We moved it up, because my matron of honor has to go to a conference. I've been trying to get hold of you, baby bro, but you weren't home."

"You could have e-mailed me. I pick up my e-mail most days."

She scoffed. "E-mail! Ha! You got all the computer smarts in the family. I tried to get online, but something went wrong in my mailbox, or whatever, and those poor boys on the tech support line have just given up on me, I swear."

Cole rolled his eyes.

"But come in, come in! All of you. Bring your dogs. Bring your bathing suits. I have a terrific pool. Mark is at work, but he'll be thrilled to come home and find someone to talk to besides me. And, oh my! Ernie, is it? That's quite a camera you have. Are we on the news or something?"

Jane liked Cole's sister. Obviously, she had megabucks and enjoyed success in what she did, but she was as down-home as a Cornville cowboy. When Angela explained to her about Ernesto and the camera (permanently mounted on his shoulder, it seemed), waxing eloquent about the art of the documentary, the agony and the ecstasy of canine sports, and so on, Nancy sent Cole a subtle eye-roll that proved such things were truly genetic. At that moment, Nancy could have been a grown-up Teri. But subtle as it was, Angela saw it and laughed.

"Okay, I get carried away. But you don't mind us shooting, do you?"

"Heck no. I've always wanted to be on TV."

The interior of the house was as gorgeous as the exterior. They each had the luxury of a large bedroom. Three huge bathrooms provided a welcome change from the motor home facilities, where anyone sitting on the pot had their feet in the shower stall. And although Nancy might not share her brother's computer savvy, in the kitchen she was an absolute wizard. She insisted upon feeding them a dinner fit for royalty.

"It's the cook's night off," she told them as they arranged themselves around a gorgeous mahogany dining room table. "Getting to use my own brand-new gourmet kitchen is a treat for me. And you people are just the excuse I need."

"You have a cook?" Jane said, both awestruck and envious.

"I have a cook," Nancy confirmed. "A little Chinese lady, and such an artist with food. She's been with me for about five years." Nancy laughed. "I know it's a ridiculous luxury, but when I'm working on a deadline with the strip, which is about always, I tend to not exercise, not feed myself, not clean the house, or anything else. So I gave up a long time ago and hired people to do what I should be doing."

"Don't let her fool you," Cole said. "It has nothing to do with her being focused on work. When we were kids, her room always looked like a tornado had just blown through. And the only thing she ever made in the kitchen was a peanut butter sandwich."

"Well, at least I've learned to cook," Nancy threw back, pointing her knife toward the wonderful pot roast she had served. "And have you learned to do anything more practical than computers? He never could get his nose out of computer this and computer that, games and programs and whatever. Either that or he buried himself in some math problem. Never even played football like a normal kid."

"Yeah, football got *me* such a long way in life," laughed Mark, who had come home just before dinner and, as Nancy had predicted, welcomed the unexpected guests with open arms. "I played quarterback all the way through college, aimed my whole life toward getting drafted by the pros, and ended up with a liberal arts degree and no job. The only thing I could put on my resumé was a tendency to fumble the ball on the ten-yard line. Damn!"

They all laughed, because it was obvious that Mark had done well for himself in starting up a recreational equipment business.

After dinner, they drifted into the living room to enjoy pie and ice cream. Nancy wasn't one of those people who quailed at the thought of crumbs on the carpet or an occasional dollop of chocolate marring her leather furniture. Nor did she mind dog hair accessorizing her living room décor, because she invited the dogs—even baby Dash—to join in the after-dinner socializing.

Jane took her dessert to a cozy spot on a small loveseat beside the fireplace, which was now serving as a frame for a colorful spray of mixed flowers. Shadow and Idaho crowded against her legs, panting from an exhilarating run in Nancy's backyard. Teri sat cross-legged on the carpeted floor with Dash in her lap, while Dobby laid claim to a plush pillow on the window seat overlooking the yard. Rick sprawled his generous frame on one of the big leather sofas that were arranged in a "conversation group" in the center of the room. Angela sat in a chair on the other side of the fireplace, as far from the vet as the room allowed. Every once in a while she sent a surreptitious glance his way.

Nancy circulated around the room, making sure everyone had enough ice cream and cake. "Coffee!" she exclaimed. "I forgot the coffee! What a dunderhead!" Then she spotted Cole just coming into the room. "Bubba boy, be a good sport and go turn on the coffeemaker, will you."

Jane couldn't help but laugh. "Bubba boy?"

Cole grinned ruefully. "Nancy, I'll get you for that." But he turned back to the kitchen as his big sister had ordered.

Teri was anxious to show off her new puppy, especially since Ernesto had his camera going in an unobtrusive corner of the room. She insisted that everyone watch her little friend show off his new skills at sitting and lying down on command.

"Jane's a famous dog trainer," she boasted. "And she's teaching me how to be a trainer, too."

"Not famous," Jane corrected. "And what did I tell you about getting Dash excited right after he eats? You'd better take him out into the yard for a few minutes."

"Right," Teri agreed, then informed Nancy and Mark, "Dash is only nine weeks old, and he almost always pees outside, where he's supposed to. That's because I'm training him."

Cole came back in and dropped down beside Jane on the loveseat, casually draping one arm behind her. "Well then, Miss Dog Trainer, you'd better get that puppy outside like Jane told you, or you'll be giving us a demonstration of how to clean a carpet. Got it?"

Teri grinned and lifted the pup into her arms. "Got it."

As Teri trotted happily toward the backyard, Jane wondered if the arm draped casually along the back of the loveseat was accidental or deliberate. She saw Nancy give them a thoughtful glance, even though Cole's attention seemed to be anywhere but on Jane.

"Coffee's making," he told his sister, and somehow the encircling arm slid from the back of the seat to rest gently on her shoulders.

An accident, Jane told herself. Definitely an accident. Yet that arm gave her a peculiar feeling in the pit of her stomach, a region heretofore reserved for hunger pangs and competition jitters. It was a warm feeling, overall, spiced with a touch of unease. She and Cole were not an item, after all. Since that kiss on the lakeshore at Antelope Island, he had completely behaved himself—behaved like a friend. A good friend. A friend who cared. A friend who kissed really, really well. But they were not an item. She should not be getting warm feelings from such a simple gesture.

"So, Jane," Nancy said with a curious smile, "Cole tells me that you and he are competing for the same prize."

That made them sound so connected, so Jane clarified. "Cole and I and about a thousand other people."

"You mean my baby brother is actually good at something that doesn't involve a keyboard or calculator?"

Jane couldn't help but give Cole a teasing grin. "His dog is very good. That's all I'll say."

"But she thinks *her* dog is better," he said.

"My dog at least is big enough to not regard a clod of dirt as a major hurdle."

He smiled and squeezed her shoulder. "I told you she's prejudiced," he said to his sister. "Stubborn, too."

Nancy raised a brow. "Is that what you told me?"

An even wider grin spread across Cole's face.

They had been talking about her, Jane mused somewhat uneasily. What exactly had Cole told his sister? His face didn't give a hint, and Nancy just smirked. Was that a big-sister smirk, or something else?

Jane became even more conscious of the weight of Cole's arm lying across her shoulders. That arm seemed almost possessive, a mark that she belonged to Cole and therefore belonged in this picture of family affection. One part of Jane felt terribly out of place, and another part wanted to try the belonging on for size.

This family scene was unlike anything Jane had experienced growing up. She didn't have siblings, and her parents, while affectionate and caring, had maintained a distance they thought belonged between generations. No joking or teasing had lightened their relationship. Jane suddenly envied Teri growing up with a father like Cole and an aunt like Nancy.

"Hey, Jane," Nancy said. "How about giving me a hand battling the mess in the kitchen?"

"Sure thing." With mixed relief and reluctance, Jane slipped from beneath Cole's arm, ignoring the brief squeeze of his hand as she left.

"I'll help, too," Angela volunteered.

"No need," Nancy told her. "Sit down and enjoy the ice cream. And if you let Ernesto near my dirty kitchen with his camera, I'll have to do something very uncivilized to the poor man."

Angela laughed and settled back into her seat on the sofa. "As long as you keep feeding me ice cream, your word is law. This stuff tastes positively homemade."

"It is homemade," Mark told her. "We got one of those electric ice cream makers as a housewarming gift."

"Oh, my," Angela purred, taking another bite. "I'm in heaven, even though I'm going to have to pay for this with at least an hour with my new aerobics tape."

"Don't do it, Angie," Rick warned her. "You'll end up a Skinny Minnie like Jane there. No offense, Jane."

Jane laughed. "None taken. And don't worry about Angela. She never carries out her threats to exercise."

"Hey!" Angela objected, but Jane escaped to the kitchen before Angela could work up a good head of steam.

Safe in the kitchen, Jane and Nancy shared the laughter. "That's quite a motley crew you have there," Nancy said.

"Not *my* crew," Jane denied, stacking the dirty saucepans and skillets from the stove. "Angela and her canine reality series keep collecting people along the road."

Nancy started hot water running in the sink. "You all seem to have a good time together."

"We have our moments," Jane admitted, her thoughts running through highlights of their trip. Most of those highlights involved Cole.

As if picking up on Jane's thoughts, Nancy shot her a curious look. "Have you known Cole a long time?"

"Oh, heavens no!" Jane said too quickly. "We got acquainted at a couple of agility trials, and then his motor home broke down, so we offered him a ride."

Obviously not taken in, Nancy replied with an inarticulate "Hm."

"We're friends," Jane told her. "Just friends."

"Uh-huh," Cole's big sister said with a smile. "You know, I don't think I've seen Teri so animated since Mandy died. She took her mom's death very hard."

"Any kid would, I would think." Jane dumped the dirty cookware into the sink.

"True, but most kids recover faster. Teri sort of just sank into herself. But look at her now. That grin of hers is so big it's almost bigger than her face."

"It's the puppy. Dogs can do wonders for people who hurt."

"So I've heard. Pet therapy in hospitals and nursing homes is all the thing now, isn't it?" Nancy picked up a greasy skillet and smiled at her grease-distorted reflection. "But love can do wonders, too. The kid adores you."

Jane snorted. "She likes me right now because I finagled a puppy for her."

"Maybe," Nancy conceded. "But how about Cole? He looks at you as if you're something better than my home-made ice cream."

Jane nearly dropped the stack of dirty plates she was carrying. She recovered her grip on the china, gave Nancy a stern look, and told her, "Cole isn't doing any such thing. We're friends, like I said."

Nancy chortled. "Friends with benefits?"

Jane set the stack of plates carefully on the counter. "No benefits. What? You have it in for your poor brother?"

"I'm happy he's looking at someone again, someone nice like you."

Jane made a rude sound.

"You can't deny it! You have a soft spot for him, don't you?"

"No." Jane focused on putting the rinsed plates into the dishwasher.

"I can tell. You do. And Teri likes you. That's very important."

"Nancy, you're out of your gourd."

Nancy laughed, not at all intimidated by the tone that could quell a Rottweiler. "No I'm not," she said merrily. "A woman in love, like me, can spot another woman in love. You and I have a lot in common. I can tell."

Jane looked around the big kitchen with its terra-cotta tile and shiny appliances, looked out the window at the pool with its terraced fountains, glowing in the night with soft underwater lighting. Then she thought of her own humble home—ex-home, that is—which she had loved dearly, but was a galaxy away from the universe where Nancy Forrest lived.

"What," she asked, truly curious, "do you think we have in common?"

"Oh, lots!" Nancy squeezed out a scouring pad to go to work on a particularly grungy skillet. "Look at us—both women who are not, let's face it, in the first bloom of youth."

Jane smiled at that. "I don't remember ever really being in bloom."

Nancy shook her head. "Well, some of us bloom late. You're what? Twenty-eight, maybe?"

"Thirty." It was the first time that Jane could remember where someone had erred on the minus side of her age. Chalk up a point for the makeover.

"Okay, you're thirty. I'm thirty-five, so I held out longer than you did. But we're both mature women, strong, independent, competent, both very defensive of our independence and privacy and all that."

Jane was impressed. "How do you know all that about me? We only met a couple of hours ago."

Nancy laughed and placed a gleaming skillet in the drainer. "I'm a cartoonist, and I'm used to observing people to get material for my strip. Besides," she added with a soft smile, "I see myself in your eyes—myself when I first met Mark. I fought the temptation to let some man have power over my life. Frankly, the idea terrified me. And I also couldn't believe that someone like Mark could sincerely fall for someone like me."

"What do you mean, 'someone like me'?"

Nancy just smiled, and Jane really didn't need an answer, because she knew. How many times had she poohpoohed the thought that Cole—good-looking, smart, fit, and eminently eligible—would be attracted to Jane Connor. Not the Jane Connor of the breezy hairdo and Angela-assisted makeup, but the Jane Connor who washed down smelly kennels, brushed out dirty dogs, and provided maid and meal service for a varying menagerie of dogs and cats.

But Nancy was the real thing, successful and attractive, with a little plumpness that added to, not detracted from, a soft, feminine appeal. She was what she was, not someone who had been dolled up for the benefit of a television audience, not some Cinderella who would give up all the fake veneer—the expensive haircut, the mascara, and the flattering clothes—as soon as Angela and Ernesto took the camera away.

"You're someone that any man would be attracted to," Jane told Cole's sister.

Nancy laughed and shook her head. "And look at *you*, with that figure, those great green eyes and flamboyant hair. And the great smile. You have one of the prettiest smiles I've ever seen."

Jane's mouth fell open.

"Don't see yourself that way?" Nancy nodded. "Most of our uncertainties, I've learned, come from the inside, not the outside. And most of our defenses, as well. You and I both have grown a thicket of thorns around us that anyone has to negotiate to get to our hearts. Not just guys. Anyone."

"That's—"

Nancy's raised brows stopped Jane mid-denial. How could this woman know? But she did know. Jane had two good friends in this world—Nell and Mckenna. And both of them had teased her endlessly about her reluctance to let people get close to her.

Nancy answered her unspoken question. "I know because we're so much the same. Like I said, I recognize myself in your eyes, Jane. Except that I got smart and surrendered, and now I've discovered that independence doesn't hold a candle to happiness, and a couple is more than just two people living together. It's a synergy that's so amazing that it can't be described; it has to be experienced."

Nancy's passion in her conversion was almost spell-binding. If she'd been an evangelist, she would have been right up there with Billy Graham. Jane had to fake a chuckle to break the spell.

"It's so wonderful that Mark came along for you," she told Nancy. Then, with a crooked smile, "But Cole doesn't want to 'synergize' with me, Nancy. You're just so in love that you want love to happen for everyone. Your brother's an absolutely great guy, and you shouldn't worry about him. He's going to find someone really special to bring into his life and Teri's. But I'm not that someone."

Why did that thought make Jane feel heavy inside?

Nancy nodded and smiled. "Still fighting the battle, are you? Believe me, Jane—if you win this particular battle, you lose. You really, really lose. Take it from a veteran of the same battle." She placed the last scoured pot in the drainer and threw Jane a towel. "So welcome to the family, Jane, and dry."

chapter 20

THE ARGUS Ranch Facility for Dogs outside of Tacoma, Washington, was a dog exhibitor's dream, and a producer's as well, Angela decided at the end of a walk around the place. The walk had taken some time, because the grounds included meadows, training buildings, two covered arenas, parking lots, an RV lot where the Enterprise happily rested with full hookups, and a modern "ranch house" that boasted all the comforts of home. The Argus manager, a top-flight agility competitor and judge in her own right, had given Angela a tour of the place when she had explained that Argus Ranch would be featured in *Winner Take All*, not only with footage from this weekend's agility trial but from the grand finale in August, when top competitors from across the nation would gather here to run their hearts out in the Solid Gold Invitational.

Actually, Merlyn, the manager, hadn't been that impressed with the prospect of being featured in a canine reality show, but she was a friendly sort and had been very cooperative, taking Angela through the ranch house, training buildings, and the exhibitor dormitory, then giving a preview of how the Solid Gold event would be laid out among the different arenas. The manager knew Jane by reputation, and remembered Cole and Dobby from a trial she had judged last winter.

"Jane's a tough competitor," Merlyn commented as they walked toward the biggest arena. "And she's a great representative of the sport. You couldn't have chosen a better subject for your—you did say this was a documentary?"

"Yes, a documentary. Sort of a blend of documentary and entertainment."

"Ah. Well, Jane will be good, no matter. And Cole"—she smiled the same smile that Cole seemed to inspire in so many women—"Cole is unique with that little papillon of his. Not many guys could work that well with a toy breed. You're going to have an interesting show."

The woman didn't know the half of it, Angela thought smugly as Merlyn left her on her own in the big arena, where the Excellent Standard class and Novice Jumpers had already begun. An hour earlier, Cole and Dobby had put in an outstanding effort in Standard, with Dobby bouncing over the jumps and streaking through the tunnels like a little whirlwind with fur. One would think that a fragile little dog like Dobby would hesitate on the dog-walk or A-frame, which must look like a ten-story building to such a tiny creature. But not Dobby. Put that little dog on the starting line of an agility course, and she transformed from a pillow princess into the canine version of Wonder Woman. Jane was going to have her hands full dealing with the Cole/Dobby challenge—in more ways than one, Angela mused with a grin.

Ah, the rocky road of romance. Cole was playing Jane just right, Angela thought. She had watched them carefully that morning as they returned from their jog. Jane had been red-faced and sweaty, with her hair pulled back into an unattractive, stubby ponytail, yet Cole courted her through every glance, every casual touch. Jane didn't even seem to know she was being courted—or maybe she was just too stubborn to acknowledge it—but to Angela's way of thinking, a man who showed interest even before a woman did her hair and makeup was definitely a serious player. Bringing Cole on board their expedition was not only a stroke of brilliance for the show, but a real favor to Jane as well. Though Angela didn't expect Jane to admit it any time soon.

But that brought the other addition to their convoy to mind, and Angela didn't really want to think about Rick. Since that incredible kiss behind the motor home, thoughts of Rick had plagued her, muddling her mind and making her stomach tighten. Damn him, the man simply did not behave like a normal man should. Men were supposed to like casual sex. It was some kind of universal law. The big bozos had to be trapped into anything more serious. But this big bozo had turned down a perfect chance to get her in the sack with no strings attached. Because he said she was too good for a one-night stand? Bull! Angela could have understood him backing off and making excuses because she didn't appeal to him. But that kiss proved otherwise. And he kept hanging around, convoying with them, eating with them, making himself a part of the group, placing himself where she couldn't help but talk to him, argue with him, be with him—dammit! And all the while he watched her with that infuriating smile on his incredible mouth, like he was waiting for her to repent her foolish ways and fall into his arms for a "serious relationship."

Serious relationship, bullshit! Been there, done that, and barely survived the emotional shredder. What Angela needed to do was forget about Rick and his incredible mouth and infuriating smile, and concentrate on Jane, who was warming up Shadow on a set of practice weave poles at the far end of the arena.

"There you are," Ernesto said as he walked up, camera on his shoulder as always.

"Here I am, of course. Where have you been all morning?"

"Getting some background shots of the ranch. Quite a place, eh?"

"Tell me you didn't miss Cole's run this morning. It was spectacular."

"I got it."

"And did you get a shot of Jane watching with that wistful look on her face?"

"What wistful look?"

"Ernie! How could you miss that? That woman wears her feelings on her face like I wear makeup! How could you not get that?"

"I figured she was entitled to some privacy. Think about it, Angela. You didn't much like it when I shot you yelling at Rick a few days ago. Or when I caught that little tête-à-tête beside the swimming pool."

"I was not yelling at Rick," Angela insisted through gritted teeth. "And it was not a tête-à-tête. Anyway, that's different. I'm the producer of this series, not the star. I don't belong on camera. Jane does, with everything she does and feels. Especially when she feels. Audiences like drama with their sports. Drama, conflict, and romance."

Ernesto sighed.

"You did follow them on their jog this morning, right?"

"There's no drama, conflict, or romance when they jog, Angela. They run, talk, sometimes laugh. That's all."

"Running, talking, laughing are important. It's the subtleties that make these things real. Don't let up."

"You know," Ernesto said, "Jane's not going to like it when she sees some of the stuff we've shot."

"Jane's a sport," Angela assured him. "She and I have talked this out, and she knows what the score is. Don't worry about her. She's a big girl. And speaking of Jane, she doesn't look too pleased over there at the practice weave poles with Shadow. Get that, Ernie. She never has trouble with that dog. This is new. So go catch it."

"If she sees the camera, it'll just add to her problems."

"Then don't let her see the camera," she instructed, exasperated. "Sheesh! Do I have to think of everything?"

JANE TRIED hard to keep her cool with Shadow, but the golden retriever was making it hard. Usually so compliant and enthusiastic, Shadow was paying only minimum attention to the line of twelve weave poles set up for practice. For the third time he had "popped a pole," or missed one of the poles in his fast in-and-out weave. And the weave wasn't as fast as it should be.

"What is wrong with you today?" Jane demanded in a low voice, but the tone made Shadow's ears fall. "By now you should be able to do these poles in your sleep, if you would just pay attention."

The dog looked longingly toward the door, which beckoned with a warm square of white sunshine.

"Play in the meadows later," Jane promised. "Work now. Your turn is coming up."

Shadow whined and looked once again toward the door. Who said dogs couldn't talk?

"Do you miss Teri and Dash?" Jane asked. "Is that it?"

When they had left Spokane the day before, Teri and her puppy had stayed behind for a visit with Cole's sister—to help Nancy get ready for the wedding, Teri had boasted.

"You miss that puppy climbing all over you and all those supposed conversations you had with the kid?"

Shadow wasn't saying. He might carry on conversations with Teri, as the kid claimed, but lately he hadn't been talking much to Jane.

"Just a couple more practice weaves," Jane told him. "Then we'll take a break."

Shadow did another weave, perfect but slow. Then another where he missed the first pole. Jane gritted her teeth, reminded herself that continuing on this bad note would do more harm than good, and snapped the leash to the dog's collar to take him outside. "Maybe sniffing a few trees will put you back on track, eh?"

Fifteen minutes later, when they shot off the start line, Shadow's mood had changed from distracted to determined. He sailed over jumps as if he had wings on his feet, sped through the tunnel, drilled the tire jump, cleared the triple with six inches to spare, and flew over the A-frame and dog-walk without missing a single beat. Every turn and jump was a thing of beauty. Every foot landed precisely where Jane wanted it to land, every shift of weight came just at the right time. Jane and her dog were once again a team as they crossed the finish line in record time, with a perfectly clean run.

Jane whooped with joy and launched herself at Cole, who had been watching from near the exit gate. While Shadow jumped up and down in excitement, Cole pounded her on the back in congratulations. Almost losing her balance, she grabbed hold of him to steady herself. The small intimacy inspired a blush above and beyond the heat of exertion.

"Oops!" she cried, extricating herself. "Sorry, Cole. Got carried away."

"Great run!" he told her with a big grin. "You might even have beaten us."

She laughed. "You can be sure that we beat you. I think that's about our best." She tingled where they had momentarily been welded together. Good thing she had a few hours before running Jumpers class. Now she was as distracted as Shadow.

"It's all that jogging I've been forcing on you," Cole claimed. "So some of the credit belongs to me, you know."

"None of the credit belongs to you," Jane countered, grinning.

"Want to grab a bite?"

The bite that leapt into Jane's mind had nothing to do

with hitting the food concession. Don't go there, she warned herself.

"Uh, actually, I need to work a bit with Shadow. This last was a good run, but he's been giving me fits on stuff he should have down pat."

Cole shook his head and smiled. "Edged out by a dog. Jane Connor, you're a difficult woman."

She grinned. "Never said that I wasn't."

Jane forced herself not to watch Cole leave, and instead tugged Shadow toward the big outdoor arena where several other handlers were working their dogs over practice jumps. She figured a few minutes of obedience work might remind Shadow where his attention should be. It might do to remind Jane where her attention should be as well.

"Hey, Jane!"

Jane looked around to see Merlyn Anderson, the Argus Ranch manager, hailing her from the ranch house.

"Hey, Merlyn. What's up?"

"We had a couple of cancellations on dorm rooms. You were telling me this morning that living in an RV is getting old, so I thought maybe you might like to sleep in a real room while you're here." Her eyes twinkled mischievously. "Since you're going to be a star, or so I'm told, we have to treat our stars right, don't we?"

"Don't start!" Jane warned. "I get enough of that star business from Angela."

Merlyn laughed. "The room is there. Take it or leave it. I have three cancellations, so you're not putting us out."

The very thought made Jane want to sigh with pleasure. A real room, with plaster walls and a bathroom where her backside wouldn't hit the door when she bent over to wash her face in the sink. "It's a deal, Merlyn. Thanks. I can take the dogs in with me, right?"

"Take the dogs, take your friends—I don't care. Be my guest."

. . .

JANE DID take the dogs with her when she temporarily vacated the motor home. And it turned out that she took her friends, too, because when she dumped her duffle bag in her room and went walking about to explore the dormitory, she recognized a jumble of familiar voices. Following the sound, she climbed the stairs to the second-floor "common room"—a living-room—style area with easy chairs, sofas, and a homey fireplace. There she found the entire motor home crowd that she had looked forward to shedding for the night, along with Merlyn, a host of exhibitors she knew only slightly, and the ever-present Rick Tolleson.

Jane laughed ruefully as she came into the room. "I knew that was Angela's laugh."

"There you are!" Angela proclaimed. "You thought you had escaped, didn't you?"

Rick was keeping track of Angela, Jane noted, with the same determination that Angela showed in ignoring him. Jane wondered again what their quarrel had been. Every time she had asked Angela about it, she got a huffy reply along the lines of "Men are such assholes!"

Jane, feeling a bit wicked, couldn't resist stirring the pot a bit. "I see Rick is here," she mentioned to Angela.

"Is he?" Angela replied loftily.

"Uh-huh. Is that Sally Croft with that nice German shepherd hanging onto his every word?"

Angela sniffed. "You're the only person I know who can't identify a person without making note of which dog that person has."

Which was a dodge if Jane had ever heard one. "You know, Rick is considered quite a catch by just about every single woman in the dog world."

Angela leveled a narrow-eyed glare at her. "You have romance concerns of your own that you should pay attention to, Jane, rather than sticking your nose in someone else's affairs."

"Ah," Jane said, smiling. "That's your gig. Right?"

"Feeling feisty tonight, are we?"

"I did have a couple of good runs today."

"Maybe you should take some of that feist over to Cole. I think he was looking for you earlier."

"Cole?"

"Uh-huh. Over in the corner. Take your eyes off of Rick for a moment and pay attention to your own man."

"Cole is not my man," Jane said, annoyed.

Angela smiled complacently.

Cole was indeed in the corner, standing by a table laden with bottles. He was pouring—was that what Jane thought it was?

"There you are," he greeted Jane.

"Is that what I think it is?" Jane asked.

"Merlot, chardonnay, or zinfandel," Cole said, holding up a bottle and pointing to several others. "Take your choice."

"What is this? A party?"

Cole presented her with a full glass. "It is a party," he confirmed. "You are looking at a man who has been invited to the Solid Gold Invitational."

"What?" Jane almost spilled her wine.

"My old business partner checks my post office box in Albuquerque every day. Guess what came in the mail?"

Jane was stunned. Happiness for Cole instantly went to battle with outright envy. "I ... that's ... ohmigod!" She set the glass of wine on a nearby table, grabbed Cole by the hands, and jumped up and down. "That's incredible! Cole! That's so great!"

One of the exhibitors whom Jane knew only as a border collie handler inserted herself into the congratulations. "I got an invite, too. So we're celebrating."

"That's wonderful!" Jane refused, absolutely refused, to

give in to selfish, spiteful envy. And she refused to look toward the camera that Ernesto had produced. The man could conjure a camera out of thin air. After all this time on the road with him, Jane should expect that.

Everyone ended up talking at once, congratulating the two invitees, rehashing past agility runs, both their own and others', speculating about who else might soon be getting a note from the Solid Gold organizers. Someone had gone overboard buying the wine, because the supply seemed endless. Several full bottles remained even when the celebrators started drifting away, back to their RVs, motels, or dorm rooms, and not because anyone had been judicious in their drinking.

By the time the room had nearly emptied, the hour was still relatively early. Ernesto and his camera were gone, so Jane felt free to let the warm buzz of wine soften some of her defenses. Angela and Merlyn had hit it off, it seemed, because they sat together on the raised hearth of the fireplace, deep in conversation. Cole was busy fielding advances from a tall, rangy woman with a Texas accent and a rather braying laugh—maybe it wouldn't sound quite so much like a donkey hee-haw if Jane hadn't downed half a bottle of merlot.

Jane leaned back into the soft sofa cushions and closed her eyes. When she opened them, Cole sat beside her and everyone else had gone.

"Looks like the party's over," she said. "Look at the mess."

"I told Merlyn we'd take the stuff down to the kitchen. She says staff will wash it up tomorrow."

Jane yawned. "You volunteered *us*?"

"I knew you'd want to help."

"Right." Suddenly, she felt all soft inside. "Hey, Cole. Congratulations. I mean it. I couldn't be happier."

"Really?"

"Okay, I *could* be happier, but only if it were me."

He laughed. "I'm starting to make a list of possible

places you can take me to dinner. What kind of food do you like?"

She grabbed a sofa pillow and swung at him. "Don't start counting your chickens. I'm going to get one of those invitations any day, you know."

He laughed, caught the arm that swung the pillow and tugged her forward into a hug. "You will," he said, serious now. "No one doubts it, except maybe you."

The warmth of his arms surrounded her, and Jane melted. The feel of his body, his wine-scented breath in her hair, his mouth brushing the back of an ear—those things became the focus of her entire attention. For a moment, she forgot about agility, the ashes of her life, the uncertainties of the future.

But then he pulled away, smiling ruefully. "Dishes," he said. "Duty calls."

Dizzily she floundered back to reality. "Oh, yeah. Dishes."

Downstairs in the kitchen, Jane filled the sink with soapy water, despite Merlyn's assurance that the staff would wash up. Maybe it was an excuse to extend the time she had with Cole, or maybe she was just restless, unwilling to return to her room, where Shadow and Idaho stretched out contentedly on the twin beds. Without a word of protest, Cole picked up a dishtowel and began to dry. They didn't speak, though in truth there was a lot that could be said. But the bond that had been growing between them had strengthened this evening, and now it stretched between them with a vibrancy that needed no words for its support.

But when the last glass was washed and dried, Jane found herself at a loss. She was still warm from the wine, muzzy with a strange longing that had nothing to do with her drive to win the Invitational.

Cole hesitated as well. Jane wished she knew what he was thinking.

"Finished," he said.

"Right. Well...I need to take my dogs out for a walk. Then turn in." The words felt empty. What did she really want? Jane didn't know.

"Mind if I join you?"

"Of course not." Such an ordinary exchange of words, but it sent a thrill of nervousness through Jane, a jumpiness that rivaled her precompetition jitters.

They fetched Idaho and Shadow from Jane's room, then, to Jane's surprise, went three doors down the hall to get Dobby from another room.

"I decided to take a vacation from the motor home as well," Cole explained.

"Well...that's nice."

Come on, Jane, you can do better than that.

"All the comforts of home here."

Their conversation wasn't exactly sprightly, but a tense sort of vibration hummed in the air between them as they walked through the cool July night to one of the ranch's open meadows, where floodlights lit the grass. There they turned the dogs loose and let them run, sitting side by side on a bench to watch. Cole's arm snuck around behind her, just as it had in Spokane, and Jane couldn't resist the urge to lean into him and rest her head on his broad shoulder. Somehow it seemed right and natural. Their breathing synchronized, and Jane could feel his pulse beneath her cheek. The temptation to turn her head and press her lips against his neck caught her by surprise, making her wonder what his reaction might be if she did such a thing. As if he could read her thoughts, Cole tightened the arm around her shoulders. He shifted, looking down at her, but she didn't meet his gaze. In her current mood, that would have been much too dangerous. No telling what stupid thing she might do if she actually got sucked into those dark chocolate eyes.

Clouds hid a full moon, and rain threatened. Soon, a cold drizzle sent them back to the dorm, where they wiped the dogs' feet, and their own, and separated to go to their own rooms with a simple "Good night."

In her room, Jane took a shower and donned the over-sized T-shirt that she slept in. The bedside clock read eleven o'clock—late for her. No doubt she would be tired and a little hungover for her run the next morning. Strangely, she couldn't work up much anxiety about it. As she shooed Shadow from her bed and lay down, her mind wouldn't turn off. Nothing seemed quite the way it should be. Her usual assurance that she was following the correct path—the only path—had somehow faded, leaving her with an uncomfortable feeling of uncertainty.

Uncertainty about the Invitational. Was it right for her to pin her whole future on such an unlikely victory, closing her eyes to all other possibilities? Possibilities like . . . no, she wouldn't think of Cole as a possibility. That was just silly.

Uncertainty about what kind of future she actually wanted. After this summer of travel and constant compan-ionship, could she return happily to the isolation of a ken-nel, with dogs and cats the only ones to keep her company?

And the most alarming uncertainty—was she being stu-pid about Cole? Would she ever again have the opportunity to be with such a great guy, someone who drew her so strongly in so many ways, someone who seemed to be drawn to her as well? She thought about Cole's sister Nancy, who in some ways was so similar to Jane. Nancy had changed her priorities, taken a chance, and hopped on the couples train. How happy she seemed, for now, at least.

If you win the battle, Nancy had warned, then you lose.

So why was Jane fighting so hard? Was she lying here alone in the dark out of cowardice? Suppose she went to Cole, had a fling, and gave in to the attraction. That wasn't necessarily a life-changing event. They were adults, after all. They could be together without taking over each other's lives. It could be a casual thing, a temporary thing, a fun thing.

That was the wine talking, Jane warned herself. She should stay right where she was, alone in the dark, and go to sleep.

Coward, the wine accused. Or maybe it wasn't the wine. Maybe it was a Jane that had hidden until this strange summer had set her free. *Go ahead,* the new Jane tempted. *Get up. Go knock on his door. Maybe he's lying there thinking about you.*

Don't you dare, the old Jane said. *Lie right where you are. Go to sleep.*

The new Jane scoffed, *Then you'll never know, will you? You'll be a dried-up old maid, and never even know what could have been, what you missed.*

Frustrated, she turned over and pounded her pillow. Idaho raised his head and looked at her. The glow of the ranch floodlights coming through the window caught in the border collie's eyes. Plain as day, the dog said, "Go for it, kid!"

"No!" Jane groaned. "I will never drink wine again. Never."

Shadow whined, but Idaho, the old dog who knew her so well, just looked at her.

"I'm not the type," Jane told the border collie. "He'll think I'm a fool."

A soft woof was her only answer.

"I am going insane."

Nevertheless, she swung her legs out of bed and got up, just to see how it might feel to at least start the journey. Then she got her old fuzzy robe out of the closet and pulled it on—quite a sexy piece to wear while calling on a man. Not that she was going to carry through with this madness. She was just . . . just . . .

Coward! the new insane Jane said, or maybe it was Idaho.

She *was* a coward. Jane admitted it. And she certainly wasn't going to go knock on Cole's door in the middle of the night. Certainly she wasn't. That was beyond insanity, even if Idaho did think it was a good idea.

So two minutes later, when she raised her hand to knock on the door three rooms down from hers, it almost caught her by surprise. She felt as if she were outside her own body, watching, with no control over what this new Jane did.

The door opened, and there stood Cole, in running shorts and nothing else. Jane swallowed hard. "Uh...hi," she said.

His smile warmed her to the bone marrow. "Jane."

What the hell did a wanton woman say at such a time? Her knees were turning to water, and her throat threatened to close out of sheer terror. "I was...just lying there...in the dark..."

He took her arm and pulled her forward into the room. "And you wondered if I wanted company?"

"That's it. I wondered if you wanted company."

The door closed with an irrevocable click, and Jane's heart started to race.

"So..." He looked at her hard, as if trying to see through her skull into her mind. "Maybe you were wanting company, too?"

She tried to breathe. "I...maybe don't know what I want. But...I just...I decided that...you and I, maybe, needed to be more than just friends. And that I was being silly, ignoring that I feel, well, a lot for you."

He smiled, and his hand slipped down her arm to grasp her hand. "You feel a lot for me?"

"Uh...yes."

"That's good," he said. "Because I feel a whole lot for you, Jane."

All the air ran out of her body. "You do?"

"I do."

"So maybe we could just...you know."

His smile grew into a wicked grin. "I do know."

"Just between you and me."

"Certainly between you and me. Very much between you and me."

And then there was no more time for talking.

IN THE RV lot, Angela found herself with a rare evening of privacy. Ernesto had turned in early. Jane and Cole had taken rooms in the dorm. And Angela rattled around a motor home that suddenly seemed too large.

Not that she minded. She wasn't one of these people who had to have company all the time. Though not having anyone to talk to felt strange. But then, she could talk to herself, Angela supposed. After all, she was her own best listener. She was the person who best understood herself, the person who had the most interest in what she had to say.

"So, how's tricks?" she asked herself.

"Tricks are pretty good, thank you," she answered. "We had a nice party tonight. The filming is going well. We have a cast of interesting characters and adorable dogs, and the suspense is growing. This series is going to make me a name."

Was work all she had to talk about? Angela wondered.

"Of course I can talk about other things," she declared aloud. Thinking hard, she tried to come up with something. Something positive. A lot of things in her life were untouchable, either to think about or to talk about, such as her ex-marriage to her rat-bastard ex-husband. Her childhood as the neighborhood fatty wasn't fit for conversation either. And as for the present, besides work, she had ... Rick?

She made a rude sound. "Forget that!" she told herself. "You really don't want to go there, Angela. That man is a mistake waiting to happen. He's a big, sexy pest."

A knock on the door interrupted her conversation with herself. Probably Ernesto, she thought, wanting a late-night snack.

The door opened not to reveal Ernesto, however, but the big, sexy pest, looking sexy as ever in a loud Hawaiian shirt, knee-length shorts, and adorably tousled hair. Angela wondered if just thinking about him had brought him here to plague her, like some wicked djinn.

"Hi there," he said cheerfully.

She didn't bother with politeness. "I thought you got a motel room in town."

"So I did. But I noticed that your roomies all escaped to the dorm, so I figured you might need some company." From behind his back, he brought out an offering.

"You swiped wine from the party?"

"That cheap stuff? Hell no. I bought my own. Only the best for you, my lady."

Angela sniffed.

"So, can I come in?"

"I suppose." This was a disaster in the making, Angela told herself, but there was a limit to how rude even she could be. Besides, turning down an excellent bottle of wine was a crime.

Rick came in and made himself comfortable on the sofa. He'd been in the Enterprise often since joining the convoy, but tonight he looked too big for it. His broad shoulders and six-foot-plus height made the motor home seem close and small. Rick looked, Angela reflected, like the legendary Tarzan might look sitting in some prim lady's stuffy parlor.

"What is this wine you're bribing me with?" She took the bottle from him and noted a very fine label. "You're having some, right?"

"You bet."

Angela got two wineglasses from the cupboard and poured.

"You're headed to Houston next?" Rick asked, taking the glass she handed him.

"That's right." She took her own glass and sat on one of the dinette chairs, about as far from Rick as she could get and still be in the same room. "Five huge trials. Cole got his invitation to Solid Gold, so now our girl has to get some more points to get there as well."

"Your precious show depends upon it, eh?"

Angela shrugged. "She'll make it. Jane isn't a quitter."

"No. No quitters allowed in this game."

Angela gave him a cautious look over the rim of her wineglass. "What is that supposed to mean?"

He just smiled. "You know, you're one of the most suspicious women I've ever met."

"I am not."

"You are. You examine everything for hidden meaning, potential trouble, veiled threats."

"That's how one stays on top in this world," she replied.

"Staying on top is a lot of work," he said, sounding more mocking than sympathetic. "Here, Angie, let me top off your wine."

Angela reached out her glass, and he poured. "Are you trying to get me looped?"

"Could be. Maybe I'm here to take advantage of you."

She snorted. "Small chance of that. As I recall, I tried to take advantage of you not too long ago, and you took a pass."

He leaned back on the sofa, appearing completely relaxed with his arms stretched out along the back and one ankle resting on a knee. His eyes perused her lazily, warmly, and Angela could feel a tentacle of heat uncoil inside her.

"Maybe," he said in a quiet voice, "I got lonely."

She wasn't ready to let him off the hook. "What happened to the protestations that I'm just too good for a one-night stand?"

"Maybe I've realized that all relationships start out with just one night."

"Maybe you're a dog barking up the wrong tree. I don't take well to strings, Rick. And from what you've said so far, you're positively wrapped in strings that you want to get someone else tangled up in."

He shook his head with a "Tch, tch, tch. What did I say about suspicion? Here I'm offering myself on the altar of passion, and you do nothing but throw accusations." Then his tone became serious. "Angie, sweetheart, just take me at face value for tonight. You're like a magnet, and I'm tired of fighting the pull. Can we just take things as they come, enjoy each other, and not worry about strings or a future? For now."

She was a magnet? Then why did her blood start racing through her veins whenever she looked at this guy? Rick was trouble, Angela reminded herself. They didn't want the same things, and he wasn't really surrendering so much as calling a truce.

But she wanted him. She had wanted him since she had first seen him at the trial in Carson City. The night was lonely. Her life was lonely. Was it such a crime to ease the loneliness for just a few hours with a bit of closeness?

The closeness wouldn't stick. It never did. But that was the price she paid for the wanderlust that ruled her life.

He patted the sofa beside him. "Come sit by me, darlin'."

Angela did more than that. If she was going to do this thing, then she would take the lead. She would be in control. Lifting one brow in challenge, she unbuttoned the top button of her shirt, then the second. "Do you really want to sit, *darlin'*?"

chapter 21

JANE WOKE to a fantasy that once had existed only in her imagination, and then only in what she considered her weaker moments. But as she rose from sleep to wakefulness, the fantasy, the dream, solidified into reality. She really was lying crowded into a narrow twin bed with Cole Forrest wrapped around her, his bare arm thrown across her—ohmigod!—bare breasts, their legs entangled in a way that was a good deal more than suggestive.

The memory of what had occurred between them the night before seemed more like a delicious dream than a real memory. But that intimacy, that unexpected rhapsody of pleasure, had actually happened. Amazing. She should be mortally embarrassed to be lying here naked with an equally naked man, but she wasn't. Maybe later she would be. Maybe later things would get awkward between them. But right then, pressed close against Cole, feeling the rise and fall of his bare chest against her naked back, she wanted just to stay there, cocooned in their own little world.

"Are you awake?" came a whisper in her ear.

"Yes."

His arm dropped to her waist and tightened. "How do you feel?"

Jane smiled. "Good. Weird."

He laughed. Curled in the middle of the room's other bed, Dobby opened one eye and regarded them sourly.

"I don't think our chaperone approves," Jane said.

Cole nuzzled her neck. "Our chaperone can mind her own business."

The feel of Cole's warm lips on her skin sent a wave of unfamiliar delight from head to toe. "Oh, my," she whispered.

"Your skin is like silk. Did you know that?"

His hand moved to her hip. Her bare hip. Jane sucked in a breath. This was leading to more. Was she ready for more?

"Cole?"

"Hm?"

"I . . . uh . . . have to take my dogs out. And . . . and . . ."

He laughed. "Okay, Miss Practical, we'll save this for later."

The idea of doing this again, and maybe again and again, made Jane's heart beat even faster. They had crossed a threshold. Where did things go from here? Or did they go anywhere? This was a fling, she reminded herself, not a lifestyle change.

And she needed to get back to real life, to collect her dogs and take them out for their morning business. And then she had a trial to run, an invitation to earn.

Later she could think about any changes the night might have wrought.

TERI WAS eating a bowl of oatmeal with sliced bananas when the phone call came.

"It's your dad," her aunt Nancy told her, and handed over the phone. "And when you're through, you'd better get into the backyard and talk to your puppy. Last I saw, only his tail was visible above the hole he was digging."

Teri slurped the last of the oatmeal from her spoon, took the phone handset, and headed for the backyard. "Hi, Dad! How's Dobby?"

"Dobby's great." On the other side of the line, her dad's voice sounded really happy.

"Dash is good, too. Except he's digging holes in Aunt Nancy's backyard. And yesterday he peed in the hall. Dash!" she shouted. As her aunt had said, only the tip of a little golden tail showed above his excavation. "Quit that and come here!"

Dash ignored her.

"Are you doing what Jane told you to do with his crate training?" her dad asked, just as if he could see the puppy misbehaving.

Teri sighed. Maybe, without Jane to remind her, she had been a little lazy about that. Funny that she missed Jane and Shadow and Idaho almost as much as she missed her dad and Dobby. Especially Jane, because Jane always made sense of dog stuff and made Teri believe she could really be a dog trainer some day.

But it wasn't right to miss Jane that much. What would Teri's mom think?

"Aunt Nancy helps me," Teri said.

"Of course she does, but your aunt Nancy doesn't know dogs like Jane does."

Why did her dad's voice sound funny when he said Jane's name?

"Okay," Teri said. "I'll try harder."

"That's my girl. And guess what? I have great news. We got invited to Solid Gold—you, me, and Dobby."

Really it was her dad and Dobby that got invited, but her dad sounded so happy that Teri didn't remind him of that.

"Is Jane going, too?"

"I'm sure Jane will get invited too. She's the best there is."

Teri didn't know quite how to take that, and there was a funny silence on the other end of the line that showed her dad was thinking about something. Maybe thinking about Jane. Something funny was going on here, just as Teri had always suspected.

Her suspicions were borne out by her dad's next question. "Teri, you like Jane, don't you?"

Teri hesitated. Dash, covered with dirt, had climbed out of his hole and was trotting toward her. Jane had helped her get Dash, and that was very big. And Jane was a dog trainer. That was big, too. The other ladies that had tried to latch onto her dad weren't as nice as Jane, and they didn't have cool dogs.

But Teri shouldn't be liking Jane too much, and neither should her dad. And it was beginning to sound as if her dad liked Jane too much. So Teri had to be careful.

"Jane's okay," she conceded.

"Just okay?" Her dad sounded disappointed.

"She's nice," Teri said with a hint of belligerence. "But she's not my mom."

More silence, a silence that sounded heavy over the phone. "Teri, no one except your mom will ever be your mom. That doesn't mean that you can't like someone, or even love them."

Teri didn't want to talk about this. "I have to go fill in Dash's hole. And then wash him off. He's all covered with dirt."

Her dad didn't push it. "We'll be by tomorrow to pick you up. Then you and I will talk, okay?"

"Okay."

"Tomorrow, then."

Teri bit her lip. "Dad? Told ya Dobby could do it. Give her a kiss from me."

"Sure thing, sweet pea. See you tomorrow."

When Teri pressed the button to end the call, her tummy

felt funny. Things were changing. Too much was changing. Making a face, she sat down on the brick wall that enclosed a flower bed, picked up her dirty, mischievous puppy, and hugged him to her.

SITTING ON the bed that Jane had recently left, in the little dormitory room where he—perhaps—had changed the direction of his life, Cole flipped his cell phone closed and frowned. He knew his daughter well enough to detect uncertainty and tentative rebellion in her voice.

For a kid of eight, Teri had a finely honed talent for reading situations and people—especially for reading her father. Perhaps better than her father read her. It hadn't occurred to Cole until this minute that his friendship with Jane might spark resentment in Teri. He should have been smarter. Now that he looked back on it, his daughter's up-and-down mood swings did coincide with his increased attention to Jane, even though most of the time Teri seemed to admire Jane.

Cole felt a familiar frustration dim the glow left over from an incredible night. It would take a genius to understand the workings of a bright eight-year-old mind. If Mandy had lived...

But Mandy hadn't lived, and for the first time since losing his wife, Cole had met someone who excited his interest. He didn't want to put Teri through the emotional roller coaster of becoming attached to someone and then losing her—yet again—but his hopes for Jane... well, his hopes for Jane weren't quite solid yet, but they were certainly getting there. In this day and age, one night of intimacy didn't automatically mean two people were headed toward a permanent relationship. But Cole knew a good thing when he saw it. A chance at love was a gift that didn't come along often, and when it did, only a fool let it pass.

He would figure out how to help Teri welcome a new person into her life. If he could only convince Jane that *she* needed a new person in her life.

JANE STOOD at ringside watching Cole and Dobby make their run in the eight-inch division of Jumpers class. Amazing, she thought, how the persnickety pillow princess transformed herself into a flying furball the minute she set paw into an agility ring.

Almost as amazing as Jane transforming herself into—what? Seductress? Slut? Did she have regrets? Not a one, she assured herself. But today she did feel different, not quite herself, fuzzy around the edges, and restless in a way she couldn't quite define. No doubt it all had something to do with unexpected passions. "Passion" had never been a word Jane associated with herself, but apparently she didn't know herself as well as she had thought.

What did she do now? Did she do anything, or just let things take their natural course, let passion play itself out and separation cool the flames? The question was too big to think about just then. She had a job to do, a future to secure. Later she could think.

Jane met Cole as he exited the ring. Dobby jumped into his arms, and Jane was tempted to do the same. Too bad she couldn't, but she had to keep her feet on the ground in more ways than one. Right now, though, she would indulge herself, enjoy the thrill that warmed her when his arm slipped around her, and when his white teeth flashed in a smile. She had seen that smile the night before, and she knew it was for her, not for his perfect run.

"Well, that was just gravy," she told him as they walked together toward the food concession. "Tell Dobby she doesn't need to be perfect now that you have that invitation. In fact, if she has any mistakes planned, she should get them out of the way before she comes back at the end of August."

"She's just having fun. That's the whole point, isn't it?"

"If it isn't, I guess it should be. Are you going to buy me a cup of coffee to celebrate?"

His smile grew just a bit lewd. "And we're celebrating...?"

Heat rushed to her face. "Dobby's perfect run."

"Not anything else?"

She took a swipe at him. "Okay, you were pretty perfect, too."

"You're talking about agility, right?" He took her arm and pulled her over for a quick kiss, then said in a low voice. "Not last night?"

She laughed and pushed him away. "You're trying to embarrass me. That's not fair."

More serious now, he said, "I'm trying, in my own awkward way, to let you know that last night was special. And I think we need to have a talk."

Oh, no. Not now. She couldn't think about it now. So instead, she stood on tiptoe and briefly pressed her lips to his. "I have to run. I need to work Shadow before our turn comes up in Standard. Later."

She escaped. Later she would think about last night and the jumble of feelings that threatened to trample her. Later.

But some distractions didn't easily get shoved to later. They intruded at the most inconvenient times, like when Jane was drilling Shadow in a warm-up before going to the ring. And again when she and Shadow were running the course, throwing Jane off her timing and concentration. Their run ended up good, but not terrific. They won the twenty-four-inch division, but fell short of the overall victory that Jane had wanted.

Strangely, Jane didn't get down about her less-than-perfect performance, as she usually did. Her priorities were shifting. That wasn't good. Now more than ever she needed to keep her eye on the ball. But she couldn't get terrifically upset about that, either.

What she most wanted right then, she realized, was to have Cole smile at her as he had that morning. She wanted to walk out in the meadows with him, with the dogs gamboling around them. She wanted to sit down to dinner—it didn't matter where—and see his face across the table from her, just as it had been for these last few weeks.

What had happened to her? What was she doing? If she wasn't exactly herself, then who was she? But she wouldn't think about it now. She would think about it later.

After the awards were handed out, they packed the motor home and headed out for the next set of trials—a five-day extravaganza of agility at the huge Astrodome in Houston. Rick had left the convoy, telling Jane that he had to take his trailer in to have the wheel bearings packed.

"We'll miss you," Jane had told him.

"Maybe *you* will," he had said, sounding huffy. Then he'd given her a chagrined smile. "Sorry."

"Shall I tell Angela good-bye for you?" she had asked, blatantly prying.

"Don't bother" was his terse answer. "We already said our good-byes."

So that was it, Jane thought. Angela had finally driven him away, which might be the reason that the producer had looked like a thundercloud all day, muttering under her breath and snapping at anyone who got within range.

"I don't suppose you're going to tell me what happened?" Jane said to Rick.

"Ask Angie," he replied with a snort. "The world's most stubborn, obstinate, chickenshit excuse for a woman."

Jane decided to pass on that one. She had troubles enough of her own.

They got on the road, with Angela driving, Cole riding shotgun, Jane fixing sandwiches in the kitchen, and Ernesto following in his van. Now that they were all together again, there would be no more private moments with Cole. The next day, they would pick up Teri and Dash, and their little rolling family would be once again complete.

Cole had said that they needed to have a talk, but when could they talk, surrounded by people, hounded by Ernesto's camera? And did Jane really want to hear Cole's thoughts on the line they had crossed? Did she want to say anything before she had a chance to think?

Words, if they were the wrong ones, were hard to take back, while a silence, though frustrating, left unsaid possibilities to explore. Perhaps it was a good thing that she and Cole had to put on the brakes for a while.

They had gotten a fairly late start from Argus Ranch, and once their cavalcade had conquered the challenge of the Cascade Range, dark gathered quickly. They set up for the night in a Kampgrounds of America campground just outside of Ellensburg, Washington, which gave them only a few hours' drive to Spokane to pick up Teri the next day.

It was a weary crew that maneuvered the motor home into its assigned space and went through the routine of hooking up to the amenities—water, electric, and sewer. Angela was downright sullen, avoiding conversation. Ernesto, also, was quiet.

After they were settled in, Cole took his laptop to the KOA office to use the Internet connection, and Jane decided to take Shadow and Idaho—who seemed almost as weary as the human part of the crew—for a walk. She hesitated for a moment, wondering if she should wait until Cole returned, so he and Dobby could join them, but did she really want to be alone with him right then? She did, Jane discovered. And yet she didn't.

What a confused, wishy-washy moron she had become!

The campground was well lit, and the dogs enjoyed stretching their legs and sniffing around the ground. Jane enjoyed the privacy, which had been a rare commodity since she'd become Angela's latest "star." The only one whose company might be superior to privacy was—*Don't go there!* she warned herself.

"Hey, Jane," spoke a quiet voice behind her.

She turned to find Ernesto trailing her. The dogs greeted him enthusiastically, and he absently ruffled their ears. But his expression was serious.

"I...uh, wanted to have a word."

Jane couldn't help but sigh. "What is it, Ernie? Have I been showing too much of my bad side to the camera?"

He smiled. "You don't have much of a bad side that I can see." Then his smile faded. "I wanted to just, well, give a word of caution. About Angela."

Jane frowned. "What about Angela?"

"Angela's a good friend of mine, besides being my boss. She and I have done a lot of projects together, and she's good people. I know that for a fact. She's helped me out of a bind or two."

"I know she's good people, Ernie. You don't have to tell me that. So what's the deal?"

Ernie grimaced. "The deal is that you—you and Cole, that is—need to watch yourself."

Jane felt heat rise to her cheeks. It was one thing to indulge in a fling with Cole, and another thing—a horrendously embarrassing thing—to have others know their private affairs. "What do you mean?" she asked cautiously.

"I mean that Angela likes to put a personal slant on all her projects. Hell, she can have an audience breathless over the courtship of a wombat. Think what she can do when people are her subjects."

Jane jumped to a horrific conclusion, then dismissed it. There were no cameras in the Argus dormitory. She and Cole were safe. Weren't they?

"I'm not always real comfortable with where Angela wants the camera to go. But she's the boss. She's the one who has to sell this stuff to the network, and she's the one who takes the heat if the series bombs. So I do what she tells me to do."

Jane didn't like the sound of this. "What exactly are you referring to, Ernie? You're going out on a limb to warn me about something, so you might as well go all the way out and get specific."

Ernesto looked unhappy. He scowled, looked at the dogs, at the ground, then finally met her eyes. "Come with me, if you want. Maybe you should see this."

Jane followed him to the van and squeezed in beside him, between his cot, two shoulder-mounted cameras, and the editing equipment.

"Sit down," he invited, pointing to the stool in front of the editor. Then he retrieved several discs from storage and slipped the first one into the machine. "Watch," he told her.

Jane watched for a full half hour, growing more distressed by the minute. She'd had no idea how accurately a camera could see into people's souls. Simple things—a look, a smile, a casual touch—showed incipient romance much plainer than she'd seen it when she had lived the action depicted on the screen. This wasn't a fling with her and Cole. This was more like the real thing, like love. What Jane saw on that screen was blossoming love.

There was that awful blunder when she had barreled into him after a run. How had the camera gotten that close-up? Cripes! Even there, lying on the ground with Cole, she had looked smitten. And here was the evening in Reno: Greta, Sybil, flirty Sheila and her hubby sitting around the table without Cole and Jane—but here they came, walking into the restaurant together after that interlude in his motor home, right after that almost-kiss. And just look at the expression on her face. And his eyes! His eyes followed her every move.

A dozen more scenes made her heart stop: Jane and Cole in the Enterprise, Jane and Cole coming back from a jog, laughing. Jane and Cole walking an agility course together, heads bent close, discussing strategies. And worse, much worse, there they were that very day, walking toward the food concession at Argus Ranch, with Cole stealing a kiss. Walking off with their arms around each other.

If Jane had checked each day's camera takes, this never would have happened, because she would have put an end to it. But after the first few days of fascination, she had stopped watching the daily material. At first she had been eager to see her own handling mistakes in the ring, so she could correct them. But that had grown old very fast, and there had always been something else to do when Angela and Ernesto huddled together in the van to evaluate what they had caught on camera. But now...now...There seemed to be more in this series about her and Cole together than about the dogs and agility.

Something akin to illness roiled in her stomach. How could she have been so stupid? The whole country was going to feast their eyes on her most private, vulnerable moments, and they were going to consider it entertainment. This wouldn't do. This just would not do!

"Anyway," Ernesto said, casting a dubious look at her face, "I thought you should know what was up. It's going to be a great series, both about the dogs and about you, but, well, you've never seemed too thrilled the camera was butting into your business even when it was just dog business. I figured you didn't know the direction Angela was going."

Jane tried hard to keep her voice under control, but a quiver betrayed her. "Thank you, Ernie. I know you could get into trouble for showing me this."

"Nah. Angela and I have worked together too long. She won't get on my case. She needs me too much."

Feeling as though she'd been hit by a baseball bat, Jane stumbled out of the van and straight into Cole, who was just coming back from the office with his laptop tucked beneath his arm. With the other arm he stopped her from barreling into him. His hand slipped down her bare arm in a brief caress that inspired near panic. She didn't have time for this, shouldn't have let it even begin.

"What's wrong?" He regarded her expression with concern.

She expelled a pained breath. "I'll show you what's wrong. Follow me."

She led him into the van and loaded the damning evidence into the viewer. Demonstrating the better part of valor, Ernesto excused himself and left them to it.

"Do you see this?" Jane demanded indignantly. "Do you see the direction Angela has taken this series?"

But Cole seemed more bemused than upset as he watched their story play out on the video. Some narration had been added, and he even laughed at some of Angela's more humorous observations.

"You're laughing!" Jane said, almost frantically. "How can you laugh?"

"Well, her comparing Dobby to a teacup-size border collie is clever."

"Forget Dobby. How about her portraying us, you and me, as some sort of soap opera story of the dog world?"

Cole shrugged. "If any of my friends see it, I'll get ribbed. Probably you'll get the same treatment."

"Ribbed? Is that all? Cole! Angela is laying us bare for the whole nation to see!"

He chuckled. "Laying us bare? I don't think Ernesto caught that part. At least I hope he didn't."

She almost choked with mortification, and Cole winced.

"Hey!" He reached out and touched her cheek, and Jane flinched. "Jane, you're upset. Okay. I can see where you might be surprised by all this. But you know, after this series makes its run on television, no one is going to remember who you are or who I am. People who watch this sort of thing will be more interested in the dogs than in you or me, in spite of what Angela thinks."

He didn't convince her. Moaning with frustration, she sat down on Ernesto's cot. "I just...just...I can't do this. I really, really can't."

Cole regarded her narrowly. "You can't do what?"

Jane herself was a bit confused. She just knew that watching herself and Cole on that screen felt wrong. Very wrong. She was tired. She was angry. And more than anything, she just wanted her own familiar life back.

Cole sat down beside her and repeated, "You can't do what, Jane?"

"I can't do—" She flung her arms out in a gesture that encompassed not only the van, but the whole world she had stepped into when she first prostituted herself to Angela's project and Angela's notions about audience voyeurism.

"You can't do *us*," he concluded. "Is that it?"

Hearing it spoken out loud sent a stab of pain through her heart, but that was certainly part of what she found daunting.

He took her silence for agreement. "Jane," he said gently, "you're not giving us a chance."

"It's not you," she said miserably. "It's...it's just really bad timing. Besides, you don't know who I really am. I'm not what Angela created here, the flippy hairstyle, the makeup, the clothes. I'm plain. I haul dog food and clean kennels for a living, and my hair is burning-bush red instead of whatever this color is that they made it."

He shook his head. "Do you think any of that matters to me? You think I don't know you? I do know you, Jane Connor. I never would have let you get into my heart unless I did. And I especially wouldn't have let you get into Teri's heart."

That scared Jane even more than watching the video. Some part of her stood aside and acknowledged that she might be making a Himalayan-sized mountain out of a divot-sized molehill, but once the ball of panic got rolling, she felt helpless to stop it.

"You don't understand!" she declared. "I tried to explain it at the very first. I can't take time for this. I thought last night was a fling, just a casual, temporary insanity. But now that I see what led up to it . . . I can't do this! I am going to win the Invitational, and I can't afford a distraction. I have to win, Cole."

"Why do you have to win?"

He didn't know about the ruins of her life, and she was reluctant to explain. She didn't want him to feel sorry for her, or to think she was some kind of heroine. Somehow that would pollute their friendship, if friendship is what they had.

"I just have to. It's something I have to do. And being with you . . . and all of this . . ." She waved a hand toward the screen. "I just can't."

His features hardened. "Maybe you're right. Maybe I don't really know you. I thought you were someone safe to love, someone who would be good for both me and Teri. And here you resent our relationship because it distracts you from winning a goddamned agility trial?"

She bit down on a reply. When he put it that way, it sounded very harsh. He didn't say anything more, just looked at her with disappointment in his eyes, then got up and left the van. Jane dropped her head into her hands. Maybe she was allowing some devil inside her to push her over the edge of terminal stupidity. And she couldn't help it. She couldn't help it.

God, how she wanted her old life back.

THE RIDE to Spokane the next day was a silent one. Jane and Cole didn't speak beyond what was necessary for two people confined in a thirty-four-foot tin can rolling down the freeway at seventy miles per hour. Angela wasn't her usual bouncy self either. The producer's mood, in fact, had induced her to empty the cupboards of junk food, without a single mention of intending to do penance with aerobics, sit-ups, or any other calorie-burning activity. In short, Jane had never seen her so down.

But Jane had little time to worry about Angela. She was too absorbed in her own personal drama. She hadn't realized before this how much she had valued Cole's company, their conversations, the teasing speculation about who would have to pay the exotic dinner bet they had made.

Jane should have remembered one of the primary reasons she didn't take up with men, that every person she had watched skip down the road of romantic entanglement spent more time in misery than joy. She should have remembered. Poor, sweet Nell had been duped in the worst sort of way by the man she fell in love with. Jane recalled every detail of Nell's meltdown when she had learned the truth, poor girl. It didn't matter that they had made up in the end. Nothing could be worth the misery that girl went through.

Mckenna, also, had twisted in an ill wind of uncertainty and doubt with the man who had finally won her.

What had possessed these two otherwise sensible women to bludgeon their way through to a happy ending was beyond Jane. Sunk in misery, not knowing if she was being sensible, selfish, cowardly, or wise, she wished she had never allowed herself to weaken under the blandishment of Cole's attentions. His attentions, the dark, warm eyes, the endearing lift of his smile, his unashamed tenderness for his kid, and an oh-so-tempting tenderness for her.

Stop it! Jane told herself as she stared out a window at the passing monotony of eastern Washington. What had she done to herself, that her mind was so stuck on coming back to what it shouldn't? All summer she had been playing at this, believing that she was sticking her toe into the water of a mild flirtation, a tentative experiment in casual romance. Now she had been slapped hard with the truth: She hadn't dabbled in the safe shallow end of flirtation, she had dived headfirst into something much more serious. She wasn't ready! She had things to do. Important things. And—face it!—she was yellow-belly scared.

Dealing with the complications of having a man in her life just didn't fit into Jane's plan for herself.

They arrived at Nancy's place midday, where Teri and Dash both rushed from the house to greet them. Shadow and Idaho, who had seemed as down in the mouth as the human members of the Enterprise crew, perked up and ran around the lawn with tails wagging and tongues looking for someone to lick. Dobby roused herself from her pillow in the motor home to join them, running about the yard, squeaking in excitement, and finally jumping into Teri's arms as if the little girl had been gone for weeks instead of a few days.

Teri, Dobby, Dash, and Cole had themselves a group hug. Jane watched, trying not to let her heart ache with envy. She had missed Teri, Jane realized with surprise. She hadn't realized how firmly the little know-it-all potential dog trainer was seated in her heart—another revelation, maybe, that Jane didn't know herself as well as she had thought.

After the family greetings were over, Teri took Dash over to Jane. "I taught him to roll over. You want to see?"

"Sure," Jane said.

Dash dropped to the grass on Teri's command, which Jane thought was quite good for a pup his age. But when Teri told Dash to roll over, he simply regarded his mistress with a puppy grin.

"Roll over, Dash!"

Grin with a lolling tongue.

"Usually he does it!" Teri complained.

Jane laughed. "Welcome to the world of dog training, kid."

Teri made a face, then gave Jane a slightly chagrined look. "You were really nice to get my dad to let me have Dash. I know it was you who did it. My dad says that when somebody does something nice, we have to say thank you."

"Your dad wants you to be happy."

Teri nodded, but gave Jane a worried look. "My mom would have wanted me to have Dash. She would have. She was the world's best mom, and my dad loved her a lot. So did I."

Where did that come from? Jane wondered. "Of course you did," she agreed.

Nancy interrupted the puzzling conversation by sweeping Jane and Teri toward the group. "You're spending the night, aren't you?" Nancy asked them all. "I have a wonderful chicken cooking for dinner. You have to stay. And Ernesto, Mark wants to show off his new digital video recorder to you." Then in a lower voice, because Mark was just then coming out to greet them, "Maybe you can show him how to use it correctly. He doesn't have a clue."

Everyone agreed they should spend the night, and Jane felt relief, because in everyone's friendly chatter, tensions melted and moods lightened. And one more night of reprieve from sharing a bed with Angela could only be welcome.

"What's wrong between you and my brother?" Nancy asked in a low voice as she and Jane followed the group into the house.

"Nothing," Jane lied.

Nancy gave her a look, shook her head, and lamented, "Oh, Jane."

After lunch, Cole took Teri into Spokane, and Mark went with them. "They have a zoo in this town," Teri told Jane as they left. "My dad told me so."

"Have fun," was all that Jane could say as she was left behind. She tried to ignore Nancy's sympathetic look.

Apparently, however, the trio didn't go to the zoo, because when they returned, Mark was alone in his Honda Accord, and Cole and Teri followed in a motor home. It wasn't much bigger than the one that had given up the ghost in Nevada, but this one gleamed with newness, and its engine hummed like a well-tuned instrument singing out for the road.

Their little band was truly breaking apart at the seams.

NELL WAS watching the evening newscast when the phone rang. She had to push Piggy off her lap to get up and answer it.

On the other end of the line, Jane answered her greeting.

"Jane!" Nell exclaimed. "Where are you? How are you? You haven't called in an age. It's Jane!" she told an attentive Piggy.

"Not quite that long," Jane denied.

As if her big corgi ears could pick up Jane's answer over the phone, Piggy woofed indignantly.

"Piggy thinks it's been too long."

"Well, then it must have been. Certainly Piggy can't be wrong."

Nell laughed. "I'm really glad you called. I've been trying to call your cell phone, but I can never get through."

"That's because we've been rolling through places that truly qualify as the ends of the earth. Right now I'm just outside Spokane. We're headed for Houston."

"You sound tired, Jane."

There was a hesitation on the line, then, "I am, I guess."

Neither the tone nor the words sounded like the Jane Nell knew so well. "What's wrong?"

"Nothing's wrong. You're right. I'm tired. We're at Cole's

sister's house. You remember I told you about Cole and his daughter?"

Yes, Nell did remember, and her ears had perked up when she had heard Jane speak of Cole in particular. In fact, she had nursed a frail hope in her heart that Jane and this Cole fellow might hit it off—he sounded like a good guy. "Sure, I remember."

"They've been traveling with us, you know. But now they've bought a new motor home and are taking off for some vacation time. Cole got his invitation to the Solid Gold trial a couple of days ago, so he's set."

So that was it, Nell thought. There had been something there. She could hear it in Jane's voice. And for some reason they had split. Poor Jane. Nell was well acquainted with the pain one could feel when the superhighway to love suddenly turned into a rock-strewn donkey path.

But Jane was still talking. "So Angela, Ernesto, and I are going on to Houston. Five trials at one site." Her sigh sounded weary. "You know, after this summer, I don't know if I ever want to see the inside of an agility ring again."

Nell guessed that it wasn't the agility that had Jane down. But she was forgetting the most important thing! "Jane! How could I forget? I should have told you at the very first. I checked your post office box today and you got your invitation to Solid Gold! You're in!"

A stunned silence met the announcement.

"Did you hear me?"

"I heard you," came Jane's soft response. "I'm just... wow! I'm in."

"Yes! You're in. So why not come home instead of going to Houston? I'll bet you can use the rest. That producer of yours has to have enough film by now to do three series, at least."

"More than you know," Jane said in a sharp tone.

"Come home, Jane. We miss you. You and the dogs can rest, and then you can go win the Invitational. Come home."

Ten minutes later, Nell was on the phone to Mckenna Markham, the other third of their friendship trio. "Think fast," she told Mckenna. "Jane is headed home. And if she tumbles to what's going on, we're in deep puppy doody."

chapter 22

HOME WAS no longer home for Jane, but just the same, being back in Arizona, in the Verde Valley, meant stepping back into familiar territory and meeting familiar faces. The moment that she'd slid into the seat of her own familiar van, which all these weeks had been parked at Angela's place in the suburbs of Phoenix, Jane felt the knots inside her start to relax. And the dogs' tails wagged furiously as they dove into their own familiar kennels.

"Not quite as comfy as the big motor home, eh?" Jane asked as she closed the kennel doors. "But a lot safer. And much safer than riding loose in the backseat of the rental car."

They settled down happily in their crates, despite being spoiled by riding loose for weeks in the motor home, loose again in Jane's rental car as they drove south from Spokane, then loose yet again in the taxi from the Phoenix Sky Harbor Airport, where Jane had turned the car in. The taxi driver had just about had a heart attack when the two dogs had climbed into the cab, but he'd mellowed when Jane had informed him they were "movie star dogs." It wasn't totally a lie. Shadow *was* going to be a star once Angela's series showed up on TV, or so Angela kept saying.

Even the thought of Angela and her blasted series didn't dim Jane's pleasure at being back in home territory. The two of them had had words before Jane had hopped in a rental car and hit the road. The first words were about Angela's Peeping Tom tactics.

"This is Show Business!" Angela had insisted, definitely with capitals on both sacred words.

"It's invasion of privacy!" Jane had countered. But she hadn't gotten anywhere. Angela was the producer. Jane had agreed to do the show. And Rising Star Productions had pretty much been supporting Jane and her hungry dogs all summer. So that had been that.

The second exchange of words was about Jane's leave of absence, so to speak. Angela had wanted to continue filming.

"You can continue filming at the Invitational," Jane had told her firmly. "Shadow needs a rest. I need a rest. If you want to give your audience the drama of us ending up in that final cut, with everybody running their hearts out for all that money, then don't push."

Jane had learned something about Show Business, after all, and one of those things was that last-place finishers don't draw the crowds that the contenders do. So Angela had reluctantly given her blessing, wished her a good vacation, and said she would see her back at Argus Ranch in three weeks.

Cole would be at Argus in three weeks also, Jane knew. But she wasn't going to think about Cole. Whether Jane had been wise or foolish in her decision to ditch him, Cole was water under the bridge, yesterday's news, cold potatoes, or whatever other cliché Jane could think of that meant he was out of her life.

Except that he *would* be at the Invitational.

"I won't think about that," she told Idaho and Shadow.

Their only response came from tails thumping inside the kennels.

JUST ONE day after Jane's arrival home—or rather at Nell's home, where Jane occupied the guest room over the garage until she could once again get a home of her own—Nell planned a welcome-home barbeque.

"I don't need a party," Jane objected as they sat at the kitchen table eating eggs and toast.

"Of course you need a party! You've been gone for ages, and you come home with an invitation to a prestigious agility event like—what was it?"

"Solid Gold." Nell wasn't really into agility, or any other dog sport, mostly because fat little Piggy couldn't be bothered to get off her dog bed and do anything that required energy.

"That's right. Solid Gold. Besides, I need an excuse to initiate Dan's new super-duper outdoor grill."

"Okay," Jane conceded. "What time?"

"I told everyone two o'clock."

"That gives me time to go over to Cornville and take a look at my place."

A piece of toast stopped halfway to Nell's mouth. "Oh, Jane! You don't want to do that. You'll just get depressed. Nothing has changed there since you last saw it."

Jane had to admit that last time she saw the remnants of her home and kennel a few days after the fire the sight had been very depressing.

"Except that a friend of Dan's who has a bulldozer cleaned up the place a bit. For when you're able to build, you know. And Mckenna persuaded the city to haul away some of the worst of it. But you don't want to go there now. I thought we might go up to the medical center this morning. You know, they really miss Idaho. The nurses ask after him all the time. Then we'll come back and get ready for the barbeque."

Jane let herself be convinced. Visiting patients at the hospital was a much happier prospect than brooding in the ashes of her old life.

At the Verde Medical Center, Idaho seemed happy to be back into the hospital routine. The staff all exclaimed on his return, scratched his ears, gave him cookies that they saved for the therapy dogs, and generally let him know his presence had been missed.

Jane had been missed also. "You look great!" said Stephanie, a nurse in Critical Care. "I love the hair. It makes you look so young."

Jane had suffered a few qualms about appearing before her old acquaintances with the new look, but there was nothing to be done about it other than brush up the breezy hairstyle, dress up her face a bit with a dab of makeup, and hope everyone realized that she was still the old Jane.

Not that she was totally the old Jane. The new Jane was getting her way more and more. She had gotten into the habit of actually checking her appearance before leaving the house, selecting clothes that matched rather than grabbing any old thing out of the drawer.

Other changes didn't show on the outside. She used to stride through life with a certainty of purpose, a comfortable conviction that she was where she belonged, doing what she was meant to do. But these days that certainty eluded her. Her life was in flux, her future up for grabs, her convictions more like putty than steel. And in a corner of her heart lurked a man and a little girl whom she couldn't forget.

But going around the hospital with Idaho, Nell, and Piggy brought Jane's own problems into perspective, as it always had. The quiet courage of people in the worst of circumstances, hooked up to blinking, beeping machines, imprisoned in a web of tubes, unable to walk, or run, or even tend to the most basic functions of life without help, made Jane appreciate just how fortunate she was. Most were delighted to have a cold border-collie nose prod affectionately at a hand, or to have a fat corgi cuddle for a few minutes on their bed. Idaho entertained with silly tricks—a waving paw, a bow, a roll-over. Piggy just cuddled. And the patients reminded Jane that considering the big picture of her life, she had little to complain about.

That afternoon's barbecue also reminded her that she had little reason to feel sorry for herself on any account. Her home might be ashes, her body bone-tired from a summer of stress and competition, her love life a disaster of her own making, but she had friends who cared about her, who gave with no expectation of getting back. She had Shadow and Idaho, who loved her regardless of what she did. So she reminded herself as she sat on Nell and Dan's back porch, smelled the delicious aroma of barbequing ribs sizzling on the grill, and watched the dogs gallop across Nell's grassy fenced acre along the Verde River.

Beside Jane, Mckenna lounged in a deck chair, her long legs bared by a pair of abbreviated shorts that only Mckenna could wear. She took a long sip of her iced tea before turning lawyerly eyes upon Jane.

"So who is this fellow who hitched a ride with you halfway across the country?"

"He didn't hitch a ride," Jane said.

"You know what I mean."

"He's just a guy. Another agility competitor."

A thoughtful "Hm" was Mckenna's only reply.

"He has a daughter," Jane said, hoping to defuse Mckenna's overactive curiosity. "And a papillon. Would you believe? The man competes with a papillon!" She tried for just the right mix of casualness and disinterest. "Actually, he's the same guy who beat Shadow and me at Flagstaff in June. In Utility class."

"Is that anything like agility?" Mckenna, like Nell, wasn't exactly into dog sports.

"No."

"Versatile fellow, then. Good-looking?"

"Sort of." If you considered chiseled features, a thousand-watt smile, and eyes like pools of rich chocolate good-looking. If you considered broad shoulders and lean muscle and big, wonderful, gentle square hands good-looking. Jane had always set a lot of store by good hands.

"Nice?"

Smart, funny, down-to-earth, generous, and not afraid to show his own uncertainties—very unusual in a man. "Nice enough," Jane conceded.

Mckenna lowered her trendy dark glasses and skewered Jane with a knowing look. "That far gone, are you?"

"No!"

Mckenna just smiled. She wasn't one of the state's most lethal attorneys for nothing. The woman could read more into two casual words than most people could get out of a two-page confession.

"If you end up having a formal wedding," Mckenna warned, slipping her dark glasses back up her nose and stirring her tea, "don't expect me to wear some bridesmaid outfit straight from Barbie's wardrobe. Not even for you would I wear teal taffeta. Or any other color taffeta, for that matter."

Jane laughed. "No worries, there, Mckenna. Absolutely no worries. There is not a wedding in sight."

Everyone happily spent the afternoon eating sloppy ribs and potato salad, drinking beer, iced tea, sodas, and the wine Mckenna and Tom had contributed. They played Frisbee with the dogs, tossed horseshoes, traded news, and generally kicked back in the hot Arizona sun.

As the afternoon wound down, Jane collapsed into a deck chair to watch Tom, a county prosecutor, and Dan, an ex-cop, ex—private eye, and current law student, in animated discussion (actually more like argument) over the fine points of some legal case. Nell and Mckenna sat on the porch with Jane, talking about the success of the statewide pet therapy network they had all been involved in organizing, and occasionally prying into the more personal aspects of Jane's summer—without success.

Jane felt tension seep out of her like air leaking from a dangerously taut balloon, easing the tightness that drew her muscles into painful knots, making every breath come easier. With new interest she watched her friends, Nell and Dan, Mckenna and Tom. Both women seemed to have a glow that hadn't been there when the three of them were all single and committed to personal independence. They laughed more. Some of Mckenna's edge had softened. Nell's ever present optimism had deepened from a hopeful veneer to something deeply genuine.

"Let me ask you something," Jane said to Mckenna. "You're married to a middle-class civil servant, and you're working out of a storefront office with linoleum floors and furniture from Goodwill. Do you ever regret giving up that high-powered job defending society's well-heeled evildoers, your fancy car, gorgeous house, and designer clothes to marry an ex–rodeo cowboy?"

Mckenna hooted. "God no! If you remember, that high-powered job had me living on high-blood-pressure pills and dodging through an obstacle course of backstabbing colleagues."

"At the time, you claimed to love it," Jane reminded her.

"True, and when I lost it, I surely did think that I wanted it all back. But when I fell for Tom, I found out that what I had thought was happy wasn't really happy. Tom taught me happy. So now sometimes I work a sixty-hour week in a storefront office for clients who sometimes pay and sometimes can't, but I go home at night to a guy who makes me smile. And I go to sleep at night without wondering if I'm doing anything worthwhile with my life." She smiled in Tom

Markham's direction, and her eyes softened. "He does make me smile, bless him, and now I wonder how I survived that other life."

Mckenna's eyes turned on Jane, stabbing deep. "So let me ask you, Jane, what did you have that was so great that you can't give it up for a stab at love?"

Jane tried to laugh. "You're imagining things, Mckenna."

"I've never known you to be afraid of anything," Mckenna continued, ignoring the denial. "But then, I guess I've never really seen you with a guy, either."

"This case you lose," Jane told her with a false smile. "You're way off the mark."

"Uh-huh," Mckenna said with a smirk.

Jane hated Mckenna's smirk. That smirk meant she knew that she was right.

"Besides," Jane insisted, "I'm not afraid of anything." Except maybe not winning that damned Invitational, not having the money to rebuild her life, or discovering that her old life wasn't enough anymore, now that her eyes had opened upon other possibilities. Oh, no, Jane thought to herself cynically, she wasn't afraid of anything.

WHILE JANE sat in a deck chair on Nell's porch, Cole and Teri stood on a ledge a hundred miles north, looking out over the yawing chasm of the Grand Canyon.

"That's really big," Teri said for about the hundredth time since they had arrived two hours ago.

"Told ya so." Cole echoed his daughter's favorite phrase.

Teri looked at the guide book. "This says the rocks at the very, very bottom are more than a billion years old."

"That's old," Cole agreed.

"That's older than the Constitution."

"By quite a bit."

"Older even than you!" she said with an impish grin.

"By quite a bit more. Be nice, Miss Smarty Pants, or I

won't buy you that ice cream cone that's going to cost me an hour standing in line."

"I'm nice," Teri declared. "And Dash wants an ice cream cone, too. A chocolate one."

"Dogs aren't supposed to eat chocolate," Cole told her. "It could make Dash very sick. My guess is that any kind of ice cream would make him sick."

"What about Dobby?"

"Dobby, too."

Dobby and Dash, both securely fastened to leashes, watched the exchange with great attention. The dogs weren't much interested in the Grand Canyon, it seemed, but both appeared to know the words "ice cream."

"Let's walk along the rim path a ways," Cole said, "and then I'll stand in line to get us some ice cream."

They strolled along the paved trail, the dogs trotting along beside them. Summer tourists crowded the pathway, conversing in at least a half dozen different languages, gawking at the scenery, trying to capture the beauty with cameras and video recorders. Children and adults alike laughed at the antics of squirrels, chipmunks, and birds who had perfected the art of begging. Dash and Dobby got their share of admiring looks, and more than one admirer asked to pet them.

"Dash is being good," Teri said proudly. "He's just about the world's most perfect puppy."

"You should send a postcard to Jane and tell her so."

Teri made a noncommittal sound.

"After all," Cole reminded her, "Jane was the one who taught you how to teach Dash."

Teri held her silence for a few moments, staring out over the vast landscape. Then she asked, cautiously, in a voice that sounded more adult than child, "Do you miss Jane very much?"

The question caught Cole by surprise, so much so that he almost gave an honest answer. The truth was that he missed Jane a lot. It was amazing how that prickly, stubborn woman could grow on a man in such a short time, just a few weeks really. He missed seeing her in the morning, with her hair all askew and wearing that ugly T-shirt she slept in. He missed jogging with her, even her moaning about aching muscles and decrepit knees. He missed her quick flashes of humor—and temper. He missed the smiles she had given to Teri, and to him. And he really missed the opportunity to watch her when she didn't know she was being watched, when she was just herself and not worrying about him or anyone else. She was more graceful than she knew, more feminine, even though strength and efficiency defined almost every move.

Most of all, he missed talking to her, teasing, arguing, sometimes agreeing. Not many women were as unaffected, as natural, as bright.

And oh, yes, he missed making love to her. Their one and only encounter had created an instant addiction. No other woman would satisfy that craving. Only Jane.

But Jane, with all her strength and brightness, had closet monsters that she hadn't yet overcome. And apparently, sharing herself with another person, a person who loved her, was one of them. What a waste it was—a sad, sad waste.

But Teri had her own monsters. And Cole wouldn't unload his problems on his daughter. "Jane was a good friend," he told the little girl. "But she had things to do on her own, and so did we."

"You liked her." Teri's tone held a hint of accusation. She looked up at him intently.

"Sure, I liked Jane," he replied. "Didn't you like Jane?"

Teri looked down, but Cole had caught the flash of guilt in her expression. Parents learned very early to detect guilt on a kid's face.

In a sudden flash of understanding, Cole saw the problem. This problem went beyond Jane. If Cole ever wanted to get on with his life, and if he wanted Teri to get on with hers, this was something he had to deal with. Sometimes he wished he had read those books on child psychology that Mandy had gotten from the library during her pregnancy.

They came to a bench shaded by a twisted cedar. "Teri, sweet pea, sit down."

She sat, her mouth twisting uneasily this way and that.

"I want you to be real honest with me, no matter what you think I want to hear, because whatever you say, honey, you're not being bad, and you're not going to get in trouble."

"How about the ice cream?"

"You'll still get ice cream."

She heaved a resigned sigh.

"So answer me this, kiddo," he said. "What do you think about Jane? You got to know her pretty well, and she helped you get a dog of your very own, and she helped you train him. Did you really like her?"

Teri worried at her lower lip and looked away. The sigh came yet again.

"Come on, sweet pea. I think maybe this is something we should talk about. I liked Jane a lot. But I want to know how much you liked her."

"I don't think you should have liked Jane a lot," Teri said with a hint of belligerence.

"Okay. Why is that?"

"You love my mom. You've never looked at other ladies, because you still love my mom."

Yup. There it was. "I do still love Mom, Teri. I'll always love her."

"Then you can't love Jane."

Love. From the mouths of babes . . . Had his attraction to Jane reached the level of love?

But that wasn't exactly the problem at hand. "So you think I can't love Jane because I love your mom, is that right?"

The emphatic nod of Teri's head made her ponytail bounce.

"And I suppose you can't love Jane, either, because you still love your mom?"

"It might hurt Mom's feelings," Teri explained, looking up at him with moist eyes. "You said she's always with us. You said she looks down from heaven and knows everything we do."

Damn! Cole thought to himself.

"And I know that it's true. Because I can hear Mom talking to me sometimes. And when we met Jane and Shadow, Shadow talked to me sometimes, because Mom made it so he could, I think. 'Cause usually dogs don't talk to people much. Shadow always told me to be good and things would work out okay, so I figure Mom told him to say that, because that sounded kind of like Mom."

This probably was more than he wanted to know, Cole decided.

"So I know Mom watches us, and we can't get another mom, because she would know, and it would make her sad."

Oh, boy. Did this call for a parent or a psychologist? Kids really ought to come with a manual, Cole thought, and half of that manual should be a cross-referenced and indexed section on troubleshooting.

Dash let out a puppy woof and chose that moment to jump into Cole's lap, something that the pup had never before attempted. Cole looked down at the puppy in surprise, and Dash smiled up at him, impressed with himself and, above all, completely trusting. On the other side of him, Teri looked up at him with a similarly trusting expression.

It was then that Cole knew what to say. Teri didn't need a shrink. Dogs did talk. And maybe someone watching over their little incomplete family had told Dash what to say.

"Teri, do you remember when you got Dash?"

Her eyes brightened a bit. "Sure I do. I remember the

very first time I saw him, with his brothers and sisters, and how he curled up in my lap and went to sleep."

"Do you think Dash loves you?"

Teri frowned. "Well, sure he does. I play with him and feed him and clean up his poop. And sometimes he takes naps with me on the bed. I know he's supposed to be in his kennel, but he really likes cuddling with me. So I know that he really loves me."

"I think Dash loves you, too, and I want you to think about that. Dash had a mom who loved him, and I'm sure he loved her. But his mom couldn't stay with him. And then you came along. You gave him a home, and you loved him, and saw that he had everything he needed. You play with him, feed him, brush him, and teach him. I don't think he's forgotten his mom, but now he loves you, too."

Teri's lower lip started to tremble, and she averted her eyes in silence.

Softly Cole continued. "Do you think that Dash's mom is sad because her baby got a good home with a girl who loves him? Do you think it hurts her feelings that Dash loves you in return?"

Teri sniffed and wiped her nose with her hand. Cole handed her a handkerchief. People with kids, he had discovered over the last eight years, always needed to carry a handkerchief.

"Will you think about what I've said?" he asked.

She got up from the bench and reached for Dash, lifting the willing puppy from Cole's lap and hugging him to her chest. "I'll think about it," she promised.

Thank you, Dash, Cole thought. *And thank you, Mandy.*

AS THE sun rode low on the hills surrounding Chino Valley, Jane unloaded Shadow from her van beside a little arena set up outside of Gloria Doolittle's house. There were few competent instructors in competitive agility in rural northern Arizona. Jane was one of them, and Gloria was another.

Gloria came out of the house to greet her. "Hey, Jane! It's really good to see you again. And what great news that you're going to Solid Gold! You go, girl!"

Jane grinned. "I feel really lucky. There's a lot of great competitors out there."

"There are. But you're one of the best."

"I don't know about that."

Shadow trotted over to Gloria and pushed his nose into her hand, asking to be petted.

"Shadow was beginning to let down in the last couple of trials we ran," Jane said, giving the golden retriever a gimlet eye. "So we're going to have to work out some kinks before we get to the Invitational."

"Well," Gloria said, "that's why we're here."

Chino Valley lay northwest of Jane's home in the Verde Valley and stood over a thousand feet higher in elevation, but summer days in August were still too hot for either canine or human activity, which was why Jane had arrived at almost dusk.

Gloria switched on the floodlights and they got to work, running one difficult course after another, drilling sequences that taxed both Jane and Shadow, mentally and physically.

At first Shadow worked fast, flawlessly, and happily, a big canine grin on his face. He had trained at Gloria's place since he was first old enough to put paw on the A-frame, and obviously he was glad to be back on home territory. After about fifteen minutes, however, he allowed himself to get distracted, and Jane allowed herself to get frustrated.

"That was exactly the problem at the Argus trial," Jane explained to Gloria, breathing hard from the last exercise.

She was certainly more fit than she had been, though, Jane noted. Jogging with Cole had paid off in fitness. Jogging with Cole had . . . no. She didn't want to think about those early mornings together. Where was Cole now? Was he still angry with her? How were Teri and Dash doing? Was Dobby losing her edge by spending too much time on a pillow?

Speaking of distractions . . . Jane pushed Cole and his family from her mind, or at least tried to. She would think about that later.

"I see what you mean," Gloria agreed. "I've seen the big guy a lot sharper."

"His weaving is slow," Jane complained. "He's looking at birds and butterflies instead of at me. He's just being goofy!"

"Well, he's had enough pressure for today, don't you think?"

"Probably," Jane said. She and Gloria walked toward the van, and Shadow, regaining his energy, bounced along beside them. "I think we need to work at least every other day, Gloria, if you have the time to spend with us."

"I have the time. But I think you might be working him a bit hard, Jane. Don't forget that at twenty months old, he's still pretty much a baby. Maybe if you took it easier on him, he might actually sharpen up."

Jane shook her head and regarded the dog balefully. "You can have a nice long vacation," she told Shadow, "when the Invitational is over." Over and in the bag, Jane added silently. With us back in business.

Back in business . . . Would that be enough to heal her life? Would spending her days at a new Bark Park, spending her evenings in a new house, watching television or reading, satisfy her? Would going to bed alone every night make her happy?

She couldn't think about that now, though. She would think about it later.

chapter 23

TWO WEEKS later, Jane and Shadow flew into Sea-Tac airport, where Ernesto met them in his van and drove them to meet Angela, who already had the motor home—which had kept the name Enterprise, even though Teri had left— parked at Argus Ranch, the site of the big event.

"So how is Angela?" Jane asked Ernesto as they drove south on Interstate 5. She was somewhat apprehensive about their reunion, considering that their last hours together had been spent arguing.

"Angela's cranky," Ernesto told her with a shrug. "But then, she's been cranky since the first time we were at this Argus place. I think she and that Rick guy had a blowup over something. She's been sort of impossible ever since."

Apparently Angela's mood hadn't improved since that last day at Argus Ranch, when she had breathed fire all day. Jane remembered Rick's sour comments when he had left. Those two were too much alike for their own good.

"So," Ernesto said tentatively. "Do you know what's going on there?"

"Not a clue," Jane admitted.

"I thought you women talked about things like that. Hairdos, boyfriends, feelings, stuff like that."

Jane chuckled. "Angela was big on talking about hair—mostly mine and why I needed to change it. But boyfriends—no." Though Angela had never hesitated to comment on Cole and play puppet master in a made-to-order romance. But that hadn't been girl business. For Angela, that had been show business.

"Okay," Ernesto ceded, "but weren't you the one who sucked that Rick fellow into our little convoy for a time?"

"Rick sucked himself into our convoy. Rick's a footloose kind of guy. He pretty much does what he wants and goes where he pleases. Trailing along after us—after Angela—was totally his idea. I just got some kicks by teasing her about it."

And she had certainly had it coming, Jane added silently.

"Whatever," Ernesto said with a sigh. "Angela's in a snotty mood. I wish your footloose vet friend would footloose himself back to Angela and fix it."

"Maybe it wasn't Rick who broke it."

"I don't care who broke it," Ernesto grumbled. "I just want someone to come in with glue to put her back together. Sheesh! She and I went up to Glacier National Park after you left to look into doing something on grizzlies, and I tell you, the bears would have been easier to live with than she was."

"Great," Jane said. "This is going to be a lovely week up here, living with her in a cramped motor home."

Ernesto snorted. "You get to live with her. I'm living in the van." He looked over at her, smiling. "Speaking of hair . . ."

Ernesto was almost as good at the non sequitur as Angela. Obviously they'd been together too long.

". . . yours looks great. Looks like you had it trimmed up."

A flush rose into Jane's face. "You're a connoisseur of hair now?"

"I'm a cameraman. I know what looks good on camera. That will look good on camera."

"Oh. Uh...thanks. I found a guy in Sedona who does good hair."

After almost two months, the breezy style had grown into blowsy. Not that Jane was buying into this hairstyle-and-makeup thing. But getting gussied up was a lot like shaving your legs. Once you started that sort of nonsense, you had to keep it up.

Angela didn't seem in quite the grumpy mood that Ernesto had complained of. She gave Jane a hello hug, then did the same for Shadow. "I missed you, you big golden star, you," she said to the retriever. "And I'm going to miss Idaho this week. He's such a steadying influence on us all. Wise old Father Dog."

Jane smiled. "I'll tell him that you said so. It'll make his border collie ego even bigger than it already is."

"You left him with your friend?"

"With Nell. He gets to compete with Nell's corgi for the prize of ruling the household."

"And of course Idaho will win?"

"Not likely. Welsh corgis are bossy little snots. Especially Piggy."

Jane put her duffle bag in the bedroom, contemplating Angela's obvious effort to smooth things between them. Anyone well acquainted with Jane—and by now, Angela knew Jane quite well—knew that the fastest way into her good graces was to show affection for her dogs. So maybe Jane should do her share in calling a truce.

When she returned to the front part of the motor home, Angela handed her a cup of tea. "Must have been a long trip," Angela said. "You look tired. But hey! I like the hair. You found someone good."

Jane self-consciously fingered a clipped lock of "Sunset Gold." "Don't take it as surrender," she warned Angela with a little smile. "At heart I'm still the slob I used to be."

"You were never a slob," Angela told her. "You were just hiding your light under a basket, or whatever that old saying is."

Jane cradled her tea in her hands and sat down at the dining table. Since they were being so friendly, for the time being, now was probably the time to smooth out some rough territory. "Angela...uh, listen. I want to apologize for going after you so hard about the stuff with me and Cole. Calling you a Peeping Tom was going way too far."

Angela slid into the seat across from Jane. "I always knew you would blow when you saw that. It didn't exactly come as a surprise."

"Well, you're right. The idea of people all over the country watching me flirt with a man—it gives me the creeps. I still hate it, but I knew when I got into this that having me, myself, broadcast over the airwaves was going to set me on edge."

Angela sipped her coffee and regarded Jane over the rim of her cup with a sympathetic look. "I guess I know how you feel. You and Ernie saw that I got a dose of having a camera on me as well, didn't you, and I'll admit it made me see this business through different eyes."

"It did?"

"Well, sure, I'm not made of stone, you know. Not that I would do anything differently, but it does make me see the other side. But anyway, you don't have to worry about it, you know, because we won't be using the romance angle. That kind of stuff works only if it has a happy ending."

Jane felt a weight lift off her shoulders—not the whole weight she had carried around for the last few weeks, but some of it, at least. "Cole and me—it wasn't that big of a deal." Even as she said it, she knew it was a lie. To her it had been a big deal. "It was just a casual thing, and even that didn't stand a chance. You know how important the Invitational is to me. I don't have time for a guy in my life."

"I can relate," Angela said, her mouth settling into an uncharacteristic downturn. "Guys always seem to come at the wrong time, or want the wrong thing...."

It wasn't her business, but Jane asked anyway. "Rick Tolleson, right?"

Angela sighed. "Hell yes. I never should have looked at the guy, you know? But I did. A deal more than look. Stupid."

Jane had known Rick a long time. In spite of his foot-loose habits, she'd never heard a whisper about him being a womanizer, a love-'em-and-leave-'em kind of guy. Poor Angela. "It didn't work out, huh?"

Angela's mouth grew into an indignant line. "Ha! The idiot dove right in and wanted—not good, wholesome sex, would you believe—but a Relationship. With a capital R. No one-night stands for him. Kept spouting some malarkey about me being too good for such a casual fling. Then, when we finally got it on, and I thought he'd finally come to his senses, I wake up in his bed in the middle of the night and find him picking out the names of our children!"

"Really?"

"Well, no, not really, but you get the idea."

Jane did get the idea, though she thought Angela picked strange things to get indignant about.

"Scared the hell out of me, you know? I was married once, and I found out that the tied-down sort of life doesn't work for me. I'm always on the move, going from project to project. I like new things, new people, new challenges. I get bored real easily. Long-term anythings just aren't my talent."

Which sounded just like Rick, Jane noted. They just might be a good pair. But she wasn't going to touch this with a ten-foot pole. She was hardly qualified to give relationship advice. As if she'd done so well for herself.

"But you know the thing that scared me most?"

"What?"

"Rick almost made me want to try it again. Walk straight into the emotional shredder. Like suicide. I almost wanted to. That was scary." Angela sighed into her coffee. "We're a pair, aren't we? Two hot women fighting off the guys."

Jane snorted. "Right. That's what we are."

"Do you miss Cole?" Angela asked.

"Of course not," Jane lied.

"And I don't miss Rick. Not a bit."

Later that evening, when Jane took Shadow out for an amble around the grounds, she reflected on the reasons that two sane, adult, supposedly intelligent women would have to lie about such a thing, both to each other and themselves. Maybe their pride wouldn't let them admit they needed someone or something they couldn't have.

Not that she missed Cole that much. Really, she didn't.

Then why, the pesky, impertinent, uncooperative part of herself asked snidely, *are you walking through the RV parking, searching for Cole's motor home?*

"I'm not!" Jane told herself.

You are. You're straining to see in the shadows, trying to remember what kind of motor home he bought.

"Am not."

Are.

"Not."

Are.

"Totally not!"

Shadow looked up at her as if she were insane.

"Okay," she confessed to the dog, "maybe I am looking for him."

But she couldn't remember exactly what kind of motor home Cole had bought—she'd been upset that afternoon, and his stupid new motor home had been the last thing on her mind.

"I don't see anything that looks familiar," she said. Shadow cocked his head to listen. "Maybe he's not here yet.

The trial doesn't actually start until day after tomorrow. Or maybe he's staying in the dorm." That dredged up memories she didn't want to have parading through her mind. Maybe when she was eighty-five she could sit back, remember that night, and smile, but not right now.

"Not that I care," she explained to Shadow. "We're going to go over by the arenas to walk. Totally away from the RVs. See how much I don't care?"

Shadow woofed softly.

But even by the arenas Jane found her eyes darting about. Others were out walking their dogs. She saw a few that she recognized, some that looked familiar only from ads and articles she had seen in some dog magazine or other. All the top people were here, that was for sure. But there was no Cole, no Teri, no little Dobby.

"What am I doing?" she complained to Shadow.

Shadow gave her a tolerant look, as if to say it was obvious what Jane was doing. She was strolling about with Shadow so that the golden retriever would have ample opportunity to lift his leg on every possible tree, bush, and blade of grass.

"They're not here. Maybe Cole decided not to come. He never cared that much about it, anyway."

That silly bet they had made—the dinner date in some expensive restaurant—had just been a tease. He hadn't cared that much about coming to Solid Gold. He hadn't cared that much about her.

But it had been Jane who'd backpedaled, who'd panicked when she had seen firsthand, with her own eyes, that she had waded into deeper water than she had known. Cole had accused her of caring less about him than winning some goddamned agility trial. He had accused her of putting a mere hobby before what they might have with each other.

He hadn't understood what Solid Gold meant to her. The Invitational wasn't just any old agility event, it was her

chance to rebuild her life. But then, how could he understand, since she hadn't told him? And she hadn't told him
because she hadn't wanted to bring him that far into her
life.

Except she had let him pretty damned far into her life
and everything else, that night right here in Argus Ranch's
dormitory.

Shadow turned quickly and blocked her path. Only then
did Jane see that she'd been about to walk into a light pole.

"Sheesh! I'm a wreck. Shadow, what would I do without you?"

Shadow wagged his tail.

"Time to head back?" she asked the dog. And then she
saw a familiar face. Not Cole's. Rick's.

"Hey, Jane," Rick hailed her. "That's you, isn't it?"

"Hey, Rick. It's me."

"I heard you got invited. Didn't see you at the big
Houston trials, though."

"I got the invite before Houston. So I figured I'd take
Shadow home for a rest."

"Probably a good idea."

"So, you're set up here? I didn't know there were going to
be vendors."

"A bunch of us. We're over there in the field where they
do the outdoor trials. All the competition this week is in-
doors."

Jane wondered if Angela knew Rick was here, and if she
didn't, should Jane tell her?

"So I guess Angie is here," Rick said, a little too casually.

"Where I go, so goes Angela and her cameraman."

"Oh, yeah. That's right. You're her current project."

"I understand her next project has something to do with
grizzly bears."

"I feel sorry for the grizzlies," he said wryly.

Jane gave him a sympathetic look, but at the same time,

she felt the need to defend her fellow female. "Angela's not that bad."

Rick shook his head. "No, of course not." He sighed. "I guess you've gotten to know her pretty well, have you?"

They took a seat on a bench across from the big arena building. Rick looked to be in a mood to talk, and Jane couldn't think of a polite way to escape acting as his sounding board.

"I guess I do know Angela pretty well," she admitted. "After spending most of a summer with someone in a thirty-four-foot motor home, you get to know them maybe better than you want to."

Rick grunted. "I guess so. She's a hard woman to understand, that one. Drop-dead gorgeous. Smart. A great gal, really. But skittish as a deer in hunting season."

"Well..." Jane began.

"You'd think a woman her age, with her brains and experience, would understand a thing or two about men, wouldn't you? Like the fact that not all men are made from the same stuff. Not all men have the same expectations of women. Not all men are so insecure that they need to keep a woman under their thumb all the time. Wouldn't you?"

"Well—"

"And wouldn't you think that she would know by now that everyone has a different style, a different need, that maybe a relationship between, say, Person A and Person B might be absolute poison, but if Person A met up with, say, Person C, they might get on like bread and butter, or chips and salsa. Wouldn't you think she would have learned that by now?"

"Uh—"

"I tell you, Jane—I live a real solitary existence, because I slip through life like a greased pig, always moving, never letting the moss grow. There's advantages to that sort of life and disadvantages as well. One of the disadvantages is that not only do you not collect any moss, you don't collect many close friendships, either. And if you're lucky enough to meet someone who might actually fit into your crazy lifestyle, and that person turns out to be too damned dense to see it, then, well, it's just damned depressing."

Jane saw what he was driving at. Poor Rick. For as long as Jane had known him, he'd been the king of jolly, smiling and joking every time she saw him. Now he looked so down he could have put a furrow in the dirt with his chin, and for that matter, so did Angela.

Don't even think about getting involved, she warned herself.

Rick sighed in dejection. "A good relationship is a thing of beauty."

Jane wouldn't know about that, but she didn't interrupt.

"It's worth working for. It's worth compromise. It's worth making adjustments to accommodate. If the potential is there, then it's worth nurturing."

She began to understand the purpose behind Rick's ode to romance. "So, Rick. Do you want me to talk to Angela? Is that what this is all about?"

"Would you?" He immediately brightened.

"No."

His face fell once again. "I thought you women loved to talk about stuff like this. Don't you?"

First Ernesto. Now Rick. Did the whole world think women had nothing better to do than gossip about men?

"No, we don't." Though truthfully, she and Angela had spent a good deal of time earlier discussing just this thing.

Then Jane had a brainstorm.

"Listen, Rick."

"I'm listening," he said in a dejected voice.

"I think you should talk to Angela."

"Angie doesn't want to talk. I don't think she even wants to get near me. You know, I didn't pull a marriage license out of the drawer and wave it at her. I just wanted to explore some possibilities of a future. But it was like showing a load of buckshot to a bunny."

"And so the bunny dove down a hole," Jane guessed.

"You got it."

"So keep your buckshot under wraps," Jane advised. "Talk to Angela about something she can't resist."

"Yeah, and that sure ain't me."

Jane slapped at his massive shoulder. "Quit feeling sorry for yourself, you big lummox. Use your brain and think. If Angela spent more time with you, she wouldn't be able to resist. Right?"

"Oh, right. I'm irresistible."

"You are!" Jane told him. "So get Angela to stick with you a while, in a situation where she's confident and in control, where she's not feeling threatened. Get her to drag you into one of her precious films—the traveling dog doctor, the New Age version of the horse-and-buggy vet."

He grimaced. "No one would be interested in that."

"You would be surprised at what Angela can make interesting."

He dropped his chin into his hand and looked thoughtful.

"That's my advice," Jane told him. "Take it or leave it."

"Humph."

"I'll send you my bill in the morning. Just call me Dr. Jane, the love doctor."

Jane guessed that he scarcely heard her. Staring into the darkness beyond where the lights could reach, he'd sunk deep into his own thoughts. So Jane patted his hand, stood, and gave Shadow's leash a tug. She'd only taken a few steps, though, when his voice stopped her.

"Good luck with Shadow at this thing," he said. "And thanks."

"Any time," she replied.

Dr. Jane, the love doctor. Right! Physician, heal thyself.

"I should have kept my mouth shut," she told Shadow as they walked back to the Enterprise.

Shadow found a bush that needed watering.

"But Rick seems so miserable," she told the dog.

Shadow paused and gave her a look.

"And Angela looks so lonely."

Together, Rick and Angela might be an absolute train wreck. Or they might fit together as perfectly as pieces of a jigsaw puzzle.

"So they ought to give love a chance, right?" she asked Shadow.

Had she given Cole a chance? Not really. But it wasn't the same. Not the same at all.

"I don't look that lonely, do I?"

An inquiring woof was her only answer.

"Of course I don't. Come on. Time for bed."

But her determined march toward the motor home didn't preclude one last glance at the RVs parked in the lot. She didn't see one that looked even vaguely familiar. Where the hell were Cole and Teri?

THE FIRST morning of the Solid Gold Invitational was glorious. A bright yellow sun shone in a cloudless sky. Green, fir-studded hills basked in mild summer warmth, not too hot, or humid, or windy. Nearly perfect. In nearby Tacoma and Seattle, tourists were getting a stunning view of Mount Rainier poised against a deep blue sky, age-old glaciers glinting in the sun.

But at Argus Ranch Facility for Dogs, no one cared about the natural beauty of such a rare day, least of all Jane, who sat in the bleachers listening to a representative from Solid Gold welcome 150 of the nation's top agility teams to the competition. Most of the spectators in the bleachers were local agility fans, plus a few die-hards who had driven or even flown in to watch. Jane recognized a fair number of Solid Gold competitors in the audience as well—all large-dog handlers. The smaller dogs were warming up in another building. This morning would see the first elimination rounds of the eight-, twelve-, and sixteen-inch classes. In the afternoon, the twenty- and twenty-four-inch divisions would compete.

The speaker was mercifully brief. He closed with a reminder to the audience that this agility event was different from any other. It didn't offer qualifying rounds toward a title or points toward a championship. What it did offer was a check for one hundred thousand dollars that would be awarded to the winner.

Dogs would compete in two elimination runs, today and tomorrow. Teams with flawless runs today would advance to the rounds tomorrow. The pool of teams who survived both elimination runs without a fault would then be whittled to a final group based on running time.

This event, the sponsor's representative declared, was the ultimate agility challenge, with the ultimate reward.

When the speaker left, the first-round judge stepped into the ring to inspect and measure the course. She was a well-known competitor and an evenhanded judge recognized for incorporating interesting challenges into her course design. She spent ten minutes marking off distances and making minute adjustments. Then the eight-inch handlers came into the ring for their pre-run walk-through.

And there was Cole. He *had* come. A herd of butterflies took flight in Jane's stomach.

He was looking good, Jane thought. Better than good. If Cole had been hurt at all by what had passed between them, it certainly didn't show.

The first competitor was a long-haired dachshund with a petite blonde handler who looked as if she could run a one-minute mile. They ran fast and clean, earning cheers and thunderous applause. The course, as one might expect, challenged both dogs and handlers with sharp turns, awkward angles, and traps designed to lure the dogs into taking the wrong obstacle. There was only one level of competition at Solid Gold, and that was Difficult with a capital *D*.

Jane applauded with the rest of the audience when the dachshund bounded out the exit gate, followed closely by the jubilant handler.

Jane only hoped she and Shadow would do as well.

The dachshund was followed by a tiny Parson's Russell terrier who knocked a bar off the triple jump. Jane saw the terrier's handler slap her hand against her forehead as they left the ring, because that handler knew the fault was hers. She had gotten the little dog into the jump at a bad angle, and it had cost her a chance at the big prize.

Next came a Cardigan Welsh corgi who streaked around the course in joyous bounds—a little too joyous. The little dog sprang from the A-frame without touching a paw to the "contact zone"—the yellow-painted section of the down-ramp that all dogs were required to touch. Too bad. It was a nice run, but that team, too, could pack their bags.

Then Cole and Dobby were standing on the start line. Cole looked relaxed and loose, much more so than Jane felt. The pint-sized Dobby looked intently at Cole's face—waiting, waiting, waiting for permission to fly off the line. Watching them poised for the go-ahead from the timer, Jane felt all the jitters of being on the line herself.

The timer signaled. Cole left Dobby and walked confidently to the entrance of the tunnel, which was the fourth obstacle. There was the first trap, because the angle of approach set the dog up to take the A-frame instead of the tunnel. The up-ramp to the A-frame was only inches away.

On Cole's command, Dobby sprinted forward, flew over the first three jumps, and flawlessly changed direction to dash into the tunnel. From there, the two of them made a very difficult course look easy. Dobby was a streak of black and white fur. Cole smiled the whole time he was running.

They exited the course to a swell of applause. Dobby sprang into Cole's arms the moment they crossed the finish line. And from somewhere in the crowd came Teri, jumping up and down, clapping her hands, cinnamon-colored ponytail bouncing up and down in a dance of joy.

Then, as if a magnet drew their gazes, their faces turned toward Jane, their smiles widened in recognition. Teri waved frantically, and Cole lifted a hand. Jane waved back, swallowing hard.

Five minutes later they caught her as she headed toward the arena door. Teri bounced up and gave her a spontaneous hug that started a glow in Jane's heart. She had to remind herself that she really wasn't a kid person.

"Jane!" Teri exclaimed. "You're here! Did you see Dobby and my dad? Weren't they great?"

"They were spectacular," Jane admitted with a glance at Cole, who hung back a bit.

"We went to Yellowstone and saw bears. And a baby bear, too. And then my aunt Nancy got married. And then we went to Pikes Peak, and Bryce Canyon where there's really weird-looking rocks, and the Grand Canyon in Arizona. My dad says you live in Arizona. Do you? I bet you've been to the Grand Canyon, too. It's really pretty. And deep."

Jane chuckled at the little girl's flood of words. "Yes, I live in Arizona. And yes, I like the Grand Canyon. I go up there lots."

Teri took her hand and tugged. "You've gotta come see Dash. He's so good. He hasn't peed in the motor home for a week. And he's losing some of his baby teeth. And he'll sit, and lie down, and stay—almost. Come see!"

Jane gently extricated her hand, giving Teri's a squeeze. "Maybe I'll come visit with Dash a little later. Shadow is running this afternoon, and I have to give him some exercise and do a bit of practice."

"Oh. Okay. Is Ernie here? Do you think he would play cribbage with me?"

"Ernesto is in the arena. I think he filmed your dad's run just in case you wanted a copy to take home."

"Can I go find Ernie, Dad? Can I?"

"May I."

Teri grimaced. "Okay. May I?"

"Yes, you may. But stay in the arena. If you don't find Ernesto, don't go wandering off."

"Okay. I promise." And off she went, leaving Jane to face Cole without the buffer of Teri's chatter.

Jane hesitated. Had Cole's eyes always been so richly dark? His smile so mesmerizing? For a moment she felt tongue-tied.

He jumped into the silence with a bland greeting. "How've you been, Jane?"

"Fine. Fine." And maybe not so fine. "That was a terrific run for you and Dobby. Congratulations."

"Thanks. Dobby did herself proud."

"And so did you."

He grinned, easing the tension a bit. "I did, didn't I?"

The grin on his face reminded her of how she had felt after a good agility run a year ago. She wished it was still that much fun. But Cole's grin faded, and he began to look uneasy. "Uh . . . Jane, Angela called me a few days after Teri and I left Spokane."

"Don't tell me she wants to do a series on you now."

He chuckled and shook his head. "No. Not that. She . . . told me why this event means so much to you, why you really need that big purse."

Jane's first reaction was anger. Angela had absolutely no regard for privacy. Then she realized that the producer had meddled just as Jane had meddled, trying to mend a rift between two people she considered friends.

"So I guess I can understand how a relationship would be playing second fiddle to something you need so much. You're thinking that your whole future depends on Shadow and this competition. I was out of line saying what I did."

Jane wasn't sure that he had been out of line, really. "It wasn't your fault," she told him. "I never should have let things go as far as they did."

A wicked sparkle lit his eyes. "I'm glad you did. In fact, I don't regret a minute of it."

Neither did she, Jane realized. She smiled. "You know, Cole, you should never play second fiddle to anything. You're too good for that. And I don't regret anything, either."

Before she could dig herself any deeper, she gave him a little wave and escaped. Now, what had made her blurt that out? Jane had always suffered from a direct line that went from brain to mouth without passing the censorship of good sense, but that little gem had caught even her by surprise.

But she really couldn't think about that right now. In about two hours, she and Shadow would be in the ring, running for Jane's future.

THE TIME was slightly over three hours, actually, a wait that stretched Jane's nerves to the limit. Standing on the line, watching the team before her run a perfect course, Jane's case of the pre-run jitters dwarfed any she had ever experienced before. She was stretched so tight that something inside was going to break any minute, she thought. And the half sandwich she had eaten for lunch was threatening to reappear.

Shadow picked up on Jane's anxiety and sat tense and panting at her side, his eyes darting from Jane to the course and back to Jane.

But before anything broke in either of them, the timer gave them the go-ahead. They sprinted off the start line, negotiated the first three jumps, then the tunnel, then turned sharply to fly over the triple. The weaves were perfect. A sharp turn to the dog-walk, then a rear-cross to get in position for a pinwheel of jumps that spat them into a sharp turn to the A-frame. Double back to just half of the same pinwheel, then a front-cross and send to the tire, and down a zigzag line of jumps toward the finish line. Through it all, Jane's heart pumped furiously while her brain went into neutral, short-circuited from sheer overload. Her body acted from instinct and months of drill. Shadow ran anxiously, looking at Jane for reassurance more than for direction, doing what he was supposed to do, but not looking happy about it.

They crossed the finish line with a clean run that won them advancement to the next day's round. Jane braced hands on her knees and tried to breathe. She scarcely remembered their performance, but a respectable time and a notation of zero faults flashed on the board above the arena.

A bit of weight lifted from her shoulders—today's weight, at least. Tomorrow was another day, and today's run hadn't been fast enough to suit her. It had gotten them into the semifinals, but that kind of speed, or lack of it, wouldn't earn them a place in the final group.

"Hey, Jane!" Ernesto hailed her. "Great run."

For the first time since joining up with Angela, Jane had forgotten about the camera. She didn't know if that was a good sign or bad.

Jane spent the rest of the afternoon with Shadow in the practice arena. The second elimination run had a different judge, and since the course was designed by the judge, tomorrow's run would have a much different feel than today's. Jane had shown under the judge more than once, and she could anticipate how the course would be set, what challenges it might offer. So they practiced, and practiced, and practiced, until Ernesto found her to say that he, Angela, Cole, Teri, and several others, including their old friend Greta, who had come to the trial as a spectator, were driving to Tacoma to have pizza.

"Want to come?" he asked.

Jane could think of nothing she wanted less—an evening looking at Cole, followed by running the next morning's agility course with the remnants of a pizza weighing her down.

"Go on without me," she said. "I'll just fix a hamburger in the motor home. Did Teri find you this morning?"

"Yeah. The kid beat me three cribbage games in a row." Ernesto grinned. "She reminds me of my youngest granddaughter."

By the time Jane and Shadow returned to the motor home, the group had left. Shadow plopped down on the floor and refused to move after eating his dinner, and Jane curled up with a sandwich and a book, trying to relax. Relaxation wouldn't come. As Cole had said, her whole future depended upon Shadow and this competition. How was she supposed to relax?

The next morning Jane felt as if she hadn't slept at all, despite having gone to bed early the night before. She and Shadow were third in the ring on the new course, with the new judge. The course was much as Jane had expected, difficult, but doable. Shadow put in a workmanlike performance, not inspired, but technically flawless. It remained to be seen if their time was fast enough to make the final cut.

It was all Jane could do to stick in the bleachers during the afternoon and watch the small dogs compete, counting the number that put in clean performances and faster times than her own. She was torn between escaping the torture of watching and the need to see Cole and Dobby run. She had about decided to flee to the motor home when Teri bounded up the bleachers to where Jane was sitting.

"Hi!" the kid said cheerily.

"Hi yourself. Come up here to watch your dad?"

"Yeah. When are you going to come to visit Dash?"

Jane felt a stab of guilt. She had no right to disappoint Teri just because seeing Cole was sure to bring on a case of red-faced embarrassment. "Maybe after your dad runs the course we should go have a visit."

"That would be great. Dash misses you."

"Well, I sort of miss him, too. I'll bet he's grown a lot."

"He has." The kid paused, and her face assumed the almost-adult gravity that Jane sometimes found downright scary. "I missed you, too."

Jane's heart sank a bit. She had missed Teri as well, even though she hesitated to admit it to herself. So she replied lightly, "Did you? It sounds as if you and your dad were too busy to miss anybody."

Teri didn't reply directly. Instead, her mouth twisted this way and that as she pondered. "Sometimes I was snotty to you. I'm sorry."

"What?"

"I really like you. See? But I thought it would hurt my mom's feelings if I really liked you, and especially if my dad liked you. But my dad told me that I'm like Dash. Dash's mom couldn't stay with him, so Dash got me. And Dash loves me. And Dash's mom would be happy to know that her puppy is with someone who loves him like I love him."

Jane couldn't think of a single thing to say.

"So my dad said that I'm sort of like Dash. And my mom in heaven would be happy if I loved a new mom, someone like you. And he told me to think about it. And I thought about it."

"Ah." Jane wondered if there was any way she could escape this conversation.

"So I thought that my mom would probably be happy if my dad could find someone, too."

"I'm sure," Jane said, taking a deep breath, "that you and your dad will find someone very special, eventually."

"Someone like you," Teri declared. "I know you really like my dad, so I thought I should tell you that I won't be a snot anymore, and that you can be a part of our family, along with me and Dad and Dash and Dobby, and you can bring Shadow and Idaho, and we'll all be happy. My mom will be happy, too."

Jane thought she might choke. If life were only that easy. "Teri—"

A welcome interruption saved her, Cole's voice, saying, "Hi, you two."

Jane didn't realize until then that she and Teri had both missed seeing Cole and Dobby run. But from the smile on Cole's face, she guessed they had aced the course.

"Did you win yet, Daddy?"

"Not yet, sweet pea." He grinned at Jane. "Teri been bending your ear about our vacation?"

He didn't know the half of it, Jane thought. His daughter had just extended an invitation into their family. She wondered what Cole would think about that.

As for Jane, she didn't have time to think about it, or to deal with the strange longings that very peculiar conversation inspired. Maybe after the Invitational she would think about it. She would have time then. Not now.

She didn't see Cole again until late that afternoon, when the competitors crowded around a bulletin board in the practice arena, waiting for the final cut to be posted. There would be only fifteen in this last group, the fastest of those teams who had survived both elimination rounds.

"Thought I might see you here," Cole told her, pushing through the crowd.

Jane was so nervous that she couldn't speak, could only give him a weak smile. He returned the smile and put a comforting hand on her shoulder. She wanted to lean into him and hide her face against that warm, solid chest. That solid chest that she remembered so well.

Merlyn—the Argus Ranch manager—marched in and saved Jane from the memory. In Merlyn's hand was the list that held Jane's future. Smiling at the tense crowd, she started to tack the list to the board, then hesitated.

"Do you want to trample each other to see?" she asked. "Or should I read it?"

"Read it!" shouted multiple voices.

Cole's hand slid down Jane's arm and he wound his fingers tightly through hers. Merlyn read fifteen competitors' names—the best of the best—who would run the next day for a purse of one hundred thousand dollars. Fifteen names. And among those names, both Connor and Forrest.

chapter 24

A WEATHER front moved into the Northwest overnight, bringing warm, sullen air to greet a gray dawn. The final round of the Solid Gold Invitational began at ten, starting with the small dogs and working up to the larger ones.

Jane pulled herself out of bed at six, feeling heavy and headachy. Angela still snored into her pillow, and the Argus Ranch grounds were quiet. Jane put a bowl of instant oatmeal into the microwave, and while it heated fixed a much more elaborate breakfast for Shadow. Some competitors wouldn't feed a dog before a competition, in order to avoid any sluggishness that came from a full stomach, but Jane thought the energy from a light, nutritious meal helped a dog deliver a superior performance.

Shadow lay on the floor, legs sprawled and head down, watching her mix kibble, herbal supplements, yogurt, and chicken broth for his meal. When she put the dish on the floor, he got up and sniffed the food, but didn't eat.

"This is a first," Jane said, though she had noted a decrease in his appetite since they had arrived. "Got a case of nerves, big guy? So do I, you know. But you'd better eat. You're going to need it."

He looked at her with soft brown eyes, then took a bite.

"That's better. Keep eating."

Shadow just looked at her. The bell on the microwave dinged. Time for her own breakfast.

Jane pulled the oatmeal from the microwave, poured herself a glass of orange juice, and sat down at the dinette. But the first bite of oatmeal stuck like cement in her throat. It made it to her stomach only when urged along by a wash of orange juice, and there it lay in a lump. Jane thought she might throw up.

Shadow whined. He hadn't taken another bite, and the kibble was turning to mush in his bowl.

"So we both have a case of nerves," Jane admitted. "I know the cure. Let's go practice."

But when they began work in the practice arena, things didn't go well. Shadow's weave pole problem had returned. Worse, he was distracted, sniffing the dirt floor, looking off into space, making mistakes that would have shamed a novice.

"What is wrong with you?" Jane demanded, an edge in her voice. Shadow had just popped a pole for the third time in a row.

She tried to gather her composure. Moving to another exercise would help, she decided. When things started to perk, then they would return to the weaves. But five minutes later Shadow missed the contact zone of the dog-walk, just because he wasn't paying attention. Then he knocked a bar from the triple jump.

Jane lost it. "Dammit! What the hell are you doing?" she shouted. "This is a fine time to get goofy, you idiot! Do you know what's riding on today's run? Do you know?"

Shadow cowered against the ground, flinching away when she came toward him. Jane stopped, horrified.

All her life she had worked with dogs, and not one had

ever cringed away from her, not her own dogs, not the dogs she had cared for and trained for others. She always taught her students that a positive, upbeat attitude was the most crucial part of training, that a dog should want to work, not have to work.

And now Shadow was looking at her as if she were the stuff of canine nightmares. His posture cried out submission and misery, his soft brown eyes spoke volumes of hurt.

Overwhelmed by misery, Jane wrapped her arms around herself and doubled over. She melted to the dirt floor, suddenly lacking the strength to stand. "Oh, Shadow! I'm so sorry! I'm sorry."

Gingerly the dog crept to her and laid a head in her lap.

How had Jane let this happen? She had abused her best friend, expecting him to carry the burden of her whole future. She had ransomed her entire life to win this stupid competition, and look what she had given up to that ransom—Shadow's trust, her own principles, and maybe more. She thought of Cole, of Teri and Dash—whom she had not visited as promised the day before.

All the things she had put off thinking about for so many weeks—important things, life-changing things. Every time she had questioned herself, she had promised to think about it later. Every doubt she had had—think about it later. Think about Cole later, about her dogs later, about her feelings later, her future—later. And now all those things came tumbling down upon her in an overwhelming avalanche. Now they wouldn't be put off, because Shadow had showed her in painfully uncertain terms just how far she had strayed from who she really was.

And here she sat, wallowing on a dirt floor, trying to comfort her weary, stressed-out dog, fed up with herself to the point of nausea.

She bent and kissed the top of Shadow's furry head. "I'm so sorry," she said again. "How could I have forgotten that you're so young? Even if you weren't still a baby, I never should have pushed you this far. My poor Shadow. If you had a brain in your head, you'd bite me and go live with someone else."

Shadow whined, looking up at her with abject adoration. Tears ran unchecked down Jane's cheeks. She was an idiot, and she didn't deserve a dog like Shadow, or Idaho either. She had never done this to Idaho, thank heaven, never gotten so desperate to win that she had lost her perspective. Now she knew how clueless she could be, and it was frightening.

"Don't tell Idaho about this," she whispered against Shadow's fur. "He would ground me for weeks."

The golden retriever smile had returned to Shadow's face. He licked her wet cheeks. But when they got up from the floor, he cast an anxious glance toward the practice equipment.

"Don't worry," Jane told him. "No more practice, and no more competition. Not until you're rested and having fun again. To hell with Solid Gold, and to hell with the big purse. There are things in life more important than money. You're one of them, and so is my self-respect—what's left of it."

Jane dusted herself off, snapped Shadow's leash to his collar, and headed out to talk to the event superintendent. Suddenly she was hungry.

ANGELA TOOK Jane's withdrawal in stride. "A good producer," she told Jane, "has to be flexible. This actually is going to make a great ending to the series. Our star puts the welfare of her dog above the need to win. We'll pull heartstrings from coast to coast. No one will expect this. It's priceless."

Jane's grimace told Angela exactly what her star thought of using her emotional trauma to pull heartstrings.

"Buck up, kiddo. People are going to think you're top

rung. And you know what? I'll bet the minute the network starts selling ad space on this series, you're going to be knee-deep in contract offers to be spokeswoman for this dog food or that puppy treat. You'll have more money coming in than you know what to do with. Or you could write a book. Everyone knows that book authors make big bucks."

Jane looked down at Shadow. "I don't think I'm going to be selling myself for money any time soon. I just need to spend some time thinking about what direction I want my life to take."

"Well, don't think it to death," Angela advised. "Sometimes life just happens, and taking it as it comes is the best that anyone can do."

Jane smiled. "I'll remember that."

"What are you going to do now? You're going to stay and watch, aren't you?"

"Wouldn't miss it. Besides," she said wryly, "I'm guessing you'll want some shots of me sitting stoically in the bleachers."

"You bet." Now she was getting it, Angela thought, noting that Jane hadn't looked so relaxed in a long time. She was happy for her. A big win at this event would have been a great finale, but Angela could deal with this crook in the road and make the series come out better than ever. Just see if she couldn't.

"What I'm going to do now," Jane continued, "is take Shadow on a long walk around the grounds, let him sniff to his heart's content, watch birds in the sky and bugs in the grass. And maybe I'll go look at the vendor booths. I don't have any prospect of money coming in any time soon, but heck, a girl can look. And so can a dog." Then she got a positively sly look on her face. "Rick is here, by the way. I saw him the other night, and he asked about you."

"Rick is here?" Angela didn't want to care. She was through with that moron. Through, through, through.

"You didn't know he was here?"

"No. Not that I care."

"Of course you don't," Jane agreed, but her smile was too knowing. She reached down and scratched Shadow's head. "Like I said, I'm going for an amble. And just in case you're interested, the vendors are set up in the big grassy area behind the practice building."

When Jane left, Angela mentally prioritized what she had to do. She had to talk to Ernesto about a new slant on the camera work. She had to do her hair and slop on some makeup. She had to go back and look at the video she had edited so far, thinking of how to make the earlier filming lead up to what would be a surprise ending.

Going to the vendor area certainly was not on her list of things to do.

And yet, after spending a full hour on hair and cosmetics, after going through three changes of outfits, Angela found herself wandering not toward the arena, where the final competition was about to start, but in the direction of the practice building, or maybe the grassy area behind it.

She was just stretching her legs, Angela told herself. She knew what kind of life suited her, and that kind of life was poison to any kind of relationship other than encounters of the most casual kind.

So why would she want to see Rick? They had said everything that needed to be said when she had booted him out of her motor home. Even though the sex had been great—okay, better than great—the man's pillow talk had headed in the exact wrong direction. Asking about her family. Talking about his sister and her kids. The man had strings written all over him, and she had known it from the first. But she had let her hormones get the best of her.

But scary as that had been, the thing that had caused the harsh words, the name-calling (mostly on her part), and the final boot, was her own lethal desire to go along, to see how things might work out, to giving the strings a chance.

That had been the scariest of all. The man was a dangerous temptation, and one slip of her resolve could lead to an ugly tangle. Angela had been there before, and she was smarter now. So she would not, absolutely would not, go anywhere near Rick Tolleson.

Yet when she looked up from her musings, her feet had carried her to within sight of the vendors. Several were arranged in a rectangle of canopies in the smooth green field.

Come to think of it, Angela remembered, she did need to shop for a gift for Jane. It was Jane, after all, who had made this whole series possible, even though she occasionally had been a pain in the ass. Angela really ought to get Jane a little something, and where better to shop than here, where every product that could tickle the fancy of a dog person was on display? Besides, she didn't see the banner proclaiming RICK TOLLESON, DVM. Maybe he had left.

So Angela ventured forward. True to her principles, she did not really look for Rick. She didn't have to, because not five minutes into her little shopping spree he found her.

"Hey, Angie."

Her heart dropped, then soared. Traitorous, stupid heart. She turned from the pendant she had been examining. "Hey, Rick. How're you doing?"

"Great. You?"

"Stupendous."

That should have been the end of it—an awkward greeting after a tumultuous parting. But it wasn't. "Come let me buy you a drink," he offered.

"A drink?"

"A Coke. Or Pepsi. Or Mountain Dew. Whatever is your pleasure."

She had to smile. "The hard stuff, eh?"

"That's right. I have a proposal to make."

An instant of panic made her heart almost stop, until he clarified.

"A business proposal. You're the businesswoman extraordinaire, the entertainment mogul, the creative genius. You should like this."

He looked good. Boy, did he look good. She loved the way the strands of his long hair, gold even in the morning's dull light, brushed against his cheek. Today that cheek was freshly shaven and smooth. When she had last seen him, he'd worn a day's heavy growth of beard, scratchy but so masculine.

She shouldn't be thinking along those lines, but it was hard not to with temptation standing right here before her in the flesh.

"Well?" he said.

Damn the man. Just by looking so hot he had distracted her from what he'd been saying. Oh, yes, a proposal.

"Okay," she conceded. "You can buy me a glass of iced tea at the food concession."

They were silent as they walked toward the concession window, but Angela's mind whirled, wondering what was up. Rick could tempt all he wanted, she decided, but her resolve was strong. She was a free spirit, and anything that tried to tie her down was poison. Rick was poison. Attractive poison. Downright irresistible poison, but poison just the same.

At a redwood picnic table beside the food concession, Rick handed her a cup of iced tea with a flourish. "Here you go, m'lady."

"Is that a beer you have?"

"Yup."

Angela suspected she should have asked for a beer. She might need it.

"Here's the deal," he said without preamble. "You mentioned something when we first met that got me thinking. You remember that day at Carson City that you and Jane brought Shadow to see me, after he'd gone bonkers and tried to skedaddle for the highway?"

How well she did remember. Seeing Rick for the first time

had nearly knocked her off her feet. He was just the kind of guy that set her senses to humming. And they had hummed. Hell, they had caroled like the Mormon Tabernacle Choir.

"You said that you would consider doing one of your documentary programs on me and my practice and how I blend conventional vet work with holistic and chiropractic. You thought folks might be interested."

She did remember, vaguely.

"Was that just a pickup line?"

"My business," she replied, a touch indignantly, "is never just a pickup line."

"Well, good then. I've decided to take you up on your offer."

Angela should have said that an idea thrown out without thinking, off the top of her head, was hardly a firm offer. But before she could say it, the producer in her took over. The idea *was* a good one, even though, truthfully, it had been sort of a pickup line.

"You can do your thing. Make me a star." He grinned engagingly. "I guarantee I'll be easier to work with than those bears you're thinking about."

She raised one inquiring brow.

"Been talking to Jane," he confessed.

Her eyes narrowed suspiciously. She suspected a plot, but then, she'd done enough plotting where Jane was concerned that she could hardly complain.

"So you think you're star material, eh?"

"Definitely star material. And I'm counting on you recognizing it, sweet Angie. But because I'm an honest fellow, I'll confess to ulterior motives right up front. I figure that if you spend enough time with me, you won't be able to resist my manly charm. And more, you'll come to realize that we were made to be together, two lone wolves wandering together."

Her heart beat a little faster. "I'd hate for you to take this on with that as your only reason, because if you do, you're going to be mighty disappointed."

He gave her a wicked, heart-stopping smile. "Oh I don't know. I'm a mighty persistent guy."

"And I'm a mighty stubborn woman."

"Well, then, maybe we'll find out what really happens when an irresistible force meets an immovable object."

She tried to say no, but the word wouldn't quite exit her lips. This was a winning situation—the lure of a salable project was almost irresistible. Rick's manly attractions had nothing to do with the temptation to say yes. They didn't, she told herself. In spite of her earlier vow not to go near him, this was business. Business put a new slant on everything. The big handsome ox could charm all he wanted, but Angela would definitely not succumb. Not if she had business on her mind. No way would she let this get personal, in spite of him and his big, broad shoulders and his heart-stopping smile. No way. At least, probably not.

She stuck out her hand. "Okay, you have yourself a deal. We'll iron out the details later."

He took her hand, his eyes bright with laughter, and something else. "A deal like this," he declared, "needs more than a handshake."

And before Angela could bolt, he bent down to plant a gentle kiss on her lips. She didn't pull away, couldn't pull away.

Oh, my, she was in such trouble.

JANE SAT in the bleachers, almost as nervous as if she were the one standing on the line. She hadn't seen Cole since the day before, when they had held on to each other and danced about with the joy of having made the final cut. But she saw him now, as if he were the only person in the huge arena. He stood on the line with Dobby, looking happy and relaxed. The team in front of them, a light-footed African-American woman who could run like the wind, along with her Parson's Russell terrier, were finishing up an absolutely flawless round.

"Hi, Jane!" Teri clambered up the bleachers to join her, climbing over the bodies and legs of other spectators. "It's just about time for my dad and Dobby to run!"

Jane scooted over to make room beside her on the bench. "They're going to do great." The terrier's time would be hard to beat, though. Each dog had two runs. A fault in either run eliminated the team. If both runs were clean, the two times were averaged. On a course with an allowed time of fifty-two seconds, the terrier had averaged forty-three.

"My dad always wins," Teri declared. Then she bit her lip. "But you'll do great, too. Shadow always does good. Maybe you'll win," the girl conceded, trying hard not to sound insincere.

"That's okay, Teri. Shadow and I aren't competing today, so we're rooting for your dad."

Teri's eyes widened. "But you made the final round. My dad said you did."

"Shadow didn't feel well this morning. He was really tired, and not having any fun. And having fun is the most important thing, isn't it?"

Teri's mouth opened, but for a moment nothing came out. Then, "Wow! I thought you really wanted to win. Didn't you?"

"Sometimes we can want to win too much. There will be other competitions for Shadow. He has plenty of time to win."

Of course, those competitions wouldn't be worth the big bucks. But no amount of money was worth what Jane had put Shadow through. And since pulling Shadow's entry, the weight of the world had lifted from her shoulders. She had built a good life before, starting from almost nothing, and she could do it again.

"Wow!" Teri said again.

On impulse, Jane put her arm around the little girl and drew her close in a brief hug. If she had been smarter this summer, she might have had a chance at becoming part of Teri's life, something she had never dreamed of wanting. Now she admitted that she might well have wanted that. Almost as much as she wanted—might have wanted—to become part of Cole's life. If she had been smarter.

But she hadn't been smart. She had blown it for the worst of reasons. Now time had passed. The passion—his, at least—had curdled. They had gotten the mutual apologies out of the way and were friendly once again, but Jane had lost much of Cole's respect when she had gone off the deep end. Or so she guessed. She had certainly lost her own respect, only she hadn't realized it until this very morning. Poor Shadow. How fortunate she was, Jane mused, that dogs were so forgiving.

Teri tugged her sleeve. "Pay attention, Jane! My dad's going to run."

"Wouldn't miss it, kid. This is very exciting."

Cole and Dobby shot off the line, negotiated a wicked tunnel/dog-walk trap, sailed through a pinwheel of jumps, bounced through twelve weave poles, and then flew over a triple jump. Dobby was running her little heart out. Even from the bleachers Jane could see the tiny tongue hanging from her mouth, the grin that brightened her mousy face. How had she ever dismissed this noble little dog just because she was the size of some kid's wind-up toy? Dobby had as much heart as Shadow or Idaho.

"Look at them go!" Jane said to Teri, who was bouncing up and down on the bench in excitement.

Their run was clean and fast. Dobby had done herself proud, and obviously pleased with herself, she jumped into Cole's arms. But they had one more round, a test of endurance as well as talent.

The second run went almost as well, with only one small misstep that threw Dobby off balance when she landed from the tire jump. It wasn't a fault, but it cost her a half second of time. At the end of her two runs, Dobby's average time placed her in third place behind the Parson's and an Australian shepherd.

"Ooooh!" came a disappointed whine from Teri. "That can't be right. My dad always wins."

Jane gave her another hug. "You know, Teri, Dobby and your dad did the very best job that they could, but the very best agility teams in the country are running today, and only one team can win."

"And winning isn't as important as having fun," Teri said, punctuating the recitation with an eye-roll.

Eye-roll and all, though, she learned faster than Jane.

Teri leaned against Jane, pillowing her head on Jane's upper arm as if she intended to stay there for a while. The girl's closeness lit a warm glow in Jane's heart. Maybe, after all this time, she was a kid person after all.

"Hey there, sweet pea," came Cole's greeting as he climbed the bleachers toward them. He had Dobby tucked beneath one arm. The little dog was positively glowing as spectators reached out to touch her and say what a good job she had done.

"Hi, Daddy. Jane said it was all right that you didn't win, because only one team can win, and there's lots of teams out there better than you."

Jane's face heated. "That's not exactly what I said, Teri."

Cole laughed at her discomposure. "Well, it's true. Most of the teams out there are pros compared to us, and I tell you, it was a heck of a good time being in there with them."

He gave Teri a buss on the cheek. "I tell you what, sweetie, to celebrate Dobby's wonderful, flawless performance, later I'll take you into Tacoma for pizza. What do you think?"

Teri's face brightened. "It's a deal."

"And right now, I see Ernesto over there breaking down that big camera, so I guess he's finished shooting for a while. Why don't you take Dobby and go over to say hi." He transferred the little bundle of black and white fur to the cradle of Teri's arms. "She deserves to ride. She's tired."

"Bye, Jane," Teri said as she proudly carried away the Invitational's smallest star. "See ya later."

"Bye, Teri."

And then Jane and Cole were alone among the throng of spectators. Cole sat down on the bleacher. Jane's heart sped up.

"Those were terrific runs," she told him. "Absolutely terrific."

"Dobby is always terrific, even when she makes mistakes. And she does, sometimes."

"Not this morning. If she'd been just a little faster . . . But you looked like you were having so much fun."

"We were."

A silence stretched between them, and Jane searched for something to say. She didn't want Cole to get up and leave.

"You pulled Shadow," he finally said. "Is he okay?"

Jane bit her lip. "He is okay, now."

No answer. She felt the silence like a weight.

"Remember what you said about my whole future depending upon this competition and Shadow?"

"Yes."

"It wasn't fair for me to put that kind of pressure on him. Shadow likes to compete, but this summer was way too much for him—running agility every weekend, on the road in a motor home when he wasn't running, no time to play or relax or just hunker down and chew on a good bone. And his stupid mom—me—scolding him whenever he made a mistake, drilling him time and time again until of course he started to make mistakes."

No comment. More silence.

"Shadow's young, a baby, really. And I treated him totally unfairly this summer. And it didn't get through my thick skull what I was doing, until this morning, when... when...cripes! I don't even like to think about it. Shadow screwed up the weaves in practice, and I cursed at him. Shouted so loud that he cringed, Cole. Actually cringed. I was so ashamed that if I'd had a hammer, I would have knocked myself over the head with it."

Cole sighed. His hand captured hers where it rested on her knee. "So you told him that he didn't have to compete and pulled him."

"Yeah."

"What about the purse that you needed so badly?"

"To hell with the money. That money isn't worth making my best friend unhappy. I'll land on my feet, somehow. I always do."

He squeezed her hand. "Best friend, eh?"

"Well, Shadow and Idaho both. Isn't that what dogs were made for? To be best friends?"

"What about people?"

"I have people friends, too. Good friends."

He nodded, looked at the arena, where a border collie was making his try for victory, then back at her. "I'm really proud of you, Jane."

She glanced his way, surprised. "Why?"

"Because you put Shadow above what you needed. I always figured you were the kind of person who put others—including your animals—first."

"You heard what I said. I made Shadow miserable."

"And now you've made him happy, at some cost to yourself. You might have won, you know. You're the best."

She chuckled. "That's an exaggeration if I ever heard one."

Jane didn't want him to let go of her hand. She didn't want him to go back to wherever he and Teri were headed, to live the rest of their lives without her. But she had to be adult about this. At least they were still friends, which perhaps was more than she deserved.

"I guess this is the end," she said with a sigh. "I hope you and Teri have a good trip back to Albuquerque."

"Yeah. About that—we're only going back there to close on the house and get our stuff out of storage. I've accepted a teaching position at Yavapai Community College in Arizona."

Jane's heart pounded so loud she was sure Cole could hear it. "Yavapai?"

"The Cottonwood campus."

"Cottonwood?" Six miles from the former Bark Park.

"That's right. You know, I learned something from you this summer. I learned that some things are worth pursuing, long and hard, until you catch them. Without wavering, without giving up when things get tough. Like you pursued Solid Gold."

"But that was a mistake."

"You were going after the wrong thing, maybe, but as I watched you, I learned that if something is worth pursuing, that something deserves serious attention."

She could hardly breathe. "Like . . . what?"

"Like you, Jane."

The breath rushed out of her in astonishment.

"You are definitely worth serious attention, and you are something too good to give up. I've done a lot of thinking about you and me, and I guess today proved to me that you really are the person I thought you were."

Now it was Jane's turn to be silent. Her throat was closed to traffic, even if she could have thought of something to say.

"Jane . . ." His grip on her hand tightened. "I'm pretty sure that I'm in love with you. And I'm hoping that once your life settles down again, you'll think about it and realize that we're a lot more than just friends."

With difficulty, she inhaled. "I...I am a pretty determined person, as you said. And..." *Breathe in, breathe out, and try to slow the racing heart*—"and I think I may have learned something this summer, too, about just what sorts of things are worth such determined pursuit. I guess a lot of my ideas are changing."

"Change can be good," Cole said with a smile. "I'm going to be camped at your back door in Arizona—fair warning. And I don't intend to let you go, Jane Connor. So you'd better get used to having a little mouse-dog around, and me, and Teri. Because we're not going to be pestering you."

Jane smiled. She didn't know exactly how she was going to build her future, but things were looking a lot brighter. "Do you know what?" she said, using one of Teri's favorite phrases.

"What?" he asked softly.

"I'm pretty sure that I love you. You and Teri and your little dog, too."

The spectators were riveted on the action in the ring, where a border terrier was running the course faster than any dog before, so they missed the action in the tenth row of the bleachers, where Jane and Cole ignored the rest of the world and said it all with a kiss.

ACROSS THE arena, Teri gave Ernesto a triumphant smile. "Told ya. I'm gonna have a new mom."

Ernesto chuckled. "From what I see going on over there, kid, you may just be right."

"Want to play some cribbage?" Teri asked.

"Only if you let me win," Ernesto said. "You've turned into a regular cardsharp."

As they headed toward the exit, Teri glanced once again toward her dad and Jane, who were talking like they had a million things to say. Shadow was going to be real happy when Teri told him about this, and so were Dash and

Dobby. And a warm glow in her stomach let her know that someone else was happy as well.

Teri looked up beyond the arena roof, beyond the gray clouds in the sky and the blue sky above the clouds, to where her mother lived in heaven. "Thanks, Mom," she said quietly.

epilogue

MCKENNA MARKHAM flipped her cell phone shut with a satisfied snap. "She'll be here in about forty-five minutes," she told Nell, who was putting finishing touches on a huge, "Welcome Home" banner. "So let's hustle."

"Better get the guys off their duffs," Nell said.

Tom Markham and Dan Travis, the guys in question, were deaf to anything their wives were saying, engrossed as they were in watching a football game on the big-screen TV in the family room.

"I see Miss Piggy's birthday present to Dan is a big hit," Mckenna said.

"Thoughtful of Piggy, don't you think?" Nell said. "She bought it just in time for football season."

Piggy, who was famous for her talent at making trouble, lay on the sofa between the men, watching every potato chip that traveled from the bag to their mouths.

"Hey, Cowboy!" Mckenna called to her husband. "We need you to take this banner over to the party and put it up."

"Now?" Tom said.

"Now would be good. Jane is almost here. She's in Cordes Junction."

Tom grunted. "She takes ten days to get here, and she had to arrive right in the middle of the Broncos game?"

"Life's tough," Mckenna agreed, comforting the poor guy with a kiss on his tousled hair. "Record it."

"Dan," Nell chimed in. "You're going to help, right?"

Dan sighed. "Right, dear."

When the women bustled off to the kitchen, though, both men's eyes followed with warm affection.

Less than an hour later, Jane pulled into Nell's driveway in her old van. Mckenna and Nell rushed out to welcome her, Idaho and Piggy not far behind. Amid hugs and greetings, Shadow jumped out of the van and pranced proudly up to Idaho, who promptly put the youngster in his place by jumping on him and knocking him tummy side up. That obligatory step over, the two dogs gamboled around the yard, happily sniffing each other, licking ears, rolling on the ground, and performing the usual canine salutations. Tom's old Labrador, Clara, joined in the play, but Piggy watched from a dignified distance. When Shadow trotted over to say hello, however, she allowed him to wash her face with his big sloppy tongue, though her almost human grimace expressed what she thought of such silly dog ceremonies.

"You look great!" Nell said, not bothering to hide her surprise. A subtle glow had replaced the strain that had drawn Jane's face the last time she had been home. Nell had expected her to be down in the dumps, considering what had happened at the Invitational. Unexpectedly, her friend looked about ten years younger, and not because of the flattering hairstyle and subtle hints of makeup.

"Why did you drive back?" Mckenna asked. "We thought you were going to fly."

"Shadow and I needed some unwinding time," Jane told them. "And I had these coupons for a car rental. So we just took our time, wandered here and there, and relaxed. I got into Phoenix this morning and picked up the van at the airport."

"Relaxed, eh?" Mckenna said. "I didn't know you knew the meaning of the word 'relax.' "

Jane chuckled. "You're a fine one to talk. Poster woman for Workaholics Anonymous."

"Not anymore," Mckenna said with a wicked smile. "Since marrying Tom. He finds all sorts of creative ways to relax."

"I'll just bet." Nell smirked.

"Speaking of Tom—where are the guys?" Jane asked.

"The guys are where we are going," Nell told her. "Big welcome-home party. And we need to go now."

"A party? Where? Who with? You guys are the only people who would come."

Nell chuckled. "Shows how much you know."

The three women, along with four dogs and one cat, climbed into Nell's minivan.

"Titi looks miffed," Nell noted, giving Mckenna's Burmese cat a wary look.

"She was sleeping beneath the quilt on your bed," Mckenna said. "She doesn't like her naps interrupted. But she would have been more miffed if we'd left her behind."

"Cats are like that," Jane noted. "Hard to please."

Piggy woofed in seeming agreement, giving Titi the Corgi Eye. Titi replied with the Cat Eye, which was just as lethal.

Mckenna pulled out a scarf and gave Jane a wicked look.

"What?" Jane asked cautiously.

"You have to wear a blindfold," Mckenna told her.

"You're kidding, right?"

"She's not kidding," Nell assured her. "This is a surprise party, so you have to be surprised."

"What kind of surprise could it be, since I know we're going to a party?"

"The kind of surprise that comes with a blindfold," Mckenna said. "So put it on."

Jane grimaced and tied the scarf over her eyes. "This had better be good," she warned.

JANE RODE along in somewhat amused acquiescence, glad to be home at last, even though she hadn't yet figured out how she was going to manage to get her life back in order. It was hard to concentrate on such mundane concerns when more interesting things—like the prospect of seeing Cole again—occupied her mind. Cole, she had decided, was definitely worth making major life changes for. Soon he and Teri would arrive in the Verde Valley, and then ... who knew?

"We're here!" Nell announced.

The minivan stopped. Doors opened. Mckenna took Jane's arm and helped her out of the vehicle.

"Can I take off the blindfold now?" She wondered what silliness her friends had planned. Whatever it was, she would have to act appropriately surprised.

"Okay," Nell said, her voice positively gloating. "Take it off."

The sight that met Jane's eyes made her jaw drop. She didn't have to act surprised. She was stunned. "What the hell is this?"

She stood on her own property in Cornville, the site that had been dust and ash the last time she had been here. Now, like a Phoenix risen from flames and ash, buildings had sprouted. To her right stood a half-finished house, a real house, with a roof, walls, windows, and a covered front porch. Spanish tiles were stacked on the roof, waiting to be laid.

"The walls will be stucco," Nell told her. "Two bedrooms, a den, a country kitchen, and a mudroom in back. I hope you like it."

Jane was dumbfounded. She could hardly breathe.

To her left, another building was rising, a prefab steel structure that appeared to enclose space enough for a football field.

"That's the kennel building," Mckenna said proudly. "You get to choose the outside facing. And we left the arrangement of kennels and all that stuff to you, since you're the one who knows what she's doing."

"How...I don't understand."

As if cued to answer her question, a troop of people ran out of the kennel building, waving and laughing. Two of those people were the husbands of Nell and Mckenna, and between them they carried a huge banner that read WEL-COME HOME JANE.

Jane thought she was going to cry. She recognized every face in the crowd—former students, businesspeople from Cornville, Cottonwood, and Camp Verde—a couple of bankers, contractors, a manager from the local Wal-Mart. She also saw clients who had boarded their dogs at the old Bark Park.

"Everyone donated," Nell told her. She herself sounded a bit choked up. "They wanted you to have this—especially the folks whose pets you saved from the fire. They heard about the insurance and got together, and presto—a new Bark Park."

"Oh, my," was all Jane could manage to say.

"Plus I made a few calls to your insurance company," Mckenna said casually.

Nell laughed. "She had them almost begging to settle up."

"But the premium—it wasn't paid."

Mckenna smiled her shark smile. "True enough, but it was a very recently lost payment, they hadn't notified you of nonpayment or cancellation of the policy, and—"

"And no one wants to find themselves in a courtroom with Mckenna on the other side," Nell said with a smirk.

"Oh, Mckenna. I never dreamed."

"We know you didn't," Nell said. "You think you have to do everything for yourself. But you don't, you know. Sometimes you have to let other people help."

Suddenly a little girl ran from the midst of the crowd of well-wishers.

"Jane! Jane! You're here." Teri trotted up and wrapped her arms around Jane's legs, nearly knocking her over. "Is Shadow here? There he is! Shadow!" As quickly as she'd charged up, she darted away. "Shadow! Dash is here. He wants to see you!"

If Teri was here, Jane thought, holding her breath, Cole must be here also. She scanned the crowd of people who had circled around her and all seemed to be talking at once. He wasn't there.

"He's behind you," Nell said knowingly.

She turned, and there he was, leaning against a pillar on the front porch of her new house. The smile on his face— and in his eyes—made her insides catch fire—a very good kind of fire.

"Hi there," he said. Or at least, that was what Jane thought he said, because she couldn't hear him over the greetings of her well-wishers.

"Hi," she said back, the sound of her voice drowned in the beating of her heart.

Tearing her eyes reluctantly from Cole, she turned to the mob of her friends. "Thank you so much! I can't believe you've done this. This will live in my heart forever."

Several in the crowd laughed. Then the owner of Figi, a schnauzer she had saved from the fire, said, "Come on, people. Be nice. Let her go to her guy."

Jane wasn't even embarrassed. She was beyond that. She broke free of the crowd and stepped for the first time onto her new front porch, into the arms of her love. "You're here," she said. The tears that had threatened since she took off the blindfold now dribbled down her cheeks.

"I told you I would be here," he said, nuzzling her hair.

"I know, I just . . . Oh, my. This is such a surprise."

He chuckled. "You owe me a fancy dinner, you know. Let's say, in Sedona?"

·She laughed. "I guess I do. But you'll have to wait a while."

"I'm not going anywhere." He tilted her face up to look at him. "You remember I said that I was pretty sure that I love you?"

Jane's heart poised on the edge of a precipice. "Yes."

"Well, I think I misspoke, and we can't have that. What I should have said was that I'm really, truly sure that I love you. Love you lots."

She rested her forehead against his solid chest, hiding her face. "I love you, too," she said into his shirt.

"What was that?"

"I love you, Cole. And I don't know what the rest of this life is going to be like, but it's going to be better than before."

"For both of us. Do you think all these people would mind if I kissed you right here and now?"

"Try it," Jane invited. To hell with privacy.

But the kiss didn't happen, not right then, at least, because a rowdy voice interrupted. "Hey, kiddo, does the hunk get all the attention?"

"Angela!" Jane squealed. "How did . . . ?"

"Oh, your friend Mckenna is very good at finding people. Ernesto is here, too, somewhere. And Rick is at the motel. He'll be over later."

"Rick?" Jane inquired, not letting go of Cole.

"My new star," Angela told her. "Oh, don't look at me like that. This is strictly business. Strictly, strictly business."

But Jane recognized the sparkle in Angela's eyes. It was the same sparkle she saw in her own eyes when she looked in the mirror these days.

"And guess what!" Angela continued with a wicked smile. "Big treat here! I have tapes of the finished series. We all get a preview! Oh, Jane, you're going to love it. You and Cole are going to be *so* famous."

Jane buried her face once more in Cole's shirt. "We have to watch?"

Cole laughed.

It was indeed, Jane thought, going to be a better life.

about the author

EMILY CARMICHAEL, the award-winning author of more than twenty novels and novellas, has won praise for both her historical and her contemporary romances. She currently lives in her native state of Arizona with her husband and a houseful of dogs.

Don't miss any of these delightful romances from

Emily Carmichael

🐕 🐾 🐕

Finding Mr. Right
___57874-X $6.99/$10.99 Canada

A Ghost for Maggie
___57875-8 $5.50/$8.50

Diamond in the Ruff
___58283-6 $5.50/$8.99

The Good, the Bad, and the Sexy
___58284-4 $6.99/$10.99

Gone to the Dogs
___58633-5 $6.50/$9.99

The Cat's Meow
___58634-3 $6.99/$10.99

A New Leash on Life
___58635-1 $6.99/$10.99

Please enclose check or money order only, no cash or CODs. Shipping & handling costs: $5.50 U.S. mail, $7.50 UPS. New York and Tennessee residents must remit applicable sales tax. Canadian residents must remit applicable GST and provincial taxes. Please allow 4 – 6 weeks for delivery. All orders are subject to availability. This offer subject to change without notice. Please call 1-800-726-0600 for further information.

Bantam Dell Publishing Group, Inc.	TOTAL AMT	$_____
Attn: Customer Service	SHIPPING & HANDLING	$_____
400 Hahn Road	SALES TAX (NY, TN)	$_____
Westminster, MD 21157		
	TOTAL ENCLOSED	$_____

Name _____

Address _____

City/State/Zip _____

Daytime Phone (_____) _____